THE CHOICE

"What happens to me when they come, if they won't issue those termination papers?" Firebird asked.

"I've given that some serious thought," Brennen said. "Would you want to go home?"

She blinked at him in disbelief before passing a hand over her aching eyes, struggling with a decision she thought had long been taken away from her. She could return home voluntarily. She could face the Electorate and proudly tell them she had come back to meet a N'Taian fate on her home ground.

They'd like that, she reflected grimly. *They have a flair for killing.*

She looked up at Brennan, who had retreated across the cell to stand against the opposite wall. "They want me dead."

"Yes." He held her gaze.

She shrugged. "It doesn't matter. At home or here."

"I doubt that any termination papers will come at first request, if that's your concern. You're too valuable to us. You could fit in among us . . . if you wanted."

Firebird interlocked her fingers and squeezed tightly. So. She had a choice. Life among the Federates, whom she'd been raised to hate, or the proud death of a Wastling, to satisfy the bloodlust of the N'Taian Electorate.

Where would she choose to live—or die. . . .

Bantam Spectra Books
Ask your bookseller for the titles you have missed

FIREBIRD

Kathy Tyers

BANTAM BOOKS
TORONTO • NEW YORK • LONDON • SYDNEY • AUCKLAND

To Karen Hancock

FIREBIRD

Spectra

A Bantam Book
June 1987

ISBN 0-553-26716-7

Published simultaneously in the United States and Canada

Bantam Books are published by Bantam Books, Inc. Its
trademark, consisting of the words "Bantam Books" and
the portrayal of a rooster, is Registered in U.S. Patent and
Trademark Office and in other countries. Marca Regis-
trada. Bantam Books, Inc., 666 Fifth Avenue, New York,
New York 10103.

PRINTED IN THE UNITED STATES OF AMERICA

O 0 9 8 7 6 5 4 3 2 1

CONTENTS

Prelude

Lady Firebird Angelo of Naetai was fifteen years old, and she was trespassing.

With Lord Corey Bowman in her wake, she squeezed and twisted through a narrow, odd-shaped opening between the outer wall of the palace and the inner partition that curved around the Electoral Chamber—a passage that would have been expressly off-limits, had anyone else known it existed.

The palace's builders, seven hundred years before, had been more concerned with appearance than security. There were many such irregularities of construction, places where the walls did not exactly meet or where they came together at peculiar angles, which created all sorts of chinks and cracks and blind passageways in Firebird's ancient home: excellent places from which to hide or spy on the unsuspecting, and Firebird had learned a great deal that way over the years.

1

Palace Security had searched out and sealed all the breaches that gave illegitimate access to the Electoral Chamber. How the House Guard had missed this one, Firebird didn't know. Perhaps they had found and closed it up once, and someone else had reopened it.

That thought made her a little uneasy—that someone else might have had the audacity to spy on this highest council in the N'Taian Planetary Systems. The fact that she herself was spying was irrelevant. In three years—if she lived so long—she would have a seat on that council by right of birth. But that a commoner, or servant, or worse, a foreign agent, might have listened, or could listen in if they knew of this place . . .

Once she no longer had use for it, she intended to remind the House Guard of its existence and have them make sure no others remained. She would not have any council *she* sat on subject to prying eyes.

Her companion stumbled, adding a soft scuffle to the drone of voices filtering through the partition. "Corey!" she hissed. "Be quiet!"

Light gleamed into the crawl space ahead through a chink in the inner wall. Beating Corey to the peephole, Firebird peered through first. In the Chamber, the Queen's Electorate hosted two ambassadors from Naetai's huge neighbor, the Interstellar Federacy. Their arrival this morning at Sae Angelo Spaceport had been tantalizingly secretive: Firebird had seen the Federate shuttle land herself, but no one would explain why the delegation had come, and the Electorate had closed this session to observers.

Both her older sisters, as Electors, were seated at the central section of that table. She glanced first at her only confidante in the family: Carradee, the blonde Crown Princess, who sat beside the throne of their mother, Queen Siwann. Carradee's smile, gently tolerant, confirmed Firebird's suspicion that the family's elder heiress would prefer to ignore the Federacy entirely. No Consort's chair now separated Carradee from the stately, silver-haired Siwann. Prince Irion had been dead almost a year, and Firebird's heart still wrenched at this evidence of her father's passing —a hunting accident. *So they said*, she thought as her gaze rested on Siwann. The Queen had mourned Irion, but governmental business had continued with hardly a pause, capably managed as before by the Electors and Siwann—a strong leader who had already become much more than the traditional Electoral figurehead.

Beyond Carradee sat the middle sister, Princess Phoena, the "beauty of the family." Though significantly taller and lighter-haired, Phoena looked nearly enough like Firebird to be her twin. Phoena's large, long-lashed dark eyes watched the Federates with intelligent intensity, and her honey-smooth complexion marked her as Angelo: royalty. She wore the habitual expression of cool, self-conscious grandeur Firebird despised. Unlike Carradee, who was willing simply to ignore the Federacy, Phoena showed open hostility. Firebird winced bitterly. That person would represent Naetai into the next century. . . .

Firebird, too, had little use for the Federacy as a political entity, but the thought of so many distant worlds —so much variety, so much technical knowledge— tortured her curiosity.

The Federacy had consolidated most of the human-settled Whorl of the galactic Arm after four centuries of catastrophe. First Sabba Six-Alpha, a binary off one edge of the Whorl, had evolved into a radiation emitter so strong all spacefaring civilizations were chased to ground while the surge blew past. Then had come the invading alien Keepers, seemingly immune to Sabba's violence.

During those centuries, while civilization deteriorated in the Whorl, Naetai—isolated at the end of the great galactic Arm—had gladly stood alone; and later, after the Keepers had gone, Naetai had made no effort to covenant to the Federacy. Proud of their culture, their noble heritage, and their independence, the N'Taians had no wish to traffic with the Federacy, which they saw as a sort of lowest common culture trying to reunite the backslid races.

While Firebird cherished the N'Taian values too, she felt certain Naetai could benefit from some technical advances of the Federacy's recent expansion. Phoena's attitude galled her.

Phoena turned aside to share a haughty glance with His Grace, the Duke of Claighbro, Muirnen Rattela, and

Firebird shifted her attention to the five strange men who stood below the U-shaped table. The two who stood forward wore dress-white tunics and carried themselves with calm authority. One addressed the Elect in clipped Old Colonial, the common speech of human-settled worlds since the First Expansion. ". . . for the mutual protection of all systems within the Federacy," he said.

Duke Rattela flicked one finger toward the man who had spoken. "It seems to me a rather unreasonable tax to levy against so isolated and well protected a system as Naetai, Admiral." Maintaining an indolent slouch, Rattela eyed the Federates with disdain. Nearing sixty, the Duke had black hair that still showed no gray, and the thickness of his jowls took up enough slack to mask any wrinkles his antiaging implants could not arrest.

Firebird's glance sprang back to the Federate guests. Behind the ambassadors, an honor guard stood at attention, two armed men in gray and one in midnight blue.

"Let me look!" insisted Corey from behind her.

Reluctantly, she yielded her observation post. These were men from other worlds—oh, to see the places they had surely seen! Firebird had just passed her first-level Astronautics exam: a "beginning" course in superatmospheric piloting, basic slip dynamics, and space medicine. She ached to explore the N'Taian solar reach, its buffer systems—and beyond, even to the Federacy.

It sounded as if the Federates hoped to establish a trade agreement with Naetai. Yet the N'Taian Electorate— the real power on Naetai, which her family served as nominal head and as voting members—was being as obstinately isolationist as ever.

A blazing shame, Firebird reflected, that's what it was. Naetai should establish relations with the Federacy—if only out of compassion. The Federates could gain so much culture in the exchange, and she'd be a sharp trade pilot. Corey could navigate, and his twin brother, Daley, was the best young mechanic in the Systems. . . .

She smiled fondly at Corey. Still staring through the chink, his face was lit dimly by the fugitive light. Black-haired and freckled, he was small for sixteen, but he still stood taller than Firebird. His silver-gray tabard gleamed faintly at the edge of the light: the uniform of Sander Hill Academy, the most exclusive in Sae Angelo City.

Together as always, they had extended their lunch break to try for a glimpse of this session.

"My turn," she whispered.

She looked enviously on the Federates. Soon, she promised herself, she and Corey would be flying the stars too, one way or another. With a shiver of glee, she envisioned herself in a shining deepspace slip ship, first activating the slip-shields that would turn its component molecules and everything aboard sideways to real space, and then the drive that would push it through the light barrier into slip-state . . .

The Federate guard in midnight blue turned abruptly to look straight at her, and she froze in horror. She had made no sound, she was certain of it! Yet he knew she crouched there, spying. She watched in fascinated terror as he stepped back from the formation to touch the arm of a red-jacketed Electoral Policeman. As he whispered in the Redjacket's ear, she caught a sparkle of gold at the edge of his right shoulder.

She flung herself away from the wall. "Corey, they saw us! You get out the underway, and I'll go back through the palace!"

Corey dashed for a cellar hatch as Firebird squeezed hastily back through the narrows, determined to evade the Redjackets. She'd done it before. Leaving widely spaced tracks in centuries of dust, she ran to the passage's end and scaled a wall of irregular stones. Panting as she pulled herself up onto a wooden crawlway, she groped for the loose board and incautiously flung it aside to peer down into the public-zone maintenance closet.

It was too bright down there. The hall door stood open, and Firebird found herself looking down into the hostile eyes of a massive black-haired man in red: the Captain of the Electoral Police, Kelling Friel.

It was too late to hide. He had seen her.

"Come down here, Lady Firebird."

She lowered herself through the impromptu trapdoor and then stood a moment, collecting her breath and straightening the tabard on her shoulders. She tried to put dignity in her expression: the Electoral Police held special authority over the Wastling class, and she had learned years ago that they responded only to regality.

"Captain." She nodded a solemn greeting.

"My Lady." He swept an elegant but muscular hand into the passway, and reluctantly she stepped out beside him. She felt no guilt for spying, only regret at having been caught.

The palace had become so still that she heard the soft jingling of his decorative sword's harness as he marched her through the Chamber's huge, gold-covered wooden doors. A second Redjacket fell into step on her other side as they approached the long table. Firebird drew a deep breath and looked up at her mother.

She knew how precarious her situation was. She was the third child of a noble house, the Queen's Wastling, and expendable.

The Wastling tradition, officially known as "heir limitation," had protected the ten noble families of Naetai for generations against the breakup of wealthy estates. It dictated that a noble couple could have as many as four children: two heirs, two Wastlings, the latter produced for insurance that the line would not die out. When the elder heir married and had a child, the Electorate issued the younger Wastling his Geis Orders: he was to find death as quickly and as honorably as possible. Outranked, outnumbered, and watched constantly by the Electoral Police, the young Wastlings had little chance of escaping that fate. As a third child, Firebird could expect to live until Queen Siwann had two grandchildren, but a Wastling who made too much trouble could be disposed of early.

For spying now, she might have her Astronautics license suspended, or she could be publicly disciplined. She shuddered at the memory of what they'd done to her last month, when she'd been caught practicing on off-limit flight sims: injected her with Tactol, a sensory stimulant that had made every movement torture for an hour. Legally, however, the Redjackets could do far worse. Even for a relatively slight offense, a Wastling could be executed.

Firebird tried to look both submissive and innocent, although she felt neither.

Queen Siwann rose from the gilt throne. The golden coronet she wore for Electoral meetings rode squarely on her coiffed silver hair; with her tailored dress suit of Angelo scarlet, the effect was that of a formal portrait come to life. "So. You have been spying upon the Electorate, Firebird."

Firebird was too proud to lie, and too loyal to betray another Wastling—particularly Corey. She said nothing, glancing side to side at the Redjackets who flanked her, elegant in their long, gold-edged crimson coats and their black trousers and caps. She felt a perverse desire to kick the both of them.

Through the cascade of her auburn hair, loose over her shoulders, Captain Friel grasped her arm. "Lady Firebird, answer Her Majesty."

Firebird glanced cautiously at the Federates, who had stepped aside, waiting to resume their negotiations. The one who had reported her stood a little apart from the others, as if observing a detail under his command. Incongruously, he looked the youngest of the three, fine-featured and alert, with light brown hair of a slightly warm, russet shade. He glanced in her direction, catching her gaze before she could look away, and the unexpected brilliance of his blue eyes made her catch her breath.

Friel tightened his grip, and she turned her attention back to the situation at hand. Surely, the Electorate wouldn't embarrass itself before the Federacy with the disciplining of a Wastling.

"Your Majesty," she said softly to her mother, lowering her eyes and praying that she had stalled long enough for Siwann to wish to get on with business—and for Corey to have escaped. "I apologize for interrupting, and I promise not to observe you again."

The Queen still stood, visibly considering whether the breach of conduct merited a charge of espionage or contempt. "You may go to your quarters," she finally ruled. "But you are confined there for the week, except for your schooling, to which you will be escorted." Her voice echoed off the domed ceiling of the ellipse. "Captain Friel, you will see to it."

Friel touched his cap in salute to the Queen and took Firebird's arm.

It could have gone worse, she reflected later. There was little to do outdoors in Sae Angelo's cold, still winter, her suite was pleasant enough, and she needed to practice her clairsa. But she would so have enjoyed hearing what those star travelers had to say.

Seven years passed before Naetai dealt again with the Interstellar Federacy.

CHAPTER 1

Wastling

Maestoso ma non tanto
**Majestically, but not
too much**

". . . but the inducer—*here*—bypasses the third phase of . . ."

It was no use. Firebird dropped her hand into her lap, leaned away from the banqueting table, and gazed up at the crystal chandelier of the palace's formal dining hall, letting her mind wander far from the Planetary Naval Academy scanbook that glowed on the viewer in front of her. In a week, she must be able to reproduce that schematic. But this very night, she had to appear for an interview with the Queen.

In seven years, Siwann had consolidated a vigorous rule. Carradee had married, brought her Prince Daithi into the palace household, and borne him a daughter. And Phoena . . .

Phoena burst through the swinging doors. "You nearly got yourself taken to see Captain Friel again last night, Firebird."

Phoena had not changed the slightest bit.

Firebird watched over her breakfast plate, now emp-

tied of delicacies, as her sister paced the length of the
gleaming wooden table.

"I can't believe you'd be so stupid." Phoena took a
chair with a red tapestry cushion across from Firebird and
rang for breakfast. Her golden spring gown shone in the
morning light, and when Firebird glanced from Phoena's
sparkling earrings and necklace to the chandelier overhead,
she couldn't help comparing them.

"Countervoting the entire Electorate?" Phoena snapped. "What's the matter with you? You know your place,
don't you?"

Firebird faced her sister squarely. "You know what I
think about your irradium project. If I had to do it again,
I'd still vote against the whole Electorate. You're not
building our defenses—you want a threat, a show of
power!"

"So you said." Phoena buffed her nails on the sleeve of
her gown. "We heard you very clearly yesterday."

Firebird laid her palms flat on the scanbook viewer.
"You got your commendation, didn't you? By quite a
margin: twenty-six to one."

"One." Phoena lifted an eyebrow. "In your position, I
think I'd be trying to live a while. You're lucky the
Redjackets haven't come for you. Wastlings who counter-
vote don't last. You're only in there for show, anyway. For
your *honor.*"

"Yes, honor." Firebird curled her fingers around the
viewer. "I won't compromise the things I believe in, not
even if it gives me one more day."

"Wastling," muttered Phoena. "You should never have
a vote on the Electorate to begin with."

"I'm as much an Angelo as you and Carradee. Carradee at least has a conscience."

"She voted to attack VeeRon, too."

"I know—" The swinging of the door past Phoena
caught Firebird's glance and she fell silent, toying with her
cruinn cup, as Carradee pushed through, followed by a
palace servant. A deep green robe draped Carradee's form,
now swollen with a second pregnancy.

"Carrie," Firebird murmured as the Crown Princess

sank into a cushioned chair held by the servant. "You look exhausted."

Carradee sighed and splayed her fingers on her belly. "With the little one's dancing all night, it's a wonder I sleep at all. And I'm so worried for you, Firebird. Why must you try so hard to throw away the time that's left to you?"

Phoena leaned back in her chair and fixed Firebird with dark eyes.

Easy for Phoena to smirk now, Firebird reflected bitterly, but it hadn't always been so. Phoena had been a Wastling too, until Lintess was found smothered. Firebird was three at the time and Phoena six, both already beginning their indoctrination into acceptance of the "high destiny," when it happened. A thorough investigation had implicated the programmer of Lintess's favorite toy, a lifelike robot snow bear, but, as with the death of Prince Irion years later, Firebird harbored suspicions honor forbade her to voice.

She watched the scarlet-liveried servant hurry out. "How can you condone the idea of fouling an entire living world, Carradee?" Firebird spread her hands on the tabletop. "Aren't some things worth standing against?"

"Yes. Some. Oh!" Carradee flinched and grimaced, holding her belly. "I'll be so glad when this is over."

Firebird bit her lip.

Phoena seized the opening like a weapon. "Yes. Two weeks, now. There will be some changes made in the family, won't there—Firebird?"

Carradee turned pale gray eyes to Phoena in mute reprimand, and Firebird snapped the viewer off. "I'll have longer than that. They'll send me with the invasion force. I'm a good pilot, and I'd love to fly strike. I would rather die flying than . . ." She groped for a comparison. The Wastling of another noble family had gone recently in a suspicious ground-car accident, but her grief was still too fresh to discuss with Phoena. Lord Rendy had wanted so badly to live, had lived so hard and wild.

Phoena snorted. "All right, Wastling. Waste yourself in a—a TS-whatever-it-is."

Firebird shook her hair behind her slender shoulders

and stood to leave. "I'd better get to class. We have a speaker today."

Phoena's breakfast arrived, carried by a mincing white-haired waiter. As Firebird snatched up the scanbook and swung out the double doors, Phoena called, "I'll help them put the black edging on your portrait."

Firebird ignored her and stopped in the long private hallway to gather up the rest of her Academy scan cartridges. Wistfully she shot a look down the gallery, past the spiral-legged tables weighted with heirlooms, to the formal portrait to which Phoena had referred: she had been sixteen and star-eyed when it was painted, absorbed in her piloting and her music, years away from the shadow of death under which, at twenty-two, N'Taian calendar, she now lived. The scarlet velvric gown with white sash and diadem made her look queenly, but the artist had put a characteristic, mischievous smile between brave-set chin and proud brown eyes. A scarcely tangible sadness in those painted eyes always haunted Firebird. Did others see the flaws in the courage she held up to the world, too?

She straightened her brownbuck flight jacket before the jeweled hallway mirror. *Well,* she thought, *there's one advantage to dying young: people will remember you as pretty.* Humming a defiant ballad from the Coper Rebellion, she dashed off for the Academy.

If Firebird had been born an heir, she'd have had a hard choice between the Sae Angelo Music Conservatory and the NPN Academy. She loved flying, though, and had trained long and hard to develop from a skillful pleasure pilot into a Naval officer.

She almost crashed into Corey in the crowded passway just before the special afternoon session. *"Easy,* Firebird." He stepped back, and his grin faded. "What's wrong—Phoena again?"

"Of course," she muttered. "And Her Majesty, tonight."

"Oh, that's right. I forgot." He nodded sympathetically and palmed the doorpanel for her.

The briefing room was hushed, and Firebird felt hostile anticipation in the air. She and her classmates had waited all term to meet the speaker, Vultor Korda, who had come in midwinter from the Federate world of Thyrica. Korda was one of the Thyrians' "starbred" telepathic minority, but had turned traitor and come secretly to Naetai.

As Firebird and Corey slipped into adjacent seats and loaded their viewers, a little man entered, carrying several scan cartridges himself. Physically, he looked anything but powerful: narrow-shouldered without muscle, he had too much belly straining the belt of his brown shipboards. His complexion was the fragile white of the academician or the UV-allergic spacer, and silky brown hair framed his tiny-eyed face.

She had heard rumors of the starbred. Allegedly they descended from the extragalactic Aurian race that had been devastated by plague, the *makkah*, half a millennium ago, three centuries after the first cosmic rays of the Six-Alpha Catastrophe reached Naetai. The *makkah* had killed many of the Aurian women and every male, regardless of age. Even the unborn—if male—had not been spared. Many women had fled the Aurian system for the distant whorl of star systems they called the "Starry Pool," hoping its worlds would still be inhabited by the ancient human kind from which they had once come. Thus an electrostatically shielded ship carrying twenty-seven survivors eventually made planetfall on the southern-spinward edge of the Whorl, at Thyrica.

The Aurians' talents first terrified the Thyrian humans, then impressed them, then won them over. A cure was developed for the hereditary androcidal effects of the *makkah*. Proving themselves undeceivable mediators among those willing to submit to their appraisal, those survivors' sons and daughters reunited the first worlds of the Federacy, then stepped back to let others govern.

So the story went.

Before Korda reached the center of the electronic teachboard, he twisted his lean shoulders toward the array of seats and began to speak. "So, you think Naetai can take VeeRon from the Federacy? Well, *I* happen to think you have just a chance to do it."

At Firebird's right hand, Corey fingered the edge of his desk terminal. "Slimy," he whispered.

Firebird nodded uneasily without taking her eyes off Korda. She was already guaranteed a First Major's commission on graduation by her class and flight evaluations. Top marks on this special seminar would win her a commendation, too. But Korda struck her instinctively as the belligerently insecure sort of little man who compensated for size with meanness. His kind liked to make everyone else look bad—particularly a woman at the top of her division. She shifted her weight uncomfortably, feeling her seat shift to compensate.

"I intend to teach you all you can learn about the Federacy's Thyrian telepaths: *Sentinels,* the trained ones are called. As officers, you young incompetents will be more likely to encounter them than your blazer-bait subordinates will. You won't find a more self-righteous, exclusive group if you see half the galaxy. The Sentinels virtually founded the Federacy, you know—not that it trusts them entirely. Common people fear what they can't control." He cut off their exchange of knowing glances. "Yes, I'm Thyrian too, and starbred: there are Aurians in my background. But I'm no Sentinel. No one tells me what I can do with my abilities."

Firebird went rigid. If Korda had such abilities, how much had he influenced the recent decision to attack VeeRon? She eyed him suspiciously.

A habitual glance at the tiny time lights on her wristband broke her concentration. Korda's introductory remarks concerning his own testing and training under Master Sentinels would have fascinated her on any other day, but tonight she faced her mother.

Queen Siwann had made the appointment months before, which usually didn't bespeak a matter of personal warmth. Moments of warmth between them had been so rare that Firebird could recall every one vividly. Not that she expected affection from a mother she rarely saw and hardly knew, who had feelings of her own to protect—Siwann couldn't really afford to involve herself emotionally with her Wastling child. Firebird knew and understood that.

For centuries, the Wastlings had provided Naetai with daredevil entertainers and Naval officers. Some were heroes in the history scanbooks, but none lived long enough to have children of their own. That tradition of limitation, rigorously enforced by their own elder brothers and sisters, ruled their fate. Those who refused their Geis Orders disappeared—or had fatal accidents, like Lord Rendy Angellson. Firebird wondered, sometimes, if some who vanished had survived—fled the Naetai Systems and begun new lives elsewhere. She knew one who had made the attempt: she had helped. Naturally, she had never heard from him—nor the commoner, a lovely University woman, who had gone with him. Occasionally she thought of them. Had the Redjackets found and killed them months after Firebird and Corey had reported them dead in space, or had they vanished effectively enough?

But she had chosen the path of honor, the chance to win herself undying glory by facing that destiny courageously. If only she were bound for a war to which she could give herself gladly, not a strike on her sister Phoena's behalf to help with a project she opposed. And if only Carradee's second little princess—the child was bound to be female, for inexplicably, no Angelo had birthed a male heir in five hundred years—weren't quite so close to—

When the briefing room went dark, Firebird was startled back to attention. Korda bent momentarily over the blocky media unit at midboard, then turned back toward the class. "The Sentinels in the Federate military are the ones of most concern to you, of course. If you think you see one, in battle or otherwise, shoot first and make sure of your target after he's dead. You probably won't get a second chance. Some of them can levitate your side weapon from the holster. Others have different specialties."

A life-size holographic image appeared over the block, rotating slowly, of a handsome black-haired woman who apparently stood taller than half the men in the class. "This is Captain Ellet Kinsman. She's stationed at Caroli—which governs VeeRon, by the way—and rising fast in the ranks. We rate the starbred on the Aurian Scale, according to how strongly the psionic genes that give rise to the projectable epsilon carrier wave are expressed in them. Kinsman comes from a strong family. Seventy-five Aurian Scale out of a rough hundred, which means she can do over half the tricks the pure-blooded Aurians could. You don't want to get near a person like that. Militarily, she's not much threat to you yet. She will be, when she gets some rank and experience. Memorize the face, if you have half a memory. Don't forget her."

Firebird was already memorizing as he spoke. The woman resembled her first flight trainer, Commodore Cheitt, except Kinsman's features were femininely softened, and her uniform was blue-black with no insignia save a golden star. She had seen that uniform before.

The image blurred and faded. Next she saw a man, older, also black-haired. "Admiral Blair Kinsman is her cousin. Based on Varga. The throwback of the family, about a twenty-five Aurian Scale—I think he can nudge a few electrons along a wire, if he's not too . . ."

Distracted by half a memory, Firebird missed several sentences. *Where* had she seen that uniform? She prided herself on being able to identify Federate service insignia, but this must be a rare one. Ah! The honor guard who had spotted her, that day she had spied on the Electorate with Corey for the last time—he had worn it.

"Now, this is Trouble." Blair Kinsman disappeared in a cloud of static. A younger man's figure materialized in his place, and Firebird almost gasped aloud. The guard himself! In this image he looked less incongruously young, but it could be no other—of average height, slender and well proportioned; straight chin, fine cheekbones, and hair the light, rich brown of burnished leta-wood. The image's eyes were lost in shadow, but she had not forgotten that flash of blue.

"This is Lieutenant General Brennen Caldwell. He's stationed at Regional Headquarters, Alta, but as a member of the Special Operations Task Force or S.O."—he scratched the initials onto the teachboard—"he has no permanent base or unit. Don't even get close enough to recognize him. Aurian Scale ninety-seven—they haven't had one so high in a hundred years. See the Master's star on the shoulder? Eight points, not four. Supposedly he's the first Sentinel the Federacy has considered for real rank—the Sentinels pretend reluctance to accept authority, but the situation is more complex than that." Korda paused dramatically. "Much more complex. The S.O. people rotate between the defense fleet and special intelligence assignments. Often they're sent on jobs that others have tried and failed."

Then, this was the man, now a Lieutenant General. The slowly rotating hologram did not do him justice, she thought. But the notion of a telepath at the heart of the N'Taian government, spying on them even for a day, sent a chill of horror down her spine.

"He's cute," whispered Lady Delia Stele to no one in particular.

Korda's explosive reaction startled them all. "If that's all you can think about, Stele, get out of here. Out! My time is too valuable to waste on giggly Wastlings that anybody can play with and no one will ever marry."

Delia's face, so prettily circled in blond hair, was a study in humiliation. The hostility in the room swelled nearly to exploding. Vultor Korda brought the lights back up and swung out his arms. "Go ahead and hate me. I can feel it. But I'll be alive next year and most of you will be dead. Come back tomorrow and I'll show you something that could give you another week or two." He dove for the exit.

When Firebird saw that Delia was being consoled by several girls (and, bless his heart, Daley Bowman), she slipped out into the passway and headed home. For all his sliminess, Vultor Korda had given her a good deal to think about. It roiled in her mind during dinner, which she took alone in her suite.

After calling her personal girl Dunna to remove the leavings, she retreated to her music room. A slender, triangular case lay on the carpet below the studio's small window; carefully, she drew out her clairsa by the corners of its short top arch. Twenty-two bronze-alloy strings caught the dying daylight and shone red through dangling strands of her auburn hair.

She spent the hour that remained before the interview cradling it, seated on a low stool with the transcriber running. She was writing a song that might be her last—if she lived to finish it.

The ballad honored Iarla, Queen of Naetai. A century

before, Lady Iarla, a Queen's Wastling like herself, had survived against all odds to mount the throne. Iarla had set a standard that Firebird had hoped to match; capable and compassionate, aggressive and intelligent, Iarla was one of the most respected figures in Naetai's history. The melody was the best she had ever done, and the chords that rolled from the strings of her clairsa stirred her even on a hundredth playing, but words just wouldn't come. There had been a time when she had secretly hoped to repeat Iarla's climb to glory, but as Carradee's second confinement approached, Firebird's very survival had become precarious.

After four attempts to rhyme a second stanza, she gave up in disgust and ordered the transcriber to shut itself off. She returned the clairsa to its soft case before changing into a fresh Academy uniform.

A layer of dust had settled on the ornate bedroom bureau: she needed to call Dunna in to give the suite a good cleaning. Slowly she turned around as if seeing the marble walls and costly furnishings for the first time. This had been Iarla's suite, too. That had always been a point of pride to Firebird. To be an Angelo was to be proud. With dignity that masked her apprehension, she swung down the curved staircase and across an echoing foyer to the Queen's private office.

Queen Siwann sat as stiffly as her bust in the Hall of Queens, erect in a flawlessly tailored black suit. One hand swept a platinum pen along, and the other controlled a scribepaper. Siwann had been striking in her day and was rarely caricatured, even by her enemies, except for her lofty haughtiness.

She looked up. "Sit down. I'll be with you."

Firebird complied, with the usual twinge of awe this woman commanded in her. Her Majesty's antique leta-wood desk loomed in front of a window draped with velvric curtains, giving the illusion of tiers of red wings. Gilt-lettered ancient volumes, with bindings made of the skins of all sorts of creatures, stood in dignified rows over files of tapes, disks, and cartridges along two walls. At the office's center stood a crystalline globe carved to an incredible likeness of her homeworld, but Firebird had passed it so

many times that its wonder had faded. She occupied her
waiting time trying to recall the three Sentinels Korda had
shown them, comparing detail by detail to set their features
in her memory. Would Naetai be preparing to invade
VeeRon for its mineral resources, she wondered, if that
trade agreement had been reached seven years before?

Queen Siwann laid the scribepaper down, then took a
red envelope from a drawer and flicked its corner. "I have
something for you."

"Yes, Your Majesty?" Firebird leaned forward in the
massive chair, her posture carefully correct. A graduation
gift? From Siwann? Unlikely, but . . .

"You will be commissioned next month. Assuming, of
course, that you complete all your classes."

"That's right." She hoped her mother was joking; or
maybe she didn't follow her Wastling's academic career
with the same interest she had shown in her Princesses.

"You're aware that you will then be a First Major."

"Yes." She kept her expression correctly impassive, but
she felt the skin around her eyes wrinkle into the hint of a
smile. "My flight trainer tells me I'll be assigned to Raptor
Phalanx with a squadron of my own choosing."

"I'm glad to see that it makes you happy, Firebird.
That makes this easier." Siwann handed the envelope
across the burnished desktop. Firebird fingered it open and
found a white cellopaper packet inside. "Anyone in a
combat situation risks capture. As a First Major, you would
be a candidate for particularly thorough interrogation.
Think what that would mean to Naetai." She ticked off
details on her fingers as if summing up a case against a
criminal. "You have been privy to the Electoral Council for
four years now. There is your Academy education. Your
knowledge of Angelo properties. Military facilities. Defense procedures."

Firebird slipped the small packet back into the envelope and dropped it into her lap. She had held death in her
hands, and she didn't like it. "I assume this is poison."

"Yes. You will keep it with you at all times, beginning
now. Make it an unbreakable habit. For your sake, I hope
that you will go out with the Navy and finish your days in
some—some exciting episode. I would be delighted to see

you named a hero in Derwynn's new history series. But if at any time it is obvious that you cannot otherwise avoid being taken prisoner, then your resolve to use this may be the most important thing you carry with you into battle. Must I make myself any clearer?"

"Not your orders, Your Majesty. But tell me what it is, and what it will do."

"The vernacular is Arride. It causes death by suppression of the involuntary nervous system: taken orally, it finalizes in about fifteen minutes, with unconsciousness in five. There is no discomfort. Your Aunt Firebird took it when Carradee was born, as did my mother the Queen when I was ready to rule."

Firebird nodded slightly. Such was the duty of the Queen: and she knew about her namesake, of course. The elder Firebird hadn't even waited for the Electorate to issue her Geis Orders, but had simply poisoned herself as soon as baby Carradee was declared normal and healthy.

Carradee's first little daughter was normal and healthy, too. Firebird envied her. Little Iarlet was beautiful. She was a firstborn and she would live.

She tucked the packet into the breast pocket of her Academy uniform. "Thank you, but I won't need it. I intend to have the fastest striking squadron in the Planetary Navy."

"A fine speech for a budding pacifist."

"I'll go, Majesty." She leaned forward and rested her hands on her knees. "I know what my Geis Orders will be. Just see that they put us on a military target run, not a civilian one, and I'll do my best for you."

"Yes. You will." Siwann seemed to soften. "You always do, don't you?"

Grateful for the crumb of royal recognition, Firebird nodded. "Thank you, Mother."

Abruptly Siwann pushed back her chair and stood. "Little Firebird. I haven't held you since you were a baby, and this could be my last chance. Come here."

Firebird got up, unsure of her mother's intentions. "Majesty?"

"Here." The Queen flicked her hands. "Come to me."

Hesitantly, Firebird made the circuit of the massive

desk into Siwann's outstretched arms. Only when she was not ordered away did she return the embrace.

"My baby," Siwann crooned. "My last chance to hold my baby."

They swayed back and forth, Firebird holding tightly but growing very uncomfortable. She didn't know how to react to this outpouring of sentiment. It made her feel almost guilty, as if she were taking something from Siwann that rightfully belonged to Carradee and Phoena.

It ended as suddenly as it began; Siwann pulled away, dismissed her Wastling with a gesture, and returned to her productivity printouts.

CHAPTER 2

Corey

Affetuoso
With warmth

Firebird bowed low and exited. The foyer was quiet; a puff of warm air danced through the monolithic doors from the colonnade, and she walked out into the clear summer evening.

She wandered the palace grounds, numbing her thoughts with the fragrance of the formal flower gardens and the peaceful sound of breezes rustling long, glossy leaves of the drooping fayya trees. Where the path crossed a bridge over an inlet of the reflecting pool, she stopped and leaned over the railing to throw path-pebbles at the skitters. The Angelo palace gleamed white behind her, columns and porticoes of semiprecious stone coolly reflecting the garden lumibeams. She tossed a pebble idly, and the green-gold fish flitted forward to nip at the sinking stone.

It had been a good life. She'd been wealthy. She'd traveled all over the solar reach and visited Naetai's buffer systems. She'd had good friends. *Plop!* went another pebble. Dear Carradee, now twenty-seven, had been a friend to her as well. Although besieged by eligible suitors,

Carradee had put off marriage much longer than anyone would have expected, had even given Firebird a kind of posterity by naming her firstborn for Iarla, the queen Firebird so admired. When tiny Iarlet had been born, Naetai had rejoiced, but cold dread had begun to settle in Firebird's heart. Soon, another little Princess would push her down the succession to the deadly fifth position, and the Geis Orders would be given. If only she had been born first, or even second. She would be called "Princess" like her sisters, and there would be no Geis Orders. Firebird was certain she would have made a more capable monarch than either Carradee or Phoena—or even the late Lintess. She desperately hoped Naetai would remember her as capable, and for the courage with which she faced her fate. *Plop!*

She was proud to be an Angelo, a member of the aristocracy that had seized power 350 years ago as Naetai had collapsed into anarchy after the sudden disappearance of the tyrannical Keepers. During their fifty years of systematic destructions of records and technology, the Keepers had driven Naetai into a dark age of suspicion and isolation from which it was difficult to recover. Banding together under the Angelos, who had ruled as constitutional monarchs for most of Naetai's history, the ten noble families had restored order and industry far more speedily than proved possible on the Keeper-occupied worlds of the Whorl. The aliens' reign was now history, but Naetai's distrust of offworlders, human or alien, had never eased. *Plip!* Firebird watched another stone disappear in the murky waters.

Phoena would be next to marry. She could have no children, but would be spared herself. Firebird bristled, recalling her sister's cruel words over breakfast, and turned her gaze skyward.

That bright yellow star was VeeRon, the target. The people of Naetai hadn't yet been told the real reason for the pending invasion. VeeRon's relative proximity and its orientation ninety degrees from Naetai's two buffer systems made its conquest a logical step in N'Taian expansion. But the regime had no intention of colonizing the VeeRon system: Naetai wanted VeeRon's irradium for the research of Dr. Nella Cleary.

Cleary had come to Naetai from VeeRon, offering talents in strategic ordnance research in return for absolute secrecy—and a price. In personally meeting it, Phoena had startled the Electorate by exercising a royal prerogative with Siwann's blessing, and made Cleary the wealthiest commoner on Naetai. The nature of Cleary's work was so secret Firebird wasn't even certain who knew it. The coworkers, Baron Parkai and Dr. D'Stang, certainly, and probably Phoena—but anyone else she'd asked professed ignorance (in tones that suggested they had been favored, and were sworn to secrecy). Firebird only knew the project required large quantities of irradium. A heavy-metal compound found nowhere in known space but VeeRon II, irradium had few industrial uses—barely enough to maintain VeeRon's mining colonies. If Phoena and Siwann had their way, Naetai would never again need to lower itself to negotiating with the Federacy. *Plip!*

Fortunately, VeeRon stood out almost as far from the Federate Whorl as Naetai itself, hopefully too far for a strong military defense to be economically feasible—*Plop* —or so Naetai hoped. *Plop!* The VeeRon system had no Federate military base, only a small self-defense installation and ten support depots, and if enough irradium could be seized quickly, the mission would be declared a success— but they would try for conquest.

The invasion would be under way ten days after commissioning, and Firebird knew she would be there.

Dimmer, more distant than VeeRon, she located another star in the western sky, picking it out of the Whorl: Alta. On Alta IV, a planet she had never seen, the Interstellar Federacy had its regional capital. Nine major civilizations, several minor systems, and numerous small protectorates lay under covenant to the Federacy.

And the Naetai Systems stood apart. It made the N'Taians proud, this independence. Too proud, maybe. Proud enough to attack VeeRon, only a colony of a protectorate of Federate Caroli, but the treaty ties were there. Firebird hoped the Federacy would let the VeeRon system slip into N'Taian hands—or did she?

Well, they would move soon enough. *Plop!* She was tired. *Splat!* went the rest of the pebbles into the water. She climbed the green hill between groves of drooping fayya and majestic leta trees and stepped up onto the colonnade. Between high white walls and fluted columns, a sentry in the formal uniform of the House Guard passed by on his rounds. He bowed to her and she saluted, then went in.

Vultor Korda made the following day's session very practical. "The Sentinels have developed a technique that I mentioned before. It's made them a critical element in Federate intelligence gathering. They call it mind-access interrogation."

Out of the corner of her eye, Firebird saw Corey make a quick note in his scribebook.

"It doesn't damage the subject, the way the psycho-physical methods do, but it's twice as effective. A Sentinel can send his epsilon-wave carrier inside your mental matrix and find out anything you know, if he has enough of the innate ability and can plant the proper suggestion.

"There is a way to resist access. You must concentrate on something *totally* irrelevant—such as your bootheels, or your favorite song. Then, you have to hold on like grim death when you feel your mind start to wander. You must remember that someone else is trying to direct your thinking. Let's show how it's done, Angelo."

Firebird stiffened. The very idea of linking minds, with Vultor Korda or anyone else, repelled her. But she couldn't escape without getting unpleasant, and she had heard too much about the Electoral vote already.

Korda sank onto Corey's desktop. With a slim white hand, he turned her chin to face him. "It's lots of fun. Don't be scared, Angelo. Look at my eyes. I'm going to be trying to find out your favorite color."

She complied. His tiny eyes were Totally Irrelevant Brown. The sensation started subtly, like prickles at the back of her neck, and then she felt the essence of another person approach, deep on a level of awareness she had never known existed. That "other's" presence struck her like a stale odor or a string out of tune: it was *wrong*, somehow. Suddenly she was panicking and losing control, and because he had already planted the suggestion, she saw her best clothes, all crimson.

"That was too easy. It's red, isn't it? You'll have to be quicker than that. Can you do better, Parkai?"

As he moved on, demonstrating and berating, her hand went involuntarily to the packet in her breast pocket. *Why should I bother to try?* she wondered. *I'll be unconscious before anyone can touch me.* But she wanted that commendation badly, and competitive habits that had made her a good student kept her interested in the demonstration.

In the afternoon he returned to her. "All right, Red Bird. What's your middle name?"

She hastily stopped down her awareness to a horrendously tricky passage from an etude she had recently memorized and loved to practice. As she watched the notes dance along the staff, the prickly wave touched her and ebbed away. Minor chord . . . it had three accidentals . . . descending run . . . arpeggio, two octaves . . .

Then the wave fell again with more force, and the sensation of distasteful "otherness" cracked her concentration. "Elsbeth," crowed Korda. She opened her eyes to see him backing toward Corey with an odd look in his eye. "Thought you were doing well, didn't you?"

"That *is* the idea, though?" she asked. "Or did I do something wrong?"

His defensiveness fell away. "No, nothing wrong. That's a start. We'll try advanced techniques later." He turned to Leita Parkai.

Two weeks later, on the day after commissioning, the traditional Officers' Ball took place. With the final flurry of Academy activity finished and her commendation won despite Vultor Korda's continual badgering, Firebird intended to dance. She had let the palace tresser tame her auburn mane into a ladylike coif, smooth to the crown with the back curled stylus-tight, and then she carefully pinned two new ruby rank stars onto the collar of an equally new cobalt-blue dress blouse. The effect thrilled her. Her regulation dress shoes, softened to glove weight, concealed a little sharpened stick she'd tucked into her instep for old times' sake—perhaps she could catch Corey off his guard one more time . . . later.

Nursing a goblet of wine punch and stopping at each group of partygoers she encountered, she worked her way down the gold-shot, black marble floor. Tonight the ball-room's crimson curtains were overhung in Planetary Navy cobalt-blue, and most of the ballroom's furniture and statuary had been moved aside to make room for dancers. At the far end of the expanse an orchestra filled the dais; not far behind her, liveried servants dispensed wines, sweets, and steaming, spicy cruinn. Between the blue-hung walls, beneath triple ranks of chandeliers, the aristocracy held fête.

Before she could dance with Corey, however, she would have to pay her respects to each of the Electors, all the Marshals, and nearly all her superior officers, all the while watching for Heirs with hazing on their minds. Two of her friends already wore ugly, mysterious red blotches on face and throat that made the uniform's snug collar agony to bear—and each had been seen with Phoena only minutes before breaking out.

Major—she was a Major now, a career-grade officer! Her fingers stole up to touch one star, to assure herself of its reality. The music rejoiced with her, a sweep of strings and brasses that sang in pure delight. Dreamily she gazed out over the dance floor, and so caught sight of Phoena in the arms of a black-haired officer. . . .

Corey! Firebird halted in midstep. Phoena's hand rested lazily on Corey's shoulder, and her smile was as saccharine as Firebird had ever seen it. In Corey's bland expression Firebird read resigned patience.

A tall couple swept between Firebird and Corey; by the time she regained sight of him, the dance had ended. Without hesitating she rushed forward, seized his arm, and pulled him into a particularly crowded corner. In his fresh commissioning haircut he seemed thinner and much more formal than the 'scamp she knew.

Still clutching his arm, Firebird jostled deeper into the noisy mass. "Did Phoena do anything odd, Corey? Quick!"

Corey shrugged. "She was friendly, and that's about as odd as your sister can get."

Some passing group drove the crowd closer to the wall. Firebird guarded her sloshing cup as she was pushed closer to Corey. "Don't bet on that. What did she do?" *There* had *to be something. . . .*

He shrugged, wrinkling his freckled face. "She commented on my haircut—her and everyone else—but *she* actually played with it."

Seizing Corey's shoulders, Firebird worked around behind him and pulled him down low enough to examine the back of his neck.

A thin cloth square, almost invisible against his fair skin, clung just below his hairline. Firebird tore it off and dropped it on the floor.

Rubbing at the bared spot, Corey turned around to her. "Skin patch?"

"Absolutely. That's what got to Leita and Tor. You may be fine if we got it off in time, but—"

"I *will* be fine, Firebird. She wouldn't dare debilitate commissioned officers." Corey's black eyes brimmed with mischief. "Too bad you wasted it. I'd like to see your sister in spots. I wonder what she's saving for you."

Firebird tapped one foot. "And I wonder where she's carrying them. Surely not next to her skin."

They had been working sideways out of the congested area; now Firebird broke free, pulling Corey along by his hand. "Try to watch her if you can for me, Corey. Meanwhile, I have to make about six more duty calls."

He leaned down and kissed her cheek. "Good luck— Major. And thanks."

She gave him a quick thumbs-up salute and then recollected her dignity. Massive Devair Burkenhamn, First Marshal of the N'Taian Planetary Navy, stood alone a few steps away, nibbling at a cream pastry and watching the richly garbed dancers. He had been her strategies instructor, hard but fair, an officer who treated Wastlings precisely like the others. One of the aging few who could not tolerate the youth implants a Wastling would never need, he wore a fringe of silver-gray hair around the back of his skull, far above her eye level. He was a huge man, all muscle, and Firebird still wondered how he had managed to squeeze into the tight cockpit of a tagwing fightercraft.

"Sir." She saluted, then raised her goblet toward him. "Good evening to you, and my thanks."

He returned the salute and her smile. "My congratulations, Major. Perhaps later you would dance with your Marshal."

"Of course, sir." *Major*—he'd said it! She sipped her punch to keep from grinning foolishly. "I have worked for yesterday for so long, I'm astounded to find myself on the other side of it."

He nodded sagely. "Your mother. Give her my respects."

"I will, sir. And my regards to your family." Small talk—she hated it. What she wanted to ask was, *Had Burkenhamn accepted her choice of squadron personnel?* But she held her tongue. From behind the Marshal's bulk, Phoena stepped up and tapped his elbow.

"I'm so glad to have caught you together. Firebird . . ." Phoena nodded an elegant greeting. Her spectacularly interwoven hair and kaleidocolor ball gown did not distract Firebird from the slight narrowing of Phoena's dark eyes that typically presaged some cruelty.

It might be nothing, Firebird reminded herself. *Get it over with.*

Burkenhamn bowed to the Princess. "Your Highness, ever your servant."

"Ah," said Phoena, and the bodice of her gown expanded. Body heat, Firebird guessed, created the chromatic changes in the fabric. "Thank you. I have a rather bothersome problem." She traced colorbursts on a sleeve with one gloved fingertip. "It seems that Lady Firebird might not be eligible to accept her officer's commission after all."

"Your Highness," said Marshal Burkenhamn. "Of what do you speak?"

Phoena skewered Firebird with her most condescending smile and turned her body sideways, wedging Firebird out of the conversation. "Oh, it may be nothing. Has your daughter's mare had her . . ."

Small talk, again. What is she working up to? Firebird glanced at the back of Phoena's hair as her sister prattled on. Several bright clips held the knots in place, and in a pink one . . .

Firebird squinted. The patches were hidden precisely where Phoena's automatic primping gesture would put them in her reach, in the lowest hair clip, and they looked loose enough to fall free without attracting attention. Gingerly Firebird raised a hand. At that moment Phoena spoke her name again.

". . . At any rate, it seems there has been suspicion cast on my little sister concerning the deaths of Lord Alef Drake and a commoner named Jisha Teal, last year at about this time."

Momentum carried Firebird's hand forward to pluck out the remaining patches, but her breath caught as Phoena's words registered. *Suspicion? What had been found?* One patch began to adhere to Firebird's fingers as Phoena stepped back to eye her again. Inspired even through her dread, Firebird dropped the patches into her punch cup and swirled it, remembering one of Phoena's favorite minor indignities.

And Phoena snatched the cup. "Thank you for sharing, Firebird. I was *so* thirsty." She drank half and then continued. "She and Lord Bowman reported them dead, you'll remember. I'm certain there will be an investigation. I'd have come to you sooner, Marshal, but decided to save it for tonight. Firebird hates childish pranks, but traditions are *so* important. This seemed an acceptable compromise."

Phoena drank deeply again—but Firebird's moment of revenge was ruined. She felt as if the blood had drained out of her upper body, leaving her with leaden feet and a nonfunctional brain. Heir limitation was the law; assisting an escape attempt was punishable by death. Of course Phoena would save her coup for tonight.

Burkenhamn's massive shoulders pulled back to attention. "Your Highness." He bowed again, eyeing Firebird. "You place it in my hands, then?"

Phoena shrugged. "I don't believe in involving underlings in concerns of our family."

"Thank you, Highness. I shall see that all is done for the glory of Naetai."

Phoena curtsied. At that moment His Grace, Muirnen

Rattela, touched her shoulder. "Highness, may I—" His green eyes narrowed between folds of flesh. "Highness, are you all right?"

Phoena's entire face was flushing, the shade deepening every second. She touched one gloved hand to her left cheek, on which a huge red weal rose visibly, then pulled it away as if burned. As she plucked out the hair clip she made a strangled sound. "You. . . ." She glared at Firebird. "Where are they?"

"Oh, *dear*," Firebird murmured as Marshal Burkenhamn extended a solicitous hand to the Princess. Another weal was coming up now, at the base of her throat. "What is it in the air tonight?" Firebird backed away, raising her voice a little. "Everyone's breaking out!" Nearby heads began to turn. Someone on Firebird's left snickered.

Phoena threw down Firebird's punch cup, splashing one gawking bystander, and seized Rattela's arm. Holding one hand over her face, she pulled him toward the freshing rooms. Firebird caught the word "investigation," and laughter died on her lips.

She shut her eyes. She had won, but she felt sick; her glove-light shoes felt as though they were weighting her to the marble floor. She saluted the Marshal and then fled into Corey's arms, while gossip wafted the word of Phoena's humiliation and her own disgrace throughout the great ballroom.

They retired outdoors very late. Two small moons dimly lit the palace grounds, gleaming on the meandering pool and the glade of drooping fayya trees below the colonnade. Along its edge Firebird walked with Corey, slowly now, deep in thought. Every Wastling present had congratulated her for scoring on Phoena, and wished her luck in the investigation—as had several commoners, on the sly. Her apparent popularity comforted her. But . . .

Investigation. The word echoed in her mind. If only it might be delayed until she had gone out with the NPN. Burkenhamn might yet send her out to die honorably and save her name, but the scandal would mar her hopes for—

Blow the scandal. Proudly she tilted her head, suddenly certain that Alef and Jisha had escaped. If Phoena could have told her of their apprehension, she certainly would have done that. Public suspicion that Firebird had foiled the Redjackets would only enhance her future reputation— if only she could make it to VeeRon, and end honorably.

Beside a fluted column, Corey vaulted down from the long bright porch. Silencing thought to listen closely to the fayya leaves' unending rustle and the *swish-plop* of night-feeding skitters, Firebird followed. The grassy slope yielded beneath each step; still, she kept her dress shoes on. Sae Angelo's winter would come without her this year, but not even for bare feet on summer grass would she dishonor the uniform.

Corey halted under the dark foliage of a fayya tree and turned his face to gaze down at her. He looked so serious that she almost decided not to go for the stick.

But would she have another chance? Leaning down as if footsore, she reached for her left shoe and swept up the stick. "Score." She flicked a golden pin on the front of his uniform. "Wake up, Corey."

His mouth crinkled. "Oh, Firebird. That old game."

"Old game," she echoed. "You were glad we'd played it the night Erwin decided to try to cut you up."

"All right." He reached for her with one hand. "You caught me off guard. Your point. But do you remember the score?"

Oddly enough, she did. She'd consistently doubled his points over the years at the Wastlings' private dueling game, but this didn't seem like the time to remind him. "No, I don't." She slid a hand along his shoulder and down one arm, flicking his sleeve stripe. "Nice suit, Captain. You look your age tonight." Even in the shadows, the slick dress fabric gleamed.

Corey didn't seem to be attending. "Yes, you do too," he murmured absently, raising his head to stare across the park behind her. "Well," he sighed, "we've arrived, haven't we? 'We who stand on the edge of battle,'" he quoted from the commissioning ceremony. "The victims have come of age and are ready to be sacrificed, so the others may prosper."

Firebird stepped back, frowning, her arms hanging at her sides. "Corey? . . . That's not like you."

He sighed and caught her hand again. "Firebird." She

heard an unusual sadness in the way he spoke her name. "Usually it's all right, and I'd as soon enjoy tonight as anyone. I'd like to go out with a roar, too, and never lose my hair. But . . . ." His eyes fixed on the lake again. "I'd rather live. Wouldn't you, really? Marry . . . raise a—" He pressed his lips together.

"Family?" she supplied scornfully.

"Yes," he whispered. He squeezed her fingers, and his gaze came back to hers, uncannily sober—for Corey Bowman. "A family, Firebird. I like children."

She stood silenced by the yearning in his voice and a lump that rose in her own throat. For an instant she entertained the forbidden notion of posterity—to be represented among those future generations, to not be merely remembered by them, would be sweet. . . . Hurriedly she backed away from the thought. "Children are for heirs." The words came out more bitterly than she intended. She shook herself inwardly, and the controls she'd built over the years settled back into place. "Corey, you're only hurting yourself," she said firmly. "You know better. And why tonight? Tonight we should just be happy." She pressed against him, and his hands locked behind her back. A minute later she felt him relax. His familiar, man-scented warmth made her drowsy and comfortable as she rubbed her cheek against the front of his tunic. "Do you know," she murmured after a while, "the one thing I'm going to miss?"

"Mm?" His sharp chin shifted on top of her head. "Now who's doing it?"

She stared over his arm up into the distance, to darkness the garden lumibeams could not touch. "I would have liked to have seen the worlds of the Whorl. Imagine the night sky of Alta, Corey. Stars everywhere, huge, bright stars. VeeRon will be a good trip, and farther outsystem than most people ever travel, but the Federacy has so many worlds. I'd like to see them all."

"Of course," he whispered.

"Corey." She slid a hand onto his shoulder. "I do wish . . ."

A flock of nocturnal cardees flew low over the fayya tree, twittering protest at the first pale light appearing over the walls of the palace grounds, and then the stillness returned. Firebird held tightly until the melancholy mood passed.

Corey shifted. "Tired?"

"No. Yes. No. Let's go in and see if the orchestra has fallen asleep."

CHAPTER 3

VeeRon

Alla rondo
A short work involving
alternation; in a rondo
duet, the players alternate
carrying the melody

A week after the Officers' Ball, Firebird reported to Burkenhamn's office. The investigation had fizzled due to lack of evidence: Phoena's announcement had been a hazing prank after all, skillfully chosen to humiliate and frighten Firebird. Burkenhamn had apologized; she was cleared. But Phoena's accusations and influence had earned Firebird's squadron a place on the first attack wave, a position supposedly assigned at random because of its high risk.

Phoena always was impatient to finish a task, Firebird thought wryly as she ran a spot-checking hand under the keen edge of her tagwing fightercraft's fore wing, one huge golden arrow among hundreds below the lights of the carrier's hangar-bay. *But in this case she's only given me what I wanted.*

Close behind followed her crew chief in gray coveralls, clutching his pocket recorder and calling up components for her final checkout. Seventeen minutes remained before launch for attack; the carrier would return to normal space

in ten minutes, and in fifteen drop slip-shields over VeeRon
II.

"Starboard laser cannon," he called.

She caressed the barrel, set close to the fuselage under
the wing. Finding no external imperfections, she peered
into the focusing lens.

"Go," she answered, trying to sound cool. A First
Major should be able to keep excessive excitement from her
voice.

"Shield antennae, particle and slip."

This was it! No longer practice but a check for battle,
and she was glad she'd always trained as she intended to
fight. This felt as automatic as tying back her hair.

She stroked the little projection antenna. It appeared
to be secure. "Go," she answered.

"Starboard thrusters."

She moved aft to the second starboard wing.

The checkout ran perfectly. As she struggled into her
lifesuit just prior to mounting the cockpit steps, she caught
sight of Corey—*Captain* Bowman—dangling his helmet
from one hand and waving jauntily from the stepstand
alongside the tagwing ahead of hers. She returned the wave
and climbed aboard, then checked the clock on the console.

Seven minutes until launch. . . .

Through the pale blue sky of VeeRon II they dropped
in final deceleration. The four tagwings made a tight,
beautiful diamond on Firebird's main screen, and her
fightercraft's four wings bore single cobalt-blue stripes,
First Major's colors. On her fore screen, the locale of her
assigned target began to blink. Firmly harnessed to her
g-inclined seat, Firebird braced herself mentally for combat and gave an order.

"Delia, take the generators. Daley, the field projectors.
Corey, wingtip with me across the midline."

The sleek TSR-49s broke close formation and began
pouring out scarlet ruination onto the mining colony's
support depot.

A light on her left bluescreen caught her eye—two
lights—an entire flight—VeeRon interceptors soaring

south across the flats, beyond her line of sight but clear marks on her beyond-visual-range B-V board.

"Twenty-four, we have company," Firebird warned. An energy-field projector far below and behind exploded suddenly, spewing atomizing metal fragments half a kilo into the atmosphere. She gripped her throttle rod: adrenaline made her crow aloud. "Nice shooting, Daley! Now, let's *go*. Wingtip diamond." The fightercraft pulled together until they nearly touched and then turned as a unit for the interceptors.

Firebird concentrated on her B-V display, then line-of-sight. The moment the interceptors drew within range, they began firing laser cannon, but the overlapping slip-shields of the attack squad deflected the fire. "Half-eight left . . . now!" directed Firebird, and her squad peeled neatly away from the pursuers, looped bubble-down beneath them, came up behind, and began a chase of their own. The old-line atmospheric interceptors, just as awkward as she'd been trained to expect, split left and right. The N'Taian fightercraft followed in loose firing pairs.

"No kills," she ordered. "Just disable them. Careful, I don't read slip-shields on them." Left hand on the ordnance board, she shot a bull's-eye pattern of energy bursts as she maintained her position above the hindmost enemy's tail. Had the interceptors scattered, she might have had a real fight on her hands, but they clung together like banam fruit on a tree, trying to keep their shields overlapped. *All they can really do against better ships,* she reflected. She picked off four targets, shattering one wing of each on its axis, just beyond the shield overlap that protected the fuselage. Corey and Daley shot well too, and Firebird watched, satisfied, as Delia scored last and the final interceptor pilot nursed his craft gently down to planet.

"Now, let's finish that depot!" She fingered a star on her inner collar as she brought the tagwing into a tight turnabout. If this went on, she might even last long enough to win another pair of the glittering insignia—and promotions for her friends.

In her earphone, Delia called, "Right behind you, Major!" as she pulled into slot position of the reformed diamond.

Minutes later, the depot was a glowing mass of rubble. Firebird circled her squadron back to be certain the target was totally destroyed.

"Raptor Phalanx," a distant voice rumbled in her helmet. "This is Command. We have confirmed three Federate cruisers, breaking out of slip-state just inside VeeRon IV's orbit. Continue operations; maintain constant alert."

Squill! she exclaimed to herself. *So much for strategic speculation. "Too distant to defend?" And how in Six-Alpha did they get here so soon?*

Security had failed somewhere. With superior N'Taian technology and armament, losses had been light. Even VeeRon had suffered little, under the circumstances.

But the Federates' technological edge was an "assumed" in all drills. With the odds more equal—advanced Federate craft against N'Taian numbers—the battle would soon turn grim.

She fought off a chill. It was now very likely that she would be killed. She had taken her Orders at little Kessaree's birth. But Delia, Daley, and Corey had no such Orders—yet. Perhaps she could find a way to carry hers out and protect them at the same time.

Furthermore, the Federacy's reinforcements could not reach VeeRon II for some time yet. "Twenty-four, let's take one more installation. Six-two degrees east."

"What do we do when *they* get here?"

"We run for those mountains and try to lose them in the canyons, Corey." The four golden arrows soared over the plain toward a range of glowering pinnacles.

One more . . . good, she observed—a weaponry storage dump. They would take it quickly, before the Federates could use it.

At attack velocity, they covered the distance in bare minutes. Firebird doubted the colonists had had adequate warning of their approach. Controlling an urge to keep her eyes on the sky for the enemy, she ordered, "Circle once so they know we're here. Then we go in on my mark." Below, she hoped, civilians were scrambling underground.

One lazy, graceful circle in the pale sky, golden wingtips just meters apart. Then . . . "Go!" The formation burst and reformed into a horizontal line. One pass, and the ground-to-air defenses were neutralized. Firebird wheeled the line and returned at ninety degrees from the first pass, targeting the poorly camouflaged warehouses.

She ran a loving eye over the complex control panel of her craft. Flying this advanced short-range attack fighter in real combat was as satisfying as she had dreamed it would be: watching the horizon spin around her, pressing deep into her seat as its ion-driven engines responded to her command.

Several passes later, things began to turn. Corey saw them first. "Enemy fighters at oh-eight-six-five!"

Her B-V screen picked them up an instant later. There were six of them, and they were coming in from Corey's side: two pairs and two loose wingmen. From the speed they were no VeeRon interceptors. "Twenty-four, wingtip formation and overlap double shields. Let's run for it." *All we can really do against superior ships,* Firebird thought sardonically. She wheeled her craft and punched in the drive. Her escorts, still at strike speed, roared into left wing, right wing, and slot positions just behind her.

A tiny red light appeared on the B-V board: missile.

"Get it, Delia." Firebird clenched stick and throttle and waited without breathing.

Several seconds later, Delia's calm voice came over the link. "Missile down. They won't take us that way. They'll have to waste some energy."

The pinnacles loomed closer, nearly filling Firebird's field of vision, as six ominous pips advanced across her B-V board.

In the foremost of those Federate craft, her opposing squad leader gave an order. "Intercept range, ten seconds. Delta Six, drop in and check on the colonists. Call for medical help from the fleet if you need it." His far-left wingman peeled away; five elegant black Federate intercept fighters streaked on after the tagwings. "Pull in to energy wedge. Commence fire on my mark. Standard sequence."

* * *

Firebird's squadron desperately needed maneuvering speed, but she didn't dare push for it. Once the pursuers came into firing range, her very life would depend on the double shields' ability to cover the tagwings' critical spot at the engine ports, where the heat of escaping gases warped the energy shields. The doubling took almost half the output of a tagwing's laser-ion generator, slowing its flight, but so long as the Federates' lasers were off wavelength from the N'Taians' shields, Firebird had hope of turning the counterattackers into prey.

The Federate intercept fighters closed rapidly. Firebird could see them when she craned her neck: narrow wings perched at the far end of long sleek fuselages, black as jet, flying close to unify firepower on the slip-shields. Just as Firebird decided to cancel the canyons and try to turn as a unit on the executioners behind her, they opened fire. Delia Stele, in slot position, saw what Firebird could not: all five Federate ships trained their laser cannon on Corey's fightercraft, at right wing, where his engine ports lay on the unsteady edge of the shield overlap. And, incredibly, the shade of those beams began to change.

"Twenty-four," Delia shouted. "They're *tuning* those lasers! If they hit on our slip-shield wavelength—"

At that instant, Corey strayed from perfect alignment within the squadron. His ship exploded with a sudden flash of fusion fire that was quickly left behind.

Delia's anguished voice announced it. "Corey's gone!"

For a blind moment, Firebird was lost to the battle, unable to understand or believe that Corey Bowman had died in an instant. She wanted to cry denial, even as her boards confirmed the gap in the squadron where Corey had been.

A new sound shook her back to awareness. The pursuers streaked above them with a roar, gaining altitude and circling. Their strategy made no sense, but it gave her another chance. Her squad had almost reached the canyons, where it could split, and dodge, and perhaps trap those Federate pilots. But what were they doing, up there?

Delta Leader was starbred. The blood of the telepathic Aurian race from beyond the rim of the galaxy flowed in his veins, mingled with that of his Thyrian ancestors. And his concentration had suddenly been broken by a silent scream of grief that pierced his personal shields so intensely it took him three full seconds to understand that it had originated, not in his own mind, but in one of those N'Taian tagwings.

He glared at the six glowing sensor screens on his board. "Delta Squadron, cease fire and pull up."

Normally emotion-shielded, he could not sense any individual over that range, even one in emotional extremity. One of those men must have a kind of spiritual energy so like his own that he wondered how such a genetic sport could have arisen among the N'Taians. Even among his own people he rarely found the kind of connaturality—likemindedness on the deepest level—that led Thyrians into real brotherhood. That unknown pilot would be well worth his trouble to capture, perhaps eventually to recruit. But which one?

He overflew the tagwings that were so sluggish by comparison and circled high into the atmosphere, studying the fleeing enemy craft through a visual screen skewed far from the horizon by his turn. The best probe he could extend over such a distance would catch only intense, uncontrolled—

There: an echo of the presence he had sensed.

"We want the lead pilot: alive. Delta Three, get up to relay range with the cruiser and send the catchfield team his coordinates as soon as I get them. We take the others only if we have to." Another ship veered away, climbing furiously as his compatriots dropped, following in formation as Delta Leader nosed his intercept fighter into a precipitous dive.

Fate gave Firebird little time to grieve for Corey. Her anguish was diluted by intense relief when the Federate fighters pulled up; it turned to terror when they began their second dive.

"Delia, pull into right wing. We need full overlap on those rear shields or we're *all* dead!"

In close triangle formation, the 24th Squadron continued to flee for the mountains.

* * *

Delta Leader dropped rapidly, now entirely satisfied as to which one he wanted. "We're going to come in from above and scatter them," he directed. "Stay with the leader. Chase him out into the open so we can get a clear fix on his ship for the catchfield."

Daley's voice squeaked on the intersquad frequency. "Firebird, they're coming down right on top of us!"

She made a hasty decision just short of the pinnacles. "Drop-turn right. Mark!" The triangle of fightercraft dove under, looping directly back on itself. "Eight-zero degrees!" she called, and pulled away at a sharp angle from the pursuers. On the sims, that maneuver would have easily shaken off a pair of VeeRon interceptors.

But the Federates continued to close the distance with absolute accuracy. *They're good,* Firebird admitted. She knew that they wanted to break up her squadron now, for what purpose she could not guess: they were holding fire, although closing faster than when they had taken Corey. Blast Phoena and her misconceived secret project! What a wretched thing to die for. . . .

This was the time. She would give Corey the highest tribute and go with him. The wing colors on her craft made her the likeliest of a scattered squadron to be chased, and perhaps she could create enough of a diversion to allow Daley and Delia to escape.

"Twenty-four, I'm going to dive. Split nine-zero port and nine-zero starboard, on my signal. Maintain course at full velocity until you shake these birds. Get back to the carrier if you can."

"Right, Major," Daley's voice choked.

He knows, she reminded herself. He'll take his own Orders some day. She kept her voice calm and officer-like. "Daley, you're in charge. Give Carradee my best. Five seconds." She counted them down with a sense of utter unreality. This was only a role, one she'd been rehearsing for years. "Mark!" she shouted, and made a sudden plunging, twisting turn away from her wingmen. She cut in her thrust inverters to reduce her speed. Daley streaked on to the west, Delia to the east, and once clear of them, she headed down for the dark pinnacles and shut off the braking system.

Delta Leader smiled behind his visor as the tagwings scattered across the plain. "Let the wingmen go. Stay with the leader."

Firebird checked her display. Good. They had taken the bait of her colors; all four were on her. Things were happening too quickly now for her to think beyond the moment. At attack speed, the impact should explode her ship and catch theirs in the fireball. She'd never feel it.

She switched off both shielding systems to direct the generator's full output into the engines, accelerating the dive yet more. An alarm light began to pulse on the display.

"Delta Three, stand by: point—six—two—eight and dropping fast. Get him."

A jarring, wrenching pull two seconds later nearly put Firebird through the flight harness. Shaken, she checked the controls. Everything read functional, but she was going nowhere. No! Backward! Realization slapped her as limp as a dead thing: she was caught. Somewhere above her, a powerful Federate starship projected an electromagnetic snare, a catchfield, down into the atmosphere of VeeRon II. The field had seized the fightercraft and was drawing it inexorably back into space, into the Federate ship itself.

Firebird knew her duty: the Arride packet lay in her breast pocket. A believing person, she did not fear the void. But death was a dark door, and she was frightened of the passing through, now that circumstances had given her time to think. She brought her craft back to the horizontal and shut down the propulsion; no sense in being foolish about this.

She fished out the packet and tore off a corner with fumbling, unwilling hands. It wasn't quite powder, more like tiny crystals. She hesitated, wishing there were some quicker way to have done with it. The waiting for unconsciousness would be horrible. Her handblazer would be hard to reach, though, in the cramped cockpit, and when it came down to the choice, that didn't sound any more pleasant. Wasn't there any other way? Did she really want to die? No! She did not! But capture would be far worse.

A minute slipped by. The altimeter read higher and higher, and she could now see the Federate cruiser against the starry background, looming ever nearer. Ventral sensors showed a lone black intercept fighter below her like a black shadow on the clouds, circling and climbing slowly. It graveled her. Well, it *had* been a good life. She pulled the mask away from her helmet, saluted the Federate pilot with the packet, and tipped the crystals down her throat.

They choked her. She swallowed with an effort. "Done, Your Majesty," she said aloud. Then she bowed her head and waited.

A few minutes later, a second catchfield landed Delta Leader in a small docking bay aboard the Federate cruiser *Horizon*. The space door shuttered closed. Atmosphere swirled in, then techs and a carrier crew. Near the inner bulkhead, the golden tagwing rested silently upon another receiving grid.

Eager to face his prisoner eye to eye, Delta Leader sprang from his ship and hurried to the captured fighter-craft. The N'Taian pilot showed no signs of cooperating with the arrest. As another Federate soldier sprinted along-side and activated the external cockpit release, Delta Leader drew a shock pistol and held it ready.

The bubble swung upward.

"I think he's unconscious," remarked the subordinate.

Delta Leader holstered his pistol and leapt up onto the forward, triangular wing of the golden arrow. Unconscious, he affirmed, but alive, breathing raggedly.

He pulled off the pilot's gold flight helmet, releasing a flood of dark auburn hair to spill into—

By the Word, a female! His glance caught a flutter of white cellopaper on the footdeck. "Medical crew, Lelland. She's poisoned herself." As the subordinate spoke hurried-ly to an interlink, he lifted the N'Taian's body over the cockpit's side and jumped down onto the glossy deck, cradling her, noting in rapid succession the ruby stars, the absence of ID plate, and then the petite, lovely face: small nose, delicate chin, soft red cheeks. Brushing soaked auburn hair from her forehead, he knelt and steadied her on one knee. He could bring her body functions down to nearly nothing, slow her frantically pumping heart from spreading poison to all parts of her neural system, but he hesitated. Drawn though he had been by her mental cry and its connatural pull on his senses, he had been sworn to use his abilities only for matters of highest security. Was this such a case?

Yes: a valuable prisoner lay dying in his arms. He closed his eyes and turned inward for his epsilon carrier, then took command of her body. She slipped deeper into subsleep as the medical crew arrived, and he held her there, near death itself, as they readied ultradialysis equipment. One tech cut the heavy, outer lifesuit from her. He was exquisitely aware of her will, fighting his desperately for the right to escape into the void. Her alpha matrix had a savor that intrigued him, at once strong and submissive, courageous and hopeless. Gently he lifted her onto the repulsor stretcher, and the medical attendants went to work.

The blood-cleansing equipment hissed as it activated, and he relaxed his mental stance. The N'Taian rose to normal unconsciousness and her heart began to beat again, rushing poisoned blood to her vital centers but also into four clear tubes at wrist and throat, and from there into the dialysis system. He kept his grip steady on her arm; three meds in light yellow tunics watched their instruments just as steadily. A red light flashed at one corner of the console.

It stopped.

She was out of danger. One attendant turned to him. "She'll be out for a while yet, sir. Where do you want her?"

Abruptly weariness caught up with him. He rubbed his face with one hand. "Medical deck, in a sickbed with a restraining field, and under watch. She'll be suicidal, medic. Don't lose her."

One of the attendants steered the repulsor stretcher away. Delta Leader watched intently until the little group

disappeared into a corridor. That face . . . he *knew* that
woman. He commandeered a cup of kaffa and reported to
the command bridge.

"We've taken a prisoner, Frankin," he announced over
a second cup. "First Major's insignia. Tried to kill herself
when she knew we had her."

"Herself?" echoed General Frankin, an ebullient
white-haired acquaintance from Caroli. "We don't see
many women on the attack phalanx. You're the highest
ranking Sentinel with the fleet at present. Do you want to
interview her yourself?"

"Yes."

That was exactly what he wanted.

CHAPTER 4

Sentinel

Allargando
Slowing, increasing volume

Several hours after the deadly Arride had been filtered from her blood, Firebird began her slow climb to consciousness. At first, she reached out eagerly for sensations, curious about the afterlife.

The muffled sounds around her were all wrong, though, clattery and businesslike. Furthermore, she ached all over, particularly her shoulders. This was no afterlife.

She tried to bring up a hand to rub her eyes, but her body would not move. *Restraining field?* Cautiously she opened her eyes, and something began to beep softly nearby. Her worst, her very worst, fears had come true. The suicide had failed and she had been captured. Unfamiliar medical-looking machines stood on all sides.

A med attendant in a yellow tunic, responding to the beeping movement sensor, walked over and reached down out of Firebird's view. The beeper stopped and the field released her.

"You may sit up, Major," directed the attendant in a vowel-heavy accent Firebird couldn't identify, and she supported Firebird's elbow as she pushed herself up. Walls

47

wheeled around her. Firebird sat very still, and while she waited for them to settle down she struggled to recall boarding this enemy ship.

The nurse stood in front of her. "You're all right. Do you want something to eat?"

Firebird nodded. When had she last eaten? She sat warily on the edge of the sickbed, hoping the attendant would leave her for a minute. There was certain to be something nearby that was long and sharp and deadly. Horrified by the implications for Naetai of her capture, she clung to the hope of dying silently.

But the med turned directly to a servo on the nearest wall, assembled a covertray, and handed it across to Firebird. She accepted a hot cup of some sort of broth and several large soft objects with a texture somewhere between bread and crackers. She ate slowly, cautious for aftereffects of the poison—which a victim generally didn't need to know, and she had neglected to research.

"Enough?" asked the attendant.

She handed back the empty tray. "Thanks."

"All right. You're wanted on the next level up." The attendant turned slightly. "Lieutenant."

A lean, gray-uniformed man stepped forward from where he had stood unnoticed, waiting on guard at the end of the sick bay. He held a pair of open wristbinders.

Oh, no, she thought. *Not already!* She hopped down from the bed, twisted, and tried to run, but her body remained too weak from poisoning, and she sprawled on the slick white deck.

The guard and the medic helped her to her feet. "None of that, Major, unless you'd rather be put under sedation and carried." The manacles snicked shut on her wrists.

Beaten, she stood as tall and steadily as she could and faced her captors. "That won't be necessary. I'll walk."

"That's better. This way, please." Down the glossy gray metal decks, through the narrow corridor of the huge star cruiser, she forced her feet to take her. She passed a group of six or seven pilots in Carolinian khaki, who turned and stared curiously. Her guard kept a hand on her shoulder, and she fixed her eyes straight ahead.

Delta Leader had been called up immediately when the Major revived. He made a final lighting adjustment before settling on a black-seated stool between the laboratory's doorway and a long, contoured chair. At his left side, his scribebook lay crooked at the edge of the lab bench. He aligned it. No data on this subject would go onto computer —not yet. The security of the ship's databank could be broken more easily than the special shorthand he used to jog his trained, nearly eidetic memory. At any rate, the preliminary session would primarily establish a framework, decode her particular system of mental association so he could work within it.

He had searched his own recollections for clues to her identity and where they had met, but come up with nothing. The meeting must have been extremely inconsequential . . . but he would know soon enough.

Then there was the connaturality factor: if her personality patterns were very like his own, they might need little decoding.

This could be very, very interesting.

A short flight up in a lift tube. Another corridor. Firebird's wrists hurt. With difficulty, she maintained her composure: her instincts wanted her to run but there was nowhere to go. Before a doorpanel, they stopped. Her guard pressed his palm to a black square, and as the door slid away, he saluted someone inside.

"In here, Major."

She took a step into the room. Its function was obvious. There had been a rather tough class in this sort of thing during her third year at the P.N. Academy. A long lab bench, a contoured couch, a life-signs monitor board, other scientific equipment—some completely strange to her, some very familiar.

Then the man inside caught her glance. He was familiar too—the Sentinel—Caldwell. After half a second of unreasoning delight, she felt Vultor Korda's voice echo through the still air. *Don't even get close enough to recognize him.*

She bolted for the door.

He spoke a strange, sibilant word, and her legs went stiff. She stood breathing quickly as the metal door slid shut. The hopelessness of the situation crashed around her: she was about to be questioned by the strongest Sentinel the Federacy had produced in a hundred years.

"Come back," he commanded, and her legs took her to the side of the couch.

His uniform was blue like hers, but the deep midnight blue of the Thyrian forces, and on his right shoulder she saw the golden, eight-rayed star. He sat on the black stool, body straight, one hand upraised slightly from using the Aurian voice-command. When he lowered it, she felt the ethereal cords on her legs drop away.

She tried to steady her own shaking hands. Did he remember her, too?

"Lieutenant General Brennen Caldwell." He dipped his head slightly. "Of Thyrica."

"Yes." She avoided his eyes with all that remained of her determination. Korda had warned: *The eyes: a Sentinel can use them as windows to the mind.*

After she had stood quietly for almost a minute, he said, "I need to ask you some questions, Major."

His vowels sang strangely in her ears, but she understood him easily enough. "I know."

"You will answer them for me, then?"

"No."

"That's all right. I won't count it against you."

Irritated by his serene confidence, she tensed to fight or fly.

"Sit down, please."

Her body obeyed, despite her effort to resist the voice-command.

Brennen Caldwell removed the wristbinders. "Now sit. . . ." He halted.

She glanced up at his face, dreading what she might find there, then hurriedly looked down again.

"Lady Firebird," he said quietly. "I remember now. Do you remember me?"

"Yes," she mumbled. She could feel her heart pounding, a great weight jumping in her chest as she perched on the edge of that off-white couch with its restraining field and life-signs cuffs.

"How long have you been in Service, Your Highness?" He drew away, a gesture she supposed was intended to reassure. "You were only a schoolgirl when we met before."

It seemed a harmless, even friendly, question, but she could guess at his reason for asking: to get her talking, start her remembering. She shook her head.

"I see."

She watched his booted feet, planted firmly but casually on the deck. Soon they would move, and then it would begin.

"Sit back, then, Highness," he said, but he did not command this time. She found that she could remain where she was, and she did, clenching her jaws and gripping her thighs with her freed fingers.

"Lady Firebird, please. I would prefer not to force you."

"I will give you nothing willingly." She swallowed hard, still staring downward.

The feet moved: his heels came together squarely under his knees. "Then, sit back," he said with that queer tone in his voice, and she felt herself swing around and recline on the couch. Immediately she was caught again. "The restraining field is only to help me keep my mind on my work," he intoned calmly as he secured one life-signs cuff snugly around her arm. "Don't be afraid, Major, I'm not going to harm you."

She turned her head away. It was all she could move.

After a full minute's wait, he spoke again. "How long have you been in Service, Lady Firebird?"

She pressed her eyes shut. This was the real thing and she was thoroughly frightened, a variable that had not occurred to her in the classroom. She called the difficult etude back to mind and focused inward on it with performance intensity, waiting with the fringe of her attention for that revolting, prickly feeling to begin.

But Vultor Korda had only begun his Sentinel training. Brennen Caldwell had won a Master's Star. She gasped as she was assaulted by a sensation of vast weight that seemed to press her to the floor, surging into chinks in her defenses. She accelerated the tempo of the etude, making it harder to follow, demanding more concentration.

Unexpectedly, the weight lifted. "Someone has breached you before."

A monosyllable escaped her control. "What?"

"Who has trained you in access resistance?" When she remained silent, he went on. "I'm sorry for your sake that you have training. It will only make things harder."

She stared at the metal-panel ceiling. "I have a homeland, and I love it."

"You've done enough resisting already. First you tried to atomize yourself against a mountainside. Then you poisoned yourself. You've followed your orders—Major Angelo. I have no wish to force this on you. It will not be pleasant. How long have you been in Service?"

She lay obstinately silent.

"All right," he said softly. "I do understand. If it eases your conscience, then resist, for as long as you can. But it would be more comfortable for you if you would look this way."

She responded by shutting her eyes tightly.

The weight fell upon her again, and she bound herself round with a supreme effort of concentration. For long, desperate minutes she felt like a stone on the seashore, trying to hold back the tide, as the force of his starbred will beat on her like ocean breakers. She was drowning in the darkness, terrified to breathe.

A wave fell that was sharp and warm, and the weight began to subside, replaced by a piercing sensation of Presence. She inhaled with a hiccuping gasp, recognizing the signs: he had penetrated her outer defenses. Only her ability to evade stood between Brennen Caldwell and all she knew. She tried to concentrate on a more compelling piece of music—Iarla's Song—but he shifted her focus. She found her memory fleeing down the long stairway from her rooms toward the Electoral Chamber. Desperately, she pulled away and turned it outside, toward the gardens, but her thoughts shifted abruptly again, to the military, to her commissioning ceremony. She tried to cower beneath the music of the brass band, but he forced her awareness wide open. Huge, long-faced Devair Burkenhamn bent down to pin the ruby stars to her collar, shook her hand, and presented her Academy certificate. She read the commendation over and over, in satisfaction. At one corner was lettered the commissioning date.

The assault ended so abruptly that she was left in limp disequilibrium.

With an effort she roused herself, shivering with indignation.

He exhaled deeply. "You must realize that I cannot go on that way. Surface access is gentler, but as you see, it can be complex and time-consuming. I have orders of my own, you know."

She dropped her gaze hastily from his face to his belt. He wore no holster, but a glance at his left wrist confirmed that he was armed. Korda had told them about the Sentinels' ceremonial weapon, the crystace. A tear rolled from her eye. She couldn't wipe it away, and it trickled toward her ear.

"Perhaps *this* question you would answer for anyone, Your Highness: What do your friends call you?"

"Firebird," she choked. "And it's 'Lady,' not 'Highness.'" He brushed away the tear, surprising her so much that she volunteered, "It's an awkward name, isn't it?"

"I've heard much worse," he said soberly. "My friends call me Brennen—or Brenn. Can we be friends enough for that? Even though I must—do this to you?"

She wished this half-alien would treat her like an enemy, so she could hate him. "I suppose so," she grumbled.

"Thank you, Firebird." Staring at the ceiling, out of the corner of her eye she saw him take up a stylus and reach for a black scribebook that lay open on the lab counter. "You have courage," he said as he wrote. "I appreciate that, no matter which uniform you wear."

She swallowed a trace of salt water that had run down her nose.

"Relax, now. I will be gentle if I can."

She turned her head away and tensed deliberately.

"Stubborn," he chided. He dimmed the overhead lumipanel down to nothing, leaving only a small luma behind her. Nearer and stronger the alien presence drew, surrounding and pressing her awareness like falling stone. Inexplicable lights burned around her in the darkness. She flung herself against them, trying to fight her way back to memory, to awareness of anything but that invader, but bit by bit he beat down her resistance until all thought was pinned and restrained, as helpless as her body on the couch.

His voice seemed to come from inside her. "Open your eyes." She could no more disobey it than cease to exist. The white ceiling reappeared.

"Watch my fingers," he directed softly, lifting two fingers of his left hand and placing them before her face. They seemed to shine in the dim room as he swung them slowly across her field of vision, and back, back once more, then far to one side. When abruptly he dropped them, her dazed glance was snared by his eyes.

They were brilliant, azure blue. Her last defenses crumbled like seawalls of sand, and he held them down.

Mental images began to race out of her control, dizzying and sickening her, first the Planetary Naval inventory, then ship by ship its armament and defensive hardware. Schematics and illustrations and memories of qualifying flights spun by while she cowered under the buffeting hugeness of this Thyrian's will.

It stopped. He withdrew, and she was herself again, exhausted by useless resistance. How could she stop him now? She lifted her heavy eyelids and saw him writing rapidly into his scribebook. She urged her bruised memory toward Vultor Korda. *How* had he taught her to resist? To concentrate on nothings, blank her mind of anything that truly mattered. If only she had known nothing about—

As the thought rose into her mind she felt him seize it and home on Dr. Nella Cleary, her coworkers D'Stang and Parkai, and Phoena's passionate calls for Electoral support for the secret project. Firebird struggled frantically to break control, writhing against the restraining field. "No," she pleaded.

He did not speak. The luma went out, and he bent her memory again.

The session lasted for hours. When at last he brought up the room light, Firebird felt as limp and battered as if she'd flown a mission with neither a helmet nor a harness. He left her under guard to sleep for a while, and returned a few hours later with a small breakfast.

Then, it began again. Humbled but rested now, Firebird was determined anew to resist, knowing now that she could not succeed by strength. She relaxed her defenses and let him through, watching from a distance as he called back her memory of every secret Electoral meeting she had attended.

When he began to move her focus outward, to Naetai's defenses, she began her resistance. She called up the sounds of an orchestral suite she knew and loved well, bass and treble strings soaring together like background music to the skyward rise of her awareness. Sensitized to his point of focus, she felt him touch the music. It caught him. Effortlessly it swept him along with her, back to neutral ground. She felt him press into a different part of her awareness altogether, heightening pleasurably the emotions the music touched.

He withdrew roughly.

Disconcerted, she shook loose of the music and the warm feelings he had aroused. When she could think clearly again, she opened her eyes.

He had drawn back a few feet. "Very good." His voice, although not angry, sounded tired—and definitely peeved. "You surprise me." He stared at her for quite a while without attempting access again. Then he shifted his stool. "It's an interesting thing. Mind-access almost invariably causes revulsion and a sense of foreignness. Do you feel those signs?"

Recalling the "otherness" of Vultor Korda, she grimaced. "No. I do not."

He made a few aimless marks on the scribebook, set down the stylus, then raised his fingers again. "Watch," he commanded.

But she had finished cooperating. He took no more

information on Naetai's defenses until he had exhausted her again; then, he scanned her mind like a data tape, without drugs or intimidation, and for all her resentment she was glad he did not need them, for he could have terrified her. He had discovered her single phobia: needles. Subcutaneous dispersers. Injecting instruments, so commonly used by the Redjackets and in N'Taian interrogation. All her efforts to desensitize herself had only made it worse. She guessed that the compartments at his side held dozens of the ghastly things. . . .

But he gentled her repeatedly, pausing to flood her raw nerves with warmth that carried the savor of his own presence. The mental touch of Vultor Korda had sickened her; this felt entirely different, like being plunged into a warm ocean permeated with incense.

That sensation only intensified her desperation.

Forced backward and forward in her memory, she lost track of time. At some point, as he sat writing in the scribebook and she waited for him to begin on her again, she tried to guess what he could have been and done in the Planetary Navy, and what it would have meant for Naetai.

"I wish you were N'Taian," she sighed, meaning nothing disloyal.

"And I wish you were Thyrian. Watch my fingers."

At the next respite he began to suggest that she seek asylum among the Federate forces. At first she thought he was small-talking, but he persisted, and eventually it became evident that he was entirely sincere.

Finally he closed his notes, laid the book on his lap, and leaned against the lab bench. "I'm sorry, Firebird. Forcing a mind is tiring, for both involved. Vultor Korda is a scoundrel. I have met him. He did you no favor by teaching you to resist that way, but the worst is over for you." He touched a control. The restraining field collapsed, and she stretched gratefully. "I'm finished. I will not be listening to your thoughts any longer. You are a sovereign being, and as a Sentinel I am bound to honor your privacy, except when circumstances demand otherwise."

She faced him quietly.

"You should also know," he continued, "that of all the people I have accessed for the Federacy, I have never met a person of your abilities who was so content to throw her life away in battle. I'd not see you 'wasted,' Lady Firebird." Rotating on his stool, he set the scribebook on the lab bench behind him. "You could still be a great help to us."

Firebird held down her anger. She did not wish to discuss joining the Federacy, for she was N'Taian, and proud to prefer death to treason. "I have no hostage value, General. I am 'Geis'—to be finished. They virtually signed my death warrant when Carradee's second child was born and I dropped to fifth in the succession."

"Why?"

"I've told you. I am a—"

"Why, by all that's sacred, do your people kill the extra heirs? Why not simply disinherit them?"

"Oh. I see what you're asking." She clenched both fists in her lap. "About three hundred years ago, not long after the Keepers left us, a pair of younger heirs—disinherited under the old custom—led an uprising that very nearly succeeded. They were popular; the ruling regime was not. The Coper Rebellion was bloody and long, a blot on our history, and after it was quelled, the custom was—changed. By Electoral decree."

She glanced at him. The weariness in his eyes led her to soften her voice. "Flying in a combat squadron was one of my life dreams, but I was assigned to the first attack wave to die. First-line, right into the defenses, is a common use of Wastlings. If we succeed, we win lasting acclaim. If not . . ." She shrugged. "We die honorably. No drone can take out defenses as effectively as a trained human.

"But now—my very survival confuses the succession."

Bowing his head, he steepled his fingers and sat silently. Somewhere nearby, a faint mechanical hum changed pitch.

"Would you like kaffa?" he asked.

Firebird shook her head. He touched a control above a cubby beside his scribebook. A minute later he pulled out a cup, drained it, and keyed for another.

"We cannot ignore Naetai any longer," he said. "We will be needing someone who can advise us, who understands N'Taian mindset and policies."

"You know all there is to know."

"Oh, I know what you have seen, and done, and felt recently." He frowned. "But the will that controls your decisions lies deeper than I have searched. In the same way, the Federacy might respond to a situation one way, while the Angelo regime might do something entirely different. You, understanding the mindset, might be able to anticipate them and help us avoid costly mistakes."

"I can't betray my people." She turned away. "I've done them enough harm already. If Naetai is destroyed in this war, there will be only one N'Taian to blame."

"You don't understand us at all, if you believe we would do that. We will never destroy a people, not even in a war. But do you understand that there is a difference between the people of Naetai"—he locked her eyes again, and she felt her breath quicken—"and the government of Naetai?"

"Yes, of course," she muttered.

"Are you aware of the greed, and deception, and chauvinistic arrogance that has surrounded you all your life?"

Firebird sat very still. Her cheeks felt flushed.

"To bring down a regime like that could be to win new freedom and advancement for your people—whatever their history. But for now, I understand the way you feel." He walked away, hands clasped behind his back. "Perhaps in time you'll reconsider."

She could bear it no longer. "You are speaking of my family, General. What do you know of honor? You're Federate."

"Federate I am," he said quietly, "but first, I am Thyrian."

He placed his feet apart and raised a hand. A thrill of apprehension shook her: was he about to voice-command again?

"Under normal circumstances," he said, using the hand only to gesture, "you might have been held under cold stasis until the hostilities end, but I wish to treat you differently. I am willing to sign asylum papers for you. Let them be under another name, if you can't come to us openly—I can do that for you. Let them be temporary, if

you're not ready for a commitment yet. But you need time
to make an informed choice."

"No." Firebird gripped the edge of the couch. "Thank
you, but no. I expect no more than death with honor, and
I'll be glad to have it over with."

He drew up stiffly. "If you won't accept asylum, you'll
be my prisoner. I am sorry. The brigs on this ship are even
smaller than the cabins. But you will be anonymous. Try not
to think like a Wastling for a few weeks."

She cringed under his stare. "Are you listening to me
think now?"

"No, Firebird." A ghost of a smile peered through his
eyes and then vanished. "You'd certainly know if I were:
it's an unmistakable sensation. I'll never force access on you
again, unless Federate security is at stake. Remember that."

She nodded. Her thoughts, at least, were private again.
But he seemed to read her emotions like a scanbook. At
every change of her mood, he had responded.

"You suggested another name." She sat rigidly, aware
that she had lost another small battle. "Let's make it a
common one."

He curled two fingers under his chin. "Marda," he said
softly. "No. Mari. Popular enough, but pretty enough to
suit you." He dropped his hand and let his glance linger on
her. "You like it."

She scooted backward, a little farther from him. "I do.
I've—always liked that name."

"Good. Now give it a solid N'Taian surname. You'll still
be N'Taian—a political refugee, I think. . . ."

Into *Horizon*'s log, over the vast catalog of intelligence
taken from Firebird's mind, Brennen Caldwell recorded
the name of another pilot captured at VeeRon, and on
Firebird's registry was entered "Mari Aleen Tomma."
"Mari" had never attacked a mining world in her life, never
sat on the Electoral Council that ordered the invasion. The
guilt Firebird felt about the deception was overshadowed
by her shame at having shown the Federacy everything—
certainly it was everything—that she knew.

With a promise of anonymity her only remaining

possession, she let them lock her into a shipboard holding cell about two strides across, her cobalt-blue uniform with the ruby stars—a mockery to her in the baleful light of the detention area—replaced with a green workier's coverall. And as the tide of battle turned over VeeRon, First Major Firebird Angelo huddled down upon a rock-hard cot and cried bitterly.

CHAPTER 5

Mari

Meno mosso
A little less quickly

With a full division of the Federate fleet defending the VeeRon system, First Marshal Burkenhamn elected the route of discretion and recalled his forces. Firebird was not told of that, but she guessed it. Within a day, another uniformed Sentinel took her from her cell. Few noticed them. Those who did saw only a small woman with very long auburn hair that hung loose over a green coverall, and a dark-haired Thyrian who followed protectively close behind her.

An atmospheric shuttle, a flattened oval with stubby delta wings, lay against *Horizon* like a bud on its underside. A lift shaft dropped Firebird and her guard from the cruiser's lowest level into a shuttle corridor, down which they followed a waist-high trail of tiny red lumas to a private cabin. Firebird shuddered when she noticed a line of pressure, gravidic, and atmospheric compensators on the cabin wall. Aliens had used this shuttle, and not as prisoners.

The Sentinel, Corporal Jonnis Decka, secured the lock and waved her to the window bench. Decka looked only a little younger than Caldwell, but his round face and curly hair made him seem very different. Eyeing the four-rayed star on his shoulder and wondering how his talents differed from a Master Sentinel's, she buckled a harness of black webbing across her lap and shoulders. Soon, their shuttle and four others pulled clear of *Horizon* and drifted gracefully toward Twinnich. There, at VeeRon's main settlement, Decka had told her, the Federacy had chosen to base a peacekeeping force just large enough to make the Federate presence official. In one day more the Division would begin to disperse, each element returning to its home base, with the bulk of the ships bound back for Regional Command at Alta, or for VeeRon's governing world, Caroli.

Ten squadrons of sleek black intercept fighters and a trio of tiny messenger ships escorted the shuttles. As they glided toward the red-shaded sands of the plain, Firebird withdrew into a gray haze of contemplation, staring out the viewport. Daley and Delia—had they been imprisoned too, or killed, or were they on their way back home? Her eyes watered, remembering Corey and the way he had died.

Jon Decka leaned toward the large oblong window panel. "There." He pointed. "That would be Twinnich."

She blinked back her tears and followed his gesture, out and down, as the shuttle banked. Twinnich shone and sparkled, like bright children's blocks scattered around their cylindrical bin. A slight movement of Decka's hand brought her glance back inside the cabin. His tunic's deep blue sleeve had risen far enough to reveal one end of a weapon sheath. He reached casually across to pull the sleeve down, and covered the crystace.

Once again she heard Vultor Korda's voice.

"Hollow handgrip, activator stud, sounder, and aurite crystal in the well." The slouched little man straightened just enough to sketch a rough design on the teachboard with one fingertip. "The crystal in each one of them is priceless, and we're still not sure what the chemistry is. Imbedded in the handguard is this sonic mechanism. You can hear it if you're in the same room. Like one of those little bugs that fly into your ears. . . ." He appeared to be groping for the name.

"Bloodletter," offered Daley Bowman from his seat behind Corey.

"Yes. Sounds like that. Now, do you all know why ice floats?"

Firebird and Corey exchanged bored glances.

Korda didn't miss a beat. "It's lighter than liquid water—less dense. The molecular bonds in the ice crystal expand when it freezes. Activate a crystace and the same thing happens, only more so. As a certain resonant frequency is sounded, the crystalline bonds elongate along the beta and gamma axes, and you've suddenly got a crystal as long as your arm, as wide as your hand, and with two cutting edges exactly one atom thick. That's sharp, in case you couldn't figure it out."

"So you need a twinbeam blazer," suggested Corey. "Sir," he added, mimicking Korda's unflattering tone.

"Hardly. The refractive properties of the Aurite crystal will scatter cohesive laser waves into harmless beams of light."

"Where are they made?" Delia twisted a long blond curl around her ring finger.

"They're not. The Aurians brought them when they came, and no one has figured out how to make them. Apparently the crystace was developed as a shipboard weapon before variable-power energy guns came into widespread use."

Firebird spoke up. "Does the crystal have fracture planes? How can you fight a man carrying one?"

"You shoot him before he knows you're there."

"That's all you can do?"

"You might try a shock pistol, if you're fast—or a sonic disruptor. But your chance of tuning in the resonant frequency is about as good as hitting Menarri with a rock. The pitch varies with the size of the crystal."

She glanced down to Decka's holster. It held a shock pistol, not a blazer. They did suspect she'd try to escape, then, and they intended to keep her alive. At least they hadn't bound her.

The shuttle touched down in the shady steel half-dome of a landing pod. After the other passengers had debarked, Firebird followed alongside Decka through a clear-roofed passage onto a walkway that swept them into the central tower. Inside, the sparkling cluster wore a layer of dirt: prematurely aging under colonial neglect, the premises stood littered with derelict papers and containers, dropped perhaps in the initial terror of the N'Taian attack. Even the tower had a shabby, ill-cared-for atmosphere, as though the people who worked or lived there hoped to collect their fortunes soon and move on.

Firebird walked quietly with Decka to the elevators, where a pitted steel door ground open before them. The cubicle already held a silent, old couple wearing shapeless gray coveralls, and two boys midway through their teens in torn and faded shorts. Firebird kept her eyes on the door as the others left them two by two. Finally, Corporal Decka touched her shoulder as the door opened on the fifth floor belowground.

Between two pressure-tiled passways stood a badly scratched gray desk. Two men in light blue uniforms, one dark-tanned and reed-thin, the other pale, cross-looking, and only slightly heavier, slumped behind it. As the elevator grated shut behind Firebird and Decka, the pale man snatched a cartridge from the tri-D viewer's program port while his dark partner hurried around in front of the desk, carrying a 2-D recorder and a recall pad in his gnarled hands.

"Mari Tomma?"

Firebird nodded stiffly, noting that these two avoided approaching the Sentinel too closely.

The dark man glanced down at his recall pad while she eyed his nameplate: *Tryseleen*. Tryseleen looked very much at home in the underground passway: he, too, had an air of decline under long use. "We didn't get her rank or status, in your transmission, Corporal. Military?"

"Personal registry," Decka corrected smoothly.

"Ah. She registered to you, then?" Tryseleen took Firebird's right hand by the wrist, spread her fingers, and held it against the recall panel. His tan, calloused hands scratched.

"General Caldwell," Decka answered.

Tryseleen's eyebrows arched, and he stepped away. "The Thyrian Caldwell?"

"That's correct."

Firebird tensed under their examination. Naetai had rather dubious customs regarding female prisoners under personal registry—which could signify anything from protective custody to prostitution—and she wondered if that designation carried a similar inference on VeeRon.

"Mari Tomma." The pale-skinned guard scowled, grabbed the camera from his colleague, and pressed the exposure release without warning. "Where have I seen you before?"

Her heart sank. Had she been recognized? She studied the grimy floor. Tryseleen finished scribbling on the registry and then presented it to Firebird for confirmation.

She examined the careful blend of truth and lie she and Brennen Caldwell had orchestrated:

NAME:	Tomma, Mari Aleen	Wrong.
BORN:	Sae Angelo, Naetai III, Naetai Systems (Independent)	Right.
AGE:	18.2 G.S.A.U.	That looked wrong, but she knew the computations for correcting her 22 nine-month N'Taian years to 360-day Galactic Standard Annual Units. It must be correct.
HEIGHT:	64.0 G.S.L.U.	
WEIGHT:	78.5 G.S.M.U.	Both right.
OFFENSE:	Political	Partly right.
RANK:	N/A	Dead wrong.
STATUS:	Personal registry	

He scrawled "Caldwell" below the "Personal Registry" entry and flamboyantly circled both names, then strode off down the shorter, left branch of the corridor. It took Firebird a moment to realize that she was expected to follow.

The small cell with mottled gray walls smelled vaguely stale. Tryseleen shut her in without ceremony, leaving her to examine the network of blemishes on the floor. *At least*, she reflected, *this cell is big enough to walk in.* She tried the cot and found it slightly softer than the one in the shipboard brig. Cautiously she lay back on it, stretched, and gazed up at cracks in the gray-green permastone of the ceiling.

Decka had told her that most of the Federate ships were going back to Alta, but she was to be held on VeeRon, for Brennen Caldwell of Special Operations had been given command of the peacekeeping force.

In a small, stark private room twelve stories above the detention center, Brennen Caldwell took a sip of kaffa from his half-empty cup, made a face, and thumped the cup onto his desk. It had gone as cold as Thyrian rain.

How long had he sat staring at that wall?

He cleared away the mental images that had held him hypnotized, pushed back his stool, and spun it to face out into the bedroom. Part of the inner-tower security quarters, it had no window, though the walls had been painted off-white to compensate, and a long beachscape, heavy on the purple end of the spectrum, hung opposite the desk. On the room's only other furnishing, a low cot, his midnight-blue duffel still lay open.

He would finish unpacking and then stow it to keep himself moving, keep from staring like a night-slug.

A muscle in his leg twanged as he stepped off the stool, and he stretched it before crossing his quarters.

Only a small, clear packet remained at the bottom of the carryall. Disgusted, he frowned. He'd unpacked so mechanically he'd forgotten. Through the packet's wrap, gold gleamed. Brennen focused a flicker of epsilon energy into one hand and called the packet to his fingers, then rubbed it thoughtfully. Years ago—on Planetfall Day, the festive commemoration of the Aurians' arrival . . .

. . . His memory shifted. Tarance, his older brother, dark hair still uncombed at breakfast, stood tall over him as Brennen fumbled to unwrap the small package. (A glimmer of little-brother adoration rose, and he savored it. He'd not let it pass his trained emotional controls in years.) The medallion fell free, a bird of prey plunging with wings swept back almost to touch each other. Delighted, young Brenn held it up in the bright light of the kitchen. On an impulse he flung it high. "Fly!" he called. The golden bird hovered for a moment above his outstretched hand. His mother covered her mouth, and his father blinked rapidly several times. "Put that down!" exclaimed Tarance. "You can't do that!" The medallion clattered on the center of the table. . . .

. . . He sat alone in the room he shared with Tarance. Rain drummed steadily on the wooden roof as his irritation rose: the medallion would not stay in midair. He'd been unable to repeat the unexpected trick until trained. . . .

Both brothers had been tested for epsilon potential that autumn, though at ten Brennen was much younger than the usual applicant. Tarance had tested very respectably, particularly in carrier strength, but Brennen was inducted on the spot into College.

. . . Tarance stuffed one more pair of pants into his duffel, silent in indignation, as Brenn, already wearing a sekiyr's ring, folded shirts on his own bed. Overnight Tarance had changed. . . .

. . . Young Brennen sat with Master Keeson in College, head back in a comfortable chair, struggling to focus static from a tightly modulated epsilon carrier between emotion and his awareness. The intense, painful heartbreak of Tarance's resentment served well as a target sentiment. . . .

Absently Brennen set the medallion on a corner of the gray desk. Tarance had abandoned their mutual ambition to travel the Federacy, had gone into psi medicine and bonded a wife, while Brennen rose through the lower ranks of the Thyrian forces and vaulted into Federate service. When Brennen had been winning the Federacy's Service Cross at Gemina, Tarance had begun a family.

Brennen's own romantic dream, of bonding the perfectly connatural woman the day he found her, had yielded
to control, for she was not to be found among the few
women near his age in the starbred families. His enthusi-
asm had shifted to his career as the hope faded and
vanished.

Brennen touched the medallion's beak. It pricked,
even through the wrapping. He wore no jewelry but his
Master's Star; still, he had carried this memento of youth
and family wherever the Federacy sent him.

His desk viewer still displayed a page of pale blue
characters on a deeper background. Brennen shut it down.

How things could change in an instant!

Still guarding his emotional threshold, he allowed the
hypnotic memory to return: . . . body steady, mind chan-
neled for work, he sat aboard *Horizon*, his prisoner restrained for interrogation. He caught her glance, focused
the carrier, and made the breaching plunge.

Braced for suffocating "otherness," to his astonish-
ment he found only warmth. The deeper he worked the
carrier, the more intense the sensation became. His awareness began to shift, so complete was the linkage, so natural
Firebird's reactions to challenges she recalled. His orders
took hours to fulfill: hours, deep in this connatural
matrix. . . .

Shaking his head, he cleared memory again. He should
have predicted all this from the power of her mental cry
over VeeRon. *Where did she get that strength?* Her eagerness to take a pseudonym had eased a gnawing tension and
allowed his subconscious to separate the identities: Firebird before that plunge; Mari after, the woman he knew;
and Brennen, free to know both.

But she was a provincial aristocrat, raised in a palace!

Some things are not in your grasp. The voice of
Shamarr Lo Dickin, his sponsoring Master, echoed from
another pool of memory. *Even you, Brennen. You can refuse
to walk any path, for your will and rewards are your own,
but some fates will find you.*

How would the Shamarr react to this, looking outside
the starbred for a mate? The connaturality itself did not

compel him to take the relationship further. He had controlled those youthful hopes and established a very satisfying career—and cultural factors could crush such a
friendship. Firebird knew nothing of his people, had no
inkling of the complex web of identity and ambition inside
him, into which she had torn.

But bedim the woman, he enjoyed her company.
Moreover—he smiled, recalling the memories he had
observed—she found him appealing.

. . . Soaring music of winds and strings captured his
attention, sweeping him off the focus of the interrogation.
The warm smooth slippage of her deepest feelings reso-
nated with his own. . . .

Not for years had anyone broken his concentration in
the deep, class-three access of an Intelligence-class prisoner. What were his odds of having met her in battle?
Thousands, tens of thousands to one?

Caught: his memories would neither fade nor lie quiet
under a sediment of daily experiences, not if he lived for a
century.

Other access-transferred memories clamored for attention: Wastling memories, cruelties of the heirs, and a fierce
pride in that fatal destiny. . . .

Abruptly he forced down the visions, disrupted his
emotions, and sank staring, visually and mentally blank, on
the edge of the cot.

That evening Tryseleen, finishing his shift, escorted
Firebird from her cell to a nearly vacant room so large that
it occupied a quarter of its high floor of the tower. Apparently, the lanky guard was as interested in the workings of
the Federate patrol as she, for he stood at the triple door
for some time, looking around, leaning one hand on a
pillar.

The communications center lay half-surrounded by a
long L-shaped span of glasteel windows. At its heart stood a
tri-D well, a transparent cylinder just over waist high and
two meters in diameter; a relief-figured reddish sphere
inside it mapped the surface of VeeRon II. A bank of radio
and laser-pulse interlink transceivers—Firebird counted

only four terminals—followed the well's curve. A map on the wall at her left displayed the stars near VeeRon, glimmering faintly above a long conference table surrounded by rotating stools. Its lines looked primitive to Firebird, but as the NPN had found, VeeRon was miserably equipped for defense.

A single controller occupied a transceiver terminal, and Brennen Caldwell leaned over the tri-D well, backlit in the dusk by its glow, hands resting on its edge. His pale brown hair swept with a hint of curl just below the high collar of his midnight-blue tunic. *That's longer than our regulation length,* she mused.

At that moment he turned, and it occurred to her that this Sentinel who had examined her mind so thoroughly might sense her presence. Defensively she muted her thoughts, as he left the well and crossed to the doors.

Tryseleen drew up to a stiff salute. His pale blue uniform looked slightly more dignified on his straightened shoulders. "You sent for Miss Tomma, sir."

Brennen saluted with a little less flair and extended a hand. "Brennen Caldwell. Thyrica."

"Koan Tryseleen, of Caroli, sir." The calloused hand joined Brennen's smooth one. "Recently of VeeRon." As soon as their hands dropped, Tryseleen stepped back.

"How long have you been here?"

"Six years, sir. Welcome, sir. We were cert'ly glad when you all turned up. Looked like we were going to be Naetai's next buffer system."

An amused flicker of Brennen's eyes lit on Firebird before he spoke again to Koan Tryseleen. "Off duty, now?"

"Yes, sir."

"Would you have an hour to do me a favor?"

Tryseleen, who had begun to slouch again, straightened back up with what Firebird read as pleasure. "I think so, sir."

"I understand Twinnich has a resource center. Could you withdraw five or six good cadet-level scan cartridges on Federate history and a viewer?"

"Of course, sir."

"I'd like you to bring them to Miss Tomma when you come on duty tomorrow morning."

"Very good, sir." Tryseleen cocked an eyebrow at Firebird. She glanced toward Brennen, trying to project her discomfort with Tryseleen's presence.

Brennen nodded. "That will be all, Tryseleen. Thank you."

The dark guard strode out, and Firebird wandered to the angle inside the L of the windows. There, she gazed out over the scattered low outbuildings of Twinnich. Below the sky, now a regal shade of purple, the settlement glimmered with lights, yellow and white on a hodgepodge of quonsets and rectangular bunkers. Brennen followed her over and took a stool near where she stood.

She turned to him. "Thank you for the books, sir," she said in a quiet voice.

"Brennen. I am off duty now." He matched her low volume. "I'm aware that you know very little about the Federacy. You shouldn't reject us so offhandedly."

"I'd like to know more about the Whorl worlds." *Before I die,* she amended mentally. Overhead, constellations were appearing that looked barely, satisfyingly different from those of her home. She looked at . . . Brennen, he wanted to be called, although he had not corrected Tryseleen. He too was watching out the windows, and suddenly she felt vulnerable. It vexed her. She brought her heels together and turned to stare out at the quonsets again. "So you're not chasing the Planetary Navy back to Naetai?"

"No." His voice, she noticed incongruously, was mellow but not deep: he would sing tenor, if he sang at all. "Our mission was to defend the colonists here, not to discipline your Navy. I think Naetai has learned its lesson."

The declaration startled her. This unsupported peace-keeping force presented a perfect target for an attack of vengeance and wounded pride, and as soon as the Electorate knew the situation, surely it would turn the NPN strike group around and order it back to VeeRon. In mere days, this outpost might be under attack again. How could he have missed that in her memory—and what else might he have missed? Perhaps he too had limitations.

Firebird shifted uncomfortably. If she were found alive

or under stasis and recaptured by Naetai, her trial and execution would be that of a traitor, a public spectacle such as Naetai had not seen in years.

But did she have the courage to ask for the only real alternative?

She shot Brennen a glance. If he was reading her emotional tumble he gave no sign. Loosely he perched on the metal-legged stool, both hands on his knees. "Brennen," she began. Pleased to hear her voice coming out more boldly than she felt, she plunged ahead. "If you won't release me, you owe me the dignity of letting me die peacefully here. I cannot live with the shame of treason."

He blinked. His smile flattened into official impassiveness. "Mari Tomma," he said slowly, "I want to tell you three things. First, I am astounded that the N'Taian government is willing to waste a person of your talents, and that you are willing to comply. Sometimes an officer finds it his duty to disobey an order that contradicts all reason.

"Second, you want to be admired in memory." His frown-lines softened. "Of course. But the Federacy honors its leaders too. You could accomplish so much among us.

"Finally." He flexed his hands. "I haven't the authority to sign a capital order on one of your social rank."

"Who does?"

"The Regional Council, at Alta." He challenged her with a pointed stare.

She ignored it. "Would you ask them for authorization, then?"

"Don't even request it."

"Then, give me a blade. I know how to use it."

"Mari." He sounded angry now.

Her nerve failed. She sighed. "What will my people think of me?"

He relaxed forward a little and furrowed his forehead. "Your fighter," he said softly, "was destroyed: launched from *Horizon* and crashed on autopilot near the place where you were captured. So you are free. Your people think you are dead."

Firebird let the shock charge through her as a four-ship patrol screamed overhead, then circled down to a landing pod. *Free.* She dropped her guard slightly. It would be good to live.

Brennen fingered his cuff tab. "You can have your honor *and* life, now."

"I don't want your—"

"You don't want to die, 'Mari Tomma,'" he insisted. "Your people have odd customs, but this practice of 'heir limitation' goes beyond oddity. I find it uncivilized and disgusting to raise a child for slaughter. Look what it's done to you."

She shifted her feet but went on meeting his stare.

"Where you could have become a leader of your people, you hope to be a martyr. You want to think of death and dying when there are people you could serve, could help, if you put that determination into a field of work.

"Then, you have your music. Don't you realize what a gift it is? At the very least, as a performer you could bring pleasure into hard lives. Perhaps you could lead a cultural exchange that would bring your people into Federate prominence and make Naetai a respected world. But look at you: standing there, asking me to have you killed. You're young, lovely, and talented. But branded across your mind is the word 'Wastling,' and you're proud of it."

"Of course I'm proud of it," she snapped, suddenly upset. "My honor is at stake, Brennen. It's as much my part to insist on obeying my orders as it was yours to interrogate me."

He rose from the stool, scrutinizing her. "As matters stand, you could effectively vanish; but if I issued such a request as you want through channels, it would mean the end of your anonymity, whether or not they granted the authorization to execute."

"I'll take that risk."

His jawline tensed and hardened, and he appeared to be struggling with the decision. "All right, then," he said at last. "I'll send for it now."

He walked to the nearest transceiver, and from a slot beneath it slid a sheet of scribepaper. Without a glance to the controller, he returned to where Firebird stood, and drawing a stylus, wrote quickly, using the stool for a table. He signed the paper and then handed it to her.

She read it carefully. It was apologetic and lacked command, but, amazingly, it was what she had asked of him. "When will you send it?" she asked.

"I would prefer to shred it."

She remained silent. The last thing she needed was the sympathy of an enemy.

"Now. If that's what you truly want," he said at last.

"That's what I want."

His eyes accused her, and she knew she had lied, but she said no more. Frowning, Brennen set the scribepaper into a travel roll and dropped it down a chute for the next scheduled messenger departure: the fastest means of inter-system communication, until someone developed a way to extend the range of FTL "DeepScan" communication waves.

She slid up onto a stool now herself, considering while the night deepened. She had settled matters as well as she humanly could, and Brennen had done as she had asked, against his expressed personal preference. Placated, her sense of honor sent her groping for some way to repay him—although the elimination of a Master Sentinel would be a significant score for Naetai. Undoubtedly Naetai would try again, either to destroy Twinnich or to take enough irradium from under Brennen Caldwell's nose to finish Cleary's research. If he were warned—if he had his patrols on alert when they returned—might he, with his ten little squadrons, hold Naetai again?

If he had reinforcements, she told herself, perhaps the Federacy would stop Naetai's conquest of VeeRon, and the threat of Cleary's allegedly ultimate weapon would come to nothing. She cleared her throat to speak, but when Brennen glanced at her, she turned away.

A man in pale blue limped in, carrying several rolls of print paper and a long, thin cylinder. "Where's General Caldwell?" he asked the controller.

Brennen signaled to the guard beside the door, who reached the stools while the limping man was still several steps away. "Escort Miss Tomma back to detention, please."

Numbly Firebird set her face toward the elevator—and her cell.

CHAPTER 6

Strike

Subito allegro
Suddenly fast

In the elliptical Chamber of the N'Taian Electorate on the
Angelo palace's ground floor, Count Tel Tellai excused
himself from a knot of Electors discussing hopes for the
invasion forces. Their military talk had ceased to interest
him when it degenerated into a long argument comparing
N'Taian armament to Federate. Critically Tel examined a
portrait of his ancestor, Count Merdon Tellai, which hung
on the deep red backdrop of the wall. Several shadows
seemed poorly placed, and the rendering of the nobleman's
diagonal blue sash was clumsy. The brush strokes, too,
seemed . . . hesitant. It hurt his dignity to see his family
ill-represented.

Surreptitiously Tel glanced down to assure himself that
his new tailor and dresser had done their best to match him
with his elders and the gallery of their predecessors that
stared down from the walls. Small and slight and ever
conscious that his body had given up growing before he
had, he understood the importance of appearance. His
servants had chosen a suit of elegant amber today, in
sateen. He preferred velvric, but the amber shade caught

the gold veins of the Chamber's black marble floor and its other golden appointments, coordinating him with the Chamber and making him look as if he belonged.

Satisfied, Tel turned to stand against the Chamber's inner wall, between a pair of waiting-chairs embroidered with the Drake and Rattela crests, and craned his neck in search of Princess Phoena. Barely come to adulthood, eight years behind her, he stood as the head of his family, among the best bloodlines for centuries. He was now eligible to offer a suit to one of her standing. To marry a secondborn who ranked him as Phoena did, Tel would have to give up his Eldest's right to bear children for the Tellai name, but that did not affect his attraction one whit. As a Count he held more prestige than many closer to her own age, and unquestionably Phoena noticed rank. His own seat, midway up the inner-wall branch of the table, lay separated by several of his elders from those of the Angelos on the center section. Perhaps some day he would sit higher, a member of the inner circle. But for now—

The gilded doors blew open. "Any word from the forces?" Phoena stepped between the red-coated door guards into the Chamber without waiting for conversation to quiet.

Gowned this morning in a pale shade of orange, Phoena swept forward. The sight of her drove all reflection from Tel's mind. Orange—the color of excellence in Naetai's heraldry—brought flame into her chestnut hair. If he ever collected the courage to ask her to sit for an informal portrait, he would suggest she wear that shade, it suited her so well.

He took another step away from the Electors and lifted a gloved hand to catch her eye. "Your Highness."

He had to call twice before she noticed him and walked his way. The hem of her gown seemed to float on the floor, and the plunging bodice floated on perfect skin. Tel coughed twice; the sight of so much of Phoena's flesh unsettled him. "Highness . . ." He paused, catching a breath of woody perfume as she drew near. Beside one of the thirty golden half-pillars that pretended to support the high white dome, she stopped and arched her brows impatiently. With every breath her bodice tightened. He wrenched his mind back to business. "Yes—we've received a DeepScan transmission from just outsystem. Our forces were initially turned back, but—"

"Firebird? What word of her?"

The poor little Wastling. Tel frowned, unable even for Phoena to hide his compassion. Around them, the buzz of conversation droned on: the others cared as little as Phoena that a lovely woman had left their midst forever. "No real word, Highness. They think they have identified her craft —downed—and her friend Bowman is reported missing as well. But with the distances involved, communications are dreadful. Such a lag!"

Phoena's dark eyes sparkled as brightly as her sapphire earrings. For the first time in Tel's experience, he saw her poise slip enough that she bit her lower lip. "Thank you, Tel. That's what I wanted to know." She gathered her filmy skirt to brush past him, toward her seat.

"Highness, wait!" he cried. "You've not heard the best news! We weren't chased when we retreated! Reading their weakness, we turned again, to besiege. The irradium, Phoena . . ."

She grasped his arm. "Little cousin, you have a marvelous sense of priorities. Bless you. Are you . . ." She seemed really to see him now. ". . . Are you . . . *interested* in our research, Count Tellai?"

He rested a hand on the gilded arm of a waiting-chair. "I see in it two strokes of genius, Your Highness: one Cleary's, in rediscovering the, ah, irradium principle; the other yours, in bringing her here. My interest in your mysterious secret is keen, yes."

Phoena gave a rising, tinkling laugh and released his arm. *"Everyone* wants to know my secret, Tel, and it is well worth keeping. When all is ready we will have power to spare, and the Federacy will not dare dream of subjugating us. We'll compromise with no one. But that day has not yet come. When the strike force returns, I may need support. *Quiet* support." She shot a glance up the table at Princess Carradee, who had paused to speak with another nobleman. "There are some, Tel, who are having second thoughts. Who—" She seemed to catch herself.

Hastily he murmured, "Highness, you must count on

me whatever the circumstances. My house has always
looked to the Angelos."

Again she laughed, perhaps remembering her father,
Tel's own granduncle. *A dear man,* Tel reflected with a
twinge of grief for his own sire, her father's brother: harder
than Prince Irion Tellai-Angelo, and more ambitious—but
certainly not deserving of violent death. The murderer, a
disgruntled overseer of their Tiggaree holding, had been
executed just as violently by the Electoral Police.

A high-toned bell echoed off the white ceiling. Silenced by the Call to Order, Tel bowed to the Princess. She
extended a long, perfect hand. Earnestly he took it on his
palm, closed his eyes, and touched his lips to her fingertips.

Brennen's duties at the main desk of the com center
kept him up far into the night. The controller on duty, bent
over her own glowing console, avoided his occasional
glances. He was accustomed to such standoffish treatment,
although among other Sentinels he would confess that it
depressed him. But for now the viewscreen occupied all his
attention: he evaluated his base, personnel, intelligence,
matériel. The memorizing was easy: he needed only to
focus his epsilon carrier through his memory and let the
lists scroll past. Drawing parallels and evaluations, however, and formulating plans, would take time and concentration. Though he had not previously headed so large a force,
he must act assured—inspire confidence among men and
women who would look to him for leadership. He must
know VeeRon as well as he knew Thyrica.

His "fast track," a system of rapid promotion that was
an honor in itself, demanded a stint at a defensive command
post without much risk of actual combat before his next
promotion, but this position had been dropped unexpectedly on him by Regional. It had, however, given him a
chance to hide Firebird away—even from the Federacy, for
a time—until she'd insisted on those papers.

What had she meant to say?

He pushed away from the viewer and eyed the stars,
bright in VeeRon's moonless sky. Danger had throbbed in
Firebird's emotions, there in the quiet com center. Some
specific fear had risen from her past to menace her: she had

crept to the edge of letting him inside her defenses, then fled in shame. Had she almost accepted asylum?

Chaos take the "honor" that would not let her follow her own mind!

He paused. Did he mean that?

Carefully he reviewed the wording of the message he had sent off to Alta. Certainly he had justified the request poorly—and his having sent it would buy her time to think, meanwhile proving he understood her greatest desire. She needed time, and in a war that commodity could be far too plentiful—or much too scarce. Regional would protect her once they knew she lived in Federate hands. They would demand her transfer to Alta at the very least, and most likely reprimand him for having kept her back. He knew the Councillors slightly, from several brief appearances during which he'd kept closely attuned to their emotional state. Of seven, he could count on three to—

A young corporal in Altan gray appeared from behind him, dropped a scan cartridge on his desk, and saluted. Brennen nodded thanks. The viewer glowed silently, reminding him of his own honor and ambitions.

Connaturality.

Firebird awoke rested. In the night, she found, her mind had settled. Completion of Cleary's work would spell Naetai's destruction, if the weapons were used and the Federacy took appropriate vengeance. In the end, only that issue mattered: neither her death, nor treason, nor trying to repay Brennen for having honored her wishes. Before they brought her breakfast, she called for him.

Within minutes the gray door slid open. Brennen came in, clean-chinned and uniformed in crisp contrast to her wrinkled coverall. He strode directly to her side and trapped her eyes. "Good morning, Mari," he saluted her gravely, looking down from an arm's length away.

The name caught Firebird by surprise. She groped for words.

"Did you change your mind?" he prompted. "Regarding—termination?"

"No. But you did me a kindness last night, and I owe one to you. You must watch—" She choked, stepped back, and then began afresh. "One objective of Naetai's initial attack was to secure enough pure irradium to finish Dr. Cleary's research. They'll be back to try again, if not by stealth, then by force."

His dark brows lifted, and his posture went to wide-stride, as if he were ready to jump either direction. "They understand that will mean war on Naetai itself, not just defensive action, if they openly attack the Federate military presence?"

Firebird took a second step back. "What do you mean?"

Instantly he became sober. "You don't know? That the Federacy answers any offense against a peacekeeping force by striking the offending planet?"

Firebird stared at him. "I've never heard of such a thing."

"It's not happened in years—no one has pushed the policy."

"They don't know," she whispered. "I've sat on the Electorate—they don't know."

Groaning, he turned toward the door and began to hurry out. Abruptly he glanced back. As his eyes flicked across her face, she felt him probe at the fringes of her mind. "Why did you tell me this, if you didn't know—or suspect?"

She wanted to look away but could not. Caught in his startlingly blue eyes, she suddenly doubted her own motives. Enemy or ally, she did not want this man dead. She felt no compulsion to speak, but understood that he would sense any deception in her answer.

"The . . . irradium project," she said carefully. "I don't like unlimited warfare any more than you do."

"I see." He released her from his control. Caught off balance, she bumped against the wall.

He reached for the locking panel. "I will try to contact Naetai, then, *and* get reinforcements. But there is probably not much time." As the doorpanel slid away, he pushed off from the wall. "Do you realize that you, of all people anywhere, are in the best position to fight deployment of that weapon?"

"I'm beginning to see that."

"Maybe that's worth living for. If nothing else is."

She smiled wanly.

Later that morning, dark-tanned Koan Tryseleen brought a stack of scanbooks and a broad lap viewer. "I cleaned the file," he commented sarcastically. "The super wanted to know if my kid was failing in school. I don't have a kid." Lifting the thin cartridges with a knobby hand, he read her the titles. "*Systems of the Federacy. Federacy of the Free. Transnational Government. Our Great Federacy.* You won't find any of these on Naetai."

Firebird inserted the topmost cartridge and spun its pages through the viewer. No pictures, but plenty of footnotes. It had the look of an Academy text.

"Do you know if any of these are particularly good?"

"No idea. Wait, this looks like one I had. Long time back."

"Well, thank you." She popped out the first cartridge and scrolled another. Glorious tri-Ds and rather large lettering—middle school history with a patriotic slant.

"Study hard." Tryseleen locked her in again.

Is this how Vultor Korda began? she wondered bitterly. But the scanbooks caught her. For hours, she compared indexes and contents, and scanned and read. *So*, she observed, *this is The Other Side—from The Other Side.* Although emotionally exhausted, she read until her eyes ached.

Brennen woke with the memory of a horn blaring in his ears. For an instant he struggled to identify this sterile room. A luma pulsed on the far wall, over the interlink. Fully awake in a second, he sprang from the cot and touched the luma before the klaxon could sound again. "Caldwell."

"Large slip-shield zone approaching, sir."

"Call general alert. I'll be right up." Brennen cut the interlink, zipped into a clean uniform, and took a minute to wash his face: the tingle of depilatory soap helped make up for his shortened sleep. After drying he stood motionless, focusing and composing his inner energies with a modulation exercise. Then he hurried out.

Controlled chaos filled the com room—now a war

room—complicated by the ancient, barely adequate inter-link board. Dropping into his chair, Brennen pressed a panel on the display.

"Central," said a feminine computer voice.

He leaned forward. "Caldwell speaking. Call up another pair of controllers."

"Sir."

He glanced over at the tri-D well in the room's center. Only a few bright speckles hovered over the red topo globe of VeeRon II. That would soon change.

On his left, a com tech in Altan gray sat drumming his fingers on his board. Brennen sent an energy flicker inward, and an outer cloud of epsilon static, with which he constantly and automatically wreathed himself to escape the assault of others' emotions, dissipated. He tested the waters. Chaos blared on that level too, the nearby tech's anxiety welling over all else.

Brennen cleared his throat to catch his attention. "Get me a DeepScan link to the outsystem scouts, and feed it into channel F."

"Sir." The tech's relief at finding useful occupation leaped out from the background buzz. As Brennen's static shields sprang up again, his temporary tension caused by emotional noise lessened.

"DeepScan, sir," called the tech.

Brennen picked up a headset and clipped it on. "Outsystem? Give me a status report on that slip zone."

In ten seconds a distant voice hissed in his ear. "Now passing orbit nine, sir."

"Begin regular reports when it reaches six."

This was good. From Firebird he knew that Naetai had far-less-accurate subspace scanning units, and would not spot the scouts—nor reinforcements, if they came in time.

Firebird.

He reached for the interlink board again.

"Central."

"Detention floor, please."

Firebird had not dozed long when footsteps wakened her. Disoriented, she sat up on the cot, clutching the thin blanket, and peered at a masculine silhouette in the yellow-ish light that shone through the open door.

"What is it?" She recognized the faded blue uniform, though not the man wearing it.

"Apparently, we're under attack," he answered with thinly covered hostility. "You're N'Taian, aren't you?"

"Yes—"

"I have orders from General Caldwell that you're to be allowed into the war room, if you want to observe."

This is it! she thought with a thrill of fear. She sprang from the bed and smoothed her rumpled green coverall. "Yes, I do."

"Well, don't get any wise ideas." He unhooked a singlet binder from his belt and let out a meter of its cable, then linked it around her right wrist. "If he trusts an observer from Naetai, that's his risk."

Cabled to the guard's heavy leather belt, she stepped from the elevator to a com center now vibrating with activity. All four transceivers were manned, and the controllers brusquely relayed reports along the line, onto the starmap and into the tri-D well. Both had come alive with glowing blips that signified attacking ships. The Planetary Navy circled VeeRon II like a flock of hunting kiel going for wounded prey.

Brennen spoke rapidly into a headset as she passed him. He spared her a glance and a nod and went on issuing orders. Golden sparks were scattering in the well: he was arraying his squadrons planetwide, but with a treble concentration about Twinnich, to hold off precisely the attack she had foretold.

As she and the guard took a pair of stools near the corner of the windows, her eyes swept the starry sky, searching for moving pinpoints of light that would be the attackers' fightercraft.

What a blessing to be aboveground, she reflected. *If Twinnich goes, I'll be dead with the Federates.* She glanced back into the heart of the room: enemy headquarters. *That man with the star on his shoulder is the enemy.*

Why can't I see him that way?

The answer came easily, from another corner of her

mind. *Because he has treated you with more respect than your own commanding officers ever showed. Because he wants you alive and not dead.*

Hours of waiting and tracking crept by. Only the tri-D well changed, as the scouts' reports returned. The Navy had reappeared out of slip-state at quite a distance from VeeRon's surface, and as the red swarm of blips began its series of deceleration orbits, Firebird tensed in memory. She had made that approach herself so recently (she started to count back the days, but at five, things became too confused, and she gave up). Skim lower to lose speed, but don't overload the heatshielding. Pass again, thicker atmosphere. Eyes on screens for defensive countermeasures. There had been few. That approach had thrilled her.

This one was agonizing. This was the desperate defense of an outpost that had just sent a messenger fleeing for reinforcements. Furthermore, to hold VeeRon, the Federates would be killing N'Taian pilots: Daley would be out there, and Delia.

A small, brown-haired man in the silver-gray of the Federate messenger service hurried around the controllers to the windows and pulled over a third stool. Before he spoke, he too scanned the heavens for signs of the attack force. There still were none, but it was in its second orbit and approaching the near side of the planet.

Then he cocked a bright brown eye at them. "Vett Zimmer, of Alta," he offered. "Looks like we're going to have an exciting day."

"Right," growled the guard. "I'm Deke Lindera of VeeRon. Born here. My friend"—he ran a hand along the cable—"is Mari Tomma, of Naetai."

"Oh!" Vett Zimmer drew up a bit and spoke more formally. "You're a prisoner, Mari?"

"Yes. They're being gracious enough to let me watch this, instead of waiting it out down below."

"Caldwell," Vett observed. "Right?"

Firebird glanced over toward Brennen. His back was turned. Intently he peered into the well, tracking the incoming ships. "You'll hear some disquieting things about his kind," continued the messenger captain. "But him, I like. I'm almost surprised he's not commanding from a fighter right now. In fact, I'll bet you fifty gilds he's in the air before this is over." He raised one eyebrow.

"Oh?" Did he hope she'd predict Naetai's strategy? Not for a talkative Federate messenger! "So he still flies? I had assumed he was in Intelligence."

"Both. Special Operations Task Force. Delta Squadron is one of the hottest in S.O., and he's Lead. Those S.O. squads fly a six-man formation; I've seen them in demonstration. It's something, when they pull into an energy wedge. Tight."

"What kind of demonstration?" she choked, but she didn't hear his answer. In memory she saw six black shapes through the cockpit bubble of her tagwing, heard the shock in Delia's voice a minute later. Corey! Could *Brennen* have . . . ?

She hung her head. Did it matter?

Everything grew suddenly still. Brennen touched a panel atop one transceiver, and a voice filled the room. To her surprise, Firebird knew it: Count Dorning Stele, Delia's elder brother and heir of his house, of the Third Wing, Raptor Phalanx. "VeeRon Commanding Officer, do you copy?" it barked.

"This is VeeRon," Brennen answered into his tiny microphone. "Break off your attack, or you will be liable to the most serious consequences. Repeat, break off, Naetai."

Stele spoke again. "VeeRon Commanding Officer, we will receive one negotiating party of your top people to discuss reparations for the damages suffered by our Navy. You have ten minutes in which to launch a negotiators' shuttle. We will guarantee the safety of those negotiators only."

Firebird winced. That did sound like Dorning Stele. The Count was not a trusted man, even among his own class.

Brennen leaned forward onto the console, muscles knotting in his arms. "Naetai, this base now accommodates a Federate peacekeeping force. Any hostile action on your part will be answered by the Federate fleet upon your home system. I repeat, any hostile action on your part will be answered by the Federate fleet upon *your home system*."

"You will be unable to send for additional ships,

VeeRon." The N'Taian voice sounded firm and menacing.
"We guarantee the safety of one negotiating team. We give
the rest of VeeRon no guarantees. Commanding Officer,
you have nine minutes in which to launch your shuttle."

Firebird wished heartily that she could disappear.

The bright blips continued to advance within the tri-D
well, with the majority overpassing Twinnich just to the
north. Nine minutes crawled by, and then Stele spoke
again. "VeeRon, your time is up. Have you no one whose
life you value enough to send us?"

As he spoke, a N'Taian squadron that had trailed the
others roared over Twinnich. Federate intercept fighters
pursued as the groundside guns pierced the morning sky,
but the tagwings did not double back, fleeing instead
toward the rest of the NPN. The gesture, only a handslap,
baffled Firebird.

A different speaker buzzed in an erratic speech
rhythm. Brennen made a twisting hand sign to a controller,
who switched the incoming report into the large room
speakers. "Can I have that again, Zeta?" he asked his
pickup mike.

Silence. Brennen touched another panel, and a static-
charged voice crackled loudly.

". . . fifth series of battle groups on a five-two heading
and the last one due eastward."

In the well, the glowing swarm was dispersing unexpectedly into smaller clusters.

Firebird leaned forward, listening, but no more information came. This was not the angle of attack she had
predicted! Twinnich should be the main target—it was
virtually the only military strength in the system!

Brennen turned toward her, and from across the room
she felt herself caught and pinned by his piercing eyes.
Automatically she tried to hop down from the stool and
flee. His hand came up. This time she clearly heard the
word of command. "*T'sa.*"

She clutched the stool, fighting to keep her balance as
the pressures of access and command caught her. Her
memory raced into sharp focus on battle strategy sessions.
So this was why he had wanted her in the war room! And

did he intend to betray her presence to the attackers, too, reveal her survival?

In a minute he let her go, and she knew that others had seen what he had done. She blinked, struggling to reestablish thought over her wash of fury.

Without speaking, Brennen turned back to the well. Avoiding the stares of the guard—who had drawn back to the very end of the cable—and the messenger captain—Vett Zimmer eyed her with keen curiosity—Firebird stared angrily, unable to help herself, concentrating on the line of Brennen's jaw: stern like that of a gamesman unable to play until he sees his opponent's strategy. The red speckles were far-spread now, sweeping in twenty arches toward the nightside of VeeRon II as morning light grew in the war room.

A scout transmitted a report. "Twinnich, this is Tau at nine-seven by two. The settlement at one-oh-six has been bombed. Looks like a flasher. I can't get any closer for the dust and the rem count."

Firebird recoiled. Her own squadron had overpassed that community, a hydroponics plant and a few colonists' domes, because it had no military significance whatever. Surely it hadn't been flash-bombed. Use of the photon-enhanced nuclear weapons was forbidden by all manner of treaties that even Naetai claimed to support. She'd known they were in the arsenal, as weapons of last resort, but they'd never been mentioned in drill or lecture—and these were civilians!

Brennen's Sentinel eyes caught hers in the midst of her stricken thoughts, and this time she did not resist. She felt him sweep the surface of her mind again, reading her horror and surprise.

He returned quickly to his work. The Planetary Navy was split into twenty attack groups whose courses could sweep VeeRon before converging on Twinnich. If Naetai continued to use flash bombs, VeeRon II would be open-air uninhabitable.

Brennen scattered six squadrons into pairs and sent them to intercept the N'Taian fightercraft, but as the Federates spread out to join battle, the high-altitude scouts continued to send in word of settlements bombed to dustclouds, life and structures wiped from VeeRon with callous, methodical deliberation.

One controller tuned in a Federate pilot on an inter-squad frequency. He had come upon a PN battle group and found himself outnumbered fifty times. "Heavy bomber. Cover me, Rho."

Anxious silence filled the war room. Somewhere, a pair of Federate pilots was taking on a hundred tagwings escorting a big loadship, a battle that could end only one way.

"Look out, Sig, he's released a bombing drone."

"I'm on it."

Firebird shut her eyes tightly but could not escape the image in her mind: the flash bomb's steering rockets igniting, the pilot chasing, his wingman covering him with a cone of laser fire to give him hope of destroying the drone high enough to spare the people below.

In the war room they waited, but there were no more transmissions from those pilots.

"Lovely folks, your Navy," muttered the guard to Firebird.

She didn't answer, for she felt the same, unspeakably ashamed. The Federate fleet's restraint had been rewarded by this, the slaughter of civilians, and Firebird was humiliated.

"Attack pairs, pull back." Brennen's voice rose crisply. "Re-form your squadrons at nine-oh degrees from the Twinnich quadrant."

CHAPTER 7

Stalemate

Ritardando
Gradually slackening
in speed

The long VeeRon day-cycle passed slowly, every hour bringing a few degrees' retreat toward Twinnich. When Deke Lindera was replaced by the pale guard, Vett Zimmer took a sleeping capsule and went off for some rest. Firebird was given meals with the staff, but she scarcely tasted the food. Gradually the Federate squadrons were driven back to the Twinnich perimeter. The settlement's particle-shielding dome might protect it from missile attack and radioactive fallout, but that was no guarantee against laser damage, and so many attacking ships swarmed on all sides that an overload looked bleakly certain unless the perimeter was held at a distance.

Near dusk, Vett Zimmer returned and took a shift wearing the guard belt. The horizon flashed with missile hits and laser cannon, and Firebird knew they didn't have long before the heavy bombers would begin to break through and launch the drones.

She met Brennen's eyes once more, then. They were inexpressibly sad, and she knew that he shared her grief for thousands of civilians. She spread her hands in a gesture of helpless regret, and he acknowledged it with a shrug.

A series of day-bright flashes suddenly drew all eyes to the windows. Between Twinnich and a distant mountain range, another flight of N'Taian drones had taken its bitter toll on VeeRon II. There was another explosion, and another, and as the bombs' rumble arrived at Twinnich, the mountains disappeared behind a rolling dust cloud.

She felt a hand on her shoulder and spun defensively around. "Zimmer," Brennen said quietly as he dropped his hand, "you and Miss Tomma keep away from the boards. There's no sense in my staying here any longer."

"Sure, General."

Firebird had to say some sort of good-bye. "I'm sorry, Brenn," she murmured. "I never dreamed."

"I know," he answered softly in a forgiving tone that wounded her as no rebuke could have, and then he strode out into the hallway.

"I told you he'd go. Fifty gilds, you owe me," Vett whispered, and she smiled sadly. She didn't seem to stand in much danger of having to pay.

Soon Brennen's voice joined the others on the transceivers, coordinating a defense of the little settlement that ringed the particle-shield generators with his own heaviest fire, and grouping the rest of the intercept fighters into four stout energy wedges like the one that had broken her squadron. Firebird was incredulous. Did he truly intend to counterattack?

Of course he did. Even the worst fatalist would rather die trying than waiting.

Stars came out, but few shone brightly enough to pierce the wild interplay of light that wove Twinnich's smoky sky. The Federate ships scattered, regrouped, picked off tagwings here and there, and once vaporized a pair of drones released by a bomber that hung back. It seemed to Firebird as though a band of helpless children harassed a cordon of armed giants.

It was some time before she realized that she had seen the Federates score a number of kills, and that not one intercept fighter had fallen since they had pulled in to defend Twinnich.

A triangle of hot blue engine-lights roared overhead, and Firebird followed with passionate envy. Shackled, with nothing to do but watch, she ached for the feel of her tagwing's controls. Feeling a traitor to Naetai, and to the Federates a barbarian, she had nowhere to turn, and for the first time she really wished she were dead. She hung her head, avoiding Vett's casual questioning until her eyes were startled upward by a pure white flash of dazzling intensity. Expecting a flash bomb, she found herself witnessing the immolation of an entire N'Taian squadron: the tagwings had fallen behind their lead pilot directly upon the particle shield, vaporizing with a series of implosions that lit the entire skyfield of the settlement.

Firebird held back her tears.

At last, someone on the N'Taian side apparently came to the conclusion Firebird had drawn hours earlier. The defense of Twinnich was too well coordinated to break, and N'Taian losses had continued to mount. Shortly after midnight, the N'Taians withdrew into planetary orbit, settling for a stalemate and a siege.

Brennen reappeared later in the war room, looking tired but satisfied. He snatched a meat pastry from the conference table on his way to the window. "Captain Zimmer, are you willing to try to slip for the Regional fleet? I'm wondering if that other messenger made it."

"Of course." Vett pulled off the guard's belt and held it up with a questioning glance.

"Forget it for now. Look, Zimmer, I'm not ordering you out."

"No, sir. I'm volunteering." Vett's buoyant salute so resembled Corey's that Firebird felt a bitter lump rise in her throat.

"All right. Good luck, then." Brennen clapped his shoulder, and Vett scurried off.

Two controllers were replaced by a fresh pair, and wearily Brennen took the stool beside Firebird's. He handed her the heavy belt. "I can't spare anyone else to guard you, Mari," he said, with only a trace of hostility. "Can I trust you to keep your hands clean?"

"You'd trust a N'Taian, with your staff watching?" she asked bleakly. "After this?"

"No, I suppose I'd better not." He undid the beltclasp and put it on, releasing the maximum length of the cable. "If I have to run, you *move*."

"All right." She was too tired to protest.

Beyond the windows, Vett's little messenger ship roared by. Incongruously, she thought of the fifty gilds she owed him. She suspected none of them really thought he'd make it.

He didn't. Fifteen minutes later, before their anxious eyes, his blue dot in the tri-D well vanished in a circle of bright blips. Firebird clenched her hands. At any moment, if this went on, she would burst into tears.

The besieging Planetary Navy coiled just out of reach, like a snake gathering itself for a second strike; and outside the dome that shielded Twinnich, ashen fallout settled slowly from the atmosphere.

"I need sleep and so do you," Brennen said bluntly as the next pair of controllers arrived on duty. "I'm taking you back down." He raised his voice. "Lieutenant? See that I'm paged if the situation changes."

Firebird stumbled into the elevator. Whatever tomorrow brought, it would arrive without her help.

While they rode downward Brennen remained silent, distant. The doors ground open again, and at the guards' desk he released her wristbinder and removed the belt. Handing them to Deke Lindera, he turned wordlessly back to the elevator door.

"Could I talk to you for a minute?" she called.

He stopped, and his shoulders rose and fell in a deep breath before he turned. "All right," he replied without feeling, and he escorted her to her cell.

The light glimmered on. She could see that he wanted to leave, and rest, but she desperately needed to talk with someone who understood how she was hurting. Words spilled out of her in a disorganized tumble.

"Brennen, I can't be a part of that. The ones who ordered that kind of invasion—those aren't my people. The pilots and crews—the ones who had to go out and fight—I still believe in them. But not the Electorate. Not the Marshals. The butchers," she added bitterly. "Flash bombs. On civilians."

"What are you saying, Mari?" He sat down on the foot of her cot.

"I think," she began, and then she choked. She tried again. "Brennen, you've been . . ."

No more words came out. Exhausted with tension and grief, she could hold them no longer, and she buried her face in her hands, sobbing.

At a hesitant touch on her shoulder she raised her head to see Brennen, on his feet and looking down with something in his eyes she hadn't seen before. Gone was the power of command, and in its stead was a depth of understanding she had known only in Corey.

Dear Corey, dead, as she deeply wished she were.

She fell against Brennen, clutching him and crying. His arms gathered her in as they might hold a child, and he stroked her hair with one hand.

As her tears subsided, her wounded pride began to gnaw fiercely at her. She had made an idiot of herself in the arms of a Federate General. What next?

She felt his grasp loosen as suddenly as her emotions changed, and then, reminded sharply of his starbred empathy, she was doubly stung by the embarrassment of her exhausted weakness. She pulled away from him, angry with herself, and, because of his gentleness, with him.

"I wish you'd move me uplevel," she lashed out. "Then, when they break through and flash Twinnich, at least I'll be dead with the rest of you. Do you really think you can hold them off?"

"The fleet will come. Soon enough, I hope. But I'll certainly find you better quarters, as soon as I can."

She envied his detachment. "The fleet will come," she mocked. "But meanwhile, Naetai raids the irradium mines. They can—"

He shook his head as he interrupted. "No. Not now. We have contingency plans. I cannot tell you about them, but the mines will not be taken."

"But what happens to me when they come, if they won't issue those termination papers?"

"I've given that some serious thought, Mari. Would you want to go home?"

The unexpected capitulation drained all Firebird's

spite. She blinked at him in disbelief before passing a hand over her aching eyes, struggling with a decision she thought had long been taken away from her. She could return voluntarily. She could face the Electorate and proudly tell them she had come back to meet a N'Taian fate on her home ground.

They'd like that, she reflected grimly. *They have a flair for killing*.

She looked up at Brennen, who had retreated across the cell to stand against the opposite wall. "They want me dead."

"Yes." He held her gaze.

She shrugged. "It doesn't matter. At home or here, I am Geis now."

"I doubt that any termination papers will come at first request, if that's your concern. You're too valuable to us. You could fit in among us . . . if you wanted."

Firebird interlocked her fingers and squeezed tightly. So. She had a choice. Life among the Federates, whom she'd been raised to hate, or the proud death of a Wastling, to satisfy the bloodlust of the N'Taian Electorate.

Her spirit rebelled at last. She'd hide on Alta—or Caroli—or in deep space, before giving Phoena the satisfaction of witnessing her execution.

"No," she said quietly. "I wouldn't like to go home. I do want to live. A little longer, at least."

He stayed beside the far wall, unmoving, unthreatening. "May I take you under my protection, then?"

"That makes me sound so helpless."

He answered without words, but with a sad, sympathetic smile.

"Under the circumstances, I am." She looked down at the cot. "What if that authorization to terminate comes through?"

"I simply don't give the order. Particularly if you've requested asylum."

"All right," she said numbly. She took a deep breath of stale air. "I'm officially requesting asylum, Brennen."

"I'll be back in a minute, then." He began to walk toward the gray metal door.

"Oh, it'll wait for the morning." She sank wearily onto the mattress.

Inside the doorway, he stopped. "I don't want to risk waiting. This won't take long."

He returned carrying a recall pad and a paper printed by some computer, which she read carefully. For a period of three Standard months, she was to be quartered and cared for, and granted diplomatic immunity, by the Interstellar Federacy. During that time, Lieutenant General Brennen Caldwell would be answerable for her safety and conduct, and when the period was over, other arrangements would be made. It looked very official. There was a place to record the date in her own hand: if the paper was published on Naetai, the Electorate, the Marshals, and her mother would know that she had signed after the massacre at VeeRon.

"So even if Twinnich falls," she observed as he inserted the paper into a slot in the recall pad, "there will be a record of my protest."

"I'll get you a copy to keep with you, in case that happens," he answered blandly, and drew his stylus from his left cuff. She watched him sign.

She signed below and pressed her thumb to the recall pad to confirm her signature. "Thank you, Brenn."

"I'm glad to offer it." He stepped back. Against the gray walls his midnight blue seemed almost black. "Mari, are you as exhausted as you look?"

"I haven't slept well in days," she muttered.

"May I—I could help you with that, easily, if you'd allow it."

She eyed him warily. "Sleep, only, and no coercion?"

He shook his head; she shrugged permission, and he walked forward. Gently he placed his fingers over her eyes.

She did suddenly feel as though all fear and tension had dropped from her, leaving her drunkenly relaxed and too sleepy to wonder how he had done it.

"Good night," she mumbled after him as he strode away. Irresistibly, her eyelids dropped. That was no alien, she reflected groggily, falling onto the cot. That was, very simply, a most exceptional man.

Chapter 8

Rebel

Tempo giusto
In strict time

Firebird was roused midmorning by the pale guard: fast advance ships of the Federate fleet had arrived. She watched, guarded but unshackled (to the guard's obvious disliking), as Brennen led a sortie that caught the N'Taian attackers between jaws of titanium and steel and chased them from the Twinnich quadrant. The controllers cheered, but Firebird was achingly aware that it was only a foretaste of things to come. Brennen's words had been "war on Naetai itself." It was one thing for her to accept sanctuary from the Federacy, another to consider the kind of retribution Federate technology could inflict upon her home for attacking a peacekeeping force.

Brennen didn't come in after the battle. In the tri-D well, a little golden spark left the sortie and intersected one of the larger Federate ships. She had seen enough. The battle for Twinnich was won, and until more Federate ships reached VeeRon, little else would be done. She asked to be taken below.

* * *

Several of the Second Division's ranking commanders had come ahead with the advance detail, and as soon as the safety of the people at Twinnich—the only lives left on VeeRon—had been ensured, Brennen left the battle in the command of his second and made a late-afternoon rendezvous with the officers' craft, a modified frigate, heavily armed and fairly roomy for such a fast ship.

General Gorn Frankin of Caroli seized his arm at the airlock and pulled him bodily down the dark corridor to the galley. "Caldwell! By Jin, we thought you'd taken too much killcare when that troop request got through, and I don't mind telling you if it'd come from anyone else we'd have sent the psych team instead of warships! What kind of fools attack a peacekeeping force? The clincher was that termination request. I think you owe us an explanation."

At a long, gray galley table ringed with officers, Brennen took a chair. Another Sentinel sat among them, Captain Ellet Kinsman, and as their eyes met, he sent her a quick unspoken greeting. She returned it with a burst of feelings he felt clearly, relief foremost among them, but out of respect to the others present, neither subvocalized.

"Then when we saw that VeeRon *was* under attack again," added another officer, "and how hot the debris was, we were afraid they'd sent you all to glory. I'm with Frankin. What's going on?"

Brennen thankfully accepted a hot cup of kaffa from a staffer. "First, tell me if I worded that termination request weakly enough to have it denied."

"Heavens, yes!" Frankin sank into a chair, running one hand across his shock of white hair. "It didn't sound like you at all!"

Brennen smiled into his mug.

"How in Six-Alpha did you manage to get a member of Naetai's royal family in your custody?"

"It's a very long story." He told it at length, beginning with the first battle of VeeRon and concluding with Firebird's request for asylum, and when he finished, they were silent. Lowering his static shields, he tested for their reactions.

Ellet Kinsman spoke first. Through his carefully emotionless calm he felt her surprise and cautious concern.

"You can quiet me if I'm out of line, Brenn, but what do you intend to do with her?"

"I don't know. I've only convinced her that she doesn't have to die."

"We have no orders for her disposition." Kinsman tossed her head, and her short, glossy black hair shimmered. "What will happen to her if she's sent back to Naetai?"

"Firing squad, I think." How he had hesitated before offering to return her, down in her cell!

"They're that sort, are they?" asked Ellet.

"That's no good." Frankin, tangibly pleased by the development, bounced a fist off the tabletop. "I don't imagine she's anxious for publicity, but think what an advantage she's given us toward getting those people to settle down a bit. The N'Taians don't strike me as rational sentients."

Ellet Kinsman began to comment, but Brennen silenced her with a glance that caused her to strengthen her own shields, draw up stiffly, and watch his eyes.

"Naetai, then." Frankin stood. "Full-scale attack; we *have* to take them now. Caldwell, your access intelligence will be critical."

"It's all on cross-programmable record aboard the *Horizon*."

"Yes, we requisitioned *Horizon* when we heard about your data disks. But we had no idea your sources were this good. The rest of the Division should be here within a day; that will give us just enough time to speak with Her Highness."

Brennen cast a glance around the small cabin. "Be careful with her. She's not strong enough yet to rule out the possibility of suicide. She knows what that data will mean to Naetai. She has a capacity for loyalty under circumstances that we would consider impossible, and a craving to excel. In time, she could be just as effective in *our* cause."

Despite his carefully impersonal phrasing, he felt Ellet's jealous horror flash past her control.

"Very well, General," said an officer on his left. "Have you any other advice in our dealing with this woman?"

So Sentinel reaction was beginning, and Ellet had been

the first to correctly read his protective actions. "Get her safely to Alta," he said with deliberate calmness, "as quickly as possible."

Firebird spent most of that day in study. Brennen Caldwell's likeness in Unit 78 of *Federacy of the Free* startled her: an old tri-D of a seventeen-year-old Second Captain. She checked the date and performed a rapid mental calculation: he was seven N'Taian years older than herself. By this account, he had worked up the ranks as a pilot—and a good one. "The S.O. people often get sent on jobs that others have tried and failed," Korda had said.

Even reading from a suspicious mental distance, she was intrigued. The Federate worlds were allegedly attempting to establish a reign of free commerce unparalleled since the Great Six-Alpha Catastrophe: the Federacy claimed to be founded on justice for sentients of all kinds, peace between self-governing systems, and a refusal to take life unnecessarily. On Naetai these were matters for the spiritually minded, not the government. Surely the truth about the Federacy lay beyond the middle-school oversimplification of this scanbook.

Still, she remembered her own years of idealism, and how she had grieved for her lost innocence when They— the older ones—had finally convinced her that people couldn't be governed by ideals. Her scoffing turned gradually into a wish, then a hope, that perhaps They had been mistaken.

It seemed real enough. The Federate Division had allowed the PN to retreat unassailed from VeeRon. And hadn't Brennen Caldwell treated her with decency and respect, when he could have been arrogant and cruel?

She was struggling through *Transnational Government* when Brennen came into the cell with a sealed parcel. In dress whites, he looked like a lord.

"Your uniform, Mari." He laid it on the cot. "The officers who came in with the fleet want to talk with you about those termination papers."

She clenched her fists at her sides. "What will they do?"

"Just talk. They've been in contact with Alta."

"Does . . . everyone know I'm here, then?"

"No. Only Regional Command, and these officers. But they want to discuss that, too."

She began to unwrap the parcel. "All right, Brenn. I'll just be a minute."

He left, and she dressed hurriedly. Official again in cobalt blue with the rubies glittering on her collar, she found herself standing straighter than she had for a long while. She forced a comb through her hair and greeted her reflection in the cracked mirror. *Welcome back, Firebird. You always were the rebel of the family.*

Brennen stepped back in. She saw the corners of his mouth twitch into a smile, and met it with one of her own. "I feel like an officer again."

"You look it, too." He motioned for her to lead him down the passway.

At the conference table in the war room, five more officers in white scrambled to their feet when Brennen and Firebird walked through the door. The controllers' heads turned in sudden surprise. Firebird, undeniably nervous among so much Federate authority, still felt flattered that they had met her in dress uniform.

"Your Highness." The white-haired man who stood nearest extended his hand.

She clasped it boldly. He certainly didn't look as if he had brought her death warrant. "That's not my title," she corrected gravely. "*Lady* Firebird is correct; 'Major Angelo' would also be proper."

"Please, then, sit down, my lady," he directed.

She took the nearest stool, at the head of the table: one self-conscious soldier in cobalt blue facing six in Federate white.

Brennen introduced the officers, but they seemed a blur. The nearest, General Frankin, did nearly all the talking. "I'm not sorry to tell you that the Regional Council declined to authorize your execution, Lady Firebird. General Caldwell says you have now applied for asylum."

"Yes. The matter of VeeRon has always lain between myself and the rest of the Electorate, but what Naetai has done here in the last few days lies very heavily on my conscience. I would like to help you ensure that this irradium project, for which Naetai wanted VeeRon's resources, will not be developed, as much for Naetai's sake as for yours." She glanced around the table. They scarcely reacted, and from that she assumed they already knew about Cleary's research. How quickly Brennen must have disseminated that intelligence! Frankin and the other three men looked thoughtful, although the woman Sentinel—now that she thought a bit, she recalled Kinsman from Korda's holograph—scrutinized her, and even Brennen, with something resembling reproach.

"Yes." Frankin glanced to Brennen. "We are aware of the irradium project and we share your determination to see it ended. From here, we proceed to demilitarize Naetai. I say this without malice, Lady Firebird, but your Navy will be badly outgunned."

She bristled, but she had to concur. The ache and regret awoke again.

"Do you understand that your name—your real name—will most likely be used in negotiations?" Frankin asked.

She glanced uncomfortably to the starmap, the windows, and the tri-D well, where the unoccupied pair of controllers sat with eyes to their consoles but ears to the conference table. "In what way?"

Frankin leaned forward, both forearms on the black tabletop. "Lady Firebird, your people should know that you are safe. Their impression of the Federacy is in transition. We cannot allow this challenge to peace to go unmet, but our long-term goal is mutual respect. It is our policy to strike quickly, and mercifully, and to allow our enemies to return as soon as practicable to home rule.

"We have received your claim that you have no worth as a hostage," he went on, "but your presence among us is of great importance still. Our treatment of you will have a strong influence upon the N'Taian public, as will your request for asylum. Furthermore, you are yet a potential source of information and advice."

Remembering her interrogation on board the *Horizon*, Firebird looked hard at Brennen, and he returned the stare frankly. Did they mean mind-access? she wondered. Brennen might be ordered to question her again; him, or another. She glanced cautiously at Ellet Kinsman. The

Sentinel woman was slimmer and more handsome in person than in holo.

She lowered her eyes. "So you intend to inform Naetai that I've sought amnesty?"

"We'll likely be telling them the whole story, including your final actions as a squadron leader, which speak for themselves, and what General Caldwell has called your 'astonishing' effort to resist mind-access."

Startled, Firebird looked his way. This time Brennen looked down. Pleasantly surprised, she turned back to Frankin. "Where are you sending me, then?"

"We would prefer to see you under protective custody at Regional Command on Alta. I hope that is acceptable to you."

"It is," she sighed. It seemed that she was going to see the Whorl after all.

"Very well, then. We'll meet again, Your Highness. Thank you for cooperating."

She winced at his choice of words.

Brennen stood as she did and led her away. Downlevel at the jailers' desk, he halted. "Gentlemen, this officer has accepted asylum among us and will be traveling on to Alta very shortly. Please see that she is treated with respect."

"Sir?" Koan Tryseleen's dark, rangy body straightened.

"Her name is not Tomma. I apologize for deceiving you, but it was done in the best interests of the Federacy." He glanced at Firebird. "This is First Major Lady Firebird Angelo, the Queen's third daughter." Tryseleen and his pale associate drew away as though Brennen had announced that she had a terminal, communicable disease. He laid a hand on her shoulder before she could speak and inclined his head toward her end of the corridor. She went along with him, and when the door had ground shut behind them, he took her right hand.

"Mari." He paused, squeezed her fingers, and then dropped them. "I'm going on to Naetai with the fleet as soon as I can pack, and I won't have time to say good-bye later."

In the yellowed light, she looked up into his face,

finding it hard to imagine living among the Federates without him. "Thank you, then. Watch out for yourself."

"Don't worry. Our losses should be extremely light—but that doesn't make you feel any better about what we're going to do to Naetai, does it?" He peered down sadly. "I'm sorry."

Indeed she feared terribly for her people. Impulsively she clutched his arms. "Please, don't . . ." She caught herself, choking on the plea for mercy. Naetai had opened this hopeless war. She felt helpless, horribly so. How many would die this time, as Corey had?

He offered no comforting platitudes, but his stare lingered long enough to set in her memory an expression that would haunt her for weeks: lips straight and bland, stress lines crowding his bright eyes, and a look in those eyes that might have been pain.

He took two steps through the doorway, turned, and saluted.

The door slid shut.

Chapter 9

Naetai

Marziale
Marchlike, martial

Too many arrangements needed Brennen's attention in the war room. Irritated, he pushed back an uncooperative strand of hair from his forehead and eyed his shorthand notes. General Frankin, with experience on Caroli's Board of Protectorates, was the logical man to replace him; in retrospect, it seemed odd Frankin had not received the original assignment. *Bureaucracy*, he commented silently.

For himself, he had to go out with the fleet. Even had Delta Squadron not been so ordered, he must see Naetai. From Firebird's memory he almost knew it already, but not in his own flesh. Why that mattered, he was not quite certain.

Brennen frowned. He had worked on and off with Ellet Kinsman for several years, and she had demonstrated a clear wish to share deep connaturality probing with him, but Ellet simply did not appeal to him in that way. Now, he faced a quandary. He did not like assigning her to escort Firebird to Alta, but he had no other qualified woman to send. He would have to rely on Ellet's vesting vows to keep her from shaking Firebird's emotional balance, on Ellet's intense loyalty to the Sentinel kindred and her racial pride to make a teacher of her, and on Firebird's innate curiosity to cement the relationship.

He wished he could confide in Ellet. She of all people on VeeRon might understand the insistent calls of tradition, honor, and connaturality that plagued him, but Ellet's first reaction—to public events, without even knowing of his inner feelings—had warned him away.

As if Ellet had caught his stray thoughts, he felt her draw near. Looking up, he imagined Firebird, with her delicate face and long, hot-colored hair, next to Ellet, whose strong nose and slightly concave pale olive cheeks represented classic Thyrian features, and who wore her glossy black hair just long enough to curl toward her oval face. At his own height and a little more, Ellet would tower over Firebird.

"When do we slip?" she asked aloud, leaning one arm on his desk.

"I'd like you on escort duty, Ellet. Would you volunteer?"

"Escort?"

An upside interlink buzzed raucously nearby. Brennen made certain a com tech caught it, then turned back to the black-haired Sentinel. "Lady Firebird," he said. "Minimum-security detention, on Alta."

"Alta is a choice assignment." Ellet's epsilon cloud thickened noticeably. "But since I've been working as Frankin's administrative counselor, don't you feel I should go with him?"

"Frankin will stay on VeeRon, and he'll have good counsel from the staff I'm leaving."

An aide hurried past, trailing a wide ribbon of print paper. Brennen watched Ellet without communicating, each wreathed in static no outsider would discern and through which no emotion would pass.

Ellet's face remained expressionless. "Something is wrong, Brennen. Would you show me your feelings for her?"

Sentinel ethics dictated that he must grant such a request, and Ellet would need assurance if he wanted this time to go well for Firebird. Brennen cleared his outer static shields and raised feelings that would not distress Ellet: pity, understanding, optimism. Ellet's feathery touch, connatural enough to caress—although the "otherness" felt distinct to Brennen—swept over his surface emotional presence.

She pulled back and stood erect. "Brennen, be careful."

Doubtless, knowing as a Master he was able to conceal some emotion under inner, deeper blockages she could not even sense, Ellet would guess more than he had shown her. "I am always careful, Ellet."

"Very well," she said softly. "The girl has been through torments, and she could make the Federacy a valuable resource. I will try to educate her."

"Thank you." Absently he tapped the desk. "I will ask a full report."

"You will have it."

Within a day, the rest of the Second Federate Division reached VeeRon. The last ships of Naetai's strike group fled. One small Federate shuttle picked up Firebird and a few other passengers and streaked on to Alta. From another, Brennen transshipped to the Federate cruiser *Corona*. Half an hour later the division slipped, bound for Naetai in pursuit.

The officers met after dinner on *Corona*'s bridge. Admiral Lee Danton, the only Second Division fleet officer to have risen through diplomatic channels, stood at one edge of the group before a tri-D projection of the Naetai system. The faint glow of the tri-D seemed to deepen the cleft in Danton's chin and set odd lights in his sandy hair. Within the projected sphere, two groups of tiny white and scarlet ship-images stood out against the field of space and the orbits of Naetai's six inner planets.

"So the main strike," Danton continued, "will be the largest division of our forces. The smaller groups will be deployed as follows. I will keep *Corona* just outsystem, to ensure that the N'Taians receive no reinforcements. *Elysia*, with escort, to orbit with and isolate the primary intersystem relay station. *Deng* . . ."

Leaning against a table-level communications console, Brennen waited out the tactical assignments, recording them patiently in his memory until his own name was called.

Admiral Danton turned his way. "General Caldwell, I want you and Delta Squadron with the *Horizon* and that target data on the main attack, in case there are any matters of confusion. You seem to have become our authority on N'Taian affairs."

Brennen nodded. He'd hoped for that assignment, but as a military Sentinel he had to avoid all suspicion of making unfair use of his abilities. Consequently he had to take orders.

Danton dismissed the staff. Swarthy General Vandar, who would command *Horizon*, caught Brennen's glance and beckoned him over. "You took command well on VeeRon, I'm told. I could use a second." He arched his thick brows. "And you could probably use the experience."

"On the bridge, sir?"

"Frankly, I like my bridge a little on the empty side," Vandar drawled. "Just have your squadron briefed to continue without you, if I need to call you in."

Brennen nodded.

Danton called for Vandar, so Brennen searched out his cabin, resisting the temptation to join a group of casual friends in the R&R center for Carolinian daggerplay. He felt his energy reserves still low after the VeeRon siege, and needed to get some uninterrupted rest.

He caught a full eleven hours of sleep in his cabin before the attack force's rendezvous, in which the crews were transshipped for battle. On a huge fighter carrier escorting *Horizon* he rejoined the pilots of Delta Squadron, and the carrier accelerated back into slip-state to make the final jump to Naetai.

Count Tel Tellai sat flipping the ends of his blue nobleman's sash, waiting with twenty-six other men and women around the gold-rimmed Electoral Table. An outsystem message, garbled and tense in tone, had interrupted the last afternoon session of the week. It would take several minutes for the DeepScan request-for-repeat to reach the system's fringe and a second transmission to return.

He glanced at Princess Phoena. Irritation lines did nothing for her elegant features. Today she wore an iridescent, skintight shipboard-style suit that touched several of propriety's limits, and jewels to cover what it did not. Crown Princess Carradee, in conservative mauve, merely looked concerned—and tailored Siwann held herself with utter calm.

He pulled his hand away from his sash ends and tried to emulate the Queen. He should consider the report his holdings manager had sent up this morning, regarding how last week's offseason rains might cut profits by—

The media block at center table began again to hiss and crackle. "Repeating previous transmission." The voice spoke evenly now. "A report has come in from the VeeRon strike force, Operation Pinnacle, dated four days ago. Our forces have driven the enemy back to VeeRon's main settlement and there established a state of siege."

Tel covered one hand with the other on the cool, smooth table. On his left, Muirnen Rattela gave a satisfied sigh.

"Concern grows, however, concerning an apparent slip-shield zone approaching VeeRon from galactic center–spinward by south. Contingency alert recommended, allowing for communications lag."

Tel furrowed his brow. Bad news?

First Marshal Burkenhamn stood. His huge, blue-swathed bulk seemed wasted on a man who did not need size to command attention.

"Contingency plans have indeed been drawn up by members of my staff, and our forces are already standing alert." The Marshal's rich voice heartened Tel. "However, let us remember that a slip zone can exist merely as a lingering echo of the Great Catastrophe, bouncing out of the Whorl. That, of course, is our 'best possible' scenario."

"And the worst?" The Queen remained as collected as statuary.

Burkenhamn raised the fingers of one hand. "Because no such slip zone has been observed near the Naetai

Systems, we assume that even if the Federates have sent a force to retake VeeRon, Naetai, for the moment, is safe. It is conceivable that VeeRon could already be retaken. A force large enough to achieve that could advance in this direction, and because of the buffer systems' location ninety degrees from the VeeRon quadrant, we would have little warning, if any. This *is*—" Burkenhamn tapped the table to silence a whisper at the far end. "This is, I remind you, merely a worst-case scenario. Let us remember that the Federates hesitated to approach our system at the very moment classic strategy would have suggested they strike."

"Very good." Siwann raised an eyebrow. "Continue."

Burkenhamn bowed from the waist. "Let us then turn to the possibility of VeeRon having been—"

Again the media block buzzed, cutting him off.

"Outsystem report, Noble Electors," said the clear, nearby voice. "DeepScan channel three. May I broadcast direct?"

"Certainly you may broadcast direct," Siwann snapped. A momentary stillness fell. Tel found himself holding his breath.

The distant voice babbled, all poise gone. "Subspace wake, passing the outer orbits. Alert. Very large subspace wake—"

Burkenhamn and Siwann fell on the computer terminals at their stations. Carradee's fingers splayed on the tabletop; Phoena clenched a fist and bit down on the thumb, keying furiously with her other hand. Tel wanted to hurry over to stand by her, protect her, but he sat welded to his chair.

Countdown to launch commenced. Harnessed, helmeted, and linked to life support, Brennen waited in the cockpit of his intercept fighter, all checks confirmed. Behind, cabled one behind the other inside a deep chute on the carrier's belly, sat the rest of the Delta pilots. He had boarded hours ago, strapping down before the *Horizon's* force began maximum deceleration.

"One minute to normal-space reentry; three minutes to launch. Activate generators."

Brennen obeyed the voice in his helmet with one pull

of his gloved hand, then keyed over to intersquad frequency. His inclined seat began to vibrate. Lights sprang to life on the board. "Delta Leader, generator check."

"Two, check."

"Three, check . . ."

He felt the carrier shudder. Drop point: he'd experienced it twenty times from the cockpit of a carrier fighter, but it still shook him. So many things beyond his control could go wrong at drop point, a single malfunction stranding carrier, fighters, and men in quasi-orthogonal space.

Seconds continued to melt off on his console clock, still cross-programmed into the carrier's main computer. He gripped stick and throttle, and cleared his senses one by one with focused bursts of epsilon energy.

Down went the attack carrier's slip-shields; the computer kicked his docking cables free. He pulled back on the throttle. The long chute began rushing by—dropped away —and he shot out. His overhead visual screen lit with stars. A small, white-frosted sphere lay dead ahead, growing visibly. With the momentum from the huge carrier as well as his own thrust, he carried enough velocity to make the crossing in minutes.

"Slip-shields, up," he called.

Five blips on his rear screen shimmered, jockeying into pairs.

Within an hour, Naetai's seven major spaceports were gone, and the auxiliary military bases were following. Brennen was regrouping the squadron after a pairs missile run on a rocket-fuel refinery when his helmet interlink came to life. "Delta Leader?"

"Hold," he answered. On his screen the third pair of his men swung into formation behind him, and he took the squad out of the fire zone before speaking again. "Delta Leader."

"Vandar here. General cease-fire, effective immediately. The enemy wants a conference. I'd like you along."

"Yes, sir." He switched back to intersquad frequency. "Delta Two, cease-fire has been called. Take lead and maintain high patrol." He vectored his fighter upward and accelerated back to full thrust.

Vandar and Brennen's cousin, Corporal Jon Decka, waited in an auxiliary landing bay on *Horizon*. A five-man shuttle stood ready near the edge of the platform.

"They specified three negotiators," Decka told Brennen as he slipped into the pilot's seat. "Unarmed."

Brennen returned Decka's second, silent greeting. "Heading?" he asked as they glided away from the cruiser.

"True north. They're sending a small frigate into polar orbit. Also, they claim, manned by three unarmed negotiators."

The shuttle soared toward the polar cap of the blue-green world. Brennen's left forearm rested on the edge of its control board, pressing upon a hard, slim shape in its yest-skin sheath. When he gave up his blazer, he would not be disarmed, nor would Decka.

He had no qualms about concealing the crystace. It hardly qualified as an offensive weapon. But he had discovered two laws of wartime negotiations: if a man shows up helpless, half the time he gets shot at. On the other hand, if he's belligerent, half the time he still gets shot at. He had long ago decided that he preferred to be able to defend himself.

Shortly, they docked. "That should be it." Decka slid off the pilot's seat.

Brennen reached for the latch. It yielded. The hatch swung open and he stepped through onto the N'Taian ship. On a platform to his right he laid his handblazer, then followed General Vandar toward a table that had been brought into the frigate's main cabin.

He stared in momentary surprise as the leader of the N'Taian contingent stood to greet them. No, he realized an instant later, the woman was not Firebird, but surely she was Phoena, the middle sister. Taller, fuller of figure in the best possible way, she wore her chestnut-colored hair in an ornate knot. Overdone, but lovely—distractingly so.

Decka presented his officers, then the woman introduced the N'Taians. "First Marshal Burkenhamn and General Gaelvaan. I am Lady Sellt." She pronounced Colonial with a short-vowel accent slightly stronger than Firebird's.

Angelos and aliases! Why is Phoena hiding? Brennen and his companions took three chairs across from their

counterparts as Gaelvaan poured a steaming brown liquid
that scented the air spicy-sweet into six bell-shaped cups.

From his end position, he lowered shields and examined all he could see. Deception hung in the cabin's
atmosphere, tantalizing the edge of his perception.

The Princess—he had no doubt it was Phoena, whom
he had seen through her sister's memory—was very fidg-
ety. She had hungry eyes and an angry, possessive spirit.
Now that he sat close enough to read her with a delicate,
surface emotional probe, he understood why she and
Firebird had had so much trouble. Two such strong-minded
women, in a family with room for only one, would not have
lived in peace or harmony. Phoena intended falsehood, he
was certain, and meant him harm. But unless the N'Taians
either surrendered or consented to access, he could not
confirm their veracity: Section 136, Privacy and Priority
Code. This siren would bear . . .

Watch her, he subvocalized to Decka.

Decka's smile lines darkened minutely. *Gladly*.

He read the men next—calm and steady. Military men
of long experience. They hadn't stood when they were
introduced. Were they armed, after all? No: nervous, but
straightforward. Each had the half-dressed feeling of a
disarmed soldier. Furthermore, each was ostentatiously
keeping his hands above the table.

And the crew, three of them, out of sight, although he
felt their waiting presences clearly.

Trap, he warned Decka, with a glance at Vandar. His
cousin did not respond.

Marshal Burkenhamn rose, tall behind the table, and
bowed slightly. *No*, observed Brennen, *he's unarmed.
Good*. "General, General, Corporal, let me be entirely
blunt with you, and apologize. The N'Taian Electorate has
decided to take drastic measures."

Brennen started. Something rustled behind him. From
a cargo door that had hung open a crack, the three
crewmen sprang into the cabin. Each brandished a
twinbeam rifle.

He leaped from his chair. Before he had taken three
quick steps away from the table, his crystace shimmered at
the ready. With less than a second to catch one adversary in

Aurian voice-command, he flung his carrier through the focusing point of his hand and took Phoena, who controlled the armed ones. *"T'sa!"* Energy jumped the gap. Phoena froze, standing behind the table.

But the N'Taians opened fire before Vandar or Decka could react. Jon Decka died with his eyes on treacherous beauty, and Vandar fell to the deck, one hand on his empty holster.

Brennen attacked. All three crewmen brought their rifles to bear on him, but his crystace caught and parried the killer energy beams, shimmering almost invisibly in the bright cabin lights. He had to watch every opponent at once to be on position to meet the firebolts, which arrived at the very moment they could be seen.

One guard was hit and knocked to the floor by a beam refracting off a shiny metal panel. Brennen jumped between the other two and swung the singing crystace in a wide arc, slicing one rifle cleanly in half. Then he leaped away as the other fired. The guard's shot killed his disarmed fellow.

That left only one, but Brennen sensed danger behind him. As he closed toward the still armed guard, he saw it: the N'Taian officers were going for the Federates' blazers back in the airlock.

Brennen breathed deeply, easing a portion of his mind away from Command and crystace work. Distant control of phase currents was simple enough for a Sentinel when undistracted, but he had little attention to spare, and he was tiring. Balancing the skills carefully, he feinted quickly at his opponent and then gave a nudge of epsilon energy to the airlock's circuitry.

The inner door slid shut in the N'Taians' faces, and the men stared disbelieving at the steel arch. Brennen sprang out of the remaining guard's line of fire and swung backhanded.

The force of his blow dislodged the guard's sidearm. It slid spinning across the deck. Burkenhamn, Gaelvaan, and Brennen dove for it. The Marshal was closest, but Brennen's reach far exceeded the length of his arm. With a final burst of epsilon energy he called, and the blazer flew to him.

He covered the two officers, who were battle-wise

enough to freeze immediately, and took a deep, cleansing breath to quiet his fighting fury. He used an old calming technique that consumed no epsilon effort, speculating on his opponents' parents, their friends, their children. His anger began to melt away as they faced him warily. "Lady Sellt" still stood aghast at the table, behind six untouched cups. When he released her from voice-command, she sat down with a thump.

"Over there, with her," he directed Burkenhamn and Gaelvaan. They returned to their places. "Now sit down." Brennen sheathed his crystace. "I want your hands on the table."

He took a moment to examine Vandar and Decka where they had fallen. Dead instantly, both of them, he judged. His cousin—his commanding officer . . . Once again he clamped down on his emotional control. He slipped Decka's crystace from his arm, wishing he could leave it with Jon, but claiming the irreplaceable relic nevertheless for another Sentinel.

He slid it under his wide belt, still holding the N'Taian blazer ready at his side. "Your Highness." He fixed Phoena's eye. She startled visibly but did not deny the title. "This will cost Naetai dearly. If we cannot trust you to honor diplomatic immunity, we cannot trust you at all. You force us to disable your world entirely."

"You won't get away with it, General." Her eyes steamed hatred. "You'll pay if you try, your whole Federacy. I promise. And if you think you can paralyze *me* and—"

"This ship," Brennen continued smoothly, "is returning to planet only because of your presence, and because I choose to show respect for your family. Tell Her Majesty that for me, gentlemen. Princess, were you anyone else I would imprison all three of you." He took a step toward the airlock. "Marshal Burkenhamn, I assume you are in command of your planet's defenses?"

The Marshal nodded his gray-fringed head slightly.

"If you value the lives of your people, you will evacuate every facility on your planet that could possibly be construed as strategic. Quickly. I will warn you that we captured N'Taian military personnel at VeeRon who possessed highly classified data." He fingered the lock's touchpanel. "I assume at least one of you can pilot this frigate?"

"I can," answered Gaelvaan.

"Then, take the Princess home to her mother. She needs a spanking." He plunged through the air-filled lock, rapidly securing the hatches.

As the landing seal disengaged, he accelerated to the shuttle's top speed with all shields activated. He took the moment to grieve for Decka, and for Vandar, but then immediately called up the shuttle's computer display. Vandar's murder left his second, Brennen, in the first position of planetary invasion command he had ever held—or was ever likely to hold.

Chapter 10

Surrender

Con brio
With vigor

The N'Taian Planetary Navy had utilized its respite well, and all its remaining ships were up. From the *Horizon* command chair, Brennen watched on a wall of screens as they rose to meet his forces.

The Sae Angelo quadrant's defenses fell back rapidly before his main attack. An hour later, however, on the dark side at Claighbro, his ships were gaining less territory from a fierce N'Taian defense when an alarm clamored for his attention. *Horizon's* own dorsal screen turned from blue to orange, and a voice pealed in his ear. "Rear attack, *Horizon*! Twenty marks, point zero zero heading!"

As if piloting his own fighter, Brennen automatically checked the cruiser's energy shields first. Then he touched an interlink control. "Generator room, full power to topside shields and gunnery." Another control and a number sequence. "Delta Two, this is *Horizon*. Kirzell, can your quadrant spare the squadron to defend the cruiser?"

"Yessir," a voice snapped in his ear.

He clenched a fist at the screen. Withdrawing Delta Squadron from the battle for control of Sae Angelo might cost more lives than it would save. *Where* had those N'Taians come from? They must know their mission to be suicide! He smiled without humor. How like a N'Taian he knew.

Then his dim smile faded. Had she not known all she thought she had, or had she *hidden* something from him?—a reserve unit, a secret base?

"Horizon," came a new voice from a small speaker in front of him. "Trouble here, over undersea base three. We're badly outnumbered. I need more high support."

Brennen exhaled sharply and checked a grid for the base's coordinates. A glance at the master screens showed the atmospheric forces too thin to spread further.

He bit his lip and made a fast decision. "Kirzell."

"Sir?" The interlink voice sounded closer and clearer than before, probably near striking range.

"Cancel previous order. Proceed at once to support strike group over undersea base three at grid CZ seven-one-six."

After a brief silence he heard, "Changing course, sir."

His Corporal glanced toward him from her terminal. He ignored her, checked the screens, then reached for the interlink board again. "Generator, you are authorized to draw power from all systems but weapons and life-support to maintain energy and particle shielding. Full status reports every two minutes."

The bridge went dark. Eerie silence fell. Brennen held his emotions firmly under control as he waited for impact.

A minute later the lights flared on again, and with them the screens and a cacophony from the speakers.

"Take the link, Corporal." He looked to the screens. The ordnance and shield banks had drained heavily but were rapidly recharging, and the N'Taian attack group was peeling away . . . twelve, thirteen, fourteen remaining. Then he blinked as the group changed course. *They've lost thirty percent, but they're coming back! Their commanders should be spaced!*

Three more passes before the cruiser's big guns annihilated the N'Taian attackers, and then Brennen could attend again to the atmospheric battle. It had turned, again, in his favor. Relaxing slightly, he nerved himself to a most disagreeable job.

In helpless anguish Crown Princess Carradee Angelo watched two tri-D sets built into a catfooted marble table in her cream-and-gold parlor. On the nightside of the world, lightning storms swept the skies; here on the daylight side, tall buildings stood empty, whole industrial areas evacuated to an unnatural weekend stillness—except for the alien attack ships that dropped in tight squadrons, destroyed their targets, and sped off-screen.

She watched alone; somewhere in Sae Angelo, her husband Prince Daithi supervised a communications network. Along the marble wall that separated her suite from his, several receiving units had been set on a credenza to listen in on his movements—but one by one their voices had gone silent. *This cannot be!* she moaned. *For VeeRon and its forsaken irradium mines we pay with our homeland? I've already lost a sister.*

Carradee made no effort to hold back tears the thought of Firebird called up. She had tried for so long to see Firebird in her proper light, a Wastling who should be honored to pour out her life so young, *so* much younger than Carradee would be when Iarlet was ready for rule— *Well, yes, Firebird had her nonconformist streak.* Carradee tried to smile. She would forgive and forget that streak, given Firebird's doom and the way Phoena had tormented her.

The hall door opened without warning, startling Carradee badly. A page in Angelo scarlet slipped in and shut the massive wooden panel behind him. Hastily she wiped her face dry with a silken handcloth from her skirt pocket. "Don't you still knock?" she asked wearily. "We are at war, but the world still turns, and manners help it to do so."

The boy was trying valiantly to hide his own tears. "Pardon, Highness. Please, Highness. Her Majesty is dying."

"Dying?" Carradee scrambled to her feet. "But—"

"She said you'd have only a few minutes, Highness. Please hurry!"

* * *

Brennen left the bridge when Naetai's only remaining defenses were wheelborne, after ordering downside silence to give the N'Taian government thinking time. The Federacy's deepspace forces had arrived to reinforce his battle group. He had sent reports to Danton, Frankin at VeeRon, and Regional Command. Only one duty remained, and then he would be able to sleep.

The sentry at the vault sprang to attention as Brennen stopped before his desk. "It's all over but the talk," Brennen said, "we hope. I need item twenty-six seventy-six, please."

Three minutes later he sat on his own cot, examining the parcel. Through its wrap, rough fabric showed cobalt blue and two ruby stars glittered. Firebird, wearing this uniform at their parting, had bitten back a desperate plea for her people—he had read it in the cry of her emotions. He knew she would give almost anything to buy peace for Naetai, and revealing her survival to Naetai had already been named between them as part of the price.

He pulled open the seal. From the uniform's collar he unclipped the ruby stars, then laid them in a presentation box and set it on a bedside niche. Then gratefully he began to undress.

He had pulled off one boot when his interlink buzzed. Groaning, he reached for the tab. "Caldwell."

"DeepScan transmission for you, sir. Switching on." For a moment the link crackled. "Caldwell?" came the voice of Admiral Lee Danton. "We've been discussing staff for occupation forces on Naetai, and since you're rather an expert on these people, we were wondering: Could you see yourself as Lieutenant Governor? I need a strong second, someone to do my tough jobs while I work diplomacy. It's bound to be a temporary position. After you clean house, they can move in someone from the diplomatic corps. Regional told me to push you, and suggested a step up from Delta Squadron. Want the job?"

It was a startling honor, for himself and for Thyrica— and an invitation to be hated. Yet "housecleaning" could be done fairly, and he could do it well. Being resented came with the Star.

To "push" him, though? He'd half expected to be

forced up and out of the Delta group for some time, but did Regional intend to boost his career or to catch him in incompetence? *Sentinels unnerve them all.*

He spoke to the pickup. "Sir, I accept. I am slated already to answer any official transmission of surrender. How would you like that handled?"

Several seconds later, the interlink crackled again. "Excellent, Caldwell, excellent. Speak 'for the acting commander,' and when papers are signed planetside have Mafis announce both our names. I'll make an official landing soon afterward. But if they refuse to surrender, it will be your job to convince them they should give up rather than suffer further losses."

The following morning, shiptime, Brennen's Corporal had a message on hold when he arrived on the bridge: no tight DeepScan beam this time, but a personal holo. Resting one hand on the back of his command chair, Brennen signaled the Corporal to activate the receiving unit. An image of Devair Burkenhamn sprang to life at midfloor. The Marshal waited calmly, but Brennen read defeat in his posture.

Brennen stepped onto his own transmission grid, came to attention, and nodded to the Corporal. For the first time in sixteen hours, *Horizon* broke downside silence. "Sir," he said curtly to the officer whose trap he had escaped on board Phoena's frigate. "I am speaking for the acting commander now."

"Thank you for responding, General." Burkenhamn reached beyond the projection field and brought back a long scribepaper. "I am authorized by the Crown to offer its surrender. Where and when will you meet with us to discuss terms?"

Brennen held back a smile. "Your capital city has a spaceport."

"It *had* a spaceport."

"Clear a landing pad. Meet us there, at ten hundred local time. We require a representative from your military, one for the Assembly, one for the Electorate, and, of course, the Crown."

"And we will require—"

"The surrendering party will be treated fairly, sir, but

today, terms are not yours to set. Your day will come again, I assure you. The Federacy is anxious to establish normal relations. However, if Naetai tries treachery again you will pay a high price for peace."

Three hours later, a saucer-shaped Federate shuttle settled gently on an area of Sae Angelo Spaceport that had been cleared of rubble. Watching out a viewport near the main lock, Brennen could see that the spaceport was wrecked. Most of the outbuildings had been knocked into rockpiles, the rocket craters resembled dishes of boulders, and the main terminal was glassy slag. But unlike VeeRon, Naetai had taken no nuclear shelling. The Federates' precision bombing had left the civilian skyline of the city, a curious blend of antiquity and modernization, virtually untouched, although the sky was hazy with dust.

Twenty tan-suited pilots marched down the ramp and into an escort formation, watching warily for movement among the small N'Taian contingent. General Mafis, appointed chief negotiator by Regional Command, followed the guards, carrying a silver scribebook. An albino soldier of the Dengii race from the rimward-north quadrant of the Whorl, he stood nearly two meters high, with white hair brushed sleek and a scarlet tunic that glittered with decorations.

Brennen followed, surveying the damage that had been wreaked under his command. It was an odd feeling, to almost admire destruction. The approaching N'Taian delegates, more than had been asked for, eyed him cautiously. Perhaps they had heard about his escape from Princess Phoena's ambush on the frigate; replete, he hoped, with details of voice-command, circuit control, and the rest.

He walked slowly and deliberately to one side of the circle formed by the tan-clothed guards and let his epsilon shields diffuse. Intimidation by position, his masters had taught him, controlled a crowd without overtly menacing it. This crowd, however, felt intimidated already. He rejoined Mafis.

With a long pale hand Mafis spread the papers onto a repulsor cart brought up by one of the guardsmen, and he introduced himself and Caldwell to the N'Taians. Marshal Burkenhamn faced Mafis as chief of his own delegation from his high vantage, regarding Brennen—and his crystace, which hung openly at his belt—with cool respect, and the albino with blatant suspicion.

Mafis spoke evenly. "The terms of your surrender to the Interstellar Federacy are as follows. Martial law is hereby declared. The Regional Council has appointed Admiral Lee Danton of the Second Division, Interstellar Fleet, to be your Governor. His official landing shall be at this time tomorrow. Governor Danton has selected General Caldwell, Special Operations, as his lieutenant pro tem. The N'Taian Assembly, the Electorate, and the Crown shall all hold authority under the Planetary Governor. Naetai shall remain demilitarized. The Planetary Navy is disbanded until further word, as shall be the Assembly and the Electorate. You shall hold new elections in one month."

Brennen spoke in turn. "Because we have no provision for holding a conquered state, Naetai with her subjugate systems will constitute an independent protectorate of the Federacy for the present. You will have no armies of your own, but we will not leave you defenseless." He felt their surprise, and it disgusted him. Apparently they would not have extended comparable protection to a system they had taken. He restored his shields.

Mafis continued. "This document, as we directed in our communiqué, shall be signed by four N'Taian representatives. I summon you four to sign the instrument of surrender."

Three men and a woman came to the repulsor cart, their steps raising small dusty clouds. The men signed first.

Brennen was surprised to recognize Firebird's oldest sister, a tall, thirtyish blonde who regally carried a small heaviness, waiting behind them. As he passed the stylus to her, he asked so only she could hear, "Was the Queen unable to come as we directed, Highness?"

"I am now the Queen, Excellency, Carradee Second." Startled, he eyed her. Her pale gray eyes looked red and puffy, and her hands worked nervously at the hem of her fitted brown jacket. "My mother, Her Majesty Queen Siwann, left Naetai in my hands two nights ago." She signed and stepped away.

He caught her elbow. "Your Majesty, I am sorry. May I speak with you alone, then?"

"Is this something my sister, Princess Phoena, cannot hear?" Carradee turned toward the watching N'Taian delegation. Phoena stood with the group of witnesses, eyeing the proceedings suspiciously.

Trying to manage the throne already, is she? Brennen gave no sign that he knew Phoena. "Alone, Majesty," he whispered. "For a moment."

Carradee nodded. They walked together through the circle of guards, away from the shuttle into the open, desolate field. Behind them, General Mafis began to address the assembled crowd: a special speech he had prepared for the occasion.

Brennen had asked him to take his time about finishing.

CHAPTER 11

MaxSec

Tempo I
At first tempo

As Mafis's voice faded, Brennen cleared his shields again. "How did your mother die?"

Carradee's grief and anxiety hummed, but she kept emotion out of her voice. "She took poison, sir, when it became evident to her that she had led Naetai into a dishonorable defeat."

"Arride?"

"Yes," she said bleakly. "In no other way could she save her honor in the eyes of her people."

"We have dealt with that particular poison before, Your Majesty. This brings me to what I need to speak with you about." He drew the tiny box from a pocket of his belt and handed it to her. She held it suspiciously at a graceful arm's length. "Nothing deadly, madame." He took it back, opened the lid, and returned it into her hand. The rubies flashed in the morning light.

As she examined them closely, he studied her face. Men might kill for Phoena, he concluded, but Carradee's attractiveness was subtle, touched with humility at the eyes and sadness at the mouth.

She eyed the back of one star, then replaced it in the chipbox. "These are N'Taian rank stars, General. Why are they in your possession?"

"They belonged to your sister Firebird."

Brennen stood back to survey the effect of his verbal missile. Carradee pulsed with dismay, then delight, then confusion.

She pressed her hands around the box. "We were told that she was killed in action, but you would not have these if that were true. Would you? Is she alive?"

"She is alive, Majesty."

He could see that the news pleased her, but new responsibilities crowded her mind. Firebird, now her subject, would be a grave concern. "Where is she, General? How is she being treated?"

Brennen glanced toward the crowd. Mafis was still speaking. "She is under protective custody, at Regional Command on Alta." A single intercept fighter sweeping low over the skyline caught his glance as he spoke. "She has been held as a political prisoner, but was interviewed as military."

Carradee grew paler. He felt her panic rise.

"Yes," he continued steadily. "Yes, Your Majesty, that is one reason why we were able to take Naetai without prolonged warfare. May I suggest that many of your lives were saved by her capture."

"She was taken instead of killed at VeeRon, then?"

"It was very close." He related Firebird's suicide attempts, then her capture and questioning, without mentioning his own role.

She was plainly unsatisfied. He asked, "Have you not heard of Aurian mind-access?"

"No."

"Let me show you." She was watching his eyes, and he trapped her easily. She quailed and stepped back; then, caught, she stopped resisting. He probed only deeply enough to confirm that Siwann had truly died and was not in hiding. Carradee had stood at her side at the last, sorrowing in silence.

He released her, catching her hand to steady her while

she regained her balance. "That is access of a very simple type. Your sister's memory was taken far deeper."

She swallowed, and the line of her lips became hard. "Those who did so should be punished."

"You would rather hear that she had been tortured for information?"

Carradee stepped back and studied the gray, dusty ground. When after a minute she spoke again, her words came in a flat, toneless voice. "I would rather have gone on believing that she died honorably. You and your kind are more dangerous than I had thought—Excellency. You will be a powerful lieutenant governor."

"I will only oversee the establishment of the military governorship and peacekeeping forces, Majesty. We of the Sentinel kindred are allowed use of those abilities only under stringently defined circumstances. You will see little of them now. The Federacy wishes to help your forces keep order, in the best interest of all of us."

"Perhaps you mean, 'restore' order." He detected a new tone of grudging respect in her voice as she closed her hand around the little box and snapped it shut. "Many will be glad to hear that Firebird is alive. She was popular among the people. I too wish the best for her. However, the Electorate will be deeply concerned about her survival. We do not allow extraneous heirs, sir."

"And your sister Phoena will be less than glad."

The gray eyes widened.

"We learned many things from Lady Firebird's mind," he said easily, "on many levels."

Carradee glanced over her shoulder. Phoena, in a loose, ebony suede suit, stood at the edge of the circle of guards, openly ignoring Mafis's call for unity and watching Brennen and her sister.

Carradee turned back to him. "Be that as it may, General, she must know. But let me tell her myself."

"Of course." Mafis brought his exposition to a close as they walked back toward the circle. Two guards let them through the cordon directly before Princess Phoena. "Good morning, Your Highness." Brennen gave her a slight nod.

"I have nothing to say to you—alien filth." She turned her back.

Brennen bowed toward Carradee Second and left them to their family affairs.

On their fifth day on Alta IV, the Federacy's regional capital, Ellet arrived early in Firebird's minimum-security rooms. A subtle change in her cosmetics and hair hinted at important dealings.

Sitting at the small, efficient servo table at an inner corner of the anteroom, Firebird pulled a pale green audio rod from the little program-viewer unit she'd been issued by the tower library. "Good morning, Ellet."

"What was that?" Ellet nodded toward the rod.

"Luxian music." Firebird hoped Ellet would feel her wry amusement. "It came with that assortment from the library yesterday morning. The melodies are gorgeous, but the harmony has me baffled." She set the rod back in its case. "You didn't come to discuss music, though."

"No. You have a meeting with the Council uplevel, in half an hour. Just an introduction, I believe. They have little time to waste."

"Regional Council?"

Ellet ran a finger along the rough brown stoneform wall, toward the door's inner locking panel. "Half an hour."

The tower in which both had been assigned security rooms was known as MaxSec, Ellet had explained, for Maximum Security. Eighty stories tall, its silvery walls encompassed offices, laboratories, security apartments, and shops. It was designed like a fortress, with a security system developed by the finest minds in the Federacy. Firebird was given rooms near a group of outsystem diplomats on the thirtieth floor, although—unlike those of the diplomats— her lockpanel opened only to Ellet. Escape would have been impossible. Still, Firebird had examined the broad, gridded window carefully and even given it a suspicious touch the moment Ellet left her alone. She was glad of her caution when the sting from that momentary contact left her arm limp for an hour, barely able to unpack a small kit and two changes of gray shipboards.

Within a day of her arrival, she'd been able to identify several classes of local aircraft from staring out that window over the capital city of Castille. The volume of traffic in and out of a parking bay above her window confirmed that much administrative activity was conducted in the high tower.

Why the Council, today?

News from the war, she guessed. *It's over. What's left of my homeland?*

Shortly thereafter, she preceded Ellet from the security lift into a chamber designed in majestic proportion to the responsibility carried by the members of the Federacy's Regional Council. The pale gray ceiling rose high above her, vaulted by pure white stone arches designed with an eye to mathematical beauty. There were no windows, but air moved freely. It somehow felt both ancient and modern, and as they passed across an expanse of silver-flecked stone below empty spectator galleries, Firebird felt awed in spite of herself. They ascended three wide stairs onto a platform half circled by the Council table, and halted at the center of its arc.

Behind the table sat the ruling septumvirate of this quarter of the Federate Whorl, three of them nonhuman. Firebird kept walking stiffly to mask her curiosity and distaste. One was an Oquassan alien, reminiscent of a native N'Taian amphibian, with humped back, squat limbs, and dark, rough-textured brown skin. Beside him sat two other aliens who Firebird could not identify at all, whether male or female, young or old. The white-robed human woman at the center looked oldest; to her left sat three male humans in military uniforms. A large blank visual screen hung overhead, and each Councillor sat before a small touchboard and monitor.

Ellet stepped forward. "Members of the Council, I present to you Lady Firebird of the Naetai system." Firebird, unsure of the appropriate protocol for these unfamiliar circumstances, made a formal half-bow, feeling awkward in a standard-issue gray jumpsuit and wishing for a dress uniform.

The robed woman stood. "Good afternoon, Captain

Kinsman. You are welcome on Alta, Lady Firebird. I trust you have been treated well?"

"Very well, Your Honor."

"I am Tierna Coll, formerly of the Elysian System. May I introduce Admiral Madden of Caroli, Admiral Fierrson of Kellia, General Voers of Bishda." As she continued, she turned and indicated the Councillors on the other side. "Admiral Lithib of Oquassa, Doctor Kanacka of Lenguad, and Lady Faa of Katroo."

Firebird repeated her bow, less perfectly than usual. She felt very much out of her element among aliens, even ones such as Lady Faa, who might have passed for human in dim light but for her backsloping, hairless cranium. Doctor Kanacka, a scarcely visible shimmer, unnerved her entirely.

"Our news must be conveyed with our sympathies," said Tierna Coll. "First, Naetai has surrendered." Firebird pressed her fingertips into her palms and said nothing. "We received that word late yesterday." Tierna Coll's voice rang like that of a well-trained alto; Firebird found it both pleasant and commanding. "The second news came only an hour ago. Your mother has committed suicide, Lady Firebird. We are sorry."

Firebird felt that she should respond, but her emotions seemed dead. Given the surrender and Naetai's traditions, this did not really surprise her.

Admiral Madden, second from the left, seemed to see her awkwardness. Quickly he stopped stroking his blond beard and leaned forward, spreading his elbows on the table. "We have been advised that the survival of the patrol fleet at VeeRon resulted in part from a warning you gave. I am certain that you have been thanked already, but we wish to add our gratitude to that already given."

Firebird made a small, polite bow to the kind-faced Carolinian. Caroli, VeeRon's governing world, could afford magnanimity now.

At Tierna Coll's side, General Voers stood. A row of golden stars sparkled on the breast of his coal-black uniform. "We have before us a report submitted by Lieutenant General Caldwell, now on Naetai, concerning your government's secret research. The, ah, 'Cleary/D'Stang/Parkai

Project,'" he read. "Is this a special concern of your family, Your Highness?"

Brennen was safe, then. She restrained her urge to correct Voers's unknowing aggrandizement and answered his question. "Of my sister Princess Phoena, Your Honor, and the late Queen's Electoral Council."

"You were, I understand, a member of that body?"

"Yes, General Voers."

"This report claims that you did not support the research. Why not?"

It was difficult to answer without denigrating her family. "Members of the Council, I have little official authority on Naetai, and I am not authorized to speak for the Angelo rule. But, for myself, I would like to express my regret for this unfortunate situation. I would like you to know that I am a career military officer of my own volition, but that I have grave reservations about some decisions of the Electorate." In this bright alien environment, the words sounded like treason. She glanced Ellet's way for support, but Ellet's eyes, forward on the Council, did not shift.

"My lady." The Oquassan Lithib's low, gasping voice confirmed that he was not at home in the Altan atmosphere. "This report indicates that you may be willing to consider —consider, I say—personally joining the Federate peoples. I would find that most heartening. Would you confirm that for me?"

Distracted by his appearance, Firebird found it difficult to order a proper sentence. Lithib's huge, sad eyes lay far to the sides of his high dorsal crest, and his eight digits were long and nimble-looking. *At least,* Firebird reminded herself, *he's bilaterally symmetrical.* She envied Ellet her poise among all these varieties of sentients. "The standard by which I have been taught to judge matters of policy has been, 'Is it good for the Electorate?' This broader notion— this standard, 'Is it *good?*' and no more—is very new to me. I do not understand how so many systems can peacefully share a government based on a concept like that. But it is something in which I would like to believe." Inexplicably, the alien Lithib seemed more sympathetic than General Voers, who appeared quite normally human. "My difficulty is the matter of forsaking Naetai, my home and the land of my people."

Voers leaned back and said nothing.

Tierna Coll spoke again. "That is a decision you need not face for some weeks yet. The public portions of the MaxSec library will remain at your disposal, as will newscans given Captain Kinsman, when she has finished with them. We hope eventually to be able to accord you more freedom of movement without jeopardizing your safety, but please bear with our protective custody for a time."

Some inflection in Tierna Coll's voice, perhaps her use of the royal "we," reminded Firebird suddenly of Siwann. Apprehensively she waited for grief to rise.

It did not: only relief tinged with regret, and incredulity at having survived her mother after all.

"Lady Firebird, we thank you." Tierna Coll inclined her head.

Firebird did the same. Ellet touched her arm and led her away.

CHAPTER 12

Protectorate

L'istesso tempo
**Although the meter changes,
the beat remains the same**

Sae Angelo's day was burning out in a sunset still fiery from
atmospheric dust. Brennen turned from the window back
to his bluescreen. Like most of his office furnishings, the
viewer had come from Caroli for the new occupation base.
Situated at the edge of Sae Angelo Spaceport, which was
now undergoing extensive reconstruction, the base was a
particle-shielded encampment, a tenuous foothold on a
world that still called him "enemy."

Metal shelves on one side of his desk held an array of
Thyrian pieces—Aurian relics, multicolored shellfish, holo
cubes of Thyrian rainforest—none of them his own, but
furnished to uphold the dignity of the Federacy. He had an
aristocracy to deal with.

Two items remained on his day's agenda. The first
awaited in the hall outside, with his secretary: another
aristocrat for scan evaluation, merely a surface emotional
check, for he had been instructed to avoid the use of access
except in cases of extreme suspicion.

Already he had examined the former Marshals and
several former Electors, and to a man they itched for

rebellion. Naetai needed a time of calm, a chance to begin to see the Federacy as ally.

N'Taians had a passion for independence—he had experienced that himself now, having seen the culture firsthand, heard some of the traditional stories and songs with his own ears while the performers' fierce national-istic pride radiated through his downed shields. But the Federacy did not intend to stifle that independence. Every Federate cultural unit—multiplanetary or single-continental—had its local government, its own representa-tion in regional senates. His own people answered to Alta, but that fact rarely influenced Thyrica's day-to-day affairs, internal or external. Personal and media contact with other Federate peoples, such as the aristocratic Luxians, would demonstrate this to the N'Taians—in time.

He pressed a signal onto the touchboard and then dropped all epsilon static, the better to read his subject, and waited for Count Tel Tellai.

The Count's size and soft features made him appear even younger than his nineteen N'Taian years, Brennen noted as Tellai stepped into the office's far end. He wore the blue sash of office—*father deceased only last year*, according to the file on screen—*extensive agricultural lands, children's hospital.* Otherwise dressed hat to heels in black, Tellai walked forward with measured steps, radiat-ing antipathy that created a dull, nagging unease in Bren-nen's unshielded senses. "Please take a chair, Count Tellai."

Seated, Tellai seemed even smaller. He brushed dust from velvric trousers and pulled off his narrow-brimmed hat.

Brennen eyed him: short, fine-boned, effeminate, Tel-lai looked the consummate aristocrat. Projecting the allow-able calming overtones, Brennen began. "The purpose of this interview is simple, sir. We need to know your underly-ing attitude toward the Federacy. Naturally you wish us elsewhere, but for the present we must try to work together for the good of the N'Taian people."

He had repeated the lines several times already, and read his subjects' responses. Only in privacy could Brennen scan conclusively; furthermore, he could place only one at a time under Command, should any try to attack.

Tellai didn't seem the attacking sort. Brennen pulled a stylus from his cuff and held it lightly in the fingers of both hands. "Can you recall, briefly, your feelings toward the Federacy before this crisis set us against each other? Be honest, please. You are in no danger if you tell the truth, but I can sense deception."

Tellai's long, dark lashes fell closed, and Brennen was startled by a sudden resemblance to Firebird. Was there—? He glanced again at the screen. Yes, the connection was quite close: Tellai was her second cousin.

The Count took several breaths. "I thought very little of the Federacy, Your Excellency. I have had my lands to administer, have been relandscaping the primary residence. . . ."

Brennen focused not on the words but on Tellai's underlying emotion. He caught a brief rise of regret, washed out by resentment. Not so different from the others, and apparently lacking the support of inner strength that might have made him dangerous—unlike the new Crown Princess.

For the second time that day he toyed briefly with the idea of suggesting that Carradee persuade Phoena to leave Sae Angelo for a while: take a long vacation, let calm settle.

As Tellai finished speaking, his emotions fell back into blank apprehension. Brennen rested his elbows on the desk. "In five years, the Naetai Systems will be eligible to rise from Protectorate status to full Federate covenance. The benefits of such covenance would be tremendous for your people. Assuming for the moment that this comes to pass, how would you envision your own role in such a society?"

Tellai reacted instantly. "Never in the history of Naetai has such a thing happened, sir, and it never, never will."

Brennen had to admire the dandy's outburst on behalf of his people, although fear of how Brennen might retaliate hung heavy in both their minds.

This was no ringleader.

Raising his epsilon shielding, Brennen shifted the stylus to a writing grip. "Thank you, sir. You may go."

Tellai blinked, opened his mouth—shut it—then rose and scurried to the door. Brennen pressed the key to let him out, then made one line of shorthand notes in a black scribebook.

The return of emotional silence felt coolly quiet, but he knew the pleasantness would not last. Since VeeRon, long spells in its solitary depth had begun to gnaw at him: the price of having touched absolute connaturality without bonding it.

A message remained on the Crown channel, saved for day's end to be treated with care and a possible evening followup. Carradee might reign chiefly as a figurehead, but the nobles' deference had cued him to her family's symbolic importance. Carradee had not been ordered in for an interview—nor even Phoena, the known troublemaker. Perhaps showing the Crown respect might win, if not Carradee's support, at least an inclination in that direction. Carradee would very probably still reign five years hence, when elections determined whether Naetai joined or rejected the Federacy.

He called up her message. The bluescreen cleared, then filled with pale letters.

Lieutenant Governor Caldwell, greetings.

You must be aware by now of our tradition of heir limitation. For the present we are willing to accept the Federacy's injunction outlawing it.

However, previous to the establishment of the Protectorate, a number of younger scions of noble houses were granted expensive education and training and the wherewithal to make for themselves the most honorable end possible. This was considered an investment in the nobility of our homeland.

Our sister Lady Firebird accepted such gifts, but took gross advantage of them and reportedly lives now under Federate protection. We and our Electorate deem it only reasonable in this particular case to request that the Federacy repay the House of Angelo the following expenses incurred anticipating her contribution to the glory of Naetai, which apparently were squandered . . .

Brennen blinked at the screen. Siwann's former Electors—still meeting illegally as Carradee's—meant to bill the Federacy for four years of Academy education, all jet and laser-ion fuel thereby consumed, uniform allowance including jeweled rank insignia and—a thirty-million-gild tagwing fightercraft?

He chuckled. *Wherewithal . . . honorable . . .* squandered . . . !

His entire body relaxed, and he stretched his legs: the message had broken his tension and restored his sense of proportion. The Federacy espoused respect of others' viewpoints, and perhaps to the N'Taians the request seemed reasonable. For the sake of Carradee's good feelings, he would try to settle the matter: perhaps a compromise could be arranged.

He checked her request against the reparations budget. The matter would have to be referred to Danton, he reflected soberly. He would not have it intimated that he had convinced the Federacy to buy Firebird's freedom.

Freedom. Would she take it as a gift—and did she know the meaning of the word?

The message's postscript iced the cake. The tone changed, implying a different author, and suggested the Federacy bind Firebird into servitude to pay off the debt herself.

Unquestionably Phoena's touch.

He inserted, *Can you believe this? See budget 2(C),* after the postscript and keyed it onto Danton's agenda for the following morning. Grinning once again, he shut down the viewer and waved off the room lights. Evening was his, then, to settle another matter. Rumor had reached him today that Vultor Korda, who he remembered with little respect, lingered in Sae Angelo. On his own time he would try a different kind of investigation, to satisfy himself—and the laws of Thyrica.

Sweating from the rush of frenzied packing, Vultor Korda stowed his last load of essentials into a ground car the Electorate had given him for his services. "Cheap *slugs,*" he muttered as he buried a roll of Federate gilds in the toe of one shoe. "You could've afforded an air transport,

but, ah, no, save a little credit for more important concerns
—like Nella Cleary."

Exhaust from the traffic below his apartment block
congealed in the chill air around him. Korda slammed the
side trunk shut and ran back up the steps to his studio for a
last plunge into cabinets. Breathing hard, he paused in the
doorway to look around. Angularly elegant rented furniture
lay buried under a jumble of his less vital belongings, and
all the lumas burned.

"Caldwell," he exclaimed. At least Phoena had come
to warn him! "Why did it have to be *that* eight-pointed
goody-boots?"

"Not a friend of yours?" Phoena observed from a chair
in one corner of the studio.

"Not exactly." He reached for a package of jelly
wafers, and it slipped out of his hand onto the yellow tile
floor. One end burst, splotching his discarded possessions
with purple confection.

From all others at Sentinel College Korda had hidden
his fantasies of power, biding his time, watching and
learning. When Caldwell arrived, taking annual paid leave
at an age when Korda had only begun Turn training, they
had met by chance over lunch. The following day Korda
had received a summons for reevaluation.

"Question of integrity," had been the Masters' verdict
—and Korda had been suspended—sentenced to report
every ten-day *dekia* to be treated with epsilon-blocking
drugs, lest he misuse what skills he had learned in his two
years at College.

*Scorch Caldwell and his blasted ninety-seven epsilon
harmonics!*

Temporary blocking drugs, fortunately. Only radical
cerebral surgery could strip a starbred of power for all time.
After five years of that intolerable treatment he had fled.
They would cut him—or kill him—if they caught him now,
but his abilities had returned. Korda found that living
without static shields kept him attuned to all that tran-
spired around him and saved his energy for occasional
bursts of access and Command—without distracting his
spirit from the destiny he pursued.

Indolently Phoena peeled a pale green banam fruit. "It

rather sounds as though you love him the way I respect my Wastling sister. I do wish there were a way to get to Alta. I would love to show her she cannot escape the N'Taian Electorate."

"Do you mean that?" Korda stopped midfloor and stared into Phoena Angelo's eyes as deeply as he could. Yes, she pulsed with hatred, and yes, she would pay any price to see her treacherous sister dead. And how delicious it might be if he, a mere trainee, were able to best whatever Sentinel they had protecting Firebird. Surely, they would use a Sentinel guard. "Highness, I could get offplanet easily, if you have a suggestible acquaintance on the Interplanetary Travel Committee."

"My man is in place." She straightened her shoulders and gave him a sweet smile that he read as very false. "You'd do it for me, Korda?"

"What about you, Your Highness? Don't you want to see it done, and done correctly—on the other end?" With a high-ranking escort, he reasoned, it *would* be easier to get to the Wastling. Without one, more difficult—particularly on Alta, assuming MaxSec, which he had seen once during his training.

Phoena buffed her nails on one sleeve. "I would indeed, but I cannot afford to leave my research. I'll find another to keep an eye on you, someone to help, someone with a particular . . ."

She stopped speaking, and Korda dropped impatiently onto a hassock. Phoena was always doing that, trailing off before he could catch the focus of her thought. "Grudge?" he prompted. "Against Firebird?"

"Actually, no." Her eyes narrowed, and she smiled with one side of her mouth. "I was thinking. Perhaps it would shake your 'friend' in the Lieutenant Governor's office if we sent someone whom Caldwell thinks he's beaten. That would win us quite a psychological victory, *and* rid Naetai of that cunning threat to the succession."

Korda began to puff up in agreement, but immediately he slouched again. "Caldwell has been bedimmed careful so far. He hasn't 'beaten' anyone yet, that I've heard of."

"He'll have to, fairly soon," Phoena said placidly. "I have several men working quietly to get rid of that occupation base. The first time one of my men is caught, we free him and move quickly. I have enough influence to release any ranking prisoner on his own recognizance. But could you hold up your own end? How could you get offplanet?" she asked suspiciously.

He took it as an invitation to demonstrate. Leering, he turned inward for his epsilon carrier. "How did your father die?" he asked quickly, mocking her tone of voice.

. . . Through a haze of incompletely focused energy he/Phoena saw a terrified brownbuck leap a downed tree in some far northern evergreen forest. Its motion seemed jerky and imperfect, for Korda could not control the rate of alpha flow. He/Phoena pulled hard on a rope; it sprung tight into a tripline, and almost too quickly to watch, a huge bay stallion fell, rolled, crushed . . .

Phoena flung a hand to her forehead. "It was a hunting accident. What has *that* to do with—*squill*, I have a headache. What's in your medicine cabinet?"

As Phoena plunged into the bathing room, Korda rose off the hassock. He laughed silently. Now he had something to hold against Phoena, should he need it.

And to catch that obnoxious skite from his class, Firebird—to strip her of her Altan memories, see the inner workings of the Federacy through her eyes, experience a Sentinel interrogation firsthand for his own purposes . . . He paused, listening as Phoena scattered medicine vials across the marble counter. To punish Firebird, crush her spirit and mind as the Masters had punished him, that would be sweet. Yes.

Phoena emerged, wiping her hands on a cloth, which she then dropped amid the general chaos.

"Highness," he said with a deferential nod. "When the time comes, give me the name of your contact on the I.S.T. Committee. He will see a face other than mine, no matter whom he expects. You'll arrange my groundwork?"

"You wish a false ID? Use any name you want, and I shall supply programming. But first we must get you out of Sae Angelo. Leave the mess—perhaps His Excellency the Lieutenant Governor will be looking for you."

Korda swept out an arm and motioned her to precede him out the door.

She strolled toward his servo instead. "No, I want to make some calls without using a palace line. This will suit me perfectly. Good-bye, Korda. We understand each other. I will contact you in Gorman, when the time is right."

Vultor Korda dashed back out the stairs and plunged the car down the ramp into traffic.

Alone on her tattered green lounger, Firebird pored over an Altan newscan and grieved for her homeland. Her memory, her knowledge, had helped engineer this disaster. The account on the inner section of Ellet's paper (several days old—what did Ellet fear she would do with current news?) touched her deeply. She wept as she read the grim roster of destroyed N'Taian facilities on the flimsy page. She had trained at this one, based at that one, refueled at others, and her very memories had given Brennen's forces their targets. Sae Angelo, Claighbro . . . She stopped and read the list again, frowning at the tiny print. She must have missed it.

No, it was simply not on the list: Hunter Height, two long days' ground-car drive north of Sae Angelo in the Aerie Mountains. Her family's "vacation home"—actually a fortresslike last-effort retreat. The ancient stone house sat atop a huge complex of tunnels on a granite mountain overlooking its own airstrip, and it was not listed here.

She sat bolt upright; the lounger creaked. So her efforts of resistance had not been in vain. She *had* concealed one of Naetai's minor airbases from Brennen.

Much good it had done.

Centered atop the page was a row of 2-D photographs: Brennen, Danton, Carradee, Siwann. Her gaze lingered on Siwann's picture. She would never see her mother again. Siwann was dead by her own hand, the penalty her own conscience had laid upon her for the ruin she had brought to her homeland.

Firebird grimaced and rerolled the newscan. A pity Phoena, co-instigator of the invasion, had not suffered similar remorse.

Carradee . . . An odd thought struck Firebird. Staring blankly out the window, she let it run its course. By N'Taian tradition, Siwann would have suicided once she judged her heiress fit to rule, and Firebird had always harbored a vague suspicion that Siwann was expending very little effort preparing Carradee. Siwann had intended to hold power for many years to come. Now poor, gentle Carrie would find herself thrust into a situation she could have little hope of controlling. Among the Electors, the jockeying for power would be commencing.

A week later, a packet return-marked Sae Angelo arrived. It had passed the censors unopened: an ID tape in one corner gleamed shiny brown, and below the tape had been lettered: Personal. Security I.

She took it to the inner room and sat on the edge of her narrow slideaway bed. Carefully she slit the seal and pulled out four sheets of scribepaper. One was tightly folded and heat-sealed, addressed in Phoena's flowery script. Another, unsealed, she recognized as Carradee's writing.

The other two sheets were covered with an unfamiliar masculine hand. She laughed when she saw the formal letterhead atop each page. Brennen had learned very quickly how to impress N'Taians. It read:

Office of the Lieutenant Governor
Sae Angelo
N'Taian Protectorate Systems
Interstellar Federacy

Mari—

There is a lull in affairs today; please believe that I have written at the first available moment. My title is "Lieutenant to Governor Danton"; actually, I am his bodyguard, chief of enforcement, and mentor. We are thus far impressing people with our knowledge, although the attitude prevails that Naetai is the center of the known universe, and that everyone in the galaxy must be well informed about N'Taian affairs.

We've met with hostility, but attitudes do seem to be softening as the elections approach (I've applied for my dismissal immediately afterward).

I had words yesterday with both your sisters at

the palace. The grounds are heavy with your
presence. I spoke briefly with one man on the
palace staff—an elderly butler or some such
servant—who spoke of you as I was looking
through the portrait gallery. He gave me the
impression that you were very highly thought of on
Naetai. Is that part of your problem with Phoena?

Firebird paused and stared up at the gray inner wall. It
was indeed, particularly after the late Baron Parkai had
commented within hearing of both of them that "it was a
shame about the order of succession." Phoena had had
scarcely a civil word for her since that day, more than ten
years ago now.

I may not be able to write again. Don't answer
this letter. Expense aside, I don't entirely trust the
courier service, even with an ID tape for clearance.

Yours,
B.

P.S. The portrait is lovely.

Carradee's message was warm, if officious, asking after
her treatment, warning her to maintain her dignity, and
promising "appropriate" clothing to follow.
Phoena came directly to the point:

Firebird:
So you have betrayed us all. If I ever see you
again, I shall personally remove you from the
succession.

Phoena Irina Eschelle Angelo
Princess Royale

A postscript had been added in Brennen's hand, despite
the heat seal on Phoena's paper. It read:

Not if I have anything to say about it. I apologize
for even including this, but it is important for you

to know exactly how you stand with her. If it's any comfort, she would do the same for me.

B.

Carradee's promised parcel arrived within a day, and with it a treasure: her clairsa, detuned for travel. Who had thought to loosen the strings—her girl Dunna? She almost wept at the sight of it, caressing the intricate carvings in the leta-wood upper arch as though greeting a lost friend. After a minute she set about restoring the tuning.

When Ellet brought the evening newscan, Firebird offered a short concert. "I only play for enjoyment these days." She supported the arched-triangle frame in her lap with her left hand. "Not in public anymore."

Ellet smiled tolerantly. "I have a brother who plays a similar instrument."

Firebird ran her right fingers along the strings, quickly readjusted the tuning, then played a rolling arpeggio to warm her hands. A tinkling, resonant major chord climbed the ladder of strings in two swift strokes and hung in the air while the metal strings rang out. She damped them before the chord faded away.

Shifting the balance by crossing her legs under the stool and leaning one corner on her shoulder, she freed both hands to pluck the strings and began a rollicking dance tune, the kind a young aristocrat learns as part of a "well-rounded education."

"More," Ellet insisted. "Obviously you are not the casual player Labeth is."

Gratified, Firebird began the difficult etude she had so recently memorized.

CHAPTER 13

Rattela

Sotto voce
In an undertone; whispered

To Brennen, even the outbuildings of the Rattela estate looked magnificent, fronted with white marble, their corners and doorposts carved with fruit-laden vines. The central house rose three stories to a black-shingled roof and spread long wings in each direction. *The hedges alone must keep a team of gardeners employed,* Brennen reflected as he eyed them for possible assailants. He had brought two guards, one a tall woman in Altan gray and the other a young Sentinel, but he led them up the long approach. A repulsor craft hovered silently above the grounds.

An execution yesterday had done little to improve his mental state. One Federate private, kidnapping one N'Taian girl, might have undone all the rapport Danton had worked so hard to build these two weeks. As the "strong second," Brennen had been obliged to access the soldier, confirm his guilt, escort him out to a public square, and shoot him. Brennen had not slept that night: his nerves insisted that to execute in battle was one thing, in cold blood another.

Vultor Korda, furthermore, had vanished from Sae

Angelo. Brennen had tried an aerial search for flickers of stray epsilon energy, but, as he'd feared, it had proven fruitless.

Three stairs rose before the carved, ebony-framed door. He took them quickly and knocked. A girl's face appeared on a tri-D panel that had been invisible on the white background. "Yes?"

"I wish to speak with His Grace, the Duke, miss."

"He is out, Your Excellency. Didn't the gateman tell you?"

Even in holo he could see she was lying, just as Rattela had lied when he'd claimed to be too ill to return to the occupation base for questioning. "This is government business, miss. Please have His Grace come to the door."

The image vanished. Behind Brennen, his guards watched the grounds, tense and vigilant. After a moment he extended a careful probe inside. He recalled the distinct savor of Rattela's presence from his brief scan interview, and when he felt it approach he steadied himself for a struggle.

The screen lit again, this time with Rattela's jowly face. "Your Excellency." The eyes attempted surprised innocence. "How may I help you?"

"I must speak with you in person, sir, regarding a matter that concerns you closely."

"Excellency, that is out of the question. I am in my bedchamber; I do not feel—"

Brennen angled his hand and focused a burst of energy into the door's opening circuits. As it slid aside, he shifted the focus and caught Rattela in Command, so that he froze in a shock-jawed expression, one arm half-raised.

High ceilings rose above the unmoving nobleman, and ornate white-upholstered furniture stood in carefully organized conversational arrangements. The two servants who flanked the Duke stared in confused alarm.

"Take us where we can be alone, please, Your Grace," Brennen said.

His movement made awkward by the compulsion of voice-command, Rattela shuffled toward a door on the hall's left. At Brennen's nod, the Altan guard swept the room with her stare and then came to attention in the doorway.

Inside was a man's study: weapons hung on ebony walls, and indigo leather covered the furniture. Only one exit, only one window. It would suffice. Brennen waved Rattela to a deep armchair and dropped his hand.

The Duke clutched the wings of the chair and sank into it. "Sir, I protest. This is the House of Claighbro. You have no right to force entry. I shall speak plainly with the Governor about this intrusion. I—"

"Governor Danton," Brennen said mildly, "has issued me a warrant. Evidence has been given us that this house conceals a large store of weapons. *Tactical* weapons," he added to answer the Duke's pseudoapologetic glance at several swords on the study's walls. "My greatest desire at the moment is to see you cleared from suspicion, Your Grace, but I can do so only by searching either the grounds or your memory. Of the two, mind-access will take less of your time and demand fewer of your resources." He motioned his Thyrian guard forward. When Rattela's fury exploded through his static shields, he countered with a calming wave. "He will not harm you, and we have no desire for unpleasantness. Please . . ."

Rattela opened his mouth and took a deep breath to shout. Brennen caught him again in Command. "Please do not force me to have you restrained in your own house, sir. I desire only to clear you."

He let the Command slip a little, but Rattela continued to fight, rising halfway out of the chair before Brennen could reestablish control.

He exhaled sharply. "I am sorry, Your Grace. You leave me no choice." He nodded to the Sentinel guard. Carefully balancing his energy with the other's, he relinquished control. The moment transfer was accomplished, Brennen turned inward for his carrier, modulated it, and thrust it at Rattela.

The Duke's pain and rage sizzled at him, but he held the carrier steady, probing quickly and hard for a flaw in the natural defenses of the nobleman's outer matrix.

Rattela had no idea how to resist. Brennen breached him in a second. His point of awareness plunged into heavy, distasteful pressure: strange voices, alien images, Rattela's struggle to reassert his will, and a hatred as bitter as clemis root.

"We spoke of weapons," Brennen said softly.

Vision cleared. He stood in a dim room. Crates lined two walls: oblong cases of energy rifles and smaller, blocky metal boxes that might hide anything from handguns to gravity warheads. Filed with the image was its location below the villa's main floor; the entire interrogation lasted only a few seconds.

Brennen opened his eyes. Rattela sprawled in the chair, almost convulsed in useless physical resistance. Brennen signaled his aide to let him go.

"Very well, sir," he said as the Duke composed himself. He hated to arrest the man. It would probably mean reprisals, but inaction would mean worse. "I am afraid you must come with me to Base, to answer some additional questions."

"You have no authority," the nobleman fumed. "I'll see you—"

Brennen angled a hand but did not Command.

Rattela shut his mouth and stood up. The two guards stepped to his side, and quickly the Altan woman caught one of his wrists in a binder, touched his shoulder, and marched him out.

Unhappily, Brennen followed.

Over three weeks, Ellet Kinsman had rarely let a smile wrinkle her clear oval face, and only gradually had she let their conversations (obviously manipulated to educate Firebird) touch on her own people. *But she's companionship,* Firebird reminded herself. She leaned against the wall nearest the window, careful to avoid the security grid, watching both Ellet on the lounger and the free, outside world. A high layer of tiny clouds mottled the Altan afternoon sky.

"What's the major difference between a Sentinel and a Master Sentinel, then?" Firebird asked. "Is it a matter of degree, or a different set of skills?"

"Both, at times." Ellet touched her four-rayed star, never relaxing her tutor's pose. "The line of eligibility is not drawn at any arbitrary point on the Aurian Scale, though generally those whose carrier and potential evaluations fall below ninety-three are not considered for Master's training. Some potentials shown also by outsiders influence train-ability. Focus, for example, is a function of the mind's power of concentration. I could levitate a fairly massive object if need arose and I were able to rest afterward. General Caldwell could control the rate of fall of his own body, a far more subtle and difficult skill."

"Is it—a physical center in the brain, then? A—Ellet, this is an awkward question. Do you feel the Aurians were genetically human? How did the epsilon abilities arise? A mutation?—from the Six-Alpha Catastrophe, perhaps?"

"There is a physical center, yes, low between the hemispheres. And you have studied the sciences, Fire-bird." Ellet's brows came together over her shapely but prominent nose. "Different species cannot interbreed: the Aurians were quite human."

Somehow that comforted Firebird more than she could justify. It made sense, although she had been told for years that the starbred were half-alien. But where had they come from? Ellet had not answered her other question. "The origin of the epsilon center, then? Did they practice genetic engineering?"

"That," said Ellet stiffly, "is a subject I do not discuss with outsiders, even Thyrians outside our families. We feel it unwise to encourage half the galaxy to try to duplicate what is given only to a few." Her brows lowered, and her eyes half closed.

Firebird folded both arms across her chest. "I was only curious."

"A trait you must learn to control. Every people has its racial secrets. You must respect them."

"But if people have nothing to hide, they can afford to be open." Ellet's absolute emotional control had begun to irritate Firebird. It made Ellet aloof, untouchable—whereas Brennen's gave him a comfortable steadiness.

"You speak out of ignorance," Ellet said. "Ask another question, so you can learn."

Very well—Ellet had invited this. "How is it that you show so little feeling?"

Ellet laughed, a puff of breath and no more. "Consider the question yourself. Among telepaths, broadcasting emotion is boorish—performing private functions in public. Decorum involves personal restraint, for some of the star-bred can send well, but shield themselves poorly."

"Why?"

"Talents vary."

Firebird sighed. "Range, then. How far away can you sense a person's emotion, or send the carrier wave?"

"That too varies with Aurian Scale."

"And with the strength of the one being sensed?"

"What do you mean by strength?"

"Well . . ." Firebird extended one hand, palm up. "Some people seem to overpower you when they walk into a room, and others can be invisible standing next to you. That, and—will power, intelligence—do they make any difference?"

"A little. Back to your question. Generally the width of a room is the range of a solid epsilon carrier."

"Generally that's far enough for you to do quite a bit."

"Correct."

Recalling how Brennen had probed her from across the war room, Firebird paused. Although the experience had been an infuriating public humiliation, the sensation itself had not been all that unpleasant—nor, truly, had the other sessions.

She let her gaze wander across the anteroom as she thought aloud. "Between a starbred man and woman, there must be dimensions of relationship beyond anything others experience. The potential—"

"Yes." Ellet delivered the word like a slap.

"Have you—"

"The subject is of no concern to you," Ellet said, suddenly and obviously angry. "I would like to listen to you, now. Play your clairsa."

Firebird stared in surprise. Well. It seemed she'd touched a nerve at last—but with which question? She knelt to pick up the little instrument, took a stool, and sat down.

The sonata came mechanically at first, as if she were not concentrating, but as it moved from minor to modal, she felt it sweep her away, back into the N'Taian frame of reference. Her links with her past had been weakening as her understanding of the Federacy grew; N'Taian music made her strong again.

Ellet broke into her reverie. "I must go."

"Come soon," Firebird said absently. Ellet locked the massive door behind her. Firebird kept playing.

Several days later, Ellet brought unsettling news: preparatory to the elections, conquered Naetai had sent an embassy with a firmly worded message to the Regional Council. Naetai's Electorate, the missive directed, would consider a particular gesture of cooperation to be an extremely positive sign that the Federacy was ruled by reasonable men of honor and esteem.

"But the Electorate was supposedly dissolved. What are they asking for?" Firebird asked uneasily. She and Ellet sat on opposite ends of the green lounger.

"You tell me."

"They intend to take me back with them."

"Correct. Specifically, 'The surrender of First Major Firebird Angelo, reportedly captured at the battle of VeeRon.'"

Firebird considered. On Naetai, now governed by the Federacy, she might legally be safe enough, but it would take more than Federate law to change aristocratic attitudes, and only one Heir to kill her. "I suppose they're still waiting for news of my suicide. They'll never forgive me for surviving to be interrogated—and it wasn't my fault." Ellet gave her a sharp glance, as intent as any of Brennen's. "Not my fault," Firebird repeated. She stared through the wall across time and space, seeing Lord Rendy Angellson just before he was killed in his ground car by falling debris. *Accidental death—maybe.* "I think I'd rather stay here, Ellet. It's amazing how easily one gets used to the hope of living."

Ellet rose. "All right. I'll convey your wishes to the Council, and they'll be considered along with the N'Taians' petition."

Late that evening, Ellet returned with a startling escort: the Duke of Claighbro, Muirnen Rattela, and— incredibly—her former instructor, Vultor Korda, looking more pasty-faced than ever in tight black shipboards. As the men preceded Ellet into the brown-walled anteroom, Firebird rose from the lounger, where she had been comfortably curled around her clairsa. She came to attention, rejoicing she'd not yet undressed for bed. Silently she berated Ellet for failing to warn her.

"Gentlemen." She forced cordiality into her voice. "Come in, sit down." She motioned them toward the lounger. There Rattela settled his bulk, hands on the knees of black sateen breeches, and Korda joined him. Ellet walked around behind them to lean on the windowbar.

Rattela's soft green eyes absorbed every detail of the bare little anteroom and rested finally on Firebird, who stood near the door, feet apart and hands clenched at her sides. "Suns, Firebird, this is no place for a Lady of the House of Angelo. Aren't you ready to go back to the palace?"

Rattela had left the honorific off her name; she was in disgrace, then. She sent a questioning glance to Ellet. "The Council," Ellet informed her, "has asked the N'Taian embassy to honor your period of temporary asylum, and to renew the request at its close, in six weeks."

Firebird nodded.

"But they did say," insisted Rattela, "that if you chose to return with us, they would guarantee you safe passage to Naetai."

"I see." Firebird envisioned a return to Naetai on their terms: stepping off a Federate ship, leaving behind a Federate guard who had seen her safely home, while the Redjackets waited below, beside the terminal.

She refocused her eyes on the window. Beyond the gridded glasteel panel, the lights of Castille sparkled all colors of the spectrum. Streams of cars flowed along wide avenues to an arc of low hills, then climbed to the hilltops and vanished. A little higher, she could see the wing lights of atmospheric craft; higher yet, constellations glimmered, similar to those of home, but with the brightest stars brighter and noticeably colored, and shifted to new positions. Castille by night was lovely.

"No, Rattela," she said quietly. "I've chosen to stay."

Korda leaned forward. In the presence of Ellet, who

had completed training Korda had only begun, she doubted he would try any subvocal tricks, but she watched him closely.

"I bring a message from your sister, Lady Firebird." Korda's high, strident voice became singsong: "Your people are shamed by you. The treachery you have dealt us will not be undone in many lifetimes. You would be wise to return to Sae Angelo and undo the bitterness with which people speak your name."

He did not say which sister had sent the message, but the words, obviously calculated to sting the proud soul of any Wastling, struck home, and she wavered. *Could* she go back?

All three watched her. She cleared her throat. "I will return," she said firmly. "But I don't feel that this is the time. Thank you for coming, though."

"I think you're mistaken." Korda bent down toward his bootbuckles, keeping his eyes on her feet, and Firebird tensed. That was not a natural gesture.

She shook her head and stepped backward. "It's not the time," she repeated.

"I'm not talking about timing." He shifted his hand rapidly. "You won't go back."

The slight motion of Korda's fingers probing inside his boot top put her on full alert. It was "the old game"—only now it was no game.

Korda drew a tiny weapon and she feinted left to draw his fire, then threw herself hard to the right. His shot missed. As she prepared to dodge again, she recognized the weapon: a Vargan stinger, no longer than a stylus but as deadly as a blazer if one of its energy bolts struck a vital area. Its little power cell could yet deliver four more shots.

But Korda had trained the stinger instead on Ellet Kinsman, who stood just behind the lounger with one hand stalled in midair, halfway to her blazer. "Don't even open your mouth, Kinsman," he said. "Try to voice-command me and you'll be as cold as Thyrica IX."

"Kill her!" Rattela's voice pulsed with hatred for the Sentinel.

"Maybe," said Korda. "Drop your hand, Kinsman."

Ellet obeyed, scarcely breathing. Firebird shifted one foot forward.

"Forget it, Wastling," Korda sneered. "We haven't forgotten you." The barrel of the stinger never wavered from Ellet's forehead, a scant arm's length away.

Rattela shifted ponderously, pulled his feet under as much of his weight as he could, and reached for his wide blue sash.

Firebird met Ellet's stare. What had the Sentinel been thinking, to let those two in?

"She's all yours, Rattela." Korda waved his free hand expansively.

"Lady Firebird, perhaps you retain enough of a sense of honor . . ." Rattela tried to thrust his hand under the sash, but misjudged in his eagerness.

In his moment of awkwardness, Firebird leaped for Vultor Korda. His stinger swept around, but she ignored it, holding course for his shoulders. Her action freed Ellet to speak. With one word the Sentinel had Korda motionless.

Unfortunately, it came a moment too late. Even as Firebird's momentum carried her onto him, she realized she'd been hit, although as yet she felt nothing.

She fell off Korda and glanced down. The energy bolt had struck just below her left collarbone, missing the kill zone by centimeters. The smell of scorched fabric revolted her, and she could see the bright red of her own blood through the singed edges of the hole. Her flesh began to scream protest. *So that's why it's called a stinger*, she thought shakily. She staggered to her feet.

Ellet was easing around the lounger with her blazer leveled left-handed on Rattela, even as her right hand reached toward the left sleeve where the crystace hid. "Your immunity is gone, Korda. Now you face Sentinel law." Suddenly seeing Firebird rise, she went stiff. "Firebird. You're all right."

"I'll make it. But I'm hurt."

The Sentinel's cheek twitched. "I thought he'd killed you." She twisted the stinger from the motionless Korda's grip, then grasped the Duke's hand as he pulled it from beneath his sash. It did not come out empty.

"I think this is for you." Ellet passed Firebird a mirror-bladed dagger, whose pommel was fashioned like a firebird's golden head with ruby eyes.

Firebird took it carefully; hunching forward eased the pain a little. It was a ritual suicide knife, the traditional last gift of the Electorate to Wastlings who had ignored their Geis Orders. "How appropriate. It has my name on it." She caught Rattela's glance. "Why were you so careful about drawing it? Poison?"

"A quick one," rumbled Rattela. "Do you remember what it is to be an Angelo, Firebird? Take the blade on your palm."

"Pretty, isn't it?" Ellet whispered. "It almost seems a pity to waste it."

Firebird wheeled, alarmed by the encouragement in her guardian's voice. Still holding the haft in a loose grip, she glanced from Ellet's eyes to the stinger in her hand and back again. Ellet's subtle prodding shook her more deeply than either the Electorate's gift or the burning pain in her shoulder. Confused, she bit back her protests and appealed silently to Ellet's starbred empathy with all the feeling she could focus.

Ellet shrugged, and the tableau broke. She lowered her hand. "All right, Vultor Korda," she warned, her voice so full of hatred that it frightened Firebird. "Any quick move and you *will* lose your diplomatic immunity."

Korda buried his hands in his pockets.

Ellet extended her palm to Firebird in an unmistakable "give-the-knife-back," and as she took the grip with delicate care, Ellet seemed to soften as quickly and inexplicably as she had turned menacing. She touched Firebird's charred coverall. "You lie down. I'll send a medic."

Rattela turned just short of the door. "*Your* immunity is just as temporary, Firebird Angelo. Naetai will have you back, if the Federacy wishes peace with us."

As Ellet followed the men out, Firebird drooped on the lounger and pulled up her feet. She felt shock setting in, both physical and mental. *Ellet!* her mind cried. Ellet was her friend, her teacher!

But plainly Ellet had hesitated, had let Korda fire— had nearly let him kill her.

Why? What had she done?

The throbbing grew in her chest. Pressing one palm over the wound, she closed her eyes and counted breaths.

A tall young man in yellow arrived within minutes, pushing a repulsor cart laden with medical supplies. "Let's see this," he said.

She reached for the clasps of her jumpsuit.

"No. You relax. Let me." In three strokes he cut the blackened cloth from the wound. "Just a little nearer midline and the coroner would be checking this, not me. Open your mouth."

Firebird gave up fighting lethargy and obeyed. He dropped a capsule onto the back of her tongue; it slid instantly down her throat. "That's going to make you sleep for about two days, while the tissues knit, because it will itch abominably after I clean and dress it—so get comfortable."

Was it a crime to be N'Taian? her thoughts ran on. *To be captured? Questioned by—wait—*

The drug took her instantly.

CHAPTER 14

Ellet

Simile
In like manner

Tel Tellai had visited Hunter Height before, when his father had been a guest of the Angelo family, but never under these circumstances: this time he had come as Phoena's personal escort, leaving the concerns of his estate and holdings with his employees, for a retreat of unspecified duration.

He shifted his ankles on the edge of a huge octagonal bed in the Height's uplevel master room and glanced around. Occupying most of the Height's upper story, it was oddly shaped, almost pentagonal, with windows curtained in drab brown that commanded a 120-degree view to the north, east, and southeast of its mountainous environs. Bare by his standards and entirely devoid of fine art, the wood-floored room's very spaciousness offered possibilities—and the bed on which he sat had last been occupied by his royal granduncle and the Queen of Naetai.

Phoena, gowned tonight in brilliant green velvric, stood at the bed's foot, fists clenched in graceful strength on her narrow hips. In high-backed wooden chairs across from Tel, looking profoundly uncomfortable, sat Muirnen

Rattela and Vultor Korda. Only an hour ago they had returned from their hazardous mission to Alta, and escaped Federate surveillance at the spaceport to flee to the Height.

Tel had been deeply relieved Phoena hadn't sent him: he would have gone, as his duty to his class, but it sounded as though he might not have survived. Firebird's guardian must be a most unwomanly woman!

Coals of temper still gleamed in Phoena's hot brown eyes, but she seemed to have calmed. "Well, it's in the past now," she fumed. "And it was worth a try. At least we know she has no sense of duty left at all. When that asylum ends . . ."

"Carradee can try official channels." Rattela arranged his sash ends on the hip of his maroon trousers. "It would set a most desirable precedent for our dealings with the Federacy, if we could take her legally."

"She's too slippery." Phoena wrinkled her nose. "I wouldn't put it past her to escape that, too."

"I marked her," put in Vultor Korda. The little man's reedy voice grated on Tel's ears, all the more so now that Korda had tried to murder Firebird without giving her a chance to prove herself honorable. "If His Grace hadn't—"

"Hmmph. Any medic could patch that," said Phoena. "The fact is, you missed."

Rattela cleared his throat. "Highness, that woman Sentinel was a tough one. Brutal. If I may say so, she's as dangerous as the General in Sae Angelo. My very heart sank when she stayed in the cell with us. It took courage to continue."

Phoena was not listening, but sweeping the master room with her gaze. Both thin brows arched expressively over her eyes. "This is perfect," she muttered.

"Beg pardon, Your Highness?" asked Rattela.

"Do you know," Phoena said, "if we could move others of like mind here, quietly—we could work unhampered for Naetai's freedom. The head maid insists no Federate has ever come here—I don't think they even know it exists. There would be plenty of room for a research laboratory, and the house is already staffed."

Tel pressed his palms together. "A brilliant idea, Highness. With the airfield and tunnels we could accommodate a significant amount of traffic. But would Carradee object?" He shifted his seat again, giving the rustic master room a more careful appraisal. "I can't see her giving permission without informing the Federates."

"She suggested I come here, I'm inviting friends to join me, and for that I don't need permission." Phoena sat down on the bed foot and arranged the folds of her gown with a slender, bare arm. Tel could not help but admire the way the fit of that gown and her erect posture accentuated her figure. "Hundreds of Naval officers were put out of work by the demilitarization." She scowled. "A select few could constitute a small defense force, and if any has access to military craft that survived the invasion, or weapons, we—"

"We need more than a few," Korda interrupted. "We need—"

Phoena jabbed a finger toward him. "Don't give us your 'we,' Thyrian. Thus far your help has done very, very little for our cause." She clasped her hands in her lap again. "Now, Rattela, how many do you know, absolutely loyal to us—to Naetai?"

Rattela shifted, twisting his bulk to hook one arm over the back of the chair. "All the Marshals, naturally." Tel had never noticed the pomposity in Rattela's voice before. Had *he*—no, he was too old to have been Phoena's . . .

Yes. Tel was not certain why, but in that instant he knew Phoena had had Rattela as a lover and had tired of him.

". . . And nearly the entire upper echelon of the Naval forces." Rattela spoke on, heedless of Tel's scrutiny. "And let us not forget our personal safety. The Electoral Police are with us, as well."

Phoena pursed her full lips. "Good. Good. Would you compose a message to be delivered quietly to—say, twenty of the best men you can get? Don't take them all off the top. They'd fight among each other for the privilege of giving orders. Choose four of the best, and have them select their most loyal and cautious subordinates. A core, that's all we need for now. For now," she repeated, stroking the leaf-green velvric of her skirt. "After the *elections,* tomorrow"

—she pronounced the word with distaste—"we'll know better where we stand."

Rattela rose and bowed. "Ever your servant, Highness."

"Take him with you." Phoena pointed at Korda. "Keep him busy."

Vultor Korda bowed with amateur clumsiness. "Princess Phoena, you must believe that I serve you with my very life. It would be worthless in Federate hands. Every ability I have is yours to command."

"Very well," she snapped. "Then, go and see if the servants here can be trusted. That's what Caldwell did with the Electors, isn't it?"

Rattela clenched a hand on his hip.

"And those who can't?" A corner of Korda's eye twitched as he spoke.

Phoena gave a sharp laugh. "The tunnels under the Height are deep, Korda. Do as you like. Just see they aren't found."

Tel stood at attention while the other men left the room, glad to see both of them go. "Well said, Highness." He strolled toward the chairs. Stark and simple, they seemed almost lost on the wide wooden floor. "Of course, the master suite would have to be made to suit you. So much could be done with good carpeting, fine art pieces, flowering plants—it could be made a lovely place, and efficient."

"It could."

He ran a hand over the unadorned back of one chair. "If only we did not need to hide our effort from the Queen. If only . . ." He gazed at her clear, perfect face. "Phoena, it should have been you."

Phoena sank onto the pile of white cushions at the head of the bed. Tel felt his cheeks go red. "It will be me, one day." She stroked one pillow's cording with a graceful hand. "Soon."

"Highness, I didn't mean . . ." Tel felt a tremble in his voice. "Carradee—and her little daughters, both . . ."

"Oh, never mind." She crossed her arms and shivered. "It's cold here, Tel. I don't think they've adjusted the heat for autumn yet. Would you warm me?"

She couldn't mean what he hoped. He took half a step backward, searching the walls for a climate control board.

Laughing softly, Phoena reached for the clasp on her bodice. "No, not that. I want you, Tel. Now—and in the future. Won't you serve *my* royal person, and leave Carradee to her own fate?" Her melodious voice faded to a whisper.

"Phoena, I . . ."

"But you dishonor me, if you refuse." Her lower lip seemed to quiver slightly.

"Oh, no, Phoena! Highness . . ." Tel stepped to the bedside. "I mean you no dishonor."

When Ellet returned two days later, Firebird still felt muzzy from her long sleep, but better, and the wound on her shoulder had closed. Outside the gridded window the sky loomed dark gray, as bleak as Firebird's feelings.

They pulled up stools to the table with a pot of kaffa Ellet had brought. Firebird had no small talk to offer. She drew a deep breath and steeled herself to ask questions that would probably alienate a woman who might have been her friend. Ellet, however, reading her tension with the ease of natural ability and long training, took the initiative.

"Go ahead, Firebird. You're in no danger from me."

Firebird wrapped both hands around her cup. "You hesitated to voice-command. You let Korda fire."

"Yes."

"And I assume you created that situation in the first place—you saw that the interview was allowed."

"Once I learned Korda had been sent, yes."

"Why?"

Ellet gave her a wry look. "You realize that I acted well within the boundaries of expectation, don't you?"

"Go on."

"Vultor Korda is a traitor to my people. Worse: a partially trained traitor. He was granted diplomatic immunity for his assignment to Alta by a committee of N'Taians —as was Rattela, who was evidently under house arrest, as we find out now, and shouldn't have been allowed offplanet at all. So long as Korda didn't commit certain crimes, I couldn't touch him. But he is a criminal. He deserves death. We police our own kind, Firebird, and the Sentinel who abuses his epsilon skills sheathes a crystace in his heart."

"So you wanted to catch him in an offense, but it had to be an extremely serious one. Such as murder."

"Yes." Ellet studied her interlaced fingers. "In my mind, the entrapment would have been justified. Your people are neither popular nor respected among the Federates."

"But murder, Ellet?"

"You were anxious to die not long ago, in a good cause." Ellet sighed. "There are certainly those who would question my judgment. Officially I apologize, but I'd do it again." She looked up, eyes afire. "You have no idea of the magnitude of his crimes against our people. The galaxy trusts and fears us. If we lose that fragile trust, through misuse of our abilities—it turns on us. A war of annihilation." She shook her head. "I can't believe that I had him in my grasp, and he escaped."

"Because I ducked."

Ellet looked uncomfortable. "You'll notice, please, that you are still alive. Once he had fired on you, I had a clear duty to discharge: to stop him and send both of them back. If Korda had killed you, I'd have had an equally clear duty: to kill him."

Firebird absently rubbed her shoulder. The ache had almost gone, although that side of her upper body remained stiff, and the rapidly healing burn did itch. "But it was Rattela who was going to do the killing, if I wouldn't cooperate."

"I gave you the knife. Apparently, your attitude toward suicide has changed. At any rate, my responsibility now is to protect you, under General Caldwell's orders, and I intend to do so."

"Until you have another trap to bait."

Ellet's glance darted to Firebird's eyes and held there. Firebird intentionally kept her emotions bland, thinking, *Perhaps Sentinels aren't worthy of such blind trust as the Federates seem to think.* But a person could certainly try to stay within their good graces.

"I have no intention of complaining—to anyone, Ellet.

I just want to hear, from your mouth, what you have against me."

"That's precisely why I came to talk to you, Firebird." Ellet leaned back. "Someone had better warn you that Brennen Caldwell is interested in you, and I don't mean politically."

"He what?" Firebird slid her elbows off the table. "That's ridiculous."

"Is it?" Ellet paused. "Brennen has his eye on the Federate High Command. He'll make it too, one day, if he doesn't get thrown off course by such as you."

Suddenly seeing Brennen in an alarming new light, Firebird held her peace.

"Don't worry, he'd never force himself on you. He's too much of a gentleman." Ellet's disdainful expression made it clear that she thought Firebird entirely unsuited to such a man. "But if you let him get close to you, you'll never get away. I'm giving you a chance to prepare yourself."

"What do you mean? Mind control?"

Ellet pushed her cup aside. "Of course not. If we were allowed to control people's emotions, I'd have altered yours long ago." Nevertheless Firebird envisioned a line of women eased out of Brennen's life by Ellet Kinsman. "I'm warning you," Ellet went on. "A man with Sentinel training will have found ways to please a woman without ever touching her, just as you guessed: ways that will leave her changed, unable to forget or go back. It's permissible, if she's encouraged him. I don't think you'd be capable of resisting. So unless you're interested in being a professional mindreader's wife, you'd better step carefully. And that leads to the subject of pair bonding."

"Pair bonding?" Firebird echoed weakly.

"When a Sentinel marries, he—or she—enters a permanent mental-emotional link. You can't resist it, you can't escape it. It affects the deepest level of existence. Oh, you'd keep your identity, but you'd never be the same. It's tough on outsiders, which is another reason we of the starbred families have maintained our separation."

"I assume you have plans for Brennen yourself, then. Don't change them for my sake."

Ellet arched one black eyebrow.

"I have no designs on your Master Sentinel, Ellet. None."

Snorting softly, Ellet slipped off her stool. "I see." She ambled toward the door. "Don't forget that I can read your emotions, *Lady* Firebird."

Firebird knew that her feelings at that moment were less than hospitable.

"That's all I came to say." Ellet paused with one hand over the palmpanel and looked back over her shoulder, and her voice became quite polite again. "Since I didn't get Korda, I'm glad you survived. I am sorry we can't be friends. Perhaps it's better not to even try, until the other matter is settled. After that—I hope so."

Firebird stood. "Thank you. I will think about what you said."

"Try to be objective—but you'd better think quickly. They've sent out his replacement." She left the room.

Firebird turned away from the door, feeling completely deflated. So these were the feelings Ellet had been hiding from her, all these weeks! Brennen . . . What *did* she feel for Brennen Caldwell? What had Ellet seen or felt in him? Obviously Ellet hoped Firebird would be so taken aback by her warnings that she would avoid facing Brennen entirely.

Pair bonding—deeper than the level of thought. She shuddered. Yet—the notion of being noticed by Brennen from among all women, and the chance for an indissoluble link, where before she had possessed nothing lasting, made her suddenly wistful. For all her self-reliance, she had been denied so many ordinary attachments: the loving nurture of a family, the honorable intentions of men, even the friendship of all but the other Wastlings. She had never kept a pet, fearing its torment at Phoena's hands after she died. Buried deep beneath her pride, she knew she hid a dark aching loneliness.

But—mental *bonding* . . .

Well. She walked to the tattered lounger. She would have to be careful, and keep her distance from Sentinels in general. More than ever she understood why some Federates might distrust these telepaths, even those sworn to Federate service. Entangling herself in their personal affairs had landed her in a very dangerous situation. Words Brennen had spoken to the guards at VeeRon leapt into her mind: "I apologize for deceiving you, but it was done in the best interests of the Federacy." When juxtaposed with Ellet's actions and cautions, those words took on sinister overtones. Might Brennen deceive her, or sacrifice her, "in the best interests of the Federacy"?—in the best interests, perhaps, of a man marked for the Federate High Command?

She took her clairsa from below the window and seated herself on the lounger, clutching the lovely curved frame to steady her fingers. She tuned automatically, and defiantly began with the Academy's anthem, "Beyond N'Taian Skies." But that reminded her too sharply of Corey, who alone had given and received her unrestrained support; and despite her resolve, a quick mental jump took her from Naetai to the battle of VeeRon and all that had happened after. She stared at the dull sky. If Ellet was correct, at what point had Brennen Caldwell seen in her the woman he wanted?

She clung to the clairsa, letting go of her emotions and allowing them to tumble, listening for the music they would bring. A melody came, and she shaped it: it rose in a fourth and a fifth, fell scalewise, then turned upward with a questioning minor third. She laughed uncomfortably. How could so simple a phrase betray so much turmoil? A pair of descending scale arcs fell into the second phrase, ending on a leading tone that begged for resolution. But it would not settle yet. That was all that came. She played it several times to set it in her memory.

Abruptly, she remembered the melody of the ballad she had begun for Queen Iarla. A lyric for the stubborn second stanza began to flow, as though the changes in her life had shattered a mental barrier. Firebird seized her stylus and a sheet of scribepaper and began to write it out.

Stepping off the Base shuttle in the rear main-floor garage of the MaxSec tower, Brennen took a deep breath of warm wind. Home—the only home he'd known in years. He had earned the month's leave, this time. He tossed his duffel to a Security I guard, then headed for the lift and his office on the Special Operations floor to check for mail and messages.

Inside the broad, sunlit clearing room, two plump secretaries bent over bluescreened consoles. Between them, reading a paper, stood the very person he wanted to speak with first: Ellet Kinsman. He opened his shields to greet her.

Without warning, Ellet flung down the paper. The blast of epsilon static he caught brought him up short; it was so thick it must be draining Ellet. Through it, too strong to hide, came a clear picture of Firebird and an alarming fight-or-flight sensation.

Stricken, Brennen raised his own shields and glanced quickly around the clearing room. The secretaries ignored —or had not seen—the interplay; on their left, the door to his own small office lay open in welcome. Fiercely he gestured Ellet inside and followed. Just short of his black desk he turned and leaned on its surface. Automatically the door slid shut, enclosing them both in the half-light of the narrow-windowed cubicle.

Drop the shield, Ellet.

She sank into the extra chair, black eyes glaring. "Brennen," she said aloud, "there are things you should know about Lady Firebird Angelo. She is not the person you seem to think. She is—"

"*Captain* Kinsman," he said tightly.

Ellet shut her mouth. *There was an attempt on her life, four days ago. I—*

He turned raw anger back on her carrier. "Drop the shield, Ellet, or you are insubordinate."

"Very well." She tossed her head and stared up at him. "*General.* I have broken neither law nor custom, and you would do well to follow that example."

Her static cloud dissipated, and he swept his carrier across her outer matrix. Bitter jealousy, frustration, grim satisfaction: tasting her emotional state only whetted Brennen's shocked fury. Bluntly he requested memory access; she gave sullen permission. In the space of an instant all her dealings with Firebird were transferred to his awareness.

. . . He saw Korda arrive, felt Ellet's fury at his coming and its gradual conversion to determination: with one stroke, he/Ellet could rid the Sentinel kindred of both Korda and a rival for Brennen's genes, genes which *must* not be wasted. With her thoughts he schemed to trap Korda in murder and ignored his concealed weapon. He anguished when Rattela offered Firebird the jeweled suicide knife. Firebird leaped for Korda. His heart soared as Korda fired point-blank—the traitor lay in his hands, and the rival lay dead!

. . . But Firebird got to her feet, wounded and needing aid. Ellet's frustration screamed, grating against her understanding of her duty—and his own aghast relief.

. . . Only yesterday, furthermore, he/Ellet had gone to Firebird in her bare, cell-like rooms, and deliberately poisoned any casual fondness she may have had for the starbred—for himself—with fear, and entombed it in suspicion.

Brennen stopped the carrier flow roughly enough to shake Ellet, wishing he were free to disrupt her life centers with a burst of epsilon power. "You had better leave," he whispered. "I will speak with you later, after I see just how much damage you have done."

Absorbed in misery, he did not watch her go.

CHAPTER 15

Brennen

Cantabile
In a singing style

The tone poem had been finished, and Firebird sat staring out her window, when a surge of awareness flowed over her. Gone as quickly as it had begun, it carried the unmistakable tenor of Brennen's presence. He must be very near—already. She sat stock-still for a moment longer, but the sensation was not repeated. His arrival and the untangling of events and feelings that it would bring could be moments away. She glanced nervously around. Everything in the anteroom was tidily placed, except the answers she had hoped would be tucked neatly into her mind before his return.

Closing her eyes, she recalled the nuances of that surge, trying to make it flow by again. It bespoke Brennen, but not as she had known him on VeeRon, controlled and confident. She had sensed a hesitancy at the heart of that rush of feeling, almost a tremble, as though he were afraid.

Of her?

A very long hour passed before her entry bell sounded. The MaxSec staff never rang before opening the lock, and

Ellet had not returned, but there was not the keen awareness of Brennen she had felt before.

She walked to the door. "Yes?" she called.

The door slid open. In civilian clothes, Brennen stood a long pace back. He met her eyes from the distance, undoubtedly reading her feelings but applying no pressure.

"Hello." He gave her a slight, careful smile. "May I talk with you?"

"Of course." She stepped aside, but Brennen did not move.

"May I come in?" he asked.

"Yes. Welcome back."

He walked directly to the corner table and took a stool. Baffled by the change in him, she shut the door and joined him.

He didn't look at her, but rather his hands, which he had rested on the table. Reminded sharply of the wave she had felt, she blurted out, "Was that you, Brenn, about an hour ago?"

His startled silence gave her a rush of relief. This Master Sentinel was not all-knowing. "Yes," he said when he had composed himself. "I was trying to read your emotional state before I came down. I thought I was being subtle—few people can sense a quest-pulse. But you felt it?"

"Well, yes. I wasn't doing much, just thinking. You . . ." She groped for words that would not say too much. "You seemed worried."

He stared, openly amazed. "I certainly was. I . . . The first person I met when I got back to MaxSec, fortunately, was Ellet. My friend," he said bitterly, and the label became an accusation. "She showed me what happened. All of it. I nearly choked her."

She could almost feel him seething, and was thankful that his anger was not directed at her. "As to the confrontation with Korda," she said, "I've almost forgiven her. She was tempted by too many things."

"Never." Brennen spread his hands on the tabletop. "What she knew about my feelings should have overridden those temptations. Instead, it reinforced them. She'd have been glad to see you killed." His anger quieted somewhat s the hesitancy returned. "Then she tried to frighten you with things entirely foreign to people outside the starbred families. That was brutally unfair. I intended to explain them to you, in the right time. Now I'm forced to begin with the end already known. Maybe it's best that way."

"Wait," said Firebird. "Stop."

A quizzical expression came into his eyes.

"I've missed you, Brenn. I want you to know that."

He set an arm on the table and brushed back hair from his forehead, caught off guard again. "You've been with me," he said softly. "Every memory I own is very, very vivid. If I'd had a clue, though, that Ellet would have treated you this way . . ."

Firebird shrugged.

"Those offplanet clearances never passed my desk, and they should have. I don't know how Korda did it; apparently he's more dangerous than we had thought. But Ellet took clear advantage. I should have known, or guessed. The worst of it is, she *did* act within our codes. I can't have her disciplined." He shook his head slightly. "I see she didn't frighten you as badly as she intended."

"I don't scare easily." She hesitated, remembering he would sense her feelings. "Well—she did scare me. But she might have it wrong. I'd like to hear your side."

"Shall I be plain?"

"Please."

"I will explain all you want to know, soon—as soon as possible—but first I must be sure that you know this. I am finally certain of my feelings for you." He extended a palm across the table. Firebird slid only her fingers into it, and as he curled his hand around them she tensed. "I do want you, very much. I've had my hopes since I first had you under access. Do you recall my telling you how deeply I was impressed by your talents and angered by your Wastling's ambition to die?"

She nodded. That piece of the puzzle had dropped into place during the hours since Ellet had spoken, and it had worried her.

"Earlier than that, I sensed our connaturality. There was a long turning for you, even to reawaken your interest in life. You needed to deal with the Federacy, your prejudices and lack of understanding, before you were ready to be pressured by any personal commitments. I never meant to deceive you. I've gone slowly, Mari. Sentinels enter very young and very quickly into lifetime commitments, because we read one another. I've not asked that of you."

"That's true."

"You do fear me."

"Why should I believe you will let me change my own mind?"

"I see that Ellet succeeded in one thing. You fear the very ways I would hope to please you. Now I'm afraid to show my feelings."

"I would be helpless, unable to—to back out if I . . ."

"To get away?" Angrily he echoed Ellet's phrase. "I'd never try to coerce you, overpower you, or trick you. I want to be loved and accepted for myself too, not for what I can do with my epsilon skills. If you fear them, I'll do nothing for you that another man could not."

Irritation flashed through her. "Don't you *dare* diminish yourself. Be what you are and I'll do the same."

Brennen rested an elbow on the table, leaned on it, and then straightened again. "That's more than I'd hoped for, Mari. I was prepared to be sent away. Thank you." He shifted his feet. "You're upset. Shall I go?"

"No." Firebird took a deep breath. "Tell me how things are on Naetai."

He drooped a little and looked away. "Not good," he said quietly, "but not openly bad. The Assembly and the Queen seem to be accepting the changes we have made—but the Electorate has held power too long to be cut off without disrupting the entire system, and through those channels *nothing* goes right."

"I'm sure." Firebird flicked hair behind her shoulder. "Carradee is a good person, Brenn. We have always been friends. But I assume Phoena is still . . . ?"

"Still what, Mari?" he asked gently.

"Agitating—making it all as difficult as possible."

"Oh, yes. She has a little-moon-shadow now, by the way: Count Tellai."

"Tel?" Firebird gaped. "But he's a child."

"He's just old enough to get himself into very deep

trouble for that woman. They're on vacation now, together. Anywhere but Sae Angelo."

"Did you ever see . . ." She hesitated. It hurt to ask. "Daley Bowman?"

"No," he said softly, and his forehead creased. "He is well, though. Count Wellan Bowman, I did see, and I offered him my regrets."

"Wellan wouldn't care." A forgotten bitterness seized Firebird as she remembered Corey's longing, concealed by his rowdiness from all but her, for the closeness his family would not give.

Brennen fell quiet and walked over to the window, checking his watch. She saw him catch a glint from inside the glasteel panel, lean close and examine the honeycomb-patterned security grid. It cast odd shadows on his even features.

She sighed. When would she ever go home—and to what?

He turned and smiled gently. "What if we went flying tomorrow? I've had a little Cirrus-class racing jet for four months, and I've been so busy between here and Naetai that I've had no chance to take it through its paces. I'd enjoy your company." He nodded toward the clairsa, propped again below the window. "And if you'd bring that, I'd consider myself well repaid."

She leaned on one elbow. "I'd like that. I haven't been out of here since—well, I don't mean to complain about Ellet . . ."

He frowned. "She did intimidate you. What promise can I give you that I'll respect your will and give you room for your own decision?"

Why should she believe his claims of restraint? She'd seen what he could do! Unable to think of any stronger vow by which she might bind him, she said, "Give me your word as a Sentinel."

"You have it."

"All right, then. I'd like to go out." But she felt flat, disappointed. All these weeks without seeing him, and now—just careful, distant talk? If she hoped to emerge from this unbalanced relationship unscathed she needed to keep a distance, but she was treating him as less than a friend. Would he feel her tension? She went to him and touched his shoulder. "Welcome back, Brenn." Pulling closer, she plucked up courage and gave him a quick, awkward embrace.

His eyes glinted as he drew quickly away. "Thank you," he whispered. "It's good to be back."

The parking bay lay quiet in the last moments before dawn. "There she is." Brennen pointed. "What do you think?"

The small jet at the far western end looked like a silver projectile, half arrowhead, half dagger. Gleaming, back-curved wings tapered to a knife-edged chine that swept to its nose, and a glareshielded cockpit bubble rose above twin atmospheric engines. The pilot in her leaped for joy.

"It's pretty," she said casually. "What'll it do?"

"We're going to find out." He opened the passenger entry. On her seat she found the five-point flight harness required by air codes for the most fleet-footed sort of atmospheric craft. The Cirrus racing class, whatever that specified, rose another notch in her estimation. She adjusted her harness as he laid a duffel bag and soft flask in the cargo area, then her clairsa case, and secured them all with a heavy net. "How many standard g's are you qualified for, without a gravity suit?" He climbed into the pilot's seat, so close that their legs almost touched. She laughed inwardly when she saw that his leathers were the same kaffa brown as the craft's interior, and both were trimmed in forest green.

"I don't know. Naetai doesn't use Galactic Standard. Two-thirty-seven N'Taian pressure units, however that converts. Five-eighty with a life suit."

"And you don't scare easily?" He ignited the engines. "Try me."

"All right, Major." He slid a throttle rod forward, and lazily the Cirrus glided out over the city.

Castille passed slowly below them. The cockpit afforded almost 360 degrees of vision. She feasted on the growing glow in the sky and the panorama of the capital city within its ring of green hills.

When they left the city slowzone behind Brennen

max'd the accelerator, and the thrust pressed her back and down as he pointed the sharp nose for the clouds. Firebird reveled in the feeling. He climbed at battle speed until the sky began to darken. Over-the-top in thrilling weightlessness, then Brennen nosed into a lazy, downward spiral.

"She seems to handle fairly well." He reversed the spiral. "But this really doesn't demand much of her maneuverability."

"This civilian racer climbs faster than our tagwings. No wonder we lost the war."

"This isn't entirely civilian-equipped." He tightened the spiral, accelerated the dive, and they dropped like a spinning fayya leaf, reversing again and again. She watched his hand move confidently on the rods and panels, barely tightening and relaxing. It was a tawny-colored hand, fine-boned—neither long-fingered and slender like Phoena's nor broad like her own, more typical of the Angelo line—but strong-looking, and—

Stop that! she commanded herself. *He's reading your emotions! Give in to that feeling, and eventually he'll . . .*

That only made it worse.

He turned to her, and although his voice sounded casual, something in his eyes confirmed that he had read that emotional flicker. "Are you game for some fast low-level? That will tell me what I want to know about her gravidics."

"Sure. You seem to know what you're doing."

"Hang on, then."

The next few minutes were breathtaking. He dove into a blackstone badlands area of spires and canyons and skimmed the ground at near-attack velocity, barely clearing ebony boulders, cornering at dizzying speed and doubling back with somersaulting accuracy. A natural arch loomed ahead, and the Cirrus shot through before Firebird had time to flinch.

They soared high above the ground again. "No problems?" he asked.

"That was great." Just the same, she touched the snugging control on her flight harness.

"All right. One more thing, then."

He nosed down, set into a spin, and accelerated steadily. Forcing herself to relax, she averted her eyes from the upracing ground, watching the intensity on Brennen's face as he waited, waited for the last possible moment to pull out.

Trebled gravity drove her deep into the seat as they took the bottom of the turn through the arch and soared again for the sky. Brennen shot her a glance once they had regained a respectable altitude. "Too much?"

"I didn't know that was possible." Shaken, she didn't want to admit that his dive had been far too much like her attempt to crash at VeeRon.

"All right." He straightened out and steered for a broad, striated mesa. "I think the compensators pass inspection. Let's give her a rest."

He made a casually perfect landing on dark stone and cut the engines. As Firebird climbed out, the wind whipped her hair around her face. She gloried in the lifting, falling feeling, and stretched kinks from her limbs, gladly breathing the scent of unseen flowers and faraway thunderstorms. Brennen strolled to the rim of the tableland and peered over at the glimmering yellow desert. In civilian clothes, he seemed a different man. Not a telepath, just a man who—who wanted her, who had her alone, kilometers from anywhere. She felt the skin at the back of her neck tighten at the thought.

Resolutely she marched herself over to join him. He glanced at her, pulled a hand from a pocket of his coat and pointed downward. A creature that looked uncannily like a hunting bird soared far below. As it vanished behind a hillock, Brennen turned. "Would you like to try, now?"

She froze in a panic. Now? What did he mean?

He inclined his head toward the silver racing jet, and she rebuked herself for acting like a nervous girl. Hurriedly she spun and headed back across the tableland. "I certainly would."

"The control board is totally different from a N'Taian display. Here, I'll show you." He adjusted the seat and footbars for her and went over the control panel several times. When satisfied that she had the board unscrambled, she fired up the engines and gently took it off the mesa. Her tension vanished into concentration. She dropped into the badlands at about half Brennen's speed and cruised closely along its contours, mounting small ridges and dropping into adjacent watersheds. A half-eight through and over the looming arch bolstered her confidence, and gradually she accelerated through twisted canyons, swooped back toward the mesa, pulled into a long climb over its bulk, and watched the badlands disappear behind. The mountains far ahead were shadowed green with summer. She ached to explore.

"Find a place to eat," Brennen suggested.

"It's not time to eat yet, is it?"

"As a matter of fact." He touched the panel. "If that's how closely you watch your instruments, I'm surprised you passed flight school."

She laughed softly.

"Actually, you are a good pilot, for such a new one. The NPN was foolish to waste you."

"Despite the fact that I couldn't even crash a fighter-craft properly when I was supposed to?"

Near the divide of the second range, Firebird found a round lakelet nestled in a cirque amid old-growth forest, and set down below it in the meadow. As she climbed out, Brennen pulled out the clairsa and lunch packet and swung them over one shoulder, then held out a hand to her. "Watch your step. Tripvine."

"Is that what's blooming?" Ignoring his hand, she bent down to examine the tangled groundcover. From under a round leaf she picked a tiny purple blossom shaped like a trumpet and held it to her nose. "Yes, that's it."

"They export the extract for perfume, but the stems are as tough as docking cable. I'm not exaggerating." He offered the hand again.

She took it. Carefully they walked up the vine-covered field to the lake, water and leaves riffling in a warm breeze.

"Over by the water, on one of those rocks?" she suggested. He changed direction without comment, and they scrambled over fallen trees and stones to the tallest boulder, well over twice her height.

"You first." He boosted her to shoulder height. She found a good toehold and scrambled the rest of the way up the mottled stone. Brennen tossed her the bags and then jumped to the top.

Her chin dropped.

"Does that disturb you?"

"No," she lied firmly. "Do something else."

Turning toward the shore, he lifted one hand. A glacier-smoothed boulder rolled into the air and landed with a slurping splash.

Firebird swallowed her protest. She'd asked for it. In or out of uniform, this man was Thyrian.

"We keep most of our abilities quiet in public." He sat down beside her, and his gaze went to the rocky skyline above the cirque. "They do cost us energy. It's also highly improper to use Sentinel skills unnecessarily, even in Federate service. A government that rules by fear is no government at all."

"Like the Keepers." She slid off the uncomfortable dress shoes Carradee had sent, then knelt and helped him with the lunch parcel. "I suppose it took a lot of work to learn those skills."

"It did. The Sentinel College is gruelling."

She poured clear red liquid from the flask into a pair of cups and offered him one. "Did they teach you other things, too? Arts? Science?"

"I only finished the military specialty. I was desperate to fly, and it was the only way I could afford to get into a spacecraft. At the time, I was getting so much pressure to try politics that I ignored any course of study that might have hinted I was going along with their plans for me. Now I wish I'd broadened. I would have had plenty of time."

She nodded.

"What about your Academy, Mari?"

She sipped the cool berry juice. "It must be the same everywhere. Flight. Dynamics. Slip physiology. Weaponry, systemic planetography, basic strategies. Astrogation." She slowed, trying to recall what had kept her so busy for so long.

"Interrogation and Resistance."

She glanced at him sharply. He was smiling. Very well, she could make light of it if he could. "Not enough, though."

"Poor instruction." Brennen offered a small yellow candy. "Have you ever had citrene?"

On her tongue it melted to a puddle of sweet-sour. She swallowed. "Are there any more?"

Smiling, he dropped several into her palm, then gathered up remnants of food, scattering crumbs over the edge of the boulder. Firebird wrestled momentarily with an urge to tell him about Hunter Height and its ordnance laboratory, then ate the last citrene and pulled the clairsa from its covering. Hunter Height could wait a day.

He sat close, knees pulled tightly to his chest, as she played several classical pieces. Encouraged by his unblinking attention, she closed with the theme and variations she had just composed. She made no introduction nor any comment, but his eyes seemed to come alive as she let her feelings melt into the music, and when she finished he sat without moving, just watching her.

"Did you write it?"

"Yes."

"How long ago?"

There would be no deceiving him, she reminded herself. "After I'd spoken with Ellet."

He took a long, deep breath.

"Mari?"

"Hm?"

"May I touch your mind?"

She did not answer.

"Only a touch, Mari, only a feathering. As you have just touched me."

Her neck hairs prickled again. Ellet had warned that she would never be the same, never get away if she ever allowed him to approach her. But she had good powers of resistance. *Maybe,* she conceded, *just this once, and I could still escape.*

But her voice trembled. "All right."

His eyes reflected the sky; he didn't move or speak.

Past the surface of her awareness there blew a sensation of approval so deep, so complete, that she wanted to shout aloud for the sheer joy of existence. Laughing at herself, for her fears that hadn't come true, she set the clairsa back into the padded case. "You know what I need most of all, don't you?"

"I could fill that need in you, Mari, for as long as I live."

Only then did she appreciate Ellet's warning. A person who had been stroked in that way would want more, and still more, until she was helplessly trapped. Hastily she changed the subject. "Could you really free-fall?"

"Yes. It's well within my grasp if I'm rested."

"And if I jumped?"

"I could land you. Do you want to try it?"

She hesitated. What perverse impulse had made her choose *that* subject? *But I might never get another chance*, she told herself. "Yes." She scrambled to her feet. "I do."

Thirty minutes later they faced into the gale on the windy ridge, looking down on the water, the dark forest, and the silver Cirrus, dropped like a hyperextended triangle onto the green meadow.

"Brennen," she said abruptly. "Something's been bothering me."

He lifted one eyebrow but said nothing.

"It's crazy, it—seems such a contradiction. But you Sentinels are trained in emotional control. You have to be, to face the barrage of others' feelings—that makes sense. But then how . . ." She scuffed a stone with one foot. "How can a Sentinel relax that control enough to fall in love?"

He tilted his head and thought for a moment. "We too have hopes," he said. "Subjective, personal—like everyone. Once the emotions are released we love deeply, perhaps more deeply than any others. We do not forget the wonder of finding and winning."

Gazing out into the hazy distance, Firebird nodded. "Then explain pair bonding. I'm not—committing myself, you understand, but you promised to explain some things."

Brennen sat down on a large flat stone and she took one just downwind, slightly sheltered by his body from the hair-lashing blast. "It's not as 'rough on outsiders' as Ellet

wanted you to believe, although very few of us marry out."
He took a long breath. "Pair bonding is a deep link that
manifests itself primarily in the emotions. Each feels with
the other, any time the other is near."

"The way you can read my feelings now?"

"No. Deeper, more certain, and the awareness be-
comes integrated into the other senses. There is an adjustment period, but it's not long. A few weeks, perhaps, for
you—but less for me, because I have years of mentalic
training."

"But an outsider wouldn't be taken over?"

"Absolutely not. Only . . . uncomfortable, for a time."

She studied the rocks at her feet, flat-sided fragments
of a disintegrating sedimentary layer. "I'd like to believe
you. But it's easy for you to make that statement and
impossible to prove."

He looked away. She shifted to a more comfortable
position. "Your parents are pair-bonded?"

"They were." He sounded wistful. "They were very
happy together. It took my mother years to recover completely after my father died. I ached for her. That's a
powerful argument against your having me, Mari. In my
profession, it's possible that I'd leave you a very young
widow."

"They were both Sentinels?"

"Not military. But both from starbred families, and
both trained."

"Then, how many of your people marry outside?"

"Oh . . ." She watched him consider. "Maybe one
percent, at the most. Like N'Taians, we are very wary of
new blood."

"Would it weaken you, to be bonded to an outsider?"

"Yes. You can't shield your mind from hostile influ-
ences as I can, nor have you been trained to control pain or
intense emotion."

"Which you would then pick up." She stared off down
the valley, where the stream fell away from its mother lake
like a white ribbon on deep green velvric. "It would be a
step backward for you, then."

"Not entirely. You have strengths of your own, talents

in other areas. . . ." His deprecatory half-smile surprised
her. "Connaturality of personality, you see, does not necessarily mean any degree of intelligence matching."

"I see." She caught a clear idea of one kind of match
that had been offered. Then she thought of another. "What
about Ellet?"

He nodded. "Marginally connatural. There have been
speculations about the two of us, of course, since we're in
similar work. I've been the victim of many predictions,
though. That makes your company enjoyable, Mari. You
expect of me only what I am."

Uncomfortable, she hesitated. "Under it all, I think
you're as lonely as I am."

" 'Lonely' is not quite the right word."

She picked up a chunk of rock and hefted it, watching
him and waiting.

"I live surrounded by people whom I could know,
easily." He looked down at his feet. "Yet I'm forbidden to
approach them closely enough to find real friends. Everyone outside the Sentinel kindred builds special walls
against us: either awe and too much honor, or fear and
suspicion. So no one knows me. Even you don't know my
personality the way I know yours from access. If you did,
you'd know how alike we are."

But they were worlds different, in blood and allegiance. Her mind echoed with words spoken in other times
and places: "A matter of Federate security" . . . "I'm sorry
to have deceived you" . . . "You could still be a great help
to us" . . .

"Ellet said I could cost you the High Command."

"That was a valid point." He shrugged and shifted his
feet.

"Why, Brenn?"

"My singlemindedness would be suspect," he said
drily. "Not only are you not starbred; you're not Federate."

With the rank he has achieved at his age, she reminded
herself, *he* would *have a shot at the top*. "No, I'm not
Federate. At this moment I have no country at all."

"I hope to have children, someday." He said it softly,
without warning. "A son, perhaps."

She controlled her urge to laugh. Obviously, he meant

it just as seriously as poor Corey had meant it, and in admitting that hope Brennen had made himself vulnerable. "I was a Wastling, Brenn. I wasn't supposed to have children, and I didn't try to want them." Her voice softened as their eyes met again. "You know that I come from a very long line of daughters?"

"Why is that?"

"There hasn't been a male born into the succession in five hundred years, since before the Keepers came. It's biologically unexplainable. Some people call it the 'curse of the Angelos.' The family name has survived because the men who marry in take it themselves, as a matter of rank and pride."

"If you married me, what name would you take?" he asked with surprising intensity in his expression.

"I haven't thought about it—but I certainly wouldn't expect you to become an Angelo."

"That's good."

Unexpectedly stung, Firebird's pride swelled. She saw in his startled expression that he hadn't meant to insult her, and she choked off the retort that sprang too easily to mind, but she withdrew sharply. "You wouldn't want it."

"Would you?"

"Brennen, that name has been my life."

"It almost took your life."

She could see from his tiny smile-wrinkles that he was trying to tease. "All right, I'll tell you how I feel." Tossing her stone over the side, she looked at him steadily, knowing he would read her feelings all the more easily for it. "I won't refuse you, but I can't commit myself, not yet. Not to anyone."

His eyes flicked to each of hers in turn. "You'd like to."

"Yes, I would." She forced her gaze to stay on his. Her longing for understanding had momentarily overcome her independence.

"But you still don't trust me," he said.

"I'm sorry."

"I understand," he said gently. "Because you are valuable to the Federacy, you suspect my intentions, and you have every right to do so. I too question what I'd do if it came to a choice between your interests and those of my people." He took her hand and massaged it. "There must be one highest priority in your life for which you'll give everything else—your life, your possessions, your hope— or you're not a full person."

"Don't I know it." She glanced down. "And what do you do when that one highest priority fails you, Brenn?"

"You find a higher."

Firebird nodded. Higher than the Angelo family, there had always been Naetai. But higher still were the abstracts; truth, and justice, and love: not the warmth of affection, but searing, sacrificial love. To those she could be true, whether she stood with Naetai or the Federacy.

"Meanwhile." Brennen stood and brushed rock dust from his leathers. "Would you trust me enough to jump, if I went first? It *is* the easy way down."

She snorted, appreciating the paradox he saw. She was willing to entrust him with her life in free-fall, because the worst that could happen would be a very bad landing. But if she drew too close to him, the worst that could happen was . . .

Unfathomable.

Her scramble to her feet masked a shiver. What if she bound herself to a Sentinel, and one day he turned on her? But if they were truly bonded, would he be capable of such a thing?

Undaunted, she stepped up to the cliff and peered over the side. The ridge was nearly as tall as MaxSec and just as sheer. "I hate climbing downhill. I'd rather go the easy way."

"Then, here's what we'll do." He stared downward as if picking his landing spot. "I'll go first. Once I'm down, give me a minute to rest. I think you'll feel it when I take a good kinetic grasp on you. Then don't wait too long, and be sure to jump outward far enough."

He walked to the other side of the ridge. She stood motionless, still not quite sure he meant to do it. Then he began to run, and he took a leap onto—nothing. Firebird's heart pounded as his shadow rushed to meet his feet.

Knees bent and arms outstretched, he alighted, absorbing the impact with casual grace. He dropped to his knees, resting, then got up, turned and raised an arm. She felt an invisible force take hold of her.

Hesitating, Firebird almost lost her nerve. *This is ridiculous*, she rebuked herself. She had wanted to fly since she was four, and Ellet had insisted it was easier to control another falling object than one's own body. She walked back five steps from the edge, ran forward, and jumped.

Her hair whipped behind her shoulders and upward from her head as the mountain air rushed past. It was glorious—like the swell of an orchestra. When she shut her eyes for a moment, the falling feeling went on, and on, like a dream. But she had to watch.

Brennen stood below her. Time seemed to expand: every half second of the plunge stretched to a minute. His arms opened to receive her. At last she slowed almost to a stop, caught the glitter of his eyes, and fell the last meter into his arms. She clung there, breathless.

One of his hands slipped up to her throat, tangled into her hair, and then curled around the back of her head. Firebird shut her eyes in pleasure. A gentle, hesitant kiss warmed her temple. She tilted her head back, offering her lips, abandoning her caution for a long, joyous moment to thank Brennen for this day.

Suddenly alarmed by the fervor of her reaction to the way he accepted that kiss, she felt her body quiver, then go rigid. Brennen quickly drew back. A rueful expression clouded his sapphire eyes. "Mari," he whispered. "Don't fear me. I will never try to hurt you, nor to dominate you."

"I—I know," she stammered. "I just . . ." Firebird buried her head against his shoulder, pushed away, then turned downhill toward the Cirrus jet. How could she explain that she was terrified, not of his feelings, but her own?

CHAPTER 16

Judgment

Risoluto
Resolutely

When on leave, Brennen made it a point to stay as far from his office as possible. He did prefer to sort his mail there on the S.O. floor rather than having it sent up, though, so on this blustery morning, after a thorough thousand-kilo check of the Cirrus jet he'd demanded to supervise, he concluded with a stop at the clearing station.

The pileup was diminishing. After two scrolls of the screen, he flipped through a small stack of papers: routine messages, advertisements, and pleas addressed to him but which would be better handled by Special Operations— and one innocuous-looking brown packet whose return marking caught him completely by surprise: a private message from Shamarr Lo Dickin, his sponsoring Master, apparently brought by messenger service. More than a Master, Dickin was the spiritual hierarch of Thyrica. Brennen tucked it into a jacket pocket.

Neither secretary glanced up when he hurried out to the lift. A minute later, he stepped off at the seventy-fourth floor, Security I housing, onto the brown shortweave carpet of an entry alcove. A white-clad guard stood at attention at every door down the passway. Halting at his own apartment, he thumbed the ID disk the guard held out to him. He and his guard reached simultaneously for a single broad lockpanel, and the door slid away.

Between the dining nook on his left and his private study, he walked to the edge of a deeply sunken living area whose sweep of windows overlooked much of Castille. Unnoticing, he sank onto a step and pulled the scribepaper from his pocket.

> Brennen:
>
> In the power of the Word I greet you, in our vows of service I join you, as my son of promise I embrace you. Stand firm in truth, for the path chosen today determines eternity.
>
> Is it true what Ellet Kinsman has written to me, that your heart leans toward one outside our kindred? The thought gives me no joy, yet I can guess only one reason for it. You of all men know that without absolute connaturality any bonding would bring pain, and for one of your epsilon intensity it would be crippling. You need not protest that you have bonded no wife already for this reason; indeed I know it. Life with an outsider, though, could be difficult. Hold steadfast. Be certain of the woman and yourself, and be willing to refuse her.
>
> More than that I will not say, except that you are in my awareness and surrounded by my hopes.
>
>> In steadfast love
>> Your father of ceremony
>> Dickin

Escaping breath whistled between Brennen's lips. *Ellet, interfering again!* But hoping to draw a reprimand from the Shamarr, she had won him what amounted to an expression of support.

That sobered him. He understood what he was considering: a break in his family's line, ignoring the customs that had kept the Aurian genes from dissipating. "Life with an outsider . . ." Yes. Just to start the questions, where would they live? Could Firebird make a home on Alta? She had no security clearance—this apartment would be forbidden to her. In time, would her epsilon inability wear on him, or could they work out their own ways of communicating? They might, for she was strong, intelligent. . . .

Thinking of Naetai and the Shamarr, abruptly Brennen found another Thyrian face in his mind's eye. *Korda*, he reminded himself. *Dickin should know that Vultor Korda has begun openly abusing his skills and must be dealt with.*

For the first time in her life, Princess Phoena Irina Eschelle Angelo had worked a morning with her hands— and she had found herself enjoying it, because she labored for a great cause.

Swirling a conical flask with one hand, she added enrichment broth drop by drop to a murky soup of dark green algae. Across the narrow, granite-walled laboratory, Nella Cleary hunched over the bluescreen at a massive desk Phoena had purchased to flatter her. Cleary's white laboratory coat was splotched with browned algae. Phoena glanced down. Her own coat remained spotless, of course.

"Let them wonder if we've found a way to make a sun go nova—or ionize all the water of a world," Phoena murmured, smiling as she set the flask down and reached for the last one. The stone shelf ran the long dimension of the office-laboratory, with brilliant overhead lumas to facilitate algal growth, for there were no windows: the room lay far below Hunter Height. "These little green killers will serve us just as nicely."

"Ionize water." Cleary humphed, and twisted her long body to face Phoena. "Your Highness needs a better background in the sciences. That reaction requires energy, it doesn't release it."

"That's why I'm helping you today: to broaden my education. It's nice to do *many* things well." Delicately, minding her fingernails, Phoena filled her autopette with broth and began treating the next flask. The strain was safe to handle, in this phase. Only in the presence of irradium would this algae mutate and begin to produce deadly toxin: only under hard radiation would it bloom, but under those circumstances it would multiply so prodigiously as to fill a world's oceans with poison within days.

But only for the good of Naetai's rightful rulers. Phoena smiled with great dignity. *Deadly endeavors are justified only by that end, for focusing wealth and power where it can best be wielded, not scattered to the weak.* All her life Phoena had served that ideal—more sincerely, she sniffed, than any other member of her family. It grieved her to see Carradee display such weakness.

There have been accidents before, she reminded herself. *But timing is everything.*

A bell chimed beside Cleary's desk. The stoop-shouldered woman touched a button. "What is it?" she growled.

"Count Tellai to see Her Highness, Doctor. Is she available?"

"Tell him yes." Phoena set down autopette and flask and wiped dampness from her hands on a towel. "This should be word from the Electorate."

Cleary rose and attempted to bow as Phoena dropped her lab coat on the floor. "Thank you for your assistance, Your Highness."

Phoena hurried out into the broad stone accessway and stroked the palmlock of a huge metal door. This eastern branch of the tunnel had been used for medical projects in the past, and Cleary seemed most satisfied to be installed here. She almost never came up into the daylight, although Parkai and D'Stang had grumbled loudly about sleeping underground like burrowing tetters.

Tel awaited her uplevel in the master room, pacing the deep new longweave carpet in bright-eyed excitement. Phoena found it a unique sensation to be worshipped by so true a believer, served by so ethical a priest. She met his welcoming embrace and accepted a long kiss before pulling away. "Well? Tell me—how went the vote?"

His round face crinkled with smile lines. "It passed, Phoena, even with Carradee's new Electors. The mission will go ahead, as we planned—through channels this time, as we should have tried before."

"Whatever works, works, Tel. Whom will they send to get her?"

"Phoena, this is the best part." He took both her hands. "Captain Friel of the Electoral Police, to represent Firebird's past, her obligations to her people and her family—and Marshal Burkenhamn, the very officer who administered her commissioning oath. Everyone knows what that commission meant to her. I'm certain your sister will do the honorable thing if confronted honorably."

Phoena snorted and sent a sidelong glance out the sweep of windows toward Hunter Mountain's towering triple peak. "The girl is utterly, entirely selfish, Tel. You'll see. She'll do everything she can to *avoid* the highest honor we could give her."

Tel lowered his long-lashed eyes. "I—I do feel sorry for her, Phoena, sometimes."

At last, he admitted his chief weakness! Phoena seized the opportunity to set him back on the straight path. "Tel, your nature is noble, but in this case your sympathy is unbefitting a nobleman. Firebird was raised a willing Wastling," she said patiently. "She is a traitor now, a Federate informer. She will not suicide, so to salvage her reputation among future generations—for her own sake— we must see that she is brought back. The Electoral Police will take charge of her, as is their rightful office. They will *honor* her by doing so." Phoena stared past Tel's shoulder toward the portrait of Siwann they had brought—with others—to dignify the Height, and she warmed to her subject. That last strong Queen of Naetai had left this mission in her hands, and she would not fail her mother.

For Firebird had a perverse inner strength. Phoena had known that all her life, too. This Wastling was strong enough to seize power, to destroy the ways of the Law, tear apart the fabric of N'Taian tradition—strong enough to threaten Phoena. For Naetai's sake, that must not happen.

"You won't see her imprisoned at the palace," Phoena declared, as much to the image of Siwann as to Tel. "The Redjackets have detention facilities at their lower town office: a quiet, soundproof set of quarters. They'll hold her there—question her—until arrangements can be made for a proper, public trial, with all the pomp our House can afford. Not even the Occupation Governor will interfere, if the Altans bind her over." Phoena gave a long sigh and turned her gaze back to Tel. "As much as the notion pains me, they must make an example of her. What would become of our homeland if every Wastling disrupted his family and scattered its resources? Yet her crimes have been far worse. Firebird has committed treason, and she must be punished."

Tel nodded sadly. "You're right," he whispered.

Phoena pressed one of his hands to her breast and turned around, pushing her back against him. His other hand came up to encircle her waist. "The family too will be shamed when she is led out for execution." The image in Phoena's mind—the grand procession, the final words, the fatal signal—made her breathe a little quicker. She must be certain to order a suitable dress for the occasion, to wear the appropriate jewels and present a suitably noble, sorrowing face to the media. "But it is for the good of us all, Tel. You must come to see that."

She slid around to face him. "For Naetai," she whispered. "For our people."

He kissed her long and desperately.

When Firebird learned that Brennen had access to physical-training facilities in the tower, she jumped at his offer to take her there, early in the mornings. She had had far too little physical exercise since leaving Naetai. For a week, they politely neglected one another on training time. On the sixth morning, though, as she struggled with an upper body vari-cycler, Brennen abruptly left his own station and paced toward her.

"Stop for a minute. You're trying much too hard. I know that side has been injured, but your body should relax into what you're trying to accomplish, no matter how difficult. Your effort is so loud in your mind that I can scarcely think."

She forced herself to loosen her muscles and finish the set before looking his way again. He had settled onto the nearest bench to sit forward and rest. His arms and shoulders glistened, and the skin-thin white training suit clung to his chest and hips.

She ignored the trickle creeping down her own chest. "It must be hard for outsiders to maintain their privacy on Thyrica, around so many of you people."

"Not 'so many,'" he said. "Even counting the untrained, we are fewer than two percent of all Thyrians. And part of our training—the least popular part—is the Privacy and Priority Code: when we're allowed to use our skills, when we're not, and when we must. Memorization and then thousands of hypothetical cases, two hours a day for three years."

She wiped her forehead. "Three years?"

"The death penalty is enforced for 'capricious or selfish exercise of Sentinel skills.'"

She thought of Ellet and Vultor Korda. "So I gathered."

"The moral testing before acceptance for training protects us, as well as the rest of our society."

"You said one day you could sometimes sense the direction the future is moving. Ellet never mentioned that."

"It is part of Master's training, which she has not taken. *Shebiyl* was the Aurians' word for what we see: like a branching path or a vast watershed of possibilities."

"Is it difficult to live normally, knowing all you know?"

"Define 'normally.'" He lay back on the bench. "It doesn't affect me as much as you probably think." He directed his words at the high ceiling. "I only get bits and glimpses, and I have to sort them out. Like dreams, some never come to be."

"Mm. So if you're sent on a mission, you don't necessarily know how it will go."

"Oh, Mari, no. When the will of another is involved, it's no sure guide at all."

"Such as me."

He looked her way. "Such as you."

As the weeks passed, news from Naetai became more of a rarity, for calm was settling at last. Then one afternoon Brennen brought word that shattered what fragile trust he had won.

"Mari, I must tell you something that you will like as little as I do." He stood near the door, still in uniform. If he

was distressed it didn't show, but Firebird knew how
thoroughly he had been trained in emotional control.

"Come in, then. Tell me."

Stepping forward, he said, "You have a day," then
halted. He started again. "Two ambassadors arrived yesterday from Naetai, requesting that you be transferred to their
custody."

"They can't do that. There's an entire week left on my
asylum."

"They timed this deliberately. The Council . . ."
Anger lines gathered on his forehead. "They mean to put
you on trial."

"They're not going to send me back, are they?" she
protested, backing away. His silence frightened her.
"Brenn?"

"I don't know. The Council has granted them a special
hearing tomorrow night. I won't be able to use my abilities
to help you, as badly as I would like to. I must allow events
to take their natural course. That is our law. Ellet will be
there, as well."

Speechless, she nodded.

The following evening, her door slid away on schedule
to reveal a pair of Security I guards in flawless white.
Firebird took a deep breath to calm herself and then
stepped out between them.

They took her from her rooms to the high-arched
Council chamber, cleared again of observers. All the other
principals already stood at the other end, silent as she
walked the long aisle. When she had come nearly to the
stairs, one guard touched her arm and nodded toward
Brennen and Ellet, who waited at the right side of the wide
steps. "Stand with them," the guard said.

She took the space between the Thyrians. At the other
end of the steps stood Captain Kelling Friel, wearing his
red-jacketed uniform with his black cap tucked into his
belt. Although Friel looked incongruous before the Federate council in his gold-edged crimson and black, Firebird
found that the sight of his uniform reawoke an old, disquieting response: grudging but automatic submission to his
authority.

Several steps from Friel, flanking a space evidently

meant for her, waited First Marshal Devair Burkenhamn. Knowing from his plain gray shipboards that he still could not wear the uniform, and remembering his fairness and honor, she felt a traitor.

She glanced right and left. Brennen and Ellet seemed so alike in stature and bearing that she felt out of place and unwanted among the Sentinels of Thyrica, the eyes and heart of the Federacy. They stood at ease, and if they did not dominate the chamber, at least they were at home.

Tierna Coll's white robe rustled as she rose. Once all eyes turned to her, she spoke. Her voice reverberated from the high ceiling. "We are assembled to consider the disposition of Lady Firebird Angelo of Naetai, which has become an issue of sufficient magnitude to warrant this Council's attention."

Firebird thought again how beautiful she looked in her dignity, as Siwann had looked.

"We shall proceed as follows: the N'Taian government shall speak first, as the body to which she is responsible. Then we shall hear Lieutenant General Caldwell, the guarantor of the asylum now ending, and Captain Kinsman, who served as temporary guardian under General Caldwell."

Firebird caught Ellet's movement with her peripheral vision, although she carefully kept her eyes forward. Ellet had turned slightly to study Friel and Burkenhamn with her keen black eyes. Naetai had sent an imposing pair: Friel dark-haired, the Marshal gray, but both massive.

Tierna Coll went on. "Following the guarantors of the asylum, any Councillor who wishes to recommend shall speak; then, as it is her own fate that we decide today, Lady Firebird shall take the final position of influence and honor. Are there any objections to this order?"

There were none.

"Very well. Which of you shall speak for Naetai?"

As First Marshal Burkenhamn stepped forward, Firebird groaned inside. Captain Friel placed both hands on the hilts of his ceremonial sword. Her breath quickened at the traditional gesture of censure, and she slowed it with an effort.

"Your Honors," Burkenhamn began in his rich baritone. "The Crown and the Electoral Council of Naetai request that Major Firebird Angelo surrender herself to the government which, by birth, she does represent, and which, by military oath, she serves. She is called upon to answer charges pertaining to her conduct as an officer of the N'Taian Planetary Navy. As a sovereign government under the protectorship of the Interstellar Federacy . . ." The Marshal paused for emphasis and glared at Brennen. "We do insist that our internal laws be respected."

Firebird groaned silently. They had chosen to base their demand on a key Federate practice: self-government. She struggled to think of a rebuttal, but before she could put together a coherent thought, the dour General Voers stood to speak.

"Marshal Burkenhamn, perhaps the N'Taian delegation would postulate the whereabouts of a merchant vessel called the *Blue Rain*, which left Twinnich nine days ago with a shipment of irradium ore and has not arrived at its destination, Ituri III."

Cleary, thought Firebird, *she's at it again!* A wave of dizziness washed over her as Burkenhamn's sharp intake of breath betrayed his discomfiture. He exchanged glances with Captain Friel before answering.

"Your Honor, we have not been authorized to treat on any subject but the surrender of Major Angelo."

"I believe we were speaking of honoring internal law," replied Voers, but he sat down without saying more.

Tierna Coll motioned to Brennen. "General."

He stepped forward. "Your Honors, some time ago I offered a place among us to Lady Firebird, on behalf of the Federacy. I request that the choice remain hers, to join us if she so desires."

"General," called the head of the Council. "Do you make a recommendation as to that choice?"

One of Brennen's hands clenched into a fist down at his side. "Let the Federacy remember that this is a person of talent and intelligence, whose life should not be wasted."

"Then, you recommend, General?"

Like a knot released, the hand straightened. "The decision should be hers." He stepped back.

She knew that note in his voice: he would say no more. Perhaps his own highest priority stood on trial.

"Captain Kinsman?" Tierna Coll turned slightly. "Do you recommend?"

Brennen's head turned toward Ellet, and Firebird intercepted the cautioning glance. "No," Ellet answered blandly. "Let the Council decide."

"The Council," she had said. Not "her." Very diplomatic.

"Colleagues?" Tierna Coll swept the arc with her gaze as Firebird searched for sympathetic faces.

Admiral Lithib rose on his broad stool. "Let the Lady choose," he wheezed. "It is her destiny of which we speak."

Firebird smiled at him, although she was disappointed that he'd said no more than Brennen. In the ensuing silence she heard a faint, rhythmic tapping: Captain Friel, drumming his fingers on the red leather of his sword's sheath.

"Any others?"

General Voers stood. "My colleague speaks of destiny." He nodded toward Admiral Lithib. "But a man's destiny lies more often in the hands of others than in his own. Furthermore, I too remind the Council that it is Federate policy not to interfere in local affairs. Naetai must deal with its own aristocracy, and we cannot preempt its jurisdiction over a N'Taian citizen." His voice, deep and clear, seemed to hang in the air like bells of doom.

"Any others?" Tierna Coll asked again and waited.

"Lady Firebird?"

Firebird stepped out from between the Sentinels. Facing Tierna Coll and ignoring all others lest her composure slip, she spoke. "Your Honor, General Voers speaks truly when he says that my destiny is in the hands of others. I live today because of words and actions of others here present. And while living under the protection of the Federacy, I have studied the governments and peoples whom it serves. In the eyes of the Federacy, I have read, the rights of the individual citizen of every system take precedence over all corporate rights. Therefore I ask to be heard as an individual, Your Honors. One by one, my ties with

Naetai have been falling away, and if I am allowed the choice, I will not return there yet."

Voers's dark voice rang out. "Even if to remain on Alta would mean your death?"

Would they execute her rather than continue her asylum against Naetai's wishes? Then again, perhaps they might allow her to honorably settle the matter herself, with a N'Taian dagger. She was forced to the same conclusion she had drawn weeks before, when at Twinnich she had asked for termination papers: The only fate she could not face was a traitor's public execution on Naetai.

"Yes, Your Honor. Even if it meant my death." She glanced guiltily toward Marshal Burkenhamn as she backed into her place.

Tierna Coll seated herself. "Colleagues, let us judge."

Firebird watched the Councillors confer in silent privacy, speaking via their screens and touchboards with flying fingers or the digits that served them in fingers' stead. She shivered. The chamber seemed to have grown very cold in only a few minutes. They were taking considerable time with their decision, but whether that was a hopeful sign, she couldn't guess.

Tierna Coll looked up. "General Caldwell, please come to Admiral Madden's board."

Brennen's hair, sun-bleached from weeks planetside, caught a gleam of light as he walked with what looked like utter relaxation around the far end of the table. He read the screen with an intent expression, hesitated, then reached for the board.

General Voers stood. Firebird composed herself to stand steadily to the very end. "Lady Firebird. It is on record before this Council that you would prefer to remain on Alta, even if it means your death, and not return to Naetai. Would you confirm that statement?"

Firebird tried to subdue the pleading note in her voice. "If I returned to Naetai it would surely mean my death, Your Honor. I would stay. Here, though I die, I have had a choice."

Voers returned to his touchboard, and then the seven Councillors turned to Brennen.

He gave a slight nod and soberly touched a single panel.

It seemed that everyone in the chamber shifted. Tierna Coll reached down a last time, rose to her feet, and beckoned regally. "Lady Firebird, come forward."

As Firebird slowly mounted the three broad steps to stand at the center of the table's arch, Tierna Coll continued.

"The salient points in the decision reached by this Council are as follows. One, Lady Firebird has sought and yet seeks asylum among us. Two, Lady Firebird was taken by the Federacy as a prisoner of war, during an act of war initiated by the then-independent government of Naetai. Three, Lady Firebird is yet a N'Taian subject."

As she emphasized those final words, Firebird's heart sank. She glanced helplessly at Brennen, but he did not acknowledge her. He stood with the Council; she stood alone.

"Legally, then, the N'Taian delegation is entitled to demand her return. However, the attempt on the prisoner's life here on Alta has led us to believe that she will not be granted a just trial on Naetai. Honorable delegates, do you wish to deny this?"

Firebird did not turn, but she knew Burkenhamn's voice well. "She will have a trial, Your Honor."

"We assume that your verdict has already been delivered, Marshal Burkenhamn."

The huge Marshal only returned Tierna Coll's stare.

"Very well. Lady Firebird, we wish peace with your people. If that peace required your death, you would choose to meet it here?"

"Yes, Your Honor. If you so order, I ask only privacy and a keen blade."

"No, my lady." Tierna Coll nodded to Brennen. Firebird kept her eyes on the Council table but felt him walk slowly around behind her, and after an interminable moment she heard the keen note of a crystace's sonic activator.

Aghast, she turned to face him. This was not proper! His eyes were clear, though, and his face determined as he swept up the shimmering broadsword, halting it a hand's breadth from her throat.

"Face the Council, Mari." Brennen's low voice allowed no objection.

Firebird turned her back on him and on hope. She felt all eyes on her. Surely Ellet's shone. The chamber was as still as death, except for the singing crystace.

"Honorable delegates," said Tierna Coll. "You have witnessed the confirmed choice of this prisoner: to die on Alta, rather than return to Naetai. Do you acknowledge our authority to rule thus?"

Captain Kelling Friel's voice grated with irritation. "This is entirely irregular, Your Honor. If you will not give her over to custody, we demand that she be given the means to dispatch herself in the traditional manner."

"We are aware of N'Taian suicide customs, Captain. It will not be allowed. The decision of the Council has been made, and it hangs partially upon your answer. Do you bow to our ruling, Marshal?"

Firebird's ears were full of the song of the blade. It hovered very, very near.

Burkenhamn hesitated. The end might be the same, but to a N'Taian, ceremony was almost half of justice. "We abstain from voicing, Your Honor," he said at last. "Her fate should be decided by N'Taian custom alone."

Tierna Coll smiled slightly. "Then, we declare our decision in full." Her ringing voice softened. "Lady Firebird, you are free to die here, a N'Taian subject—under *our* custom—or to return with these your people. However, we would allow you to remain on Alta, if you chose to become a Federate transnational citizen and ceased to be an extraditable alien. We ask you to make no final decision under the duress of this moment, but we do request some assurance that you are seriously considering transnationality. For the purposes of this hearing, if you will renounce your loyalty to Naetai before this delegation, which seeks justice under our authority but abstains from submitting to our ruling, we will consider our requirements met."

Firebird started. The Council *would* bar her extradition! They had deliberately forced the N'Taians' abstention by disallowing her suicide. Then, surely . . . She turned to Brennen, who stood steady and collected. Through the atom-edged blade, she still could read no feeling on his face. Beyond him, Friel hungrily fingered the hilts of his own sword; Marshal Burkenhamn stood at rigid attention, and Ellet's black eyes gleamed fiercely. She knew precisely what each expected her to say. But her destiny had been given back to her, and she thought suddenly of Brennen's words on the high ridge. As a priority, Naetai had failed her.

She faced the table. "Your Honors, I will take Federate citizenship now, if my service to you will help bring peace between our peoples."

She was gratified by the surprise, which changed quickly to satisfaction, in the wisdom lines on Tierna Coll's face. "Lady Firebird, we demand no such commitment of you. If you take an oath of allegiance to us now, you do so without duress and in full view of representatives of the N'Taian government. Are you so willing?"

"I am."

Behind her, the crystace's hum snapped off.

Tierna Coll touched several panels and met Firebird's eyes again. "You will take this oath, then."

"Solemnly I swear this day," Firebird repeated after Tierna Coll, "my unwavering allegiance to the athor—" She stumbled. "—Authority of the Interstellar Federacy."

"I do acknowledge," intoned Tierna Coll, "that Federate transnationality supersedes any citizenship."

Knowing Burkenhamn and Friel stood as witnesses, Firebird took a deep breath, then another.

"Go on," Brennen said quietly.

But Firebird remained silent a moment longer, for a lifetime of unquestioning loyalty lay behind her. She must vow away her aristocratic pride before Friel and her single-minded determination to win glory before her Marshal. It was a high price to pay, to become a full person.

But she had already chosen. She steeled herself to cross that line and calmly asked, "Would you repeat that clause, please?"

"I do acknowledge that Federate transnationality supersedes any citizenship, affiliation, or rank that I hold under any local government.

"I do swear that I shall serve the Interstellar Council

and its designates in any way, at any time, for any reason they so request, even to the laying down of my life.

"I do swear never to bear arms against the Federacy, any of its protectorates, or any representative thereof.

"Should I break this oath in any way, at any time, for any reason, I do swear that I shall submit myself to the Federacy for justice. From this day forward, I live in the awareness of this oath, both its responsibilities and its rights, as a citizen of the galaxy."

Tierna Coll slipped a paper from her transcriber and turned it upon the tabletop to face Firebird, who signed away her past with only a twinge of homesick regret. It was done.

Brennen rode back with her to the minimum-security floor.

"Do you want to come in?" she whispered.

"I do." He palmed her lock.

As the door slid shut behind them, she flicked on the lumipanel. "Shall I make kaffa?"

"No. Talk to me."

"You talk to *me*." She sank onto the raised end of the green lounger. "Was all that a trick, then? To trap them into letting me go? And why you, with the—the crystace?"

He came over and grasped both her hands. "It was no trick, I swear. They were maneuvered, but they held the critical choice in their own hands. It was a terrible risk, but it was legal. As the guarantor of your asylum, I was the symbolic nominee for the role I took. I was certain they would demand to see things done their own way. And certain . . . enough . . . that you would not go back of your own volition."

"It could have ended that way, then."

"Yes. If you had so requested, the Council would have sent you home. You're dealing with a bureaucracy, Mari. An idealistic one—but a bureaucracy all the same."

"And if Marshal Burkenhamn had consented . . . to let you . . .?"

"Do you think he could have?"

"I don't know," she whispered hoarsely. "He's a good man."

"Are you all right?" His concerned eyes peered down at her.

"I'm fine."

"I do apologize, for scaring you half out of your wits."

She nodded.

"Then, give me something, Mari. If your feelings for me had any bearing on your decision, tell me so. Or better still, show me." He drew her to her feet; and in wordless acceptance she slipped her hands behind his waist.

He held back for a moment, stroking her hair. "You already know this, although I haven't told you." His voice was curiously deep. "But I love you." His fingers locked behind her neck, and he bent down toward her lips. As he touched them with his own, first lightly but then more insistently, she felt his presence at the edge of her mind, warmer than before and stronger. *Is pair bonding like this?* she wondered.

In that moment, recalling again the overpowering sensation of mind-access, she understood how much of himself he was holding back to gentle her, and glimpsed the magnitude of what he would be able to do when he chose. Appalled, she clutched him all the tighter.

When his arms finally loosened, she turned her head and pressed it to his chest, holding all thought and tension at bay.

Then she remembered Voers's words to Marshal Burkenhamn. "Brennen."

He smiled down at her. A wisp of pale hair fell onto one dark eyebrow.

"That ship that vanished—the *Blue Rain*—I'm sure Naetai has it. They've got to be working on that irradium project again. And I think I know where."

CHAPTER 17

Return

Intermezzo con accelerando
Interlude, becoming faster

He pulled a little farther away, and she felt his scrutiny where a moment before there had been only tenderness. "Go on."

"You don't believe me."

"You're mistaken."

She swallowed a qualm of conscience. "Brennen, when you interrogated me, I was—I was a different person. I did the best I could."

"Let's worry about blame another time, Mari. Where?"

"Hunter Height. It's a . . . I'll show you, if you'd like. Access, I mean."

"I think that would be best." He motioned her to the lounger. As he settled beside her, her guilt and unease softened in the warmth of his nearness. In this matter, at least, her way seemed clear.

When he withdrew a little later, she let her head fall back. "I *am* sorry, Brennen."

He walked to the door. "Come with me. We may be

able to speak with Tierna Coll before she retires for the night."

The moment Firebird finished explaining to the tall woman in white, the door of Tierna Coll's bare outer office slid open again, admitting Ellet Kinsman. The Sentinel strode in without word or glance to Firebird or Brennen. "Your Honor, forgive me. I sensed your agitation, and came in."

As Firebird thought, *You sensed whose agitation, Ellet?* the Councillor's gaze swept from Ellet to Brennen and then back again. "I am glad you have come, Sentinel Kinsman." Tierna Coll bent down to touch a computer terminal on the room's single fixture, a secretary's desk. "Perhaps you can clarify an issue for me. Lady Firebird confesses to having concealed vital data from Master Brennen under interrogation, data which if genuine could require our immediate action. In your opinion, is this possible?"

"Her?" Ellet's control slipped, allowing incredulity into her voice. "Your Honor, this woman is no match for Brennen—in any way!"

Firebird flushed. "You have held her under access yourself, then?" Brennen asked.

"I have not. But I know you, Brennen. I know your strength—and your training—and the heritage of your family. You seem to have forgotten who and what you are." Ellet turned back to Tierna Coll. "Your Honor, Firebird Angelo of Naetai could never have deceived Brennen under access, not then. But, perhaps, now that she has had opportunity for learning to work around his abilities—"

"Your Honor, I would know deception." Brennen turned on Ellet, his face white. "And if you know my strength, you know that too. A grave danger exists to the Federacy, and I have offered my services to avert it."

The head of the Council conferred with her touch-board for a minute longer, then shut it down. "I am not convinced, General. The evidence is entirely too weak, and we must not demonstrate disrespect to the N'Taian government. Lady Firebird, we appreciate your transfer of citizenship deeply, but these weeks you have spent in General Caldwell's custody do seem to support Sentinel Kinsman's suggestion. Won't you tell the truth now, before all of us? We think it far more likely that the data gained during the original access are correct and unembellished."

Firebird bristled. "I am not inventing this, Your Honor! You are in danger—let Ellet access my memory too, if she must!"

Tierna Coll smiled mildly. "That will not be necessary. In the morning, I shall dispatch a message to Governor Danton on Naetai to check on this locality. His staff should have answers for us within a few weeks, proceeding cautiously, or immediately, should they feel the need to strike. Thank you for your concern, Lady Firebird, and your counsel, Captain Kinsman. And, General, your offer is appreciated, but your services are needed here on Alta. Please return Lady Firebird to her quarters."

Firebird's door closed behind them as she stumbled toward the servo. "Kaffa now?" she offered wearily.

"Please." Brennen took a stool and stared at the corner table. "They didn't believe me. That has never—*never*—happened before. I thought Tierna Coll trusted me implicitly. I . . ."

She pulled a pair of filled cups from the cubby and set one before him. "Perhaps she doubts *because* you're a Sentinel, Brenn?"

"They do," he whispered. "They all do. Even those who honor us. I'm certain now." His misery showed plainly in the set of his jaw and the lines between his eyes. She wanted badly to ease that hurt but could think of nothing to say, too numbed by the Federacy's rejection of her own help in the hour she had taken citizenship. This idealistic Federacy could find itself destroyed by its trust of N'Taian leaders.

After a time Brennen got himself another cup of kaffa, downed it standing, and tucked the cup into the sterilizer. "Get some sleep if you can, Firebird. I may be back, but don't wait for me." He left without explaining.

She stumbled to the back room and fell fully clothed onto her bed. *Firebird.* He hasn't called me that since . . .

The next she knew, Brennen was pulling her back to her feet and pushing another cup of kaffa at her. Trying to stand steady enough not to spill it woke her completely. Brennen vanished into the bathing room. In a minute, she peered in. All her personal things had disappeared, and he was closing a small black duffel kit.

"What are you doing?" Blinking sleepily, she smoothed the wrinkled dress tunic she had worn to face the Council.

"You and I are going to Hunter Height."

"Tierna Coll changed her mind? How did you do it?"

"She didn't."

Firebird leaned against the doorway. "You mean to go without orders?"

"Against orders," he corrected calmly.

"Brennen!" She shook her sleep-fogged head. "What do you want me to do?"

"Get us in. Identify Cleary and her collaborators. Help me get rid of it and them. Then get us out, if you can."

"But Tierna Coll—"

"She's wrong." He handed her the kit. "We both know it. And your irradium people have had too much time already, since the *Blue Rain* disappeared."

"*My* irradium people?"

Brennen snorted softly. "Sorry."

He took it for granted she would help him. "But the Council—the High Command . . ."

Handing her the duffel, he spoke slowly. "I must follow the vows I made when I was vested as a Sentinel. We are talking about an entire populable world fouled, if you understand it right. It could be Caroli, Varga, Alta."

"Alta. Phoena would like that."

"Knowing that Naetai will be eligible for full Federate covenance in five years?"

"There are N'Taians who won't ever want that."

"Mari, if Phoena's irradium project is deployed, Alta is likely gone. If Alta goes, Naetai will be . . . punished. Yet Danton would win no support for the Federacy by sending missiles into Hunter Height. Two of us, though, with my skills and your knowledge of the area, might be able to destroy the project and its developers without taking other lives. We must forestall that strike—for Naetai's sake."

She straightened.

"Are you ready?"

Firebird seized an extra pair of shipboards from the open closet. "Ready."

In the gleaming Cirrus jet, they soared out to the Interstellar Fleet's primary spaceport. An attendant took the craft into his charge at the gate of the massive clear dome, and as Brennen watched apprehensively, the young Lieutenant slid into the pilot's seat with undisguised glee.

Firebird watched Brennen's gaze follow the Cirrus to the storage hangar, laughing silently in sympathy. Then he led onto the base proper, past rows of symmetrically parked atmospheric craft and streamlined dual-drive ships that were equally maneuverable in vacuum and atmosphere: interceptors, transports, frigates, gunships, and shuttles. Her eyes widened at the display of Federate striking power, gleaming under the lights.

As they hurried along, Brennen pointed out several craft. "But the ones over by the fifth fence will always be my favorites," he said. "The old LR-2s. The greenest of us flew them in the Geminan War. They're obsolete now, but with better generators they'd serve in a crisis. Their shields were outstanding for their weight, and they do carry four cannon apiece."

"How old were you, Brenn?"

"Fifteen and crazy to fly. It's a wonder I survived. I did some mighty stupid things."

"I think I read about some of them. Unit Seventy-eight—"

"*Federacy of the Free.* They made me a hero, but I deserved to be spaced in slip for that raid on Gemina. No orders, no support ships, and nine fighter pilots following as if I were an Admiral. If a Geminan reactor hadn't melted down, I'd have killed all ten of us."

"I was a wild pilot at fifteen, too. But they didn't let me into a fightercraft until I was twenty."

"Someday you'll likely feel the same about your TSR-49s."

Inside a stuffy arms depot that smelled like institutional disinfectant, Brennen picked up a black drillcloth pack and allowed her a peep inside at a pair of wafer-thin touch activators that looked like plastic gaming cards, and a full load of miniature explosives—sonic, incendiary, and others she didn't recognize and he didn't explain. Three stylus-shaped recharges for his blazer vanished into a side pocket of the pack.

"I know the night sentry fairly well," he said softly as they zipped into high-g acceleration oversuits. "She assumes when I make a supply call it's official business. That comes from dealing with S.O. We always have to have things at odd hours. It's how I got a ship, too, and how we'll get offplanet." A woman appeared from the back room. "This looks good," he told her. "Now we need one more blazer. N'Taian issue, if possible."

He finished arming Firebird with a little Vargan stinger and a slim black bootknife. She tucked them into a g-suit pocket and followed him out.

Hundreds of near stars still shone through the arc of the dome, although the sky had begun to brighten toward dawn. They stopped at a parking row near the dome's far edge, before a thirty-meter craft with very minor atmospheric adaptations: its enormous stardrive engine dwarfed the slim, upper cabin compartment. "It's a DS-212, the *Brumbee*, designed for clandestine message delivery." He examined its rounded surface and talked his way down its length. "They've pared it down to absolute essentials for long-distance slip. It's no yacht, but it's extremely fast. It'll maintain acceleration and deceleration at several g's past what normal translight drives will give you." At the tail he straightened and grinned. "It rides like a missile."

Firebird jumped for the security handle, got her balance on the doorplate, and released the entry hatch. Brennen followed her in and secured the hatchway behind him, plunging the cabin into darkness. Feeling her way, she slipped into the first officer's chair. Brennen touched a control, and the cabin's luminescent ceiling stripes glimmered bright blue. He squeezed between the seats and into the pilot's and began rearranging the controls on the slanting display. "Would you stow the pack? There's a bulkhead compartment behind you."

She heard the familiar thrum of atmospheric ion engines beginning to respond to their lasers as she closed down a magnetic seal. Returning to her seat as he finished his checkout, she slipped into her flight harness.

"*If* we should get into a scrap," he said, "you shoot, I'll fly. Here's the ordnance board." He touched an orange rectangular panel at the center of the console, and she studied it while he raised the ship and set it in motion.

A vast, wedge-shaped sky hatch loomed ahead, edged by luminous strips. He obtained clearance for takeoff on first request, flipped the last levers, then killed the strip-lights. The atmospheric drive came to full power. Brennen released the ground brakes and they shot through the wedge, away from the base.

Firebird watched Alta dwindle, and the stars of the Whorl glowed in multicolored brilliance as the ship left Alta's obscuring atmosphere. As Brennen had predicted, they were not challenged, but still she felt uneasy. What world would she call home now? She had abandoned Naetai, and now she was helping Brennen flirt with insubordination himself.

Or was she? His Sentinel vows, he had declared tonight, took precedence over the Federacy's orders. *As Ellet's vows took precedence over his orders,* she thought with a sudden chill. One Sentinel had betrayed her for those vows already. Uneasily she wriggled in the deeply padded seat.

"Ready to slip?" he asked once they stood out far enough.

She snugged the harness. "Ready."

"Go as limp as you can. This will be more of a jolt than you expect, because we have to pick up so much speed at once. I'll max the gravidics, but they'll only take off part of the pressure."

She took a deep breath and consciously relaxed every part of her body. First the odd, vibrational sensation of the slip-shield took hold of her, and then the pressure hit. Even with the high-g suit, it was worse than she anticipated. She forced her lungs to pull in a slow breath, as gradually the gravidic compensators caught up with the thrust and her conditioned body readjusted to slip-state.

When she managed to lean forward and look around,

the stars on the visual screen had vanished. Brennen seemed entirely unaffected. "I checked the conversion factor for N'Taian pressure units. That was three-ten, perceptible. Almost thirty percent over your rating."

She took another deep breath, grateful that he had neither warned her graphically nor patronized her about the heightened effect of high pressure on women, but had spoken as a colleague in command. She called up a smile, released her harness, and yawned.

"You're done in," Brennen observed. "It's been a long night, hasn't it?" He brought the striplights back up, turned aft, and dropped one of a pair of broad shelves from the curved cabin ceiling. "Here are the bunks. But let me show you the rest of the ship. Across the way—watch your head—is the galley servo. You'll probably enjoy the food. If I complain, it's only overfamiliarity. I've been through the menu too many times."

She glanced into the washcabin—one had to back in or out of it, it was too small to turn around in—and the cargo area. "How long do your psych people think a human can travel in a compartment this size and not go off-balance?"

"The cockpit is roomiest." He let down the second bunk, little more than a black-blanketed pallet. "So you can fly it comfortably. We have life support for two for just over a month."

"You're joking."

"No. It was designed to make really long distance travel practical. The messenger service uses the DS-212 frequently, and I've spent more time in one than I care to think about." His eyes shone deep blue under the strip-lights, and suddenly she realized they were staring straight into her.

Oh, no! She flushed. *Four days alone, with my emotions naked before him?*

Then, face them, she told herself. *Ask him what Ellet meant—he has sworn to respect your will!* But she hesitated. She still could not bring herself to trust him entirely, and allowing a man to touch her—body or mind—might alter their relationship irrevocably.

But if Phoena won the round, in less than a week they both might be dead.

What *did* she feel for Brennen Caldwell?

Her cheeks warmed when she spoke. "Ellet suggested, that is—well, that you had ways of . . ." Words stuck in her throat and she sat down carefully on the lower bunk. Her hand pressed white on the bedcover.

She felt him moving toward her. When his hand touched her shoulder, she found her voice. "She said Sentinels could please one another in ways outsiders can't. Is it like—the way you touched me the day we took your Cirrus out?"

He looked very serious. "Would you like me to show you?"

Twisting her hips to turn and face him, she lost her balance and fell backward. She didn't try to get up. "I would, Brennen. I would."

He sat down beside her; she could feel the warmth of his leg pressing against her hip. A tingle of apprehension heightened an urge she could no longer pretend she did not feel.

Brennen caressed her throat, and the inward pressure of access-beginning welled up in her. This time, however, he called up neither memory nor emotion, but sensation: a gradual, inexorable arousal.

Idiot! she upbraided herself as the warm feeling of contact intensified. She tried to pull away. Immediately the strength of his presence closed firmly around her, warm and reassuring. Her eyes fell closed. Gradually the urge to struggle left her and the wash of warmth grew more pervasive, until she felt only Brennen's presence and her whole body tingling.

Then he drew the tendril of epsilon energy back, although not so far that she did not sense a lingering glow. She opened her eyes. He sat above her, bracing one arm against the bunk beside her shoulder. The star on his shoulder caught the blue striplights, reflecting streaks from its cross-rays that hurt her eyes.

"Pair bonding," he said softly and calmly, "is brought about when two connatural minds enter one another in a contact much like that, only closer—there is a total inter-weaving of the deepest emotional fiber—and then, while the matrices are locked in that way, the physical union

occurs. The simultaneous culmination seals the bond." He
pulled a long strand of hair from under her shoulder and
arranged it over her shirtfront. "That is the bond that can
only be broken by death. Only the connatural can endure
such a close approach. That is why only the connatural can
pair-bond. But connaturality, in and of itself, is not enough
to make a union. There must be love. And trust." He
stressed the word a little sadly. "Shared goals and enthusi-
asms. For each bond mate remains an individual, capable of
pleasing or hurting the other."

"And you want that—with me?"

"I have asked no one else."

She pressed her spine into the bunk's thin covering.
"First, we have a job to do. If it doesn't come off . . ."

He nodded slowly. "Even if it does, Mari, we may be in
trouble—if the other Masters rule that I have misjudged
the situation."

"Better us in trouble than both our worlds."

He gave her shoulder a squeeze, then stood and
stepped onto her bunk to swing himself into the upper.
"You're right." His voice came down to her, accompanied
by rustling noises. "We'll talk about it, when we're both
awake again."

Awake? How could she sleep? The echoes of Brennen's touch ricocheted through her mind like laser fire.
Ellet had spoken truly. She would never forget.

Carradee Second, Queen of Naetai, stood silently in
the large, ornately appointed sitting room that had once
been Firebird's. Servants had packed and stored all Firebird's possessions; in that way these rooms had cycled over
generations, briefly housing a Wastling then standing
grandly empty to honor the Angelos' guests.

I will never bear a Wastling. I couldn't take the anguish.

Carradee centered a gilded clock below a multifaceted
mirror. *Firebird would never have kept a clock like that
one—where did Dunna find it?*

These rooms would never be anything but Firebird's to
Carradee.

But if Friel and Burkenhamn succeeded—brought
Firebird back to Naetai—what then?

Sunlight streamed through high, white-curtained windows, giving the marble walls a soft sheen and setting off the dark wooden furnishings. More keenly, however, Carradee noticed the things that were gone. Scanbooks full of pictures taken on distant worlds no longer lay open on the dark fayya-wood end table; the coat-of-arms crested desk was cleared of academy trophies and scan cartridges; no flight jacket lay flung over the brocade-covered desk chair. All gone: gone with Carradee's young sister.

Burkenhamn was to report to her, Friel to Phoena, whether their mission succeeded or failed. Soon—within days.

She ambled across the room and into the adjoining study. This had been stuffed with musical paraphernalia: sold. Gone.

Firebird's formal portrait, removed from the gallery, now hung on the inner wall. Carradee reached out and touched its golden frame. She had grieved for Firebird, really grieved. Perhaps that should have made this waiting more bearable, but it did not. She didn't like to display the portrait publicly until Firebird's fate was settled. Storing it in darkness, however, would have been too much like consigning Firebird to a mausoleum, so she had hung it here herself, here in the room where Firebird had always seemed happiest—if she had to be on the ground.

The goldwork on the frame was simple, as befitted a Lady in a house of Princesses, but lovely. Carradee sighed. If they brought Firebird back . . .

Must she put her sister on trial? Arrange for her execution? Plainly Firebird would not suicide, and with heir limitation outlawed, they could not touch her for Geis Refusal. No, it would be treason. A public trial, shame on the family. How bitterly unfair that it was not done in Siwann's time, accomplished during the reign of Siwann, who had kept a healthy distance from the fire-haired imp. Unfair that Carradee would have to mourn again.

But surely the Federacy would keep her on Alta. Carradee stared at the diadem the girl in the portrait wore proudly—if a touch off-center. How could the Federates allow Firebird to be punished for an act that had been the key to their victory? Perhaps it was hope, asking her that.

Phoena's hopes, she knew, were different. Phoena's ideological retreat would be well under way now, at Hunter Height, free from Federate intrusion, as Carradee had promised.

Hunter Height—how Carradee loved the place. She shut her eyes, basking in the pleasant sadness of her small martyrdom. Here she would stay on, in bustling Sae Angelo, while Phoena enjoyed the secret, majestic old Height. *At least Phoena will cherish it, and it won't stand empty. The Lieutenant Governor was right, though; the city is far quieter without her.*

Could I attend Firebird's trial?

As Queen, I would have to. I couldn't veto an execution order if the Electorate handed it down. They'd have my crown.

Please! she whispered to the unseen Powers. *Keep Firebird on Alta!*

On the last "day" in slip at about midcycle, Firebird and Brennen finalized their plan of attack.

"The tunnel system, then, is like a long half-circle," Brennen said. "Most of the branches run east-west on the first level, north-south below that, and so on."

Firebird nodded. "Except for the Thunder Hill spur."

"We'll try that way in only if the house is too well guarded. If they do keep gas around to fumigate for rodents, I'd like to spend as little time as possible underground."

"So would I." Rising from the bunk, she opened the galley servo and stared at its contents.

"Mari?"

She turned around and caught a wistful look in his eyes.

"What will they do with you if you're caught? Have you considered it?"

"Well . . ." For an instant, her suspicion returned. Did he intend to abandon her there, use her as a distraction? "Kill me, of course. But I suspect—I think—they wouldn't shoot on sight. Phoena sponsored Cleary's research from the beginning, and she has to be there, if she has left Sae

Angelo. If I know Phoena at all, she'd love to make a spectacle of executing me."

"And if things went very wrong, and they took me?"

She leaned back against the counter. The image of Brennen powerless in Phoena's hands distressed her. "That's hard. She'd be torn between hoping to . . . to hurt you, punish you, and trying to make everything 'proper.' Are you—"

"Afraid?" he asked softly. "More so than I've ever been. Afraid to come this far and lose what you and I . . . could have had."

She found she could not answer that. "You'll come through, Brenn. With your resources . . ."

Once again he seemed to sense her awkwardness. He flipped the bunk up and out of sight, slid the fingers of his right hand into his left sleeve, and drew the crystace. She came alert with a shiver of curious awe. "You didn't get much of a chance to see this resource," he said in a lighter voice, "when I had it out at the Council hearing."

He turned the slim, dull gray dagger-hilt on his palm. Near the wide handguard she spotted a small, round activating stud; he shifted his grip, held the crystace at arm's length, and pressed it. Instantly, the resonant tone sang in her ears, and the meter-long blade appeared above the grip, catching the monochromatic light and reflecting scarcely visible shades of green, blue, and violet. Brennen swept it around to stand upright between them, and watched her through the shimmering crystal as she glanced from tip to edge to center.

Korda had described the blade's edges as of one atom's width, and Firebird finally believed him. Wonderingly she reached out her hand. Brennen gave it to her.

She made a tentative swing in the air. It was lighter than it looked, but exquisitely balanced. "What is aurite?"

"As far as I know, the Aurians never told. I don't believe it's a pure element." He took it back and pressed the stud again. "Are you hungry?"

She chose the stew, variety number three, spicy and warming. Brennen ate with a noticeable lack of interest, preoccupied with the map he had spread on her bunk.

"I could lose it here." He jabbed the long scribepaper with a spoon. "That canyon bends blind. I'll be glad to know it's coming."

"The ruggedness of the Aerie range is one reason they still use the retreat. Supposedly it can't be approached lowlevel from that direction."

A yellow light began to pulse on the console. "Fifteen minutes to final deceleration," he said.

Firebird found the g-suits and tossed him one. "Thanks." He caught it one-handed. She pulled on her own, secured the fore cargo hatches, and strapped herself in. Brennen had finished aft and already sat at his station. "Snug the harness a touch past what you'd normally use. I'm going to use the ship's maximum tolerance."

The final seconds counted off on the break indicator, and then the little craft's engines reversed with a roar. Thrown with painful pressure against the wide black webbing, Firebird glimpsed Naetai's majestic arc as Brennen leaned forward and made a course correction. *How can he do it?* she wondered as he pressed back to the seat. She could scarcely move. She had never tried to take approach orbits at such stiff deceleration.

The cabin heated palpably with atmospheric entry as the sky gradually lightened to blue around them, and they crested the pole in final orbit. Still decelerating hard, but within normal tolerance, he dropped the craft to lowlevel and skimmed the icy surface as it began to glow in the predawn light. The far northern winter's ferocious storms soon would have made this approach impossible even for Brennen Caldwell.

The ride absorbed all her concentration, leaving no mental effort to spare for Phoena or the irradium project. Like a skimmerboat on open sea, the ship rose and fell with the passes of the ice-locked range. The wild canyon turn came and went too quickly for fear.

"There it is." She pointed ahead. League Mountain, separated by a short ridge from Hunter Mountain, filled the horizon, continuing to grow until they settled gently into the snow as near the ridge as the pitch of the slope would allow. He cut the atmospheric engines and silence rang loudly in her ears.

They unbuckled and stretched. Brennen moved aft, which was now downhill. From the cargo area, he pulled two dark gray suits and handed one up to Firebird. "Thermal controls on the left wrist."

She turned around, slipped out of her gravity suit and shipboards, and stepped into the heavy pants. After struggling with the shirt, she joined them at the waist. The suit didn't hang too badly. The shirt collar fit high and snugly, the sleeves ended in skin-thin gloves. She touched a small flexible panel on the wrist and immediately began to shiver. *That's not it.* She touched a different corner. Warmth flowed through hands, feet, and body.

"Have you figured it out?" Brennen came up beside her and eyed the panel. "Comfortable?"

"A little too warm."

"Leave it that way."

She slipped back into her boots, then buckled on the gunbelt and tucked the stinger under it. As she slipped the knife into her boot, Brennen opened the outer hatch. Frigid air swirled into the cabin.

She took the drillcloth pack and jumped down, then waited in the snow as Brennen sealed the hatch, perching on the tilted doorplate and clinging one-handed to the security handle. Gracefully he leaped down to her side and took the pack.

"I'll spell you carrying that," she offered.

"The best way to work as a team is for each of us to do what he—or she—does best. Let me do the hauling. All right, my lady?"

He reminded her suddenly of a teacher she had long forgotten, one who had urged her to study music and forget the military. "Go ahead. But I'm not along for the scenery."

He smiled, and she headed up the slope across thin-crusted snow. Boot-top high, it made slow going, particularly for a man carrying a pack as heavy as that one.

"We're leaving tracks," she observed.

"We won't have to worry about it, going down the other side. Southern exposure." He plodded ahead of her, breaking trail. Her heart pounded with the altitude and unaccustomed exercise, despite her recent weeks of training. They skirted the summit on the westward side of the ridge, where the wind picked up and roared stiffly. Here, the snow had been blown away, and they began to make faster progress.

The view southward into staggered lines of rocky foothills lifted her spirits, but they dropped down quickly to avoid presenting recognizable silhouettes to any watching eyes.

About ten meters below the ridge, Firebird stopped for a breath. Behind her, Brennen whistled softly.

Hunter Height lay below on a stony knoll. The house itself, built of the granite of Hunter Mountain, was designed like a small hexagon atop a larger one; from the southern foothills, an ancient, winding road approached, and from the north a switchbacking stone lane led up from a box canyon, which ran east and west and concealed the airstrip. The knoll was ringed by a venerable stone outwall etched by lichens and the slow years of wild weather, and within the pale lay informal grounds, often battered by wind and snow, sheltered somewhat by the forested shoulder of Thunder Hill on the west.

"From the air," he whispered, "it would look like part of the mountain."

Firebird smiled smugly. "That's why your recon flights haven't picked it up."

CHAPTER 18

Hunter Height

Crescendo poco a poco
Gradually becoming louder

In the bustling thirty-fifth-floor hallway of MaxSec, a man in Thyrian blue saluted Ellet Kinsman. She returned the gesture. Who *was* he? He looked barely familiar: he must have gone through College either before her (he was *built* older, tall and well muscled) or after (but the face was so young).

"Captain Kinsman." He shone a boyish smile. "Air Master Damalcon Dardy, Thyrian forces. I'm looking for General Caldwell, and the secretary sent me to you. Is he on a security assignment?"

Older, then, and he ranked her. Ellet kept her static shield up. "Is there something I can help you with, sir?"

"I've just checked in from following up a Shuhr raid, and I'm only passing through. I wanted to introduce myself. However." He touched her arm. Both pressed against a wall to allow a man with a repulsor cart to pass. "Since this is obviously not a place for private discussion, would you join me for lunch in the officers' lounge?"

"Sir, the MaxSec lounge is expensive."

His even-toothed grin softened her reserve. "Then I will take it out of my Vital Contacts budget."

He did precisely that, presenting his ID disk to the host at the main door and insisting they be given a private booth with a view. For half the hour, while she savored a salad of genuine Thyrian shellfish, he inquired only about her own work, and she found herself warming to him.

"Caldwell, then." He spread garnetberry jam on his roll and switched to silent subvocalization. *I did mention him at the office, and I was given the distinct impression Regional has been overloading him in the hope he'll break before they have to promote a Sentinel up to High Command. What's wrong? Where is he?*

I don't know precisely, she responded tightly, and it was enough of the truth to pass. *He has gone—with the N'Taian woman, Firebird Angelo.*

Dardy set down the roll and leaned across the booth, almost tipping his kaffa cup. "What do you mean?"

Ellet maintained a stoic placidity. *When he turned up missing from duty, I put in for medleave to cover him, and made a check at the depot. He took a ship, but they are not talking.*

Dardy tapped a finger on the tabletop and glanced out the window over Castille. *Well, they wouldn't have asked him any questions,* he sent back. *S.O. is S.O. Have you reported him?*

Not yet. She pressed her folded hands hard against the table.

You're not telling me everything about this N'Taian woman.

No.

Ellet sensed a bare rise of apprehension. *She is connatural with him?* he asked.

For one moment Ellet wished for the long, slow period of "making acquaintance" that outsiders experienced. No one but another Sentinel would expect to be shown so much, so quickly and intimately—but such was their code. It had made of the starbred a people who could not easily be divided. *Apparently so, sir.*

That's too bad. Dardy made a wry face. *I would hate to see his epsilon genes wasted outside our families.*

She kept her response as stony as she knew how to make it. *This is not the end of the matter, sir.*

Dardy picked up his fork, speared a mouthful of smoked gyfish, and chewed thoughtfully. The lounge quieted momentarily as one of Admiral Lithib's Oquassan countrymen rode in on a repulsor cart, then returned to normal.

Tell me, then. Dardy laid down his fork and pushed back his plate, now entirely sympathetic. *How much do you know about where they have gone?*

She frowned. *Firebird's people are not taking occupation well,* and she raised Brennen's suspicion that certain action needed to be taken there on Naetai, although Regional ordered otherwise. *She played on his pride and won.* Ellet raised her head to meet the Air Master's eyes and sent the most painful admission of all. *She has won, sir.*

Counter to orders? Dardy looked—and felt—stricken. *Express or implied? Can Sentinel codes justify his action?*

Express orders: I saw them given. As to our codes—I cannot say. That is for the Masters to judge.

Dardy shifted his muscular shoulders to lean sideways in the booth. *It might not be too late to force him to stand back and think things through more carefully. Could they be intercepted, perhaps?—the woman apprehended for escaping custody, and Caldwell called back for questioning? Or . . . is there someone on Naetai who respects our kindred, but might wish to hold the woman there at her home?*

"Governor Danton." Ellet spoke aloud but softly, pleased with the idea. "He seemed to work very well with Brennen, and would not wish to see him in trouble, but Danton is also very close to the royal family and its wishes. The Queen wants her back." Ellet felt no compulsion to tell Dardy what that return might mean to Firebird.

"Perfect," he said. "Regional could alert Danton by the next messenger ship." *And we could maintain Thyrica's hopes to get a Sentinel on the High Command,* he added silently.

Despite having found a genuine supporter, Ellet felt a pang of loss, for Brennen's actions *had* declared his choice: Firebird, unless she refused him—or she was killed. Holding her emotions under tight reign, Ellet saluted the Air Master with her cup.

Firebird was glad for the thermal suit and stiff teknahide boots as they picked a way down slick, frosty rubble and scree toward the woods. Underfoot, little alpine plants clung to pockets of soil, turning to reds and browns with the onset of cold weather. Many glistened, edged leaf by leaf with delicate frost crystals.

Just above the evergreen forest, Brennen stopped and waited for her. She had slowed her pace to scan the Height again before they entered the trees. "There." She pointed a gray-gloved hand. "By the south wall. And another beyond the back gate."

His gaze followed her gesture.

"And there's another, walking along the west end of the grounds. See them?"

He nodded. "Three guards on morning duty."

"And infrared scanners we can't see. I think we'd better try that side tunnel, Brenn. It's farther to walk, but the house is too well covered."

"Lead on."

An hour's trudge took them up onto Thunder Hill, but at the entry site they found a huge jumbled pile of stone.

"Squill," she exclaimed softly. "They've blocked it. Recently, too." She eyed the crushed vegetation, still green.

High above her, Brennen peered down from the top of the rockpile. "We could only get in this way if we used explosives." He step-jumped down to join her. "We should conserve them for the laboratory."

"Then, it's back to your idea."

"Infrared alarms do sometimes fail. If I can shoot out the one over the service doors, we might have time to get in before they reactivate and check it."

"You're the marksman, then. I couldn't do it."

He dug into the pack and handed her two food cubes, and she crunched them dry. "Here." He dropped two more small, hard lumps into her hand.

Citrene! "Thanks." She popped both onto her tongue,

then drank a gulp of water from his bottle. He shouldered the pack again and turned back down the hill.

They walked in silence, just to the right of a bare chute scoured clean of trees by avalanches. She smelled wood smoke, and the afternoon sky over the treeless swath was purest autumn blue.

As she watched a hunting kiel soar on the air currents, a roaring streak of silver sliced the sky. Instinctively she ducked into the trees.

Brennen joined her, hands on her shoulders. "It's an active place, all right." Peering back, she saw tiny smile lines around his eyes. His apprehension must have run its course; he looked almost eager for a confrontation.

In a copse of barren, prickly bushes they rested out the afternoon, and they moved down at dusk. The high wall, once worked elegantly smooth, now wore the cracks of antiquity, and here and there stones had fallen, affording Firebird all the footholds she needed after Brennen boosted her. Lying flat atop the wall for a moment, she could see the lights of Hunter Height off through the trees, warm yellow in the lower windows and dim blue above. A scent of roasted meat on the faint breeze made her mouth water. Convinced that no one was near, she slipped down inside, rested her feet on the heavy iron handrail that circled the wall within (installed centuries ago by an elderly monarch), and then jumped backward, down to the ground. He was soon beside her, in the manicured tip of the evergreen forest.

When they reached its end, Firebird could see clearly into the kitchens. Lights still burned brightly, and white-gowned cookstaff hurried back and forth in front of the southwest-facing windows. She turned to Brennen, who stood in deep shadow behind another resin tree. He made no sign.

She looked up, startled by the almost-starless twilit sky: Naetai was a splendid recluse in the galaxy. The brightest points of the faint, familiar constellations of home winked down at her as she hid and waited. She spotted Alta in the Whorl, twinkling near Menarri, the smallest of Naetai's three moons. It looked somehow different now. She had lived under that star as a sun.

The kitchen lights went out. Firebird looked quizzically at Brennen.

He shook his head, and they waited in stillness a few minutes longer. Slow, even footsteps approached and the guardsman passed, vanishing around a broad corner.

Brennen flung himself prone and steadied his blazer on one hand. Firebird held her breath and averted her eyes from the energy pistol's muzzle.

He took a deep breath. Then another.

Then he touched the stud. A single flash fled out the corner of her eye. She waited a moment longer, until Brennen beckoned and led out at a run.

She kept close behind, flattening beside the kitchen door as Brennen tried the handle. The iron latch clicked as it released. He opened the huge wooden slab just a bit, but before they could steal through, it ground on its hinges. Brennen froze.

Firebird bit her lip.

He pressed up and pulled the door outward a little farther, then motioned her inside.

The great kitchens stood empty, lit only by cracks below the inner doors. They followed the outer wall left a few feet to the kitchen store.

Brennen zipped the gloves off his suit, then knelt and pressed an open hand to the lockbox at waist level. Firebird watched curiously. In a moment, she heard another quiet click inside the mechanism. Brennen pushed the door open. They squeezed into the pantry and closed the heavy panel behind them. A dim, pale green light sprang up beside her: Brennen's pocket luma. The tiny glowing cube illuminated a ghostly green sphere around them as they threaded their way between shelves of foodstuffs and cooking equipment.

At the end of the pantry, a palmlock guarded the cellar stairs. Brennen dropped again to his knees. "Wait—let me try," Firebird said. She pocketed her own gloves and pressed her bare right palm to the panel.

The door slid away.

Firebird shrugged and laughed softly. "Well. They didn't change the locks."

She led stealthily around the wedge-shaped stone

steps that widened into the tunnel system, where the cool air made her face tingle. After circling once, Firebird could see an orange glow beneath. Brennen pocketed the little luma. She steadied herself with her fingertips on the left wall. In a few steps more she came out in a short alcove that led to a cross-tunnel. Its left branch passed eastward, toward the area they'd agreed to check first, but Firebird remembered a large chamber at the center of the system that would have to be crossed if they traversed this level. Brennen motioned her to remain in the dark stairwell. He had drawn his blazer. Stealthily he walked forward into what seemed an unnatural brightness, then disappeared left.

She edged along the right wall to the end of the shadow, drew her own blazer, and waited. Brennen returned, shaking his head. Silently she pointed the other way. They scurried down the right branch, then made another quick right turn, down into the darkness under the Height.

After they had spiraled down another smooth stone stair past the second level, he stopped. "She's here," he whispered.

"Phoena?"

"Yes. There were men in the main chamber, talking. I didn't catch much, but that confirms it all."

"There are so many rooms along that chamber, it would've been risky to cross it anyway. Let's go without the light, as long as we can still make time."

Edging downward in total darkness, Firebird found his firm handhold reassuring. The wall vanished beneath her skimming fingers. "Here," she said softly. "Eastbound."

Firebird led now. As they drew on, a yellow glow grew stronger.

At last Brennen whispered, "Stay here," and crept on alone. She watched in the dim light, a little aggravated at being left behind. He paused, listening with some epsilon sense, then went on.

Straining her ears, Firebird heard footsteps from the west. One set, perhaps two.

"Brenn!" she called in a penetrating whisper. Before he could join her, she drew and fired toward the steps.

There was a surprised shout from up the corridor, and then silence. An afterimage of her blazer glowed faintly in her eyes.

"Quick!" he said. "There's a guard up ahead, and he's certain to have heard." They sprinted back westward, silent on muffle-soled boots.

A north-branching corridor left the straight hall. "Here," breathed Firebird. She turned right in the dark and plunged downward only moments before laser fire lit the passage.

This tunnel's floor was more broken. Brennen tripped after only a few steps. She heard the scuffle as he caught himself, then suddenly the luma sprang to life. Again she pushed herself to a run. The faint greenish glow made her hands look sickly and pale but sped their progress around the long eastward curve toward the main northbound tunnel. Several side passages led off into blackness. Their shadowy depths mocked the intrusion of light, faint though it was. Here and there, mineral crystals caught the emerald light and glittered eerily.

Once the curve had been put behind them, protecting them from following fire, they stopped to rest.

Panting, Firebird leaned against a smooth spot on the wall. "Unfortunately, now they know someone's here. If they split three ways they can have us like slinks in a tree."

Brennen was listening again. "No one's coming."

"He's reporting, then. Now we worry about gas."

"Would we have an hour to rush the east branch?"

"Probably not," she said. "But we have those oxygen sniffers. And there are several side ways between here and the airstrip lane. One is that spur that leads up under Thunder Hill. Zistane gas is heavy, and we'd be up out of danger, temporarily at least. But it's a dead end now. If they trap us in there, we're caught."

"No, we could blow our way out. But we'd lose our chance at the irradium lab. I do have an idea . . ." He killed his luma. "Get down."

Firebird dropped onto the passageway floor and pressed against the wall, fumbling for her blazer. She could see nothing. Nearby a stealthy step broke the stillness.

Then another, quieter yet. Firebird held her breath. Then rocks, blazer, and Brennen gleamed crimson as he fired.

She heard him breathe deeply, and the luma shone again, held high in his left hand as he aimed steadily up the tunnel. Cautiously, she got back to her feet.

"I felt something alive back there," he whispered.

No sound flowed down the shaft toward them. Brennen slipped her the luma and backtracked warily up into blackness.

When he came again, he shook his head. "There's no body. But I don't feel it anymore."

"Something from down one of those side passages?" She shivered.

"Does anything live down there?"

"I don't think so. But they used to tell us monster stories that kept Carradee awake for nights on end." She moved a step closer, and he reached for her hand. "Let's go," she urged, stepping out.

"Wait a minute." He pulled her back.

"You said you have an idea."

"I have," he whispered. "It's risky."

"It couldn't be riskier than waiting for zistane. What is it?"

"To split up. You should get uplevel, out of the danger of gas, and go for the researchers. If they're down here in the tunnels, they'll have to evacuate too. I'll hide and go into tardema-sleep. Once the worst of the gas clears out, I'll use the sniffers and take the lab."

She stiffened suspiciously. "This is something you'd thought of already, I think."

"Yes—and no. It was always a possibility, but I hoped we wouldn't have to try it. You will be in particular danger if we separate."

"I can take care of myself. I know Phoena pretty well and the Height even better."

"But can you kill?"

"Brennen—of course I—"

"Face to face?" He pressed her hand. "Not from a ship?"

"Oh . . . I see your point. Yes, I'm sure I can. Cleary,

D'Stang, Parkai, I can kill. Look what they've done to Naetai. To my life."

"And others whom you knew? Maybe even liked? To protect yourself and your mission?"

"I'll do it. The only trick will be getting into the tubes." Shipboard, they had discussed the hydraulic network, drilled through granite walls in a previous century to carry solar-heated water into bathing rooms, kitchens, and lower-level labs. As a child Firebird had found the abandoned hollow system, far wider than the pipes it held, and explored it over a series of summers: it had made an ideal hiding spot from Phoena (something she frequently needed). Painstakingly she had cleared away obstructions until she could negotiate the entire system, and she had kept it her own secret in this secret place. Assuming she had not put on too much weight, she should still be able to use it.

"Listen, then," he said. "Dispatch those three at all cost and without worrying for me. Tardema-sleep is a skill I have learned for just this kind of need. Figure three hours for the gas to clear enough, if they use it. Allow me roughly an hour to lay charges—starting now, if the air stays good—then half an hour to get clear enough to detonate them. In an hour and a half I'll send off a quest-pulse homed on your feelings, as I did on Alta. If you're through and off the Height, concentrate on something strongly pleasing when you feel that probe, and I'll touch off the charges. Get to the breakaway strip down in the canyon and get a plane ready while I'm on my way. If you're not clear when you feel my call, answer with fear. I'll feel it and come for you." He opened a side pocket of the black pack while he spoke. "If something happens to me . . ." He handed her one tiny touch activator card. "I'll carry the pack in as close as I can to the lab and arm the charges before I go under. Blow them if I don't call."

She touched it with one finger and drew away, shaken by his trust. "But you'd be too close to . . . *surely* it won't come to that, Brenn."

"It could. Could you do it?"

"I . . ." She swallowed. "I don't know."

"All right, Mari." He slipped the card into her hip

pocket. "You're honest with yourself. I think if it came down to it, you could. Remember VeeRon."

Within the hour, they cautiously approached the main tunnel north to the airstrip. Firebird peered out into its luminous breadth: brightly lit by everburners imbedded in glossy black walls, its floor had recently been scored by vehicular traffic. Even Brennen sensed no one nearby.

She met his eyes for what she knew might be the last time. "Thank you for everything, Brenn. I hope it works."

He took her in his arms. "Until we meet, Mari. Wherever it is." He kissed her, began to draw away, then reached for her again. She gripped him, aching, wishing uselessly that their paths had crossed in peaceful, trustful times.

He stepped away. "Start timing now. You'd better hurry."

Brennen turned back down the side passage, and Firebird headed upward at a quiet jog. The lane was as still as a tomb, and she knew it could soon be hers—if the gas came before she could cause a little trouble.

Where she reached the first level, the tunnel ended in a chamber just east of the main hall. She remembered a maintenance hatch in there, the nearest access to the hydraulic tubes. Drawing her blazer, she inched out into the chamber, listening hard. Elevators pulsing, a distant shout, her own heartbeat: she heard nothing immediately threatening, so took half the ten meters to the opposite wall at a dead run.

At a clatter of bootsteps off to her right, she dropped, rolled, and came up shooting. A red-collared figure fell heavily. She dashed to the floor-level access panel, knelt, and began popping out tracker bolts. The smooth rectangular slab loosened in her fingers. Meticulously she slid one edge outward, lifting as she moved it, leaving no scratch-marks on the black stone floor of the chamber. Then she squeezed herself into the hollow beyond. Two white polymer pipes ran up and down along one side of a shaft that could have held eight—had been intended for eight, she guessed. It was snug, particularly at shoulders and hips, but she fit. As she pulled the panel home, voices echoed out in the chamber.

Extending her arms, she grabbed one pipe, wedged her feet against opposite sides, and shinnied upward in utter darkness as quickly as she could.

The tube lay wrapped in silence. Thick stone dampened all sound above, below, and on all sides. Not even the occasional scuttering of small trapped creatures livened the hollow tonight. She wrenched herself upward another three arm-lengths, then rested a minute. Now that the first claustrophobic moment had passed, she felt far safer in this dark familiar sanctum than she had felt since leaving Brennen.

Brenn. She twisted her wrist and checked the lights on her wristband. She had already used fifteen minutes. She must hurry.

But the tube was slow going, particularly after she wriggled over into a horizontal cross-passage. At one point it narrowed so tightly that she had to shimmy back a meter, ease out of the heavy thermal shirt and pants, and push them along ahead of her, shivering and collecting scratches from the cold granite, until she passed the constriction. After that, she struggled back into the garments but left them unfastened, and soon she was glad she had done so. Three more times, she needed to shed every millimeter.

Finally, scraped and bleeding, she judged that she had nearly reached the easiest and safest place to pass into the house. Another five minutes' creeping put her at the end of the northward hollow with an upward passage directly overhead: once, it had held the feed tube to the collectors. Trying not to stir a deep pile of dust and small skeletons at the bottom of the drop, she worked herself up into a standing position, then patted the wall for a very small crack between stone and duracrete.

After a minute's search she located the crack, and then the widest prying spot, two hands lower than she expected. She had grown since first finding it. Wedging two fingers inward, holding the duracrete panel tightly, she pushed a centimeter and then waited, listening. Just past this wall had been a deep, walk-in closet used primarily by staff. No light came through the opening, so she pushed gently again, meeting a bit of gentle resistance. Sorted linens, she hoped. She gave it another shove.

The wardrobe was silent, but shouting and heavy running steps echoed in the halls. Cautiously she crept out into the dark, north-facing bedroom.

Movement caught her eye: the hall door was slowly opening. She dashed across the room toward the inner wall and pressed behind the door's path of swing. She saw the shadow cast by the hall light before she heard him: another House Guard, slinking toward the open wardrobe door.

She drew her energy pistol. One silent shot left him dead—and Firebird armed with another N'Taian service blazer. She dragged his body into the wardrobe and then crept out into the yellow-lit hall. The sound of footsteps sent her dashing for a utility room on the inner wall. Someone passed by and out of hearing. She tiptoed on, zigzagging between inner and outer rooms. What a stroke of luck Phoena had not thought to reprogram the palmlocks against her! Undoubtedly the House Guards thought they had secured these rooms already.

Behind the fourth outer door she heard two voices she'd been straining for: D'Stang and Parkai, bitterly complaining about having been dragged from their beds downlevel. Firebird smiled grimly. If they'd just gone to sleep in that extra room, they'd have been much harder to find. She checked her blazers: fully charged, both of them. She knew she wasn't much of a shot left-handed, but it would look impressive.

Firebird pressed her palm to the slick black panel and heard the latch release, resecured her grip on the blazers, and then, flinging the door wide, she went in shooting.

CHAPTER 19

Geis

Agitato
Agitated, excited

Two shocked faces turned to Firebird as she placed four silent firebolts. The shooting took her a second; recovering from the shock of what she had just done, much longer. She secured the hall door and leaned against it, breathing heavily. By the low light in the room she could see the folded bodies on two rumpled beds and beyond them three windowpanels, slatted filters closed, and a windowless outside door. Perfect. No outdoor guard would see her.

Coughing as she searched the scorched, nightrobed bodies, she found a blazer in each man's pocket. To her disappointment they carried neither disks nor research papers. Sighing, she steeled herself to slip back out into the hallway and search out Dr. Nella Cleary.

Wait. A voice from her training spoke up. *Never leave weapons behind enemy lines.* Already she carried more blazers than she could use, but she didn't want to leave Phoena's forces any additional arms.

After searching out the blazers once more, she stepped to the outer door, slipped through, and glanced around outside. All the outdoor lights burned fiercely, casting sharp grass shadows on the north leg of the outwall and obscuring the stars, and the still, cold air stung her face. Judging from shouts echoing off stone, the hunt was up—far downhill and to the south. Probably someone had spooked a brownbuck and mistaken it for a human intruder.

She laughed softly and flung two blazers toward the wall, then stepped back inside, coughing again at the scorched-flesh smell in the room. She tucked the guard's blazer into her holster and cycled her own to a fresh charge.

Now for Cleary.

Silently she inched out into the hallway. Halfway to the next room she heard running feet on the shortweave carpet, both ahead and behind. She sprinted for the next doorway, holding the blazer loosely to palm the panel quicker. The footsteps became louder.

Before she could reach the door, someone grabbed her shoulders. She spun toward her assailant and instinctively kicked upward as hard as she could. A strangled cry and a heavy thud sounded behind her as she wheeled away from the runner ahead and almost smashed her nose on a wood-inlaid wall. Rebounding, she tripped on a flailing arm and fell.

Instantly there was a knee on her back and sharp pressure against the base of her skull. "Release the gun," ordered a shaky voice above her. "Then take your hand away."

She could do nothing else. Reluctantly she abandoned her blazer and lay still, breathing quickly. The knee shifted. A well-kept, slender hand descended into her field of vision and removed her weapon. The weight lifted. Footsteps retreated across the passage, and then she heard the voice again. It seemed vaguely familiar.

"Now. Get up. *Slowly.*"

She complied, facing the dark wall.

"Hands on your head."

She locked her fingers on top of her head and waited.

"Turn around."

She came slowly around to face him—them. Two men stood before her: the smaller—very young, dark-haired, and thin, with a noble's blue formal sash across his chest—

held her own blazer trained on her; and the portly Duke of Claighbro, Muirnen Rattela, stood shaking and seething, obviously in pain. Suddenly Rattela's expression changed to utter confusion and supreme embarrassment.

"Your Highness?" He shook his head. "I beg your pardon! Why are you—"

"Wait a minute," his young partner interrupted. "That's not Phoena."

Then Firebird recognized him too: Phoena's "little-moon-shadow," Count Tel Tellai. She stood extremely still, eyeing Tellai's firing finger and wondering if she would have time to draw the guard's blazer while they stood baffled.

But Rattela smiled and wiped his palms on the white lace front of his shirt. "Well, Firebird. You came back after all. Call your friend uplevel, Tellai."

As Rattela drew a shining blue and gold blazer—blatantly ornamental but just as deadly as the service model Tel Tellai had taken—the young Count hurried into the next room. She heard his voice. "Phoena, love, you'll never believe it. We've got her." Silence. "Well, someone you've been hoping to see. You're going to be— Yes, it's she. Shall we— Of course. Oh, yes. Right away."

On a deeper level of awareness she felt Brennen's sudden, distant touch. He would know she was caught, then.

Tellai strolled back into view, beaming like a praised pet. Firebird glanced from Tellai to Rattela, weighing her chances of escape—very slight at the moment, even with the blazer and the hidden stinger. She would have to play along until Brennen could finish his own work. He would need some time yet.

Tellai rocked on his heels. "Uplevel, Rattela. Her Highness's room."

"One minute. I think we'd better spoil your sash first."

"Why?"

"Tie her."

"Surely you don't need to do that. This is a new one—a gift!" The slight young noble crossed his chest with one hand and smoothed the glowing gold-edged fabric.

"I know the Lady. Do you want Her Highness down

your throat for losing a prize like this? She'll *thank* you for sacrificing the sash."

Hastily Tellai pulled it off. While Rattela improvised a tight wristbinder, winding the excess up toward Firebird's elbows with an additional knot that strained her shoulders, Tellai removed the guard's blazer from her belt holster. Firebird submitted, keeping herself calm. She still had plenty of time.

Firebird's flash of fear had torn through Brennen and had neither cut off nor diminished. He dropped all shields, to be able to hear her—or the presence of guards. Leaning against the rough stone, he sent off the quest-pulse and let her feelings flood him. Defiance radiated from her emotional matrix with the fear.

Caught, then. But not yet threatened, and apparently not tempted to buy her life by betraying him to Phoena. Those had been his only earnest fears: that she'd be killed before they knew whom they'd taken, or that her soul hid a deeper loyalty to Naetai than he knew. She *had* hidden Hunter Height from him.

Hefting the pack, he headed up to search out the laboratory.

Five minutes later he reached the main lane and paused to "listen" again. No one was near—and Firebird remained fearful, but was more controlled now, and still safe. He drew his blazer and jogged up the main lane, following the way she had come. Where it ended in the bare chamber he turned left, hurried up a short passage, and stopped dead.

Before him rose a huge metal guardwall, its edges sealed to the stone. Light from an everburner behind his shoulder reflected off a satiny surface that looked incongruously modern in these ancient halls. His senses remained silent, except for the distant disquiet of Firebird's feelings.

He turned inward to focus a probe point, then sent it on the epsilon wave behind the locking panel. Humming circuitry surrounded his point of awareness; the sensation prickled like attacking insects. Up one course he found the resonating chamber of an alarm horn; a little further on, a high-voltage conduit connected back into the palmpanel's outer edges. It would deliver a fatal shock were the wrong person to touch it.

Brennen did not need contact. Cautiously he traced the tangled circuitry into the confirmation box. At that point, a proper handprint would be recognized, an improper rejected. He gave the point a nudge of energy.

The monstrous wall slid aside. Brennen stepped through the opening. Another pulse closed it behind him.

He looked around, gripping his blazer at loose ready. The corridor curved toward the right, walled in old stone. Along the left waited several doors, all closed.

Brennen pressed against the wall beside the first door, out of sight of anyone within. Still feeling no warning presence, he opened it, then peered into darkness. Cautiously he slipped inside. Even using the tiny luma, it took a minute's careful groping to locate a light switch. He waved it on.

A glass wall gleamed halfway across the stone chamber. Beyond robot controls, waldo hands drooped in electronic sleep. Past them lay a metal form, long and fat, an ominous shape he knew well. With a delicate tendril of epsilon energy he probed the warhead's circuits. Yes, it was one of the outmoded nuclear killers—at its heart. What then made it such a reputedly formidable—?

Irradium.

He thought he understood when he noticed the dull sheets of metal stacked alongside the half-plated bomb. Within the protection of that hardened glasteel wall, a layer of irradium could be wrapped entirely around the warhead and sealed in place by the mechanical arms. He did not understand—neither the irradium nor other changes in the warhead's circuitry, for these were outside his field of expertise—but he would remember. The warhead itself was extremely small; undoubtedly the key to the weapon lay in the sealed launching compartments near its nose. Something would be released with detonation. What? The circuits offered no clue.

Brennen slid off the backpack, carefully planning an operation more delicate than he'd anticipated. Setting off the wrong explosives, too near, might detonate the monster and its kin, atomizing the granite mountain and sending a cloud of irradium into the N'Taian atmosphere.

In the second room he found a typical office setup, its bluescreen left on. From a safe distance he fiddled with its circuitry, but it would tell him no secrets in the little time he felt he could spare. With a burst of focused epsilon static he surged all its circuits; if he were caught and his work halted, that stroke alone would slow Cleary.

He rested a minute while his carrier rebuilt, then moved on.

The third room held a number of huge, shielded crates, a shelf lined with desiccator jars and several flasks of green liquid: the air smelled oddly marine. Wrinkling his nose, he stepped back into the corridor and laid the pack on the ground.

Carefully he began distributing charges: nothing into the rooms containing nuclear materials, an incendiary onto the office chair. In the hallway he eyed the supporting walls of stone, and then, charge by slim charge, created a hidden line in the cracks that would bury the access under meters of blasted granite. He laid a second line up the center of the hall.

Had Firebird found Cleary? he wondered as he laid the largest structural charge alongside the huge metal door. At that moment the shriek of a whistle tore shrilly through the tunnel. An alarm—why so late? A signal to evacuate? Firebird's distress was coming through more urgently now.

The empty pack lay like a rumpled black pillow at his feet. Carefully he pulled out the remaining touchcard and slid it into a pants pocket, then extended a probe through the guardwall's circuits and nudged it open.

Just ahead, a uniformed man hurried up from the main lane and turned away through the chamber: he was moving at just the angle to catch Brennen in his peripheral vision, and was just too far away for voice-command. Brennen went for his blazer. The guard halted, squeezed off a wild burst, then fled around the stone corner.

Brennen let him go and slipped down a black side tunnel, hoping to find a cranny where he could safely enter tardema-sleep.

* * *

Firebird had stepped off the lift between her captors into the spacious master room on the topmost floor of the Height, just under a roof turret. Loud, excited talking in the room suddenly stopped.

She glanced around. The master room's odd shape had always fascinated her, but there had been changes made. In contrast with the utilitarian tunnels below, Phoena had made this room glitter, from springy red carpet to crystal-tiered chandelier. Even the black marble console and long, bare, metal-topped table shone like mirrors. Firebird counted almost twenty familiar people standing along the walls, below a row of formal portraits. Many of Phoena's friends were gathered here, older sons and daughters of the ten noble Houses. Among several House Guards and Red-jackets she spotted Captain Friel by his height and black hair—how had he beat her back from Alta? Where was Marshal Burkenhamn? Apprehensively she searched the crowd.

Her gaze rested instead on Vultor Korda, who stood under a long window, all but licking his lips with anticipation, tiny eyes narrowed to dark slits. Her stomach curdled. Korda had not Brennen's strength, but she thought she knew exactly what he wanted.

Phoena herself, in a flowing gown of brilliant yellow-orange, parted the line of people and walked slowly and regally toward her. Yes, Firebird admitted silently, that graceful, long-limbed (hateful, haughty) woman with the knot of chestnut hair was a beauty.

"You!" The scornful word rang in the silent room. "What—are—you—doing—here?"

Firebird stood silent, unmoving, eyeing Captain Friel, who approached with a twinbeam blazer at the ready.

Phoena drew herself up and shouted. "N'Taians, I introduce the Federacy's newest citizen. My sister, Lady Firebird." She turned to Rattela. "I just had a second report from downlevel, not half a minute ago. Parkai and D'Stang are dead."

Behind Firebird, a woman squealed. "No!"

Phoena folded her hands and held them tightly against her chest. "Yes. Was she armed?" Tellai stepped up and handed Phoena the blazers. "You searched her, of course?"

"No, Your Highness." Firebird heard a note of chagrin in Tellai's voice.

"Then, do it now," Phoena commanded icily. "Do it right. And if she moves—strip her!"

Grinning, Rattela moved in. Firebird's flesh crawled as he began to pat down the thermal suit. She kept her eyes on Phoena's face, diverting her awareness from Rattela's examining fingers and the burning urge to strike him. Clutching the fabric tying her wrists with her fingers, she willed herself motionless. She knew Phoena well enough to believe in that threat—and she was well aware of Rattela's appetite for Wastlings. The impending death of his victim woke something ugly in the Duke; she saw it in his eyes as he slid his hands up one leg. He *wanted* her to strike out.

Once Tellai and the nearest House Guards saw that she did not kick at Rattela, they too approached, each seeking into a pocket. Tellai found the touchcard and showed it to Phoena. "What's this?"

"Explosives," she hissed. "I expected as much." Phoena seized the panel. "You have a friend down there, I presume? One who kept some of the gear?"

Firebird did not speak. Brennen could well have armed those charges by this time, but surely Phoena would not risk destroying her precious irradium lab by trying a touch pattern.

A House Guard found her Vargan stinger, Rattela drew the bootknife, and Tellai presented them like offerings to Phoena. She gloated over each in turn and then passed them, along with Firebird's Federate-issue gunbelt, to Captain Friel: a tidy pile of damning evidence on the long metal table.

"It is time to carry out your Geis Orders, Wastling. Loose her." A guard cut the sash from her wrists, and Phoena smiled smugly as Firebird straightened the suit with all the dignity she could muster. "First, let's discuss your escort. Who brought you? Is he here now? I'll make it easier for you if you cooperate."

Firebird stared at her, not even tempted to answer. Phoena slapped her face, hard. Firebird reeled away, stunned and stinging. Rattela seized her shoulders and thrust her toward Phoena again.

"Who brought you? Where is he now?" Phoena repeated. After a few seconds she slapped Firebird's other cheek.

Then Vultor Korda spoke up. "Your Highness, perhaps you would like to have me examine her. Her mind should be most fertile ground by now. Furthermore, she and I have a score to settle over a certain encounter on Alta." He took a step forward. "I would enjoy that, Highness."

Phoena sniffed. "I see no point in that, Korda." Firebird would have smiled had she dared. "We have other sources within the Federacy. And *this* is obvious to me. She has always opposed me on this project, and she's here to destroy it. Clear the tunnels, Friel. Get ready to gas them and run the new Guardsman unit—in one minute. I have no time to waste."

Firebird started, amazed that Phoena had not used the gas already. Was the irradium project so close to completion that they had begun the final rush toward deployment? How much could Cleary accomplish alone?

The Captain hastened away as Phoena spoke on, running a fingernail along the inside of her left arm. "This is delightful, Firebird. Do you know what it means to me, to be able to have you executed? We can even do it at first light, the proper time for new beginnings. The north wall will be perfect. Don't you agree?" She stopped pacing and sighed. Rattela's grip shifted on Firebird's shoulders. "I've always wished I could see to this—be certain you died properly, honorably, before witnesses. In fact, just to show that the honor of the family comes first to me, I'll give you a blade now if you wish. But not poison. That's too dignified for you.

"You see"—she turned again to Korda, who now eyed Firebird from one side—"there is a sequence of honor among us. Poison and peace for those whose time has come honorably. A blade for penance or last resort. And for the criminal . . ." She drew back to include Firebird in her stare. "It may surprise you to hear that we brought a full complement of D-rifles to the Height. In such a delicate situation, I wanted to be prepared for treason in the ranks." Smirking, she pointed at Firebird. "And here you are."

Rattela stroked her throat with a damp palm.

Phoena turned to the nearest House Guard. "Check the rifle charges."

Half sick with dread, Firebird dug her nails into her hands. The narrow-band D-wave, badly distorted by metal, had been developed for surgery but had to be used with heavy anesthesia: the field built slowly, disrupting cells before disintegrating them, crazing a conscious patient with pain. Therefore Naetai had adopted the D-rifle for public execution, for which a victim would be stripped to the waist of metallic defenses. If portions of a criminal's body remained to be buried, all the better.

Still, Firebird stood steadily. First light remained hours away, and, as she had anticipated, Phoena wished to wait until long after Brennen would be free to come for her—if such was truly his intent.

Phoena seated herself at the long marble desk below the southernmost window and touched a series of panels. Firebird followed quickly, slipping Rattela's grip. Others, whispering, formed half a circle a few paces behind.

Two visual screens lit, each displaying a three-dimensional image of a stone corridor. Centered on the left screen were the double doors of the elevator shaft. As Firebird watched, they slid open. A yellow cloud began to spill out, driven by the lift's powerful fans.

Phoena gloated up at her. "Last chance, Firebird."

Firebird pressed her lips together. Either Brennen could or could not deal with the gas. She could do nothing now.

Movement on the other screen caught her eye. As the cloud billowed downward, a man in House Guard red and black dashed into range of the wide-angle pickup, eyes down, running hard, a blazer clutched at his side.

"Phoena!" Firebird gasped.

The Princess shrugged elegantly. "I signaled that there was no time to waste. I can afford to lose a guard or two if it makes the others realize they must take my orders seriously. And actually, this is perfect."

The runner stopped, finally noticing the yellow fumes drifting toward him. Raising horrified eyes to the vis-pickup, he lifted an arm in entreaty and waved the other back down the passage.

Phoena laughed. Pale and wide-eyed, Tellai laid a hand on her shoulder. Rattela, beside him, grinned.

"Now, then. This is what I wanted you to see. We're fortunate to have a subject in full view." Phoena reached forward, dragging her full sleeve on the black marble tabletop. "Friel brought me a present when he returned from Alta. 'Sonic Guardsman,' I think they call it. *Federate* technology. Watch." Her graceful finger touched a small, glossy panel below the screens. Then a second, and a third. An eerie howl rose underfoot.

On screen, the guard's eyes suddenly bulged. He flung his hands to his ears. Phoena sighed. "I thought you'd appreciate this, Firebird—with your background. Those three notes induce what I'm told is a ringing in the brain, as if the entire skull were a bell. What is it, an overtone? You should know. At any rate, it's quite paralyzing. Fatal, if it goes on too long. All the cranial arteries rupture, one at a time."

Firebird watched, panic-stricken, as the guard retched, convulsed, and then fell unconscious on the stone.

The first blast knocked Brennen to his knees and paralyzed his thoughts for two long seconds, while the second and third tones entered in deadly harmony. Pressure mounted around his brain. He dropped on rough stone. As his body curled instinctively into a fetal tuck, he struggled for recollection. He had been trained to endure sonics, long ago: he must shut down blood flow to . . .

The pain bore deeper, making thought difficult. His epsilon carrier began to disrupt. It would not modulate. It must. Must . . .

"Ah." Phoena withdrew her hand from the panel and glared at Firebird. "You're wondering if your friend is far enough down the tunnel to be safe from this, I'm sure. I had ten men installing relays all through dinner, Wastling. The entire system is covered. What admirable timing you've shown. I'd hoped to be able to test it."

As the guard's body vanished into amber fog, Phoena turned fully around. "In about fifteen minutes, the entire tunnel system will be flooded with zistane gas. If he's only shocked unconscious by the sound waves, the gas will ensure that he dies. Who is it, Wastling?''

Firebird lunged for the glossy panels and touched one off, but Rattela heaved her away. Phoena reactivated the tone. "That's enough. Guards. Restraint table." Five burly uniformed men moved in.

CHAPTER 20

Phoena

Grand pause
A rest observed by
the whole orchestra

When Brennen blinked and put a hand to his temple, he knew he had been stunned despite his effort. Silence blanketed the stone; his head pounded viciously. And the smell . . . foul . . . he coughed and took a deep gasp. It made him retch.

Far above, Firebird's fear was mounting. Her mind felt fogged now, struggling for lucidity—or was it his own that was sluggish?

Poison gas! a corner of his brain shouted from a distance. *You've been breathing it!* His fuzzed memory echoed, *Tardema-sleep!*

Yes, but how deep to send the cycle to time his waking? He turned inward and found his carrier. Another spasm of coughing shook him.

Suddenly Firebird's emotions screamed, rousing all his instincts. Screamed—and then faded swiftly to nothing. The emotional silence was complete. He sent a quest-pulse upward. Nowhere could he feel her connatural spirit.

Horror-stricken, Brennen opened one hand from the claw it had formed. He pushed it toward his pocket for the

touch activator. His stiff fingers managed to work out the
detonation sequence. If he could not achieve tardema, with
his last effort he would blow the lab.

They could not have killed her!

Struggling not to breathe, Brennen turned inward for
one more attempt at tardema.

Firebird had struggled frantically, but the guards were
too many and too strong. Two caught her hands and
dragged her to the metal table; one swept her gear onto the
carpet and bent her backward over it. Another House
Guard lunged for her feet and received a hard kick in the
teeth in his mistress's service. The next seized both her
knees and swung her around to lie flat.

An instant later she could not move, but lay staring at
the glittering white ceiling, her arms like immovable stone
at her sides. The guards' hands pulled away and she lay
panting, tears for Brennen streaming from her eyes.

"*Nicely* done," sang a female voice from somewhere
she could not turn her head to see.

Close by, Phoena's voice held a note of deep satisfaction. "*This* time she's ours, Liera." There was silence.

Something splashed into her face. It blinded her eyes
and made her fight for breath. Brandy, she guessed from
the piercing smell and the burning in her throat. She tried
to spit, could not move even her head, and had to swallow.
Only her eyelids responded—and her tongue—and she
could slow her breath. Salty tears slowly washed away the
stinging liquor.

When she could see, a pink blur resolved into Vultor
Korda's face. She averted her eyes.

"A toast!" shouted the voice of Captain Kelling Friel
close by. "Naetai!"

"Wait," Phoena called. "Finn, bring glasses for everyone. A toast indeed."

Firebird heard clinking and pouring as she blinked out
the last of the fire in her eyes. Korda moved away.

"Naetai!" the shout echoed, followed by a wash of
sudden conversation.

Then she heard Korda, whining again. "Highness

. . . Your Highness, I sense a presence about your sister that I do not like."

The hubbub stilled. "Oh?" asked Phoena's voice, distant once more. "Explain yourself, Korda."

"I can't—quite—isolate the nuances. But, Highness, if she came with anyone at all, she came with a Sentinel."

Cultured gasps and inhalations hissed on Firebird's left.

"You need not be concerned if he was trapped in the tunnels," Korda explained. "But can we afford to risk the possibility that he has not yet entered the Height and is keeping a distant contact with this one's mind?"

"What do you recommend, Thyrian?" asked Friel in a low, menacing voice Firebird knew well.

"Kill her now," Korda answered instantly. "Or at least drug her. They can neither touch nor detect the unconscious."

Phoena chuckled a little drunkenly. "I have just the thing, Korda, and right at hand. Liera. Give me your blade."

Light footsteps drew near, then Phoena's face.

"Firebird, you are about to get very, very drunk. Something I don't think you've experienced before. Have you—murderess?" she growled, and Firebird flinched too late. Another faceful of brandy flooded out her eyesight. Something thin that tasted of metal forced her lips farther apart.

Firebird cracked one eyelid open, ignoring the burning it caused. Phoena's hands held the hilt of a long dagger and a crystal decanter. Fiery liquid splashed along the blade, over her chin and cheeks, and into a fresh cut the dagger had sliced on her lower lip. Enough poured into her mouth to trigger the swallowing reflex. She tried to stop it, to pull her tongue against the back of her throat, but that only made her gulp more when finally she swallowed, a huge choking mouthful. She coughed and heard laughter. Some spewed away, but as soon as she inhaled, more liquor tinged with blood trickled down her throat. She had to gulp again. The coughing tactic worked a second time, but then the swallowing grew easier. Soon she felt muscles relaxing against her urgent wish to come alert.

Distantly, Tellai's high tenor spoke soothingly. "She's not going anywhere now, love. Too much more and you'll poison her."

"Heavens around, we don't want that." Soft laughter rippled through the master room, and the pouring stopped. Phoena's face vanished. Her voice remained close, however, becoming coy and enticing. "Tel? A thanks gift is in order, I believe. You have made me a happy woman today. Perhaps you would like to take this lovely Federate female, as a token of my gratitude."

"Phoena!" Tellai sounded genuinely shocked. "No one but—that is—only . . ."

Firebird squeezed her eyes closed, desperately fighting stupor and the agony of being unable to scream aloud.

"Not even if I would particularly like to see it?" Phoena asked.

Silence. Firebird could feel drowsy submissiveness taking hold of her too quickly to resist. So much for "the honor of the family."

"No, Phoena. Truly."

Bless Tellai. Bless the little fop's cowardly heart.

"Highness?" Rattela's voice, smooth and deadly, was not far away. A fleshy hand closed on her ankle. "I would pleasure you gladly, if you wished it done. She cannot kick nearly so well as she thinks she can."

Firebird felt her blood suddenly freeze.

"I didn't offer her to you, Rattela," Phoena snapped.

"But, Highness—"

"Are you crossing my will, Rattela?"

Firebird breathed again.

"One more toast, then," Phoena shouted. "To Lady Firebird of the Federacy. May she die like an Angelo."

A third gobletful of brandy splashed on Firebird's face, and she choked as droplets trickled through her nostrils. The struggle to breathe roused her enough to open her eyes a little; a last spark of terror revived her completely. "Now that I have your attention." Phoena stood twirling a long, curved leather-stitching needle above Firebird's eyes. "Where shall I bury this?"

Alcoholic miasma loosened Firebird's hold on even that fear. Willingly she surrendered to unconsciousness.

Voices in the master room roused Firebird into a sickening wakefulness with a pounding head and a terrible thirst, still held fast in a restraining field that reeked of stale liquor. The voices faded in and out erratically for what seemed a long time. At last, the sound of footsteps approached. The restraining field collapsed, and she felt herself pulled by the arms to a sitting position—too quickly. She crumpled forward and blacked out.

When the room appeared again she was being shaken, and she fought to stay conscious. Captain Friel gripped her shoulders, while four House Guards with weapons ready stood close behind.

She folded forward again, horribly dizzy, and a pair of guards took her arms, propping her between them. Her vision blurred. She blinked hard. She must wake up, she must! In this stupor she could barely think. Only fear came easily.

A long wash of black and orange grew before her, and when it spoke it had Phoena's voice. "Awake, Firebird? Hmm, not quite. I don't suppose you would care to meet our ancestors sozzled, would you?"

Firebird squinted, and when she saw what Phoena held in her hand she began to struggle. The Guards' hold tightened on her.

Phoena laughed merrily. "Ah, yes, you and needles. But I'm not doing this merely for a moment's fun." She drove the triple silver spike through the thermal suit into Firebird's shoulder. Firebird could scarcely breathe for the next minute, paralyzed by the old phobia.

The injection affected her almost instantly. Tactol—she recognized the sensory overload—and something more, this time. Within seconds, her head cleared. The pounding in her ears diminished to a soft pulse, while her unstrung muscles tightened suddenly and firmly. She would have tried to fling off the guards, but they secured their grip.

"Feel better?" Phoena tossed the medical nightmare

onto the metal table beside Firebird. "You look better. I
would hate to let you miss the full thrill of this hour,
Firebird. Now you'll savor every moment—as I shall."

The sensation was incredible: although her cut lip
throbbed and burned, she felt as if she could climb Hunter
Mountain in one leap, throttle all four guards at once—
now she understood why Phoena had brought up so many
of them—or tear the table to pieces with her bare hands.
But the injection had heightened her emotions as well, and
the sight of one guard's misshapen D-rifle, heavy-
chambered with a ceramic point at the barrel's end,
aroused a thrill of terror like none she had ever felt. She
would momentarily be reduced to a target. She forced her
muscles to relax.

Then she caught a glimpse out the east window. "This
hour," Phoena had said, and the faint glow beyond the hills
confirmed that less than an hour remained to her before
first light. The pulse in her ear beat quickly, like distant
parade drums. She longed to know if Brennen had been
found. She could not relinquish the hope he had escaped,
but with morning fast approaching and their timetable long
used up, if he had not come for her, he must—could be . . .

Brennen! she shrieked mentally.

Phoena spoke under her breath to Tellai beneath the
glowing chandelier. Dressed in an orange gown that fit
closely through the body and billowed out in a long dark
skirt, she looked the role of the legendary phoenix rising
from its ashes, and Firebird felt certain Phoena had chosen
the gown with precisely that symbolism in mind. Tellai, in
soft gray brocaded with silver, paled beside his regal
mistress. A sweet spicy scent filled the room from a pair of
gilt cups on Phoena's bed.

She bent forward and let a little weight rest on her
pressure-sensitive feet. "May I have a cup of cruinn?" she
whispered to the guard clenching her left shoulder. "My
mouth is full of dust."

"No." He tightened his fingers. "Be patient. You won't
be thirsty for long."

Phoena lifted something dark and limp off the bed,
crossed the vast room once more, and flung it at Firebird. A

thin black jumpsuit with zipcloth closures landed at her feet. "Put it on," she called. "And don't try anything, or I'll have you stunned and sent out to die naked."

The guards at her shoulders released her and stood, and Firebird began to peel off the thermal suit's shirt. Her scraped shoulders, scabbed to its lining, felt as if they were being combed with knives.

Suddenly her spirit leaped. North wall. On that lawn lay two blazers she had thrown into the night. Metal would distort the disintegration field—if only slightly—and if she could stay free enough to—

Another red-collared House Guard burst through the elevator door, saluting Phoena. "We've caught the other one, Your Highness!"

Firebird went stiff. The guards grabbed her again.

Phoena splayed her fingers in the air. "Was Korda right? Is it one of *them*?"

The guard drew up even straighter. "Yes, Your Highness. His so-called Excellency, the former Lieutenant Governor."

"What? Caldwell?" Phoena's shoulders sagged, as though she found it too much to believe. Tellai dashed to the lift.

"It certainly is, Your Highness. And he's alive—barely. We took him in the east lab. The zistane almost killed him, Highness. He can scarcely walk: I think he's harmless now. The rest of my detail is downlevel, disarming and collecting all the explosives they can find."

"Excellent," Phoena breathed. "Oh, excellent. Someone tell Rattela!"

Firebird stared through a whirlwind of emotion as she zipped into the jumpsuit. Harmless? Not Brennen. But . . . but surely they never would have taken Brennen if he hadn't allowed it.

Phoena hurried onto the lift and held a hand over the closing circuit. "Bring her. I don't want her out of my sight until it's over."

Yanked forward by the guards at her elbows, and trying to exude meekness, Firebird boarded the lift.

In the living area, a group of about forty had gathered

near the firebay, all wearing warm capes and coats except
one. Firebird's heart caught at the sight of Brennen standing at one edge of the crowd, his thick thermal outer shirt
stripped off. Heavy-eyed as though barely awakened, he
stood unsteadily.

Tellai bowed deeply and presented Phoena a priceless
Aurian crystace. She seized it and eyed Brennen down her
nose. "Good morning, Your Excellency," she mocked.
"What a lovely surprise. We have a little ceremony planned
in a few minutes, and I would be delighted to honor you
beside my sister."

"Let her go, Your Highness." Brennen's hoarse, weak
voice horrified Firebird. "This is my doing. I'll take the
payment."

"You'll both pay, you alien—filth." Phoena tucked the
crystace into a pocket of the cape Tellai offered. "Someone
check that skinshirt for metal once more."

Red-jacketed Captain Friel stepped forward. "Allow
me, Your Highness." He examined the undergarment minutely. "Caldwell. Lieutenant *General* Caldwell." He drew
away. "Your Highness, I've recalled something important.
On Alta, when Lady Firebird renounced Naetai, one of the
Federates claimed she had been living under this man's
guarantee of asylum. Furthermore—good glory, Your
Highness—that oath of hers was taken at the tip of *his*
sword!"

Phoena whirled around. "Ahh," she crowed. "Yes! It
all begins to come clear. I think we can draw some
conclusions about the source of your intimate knowledge of
Naetai now, Your Excellency. And you, Firebird." Scornfully, Phoena jerked her head toward Brennen. "So *this* was
the price of your treason. I should have guessed."

Firebird sputtered furiously, unable to find words that
were cutting enough, and glanced back to Brennen. His
skin was pale yellow; he had taken in a massive dose of
zistane. Understanding chilled her.

"Tie her." Phoena swirled the cape onto her shoulders. "Where's Rattela? We can't wait."

Hurriedly one of the hallway guards obeyed, letting
Firebird's bound hands fall behind her back. She winced as

the changing angle dug the cord into her skin, and looked to Brennen. Sighing softly, he dropped his gaze from the guard's eyes.

"Move," ordered Phoena. She and Tellai led out the massive eastern doors, across the flagstones and left along the winding lane that descended to the airfield.

Firebird walked the paving beside Brennen, her spirits sinking farther each time he stumbled, her tightly strung senses jolted by every step. Predawn cold flowed through her flimsy jumpsuit like ice water, and she clenched and unclenched her hands to warm them as the road fell from the Height. Near the outwall, the procession turned left again onto the long northern field, where grassy, weedy terrain made slower going. Phoena and her friends dropped behind.

Firebird spoke softly and hastily. "You all right?" Moving her cut lip felt like meeting the dagger again.

Brennen tripped once more, barely catching himself. "You woke me. Thank you."

Woke him? Had he heard her mental shriek or her terror of Phoena's needle? Firebird glanced back over her shoulder. Phoena's people followed in twos and threes, warmly bundled, few speaking. Two carried a long equipment locker between them. A rosy stripe glowed in the pale gray clouds over the spot where the sun was about to rise. "There are two blazers," she whispered, "in the grass near—"

Movement at one corner of her eye silenced her. The guards had caught up, but Brennen's quick-eyed expression hinted at hope. They passed a stake driven into the grass at the customary thirty paces out. Four of the guards halted behind them. She heard weapons clattering and refused to turn and look, but could not stop her stomach from twisting painfully.

At the outwall, two guards knotted the ends of the ropes binding her wrists to the iron handrail, several meters from Brennen.

"I'm placing your hands behind the metal," one said smoothly. "Orders. 'Fingerprints are valuable proof of decease,'" he quoted, almost capturing Phoena's tone of voice. "But this isn't so tight that you can't shift them to the front of the rail, if you'd rather have it done cleanly."

Another, finished with Brennen, reached for his black neckscarf. "Do you want a blindfold, Lady Firebird?"

She shook her head steadily. "No! Thank you." The guards sauntered back to join the firing squad, between Captain Friel and Phoena. Her gown shone like a flash of orange flame among the guards' red berets and the more somber attire of the others.

"One problem," Firebird muttered. "Our hands."

Shivering, Brennen laughed softly. "The knot is within reach of your right fingers."

Sure enough, a loop, fat and loose, lay inside her left palm. She fumbled with it, trying to force dexterity into cold, swollen, supersensitive fingers. "Why in the world did he put it there?" Blessed freedom! She stretched enough slack from her bonds to draw her hands through as the peak of Hunter Mountain gleamed suddenly orange.

"Are you up to some shooting?" Brennen asked.

"Absolutely." She eyed the rifle squad, taking up formation. "They've given me some sort of stimulant to see that I enjoy this. Maybe I'll enjoy it more than they intended."

She watched him close his eyes, head bowed, and she tensed, knowing he must gather all the strength he had left.

Tellai strode out in front of the D-rifle line, calling for the crowd to quiet.

"Ready, Mari?"

"Brenn?" she whispered.

He glanced her way.

"I love you."

CHAPTER 21

Firebird

Allegro con fuoco
Fast, with fire

"Loyal subjects of the N'Taian Queen," Phoena shouted. "Today, I have brought us—"

The ground shook with a low rumble and began to heave.

Phoena froze. Her speech ended before she finished her first declaration.

Firebird slid her hands free.

Phoena spun toward her victims and stood dazed. Firebird smiled slightly at her.

Phoena seemed to fill with life, hatred—and purpose. "Present!" she shrilled to the execution detail.

Firebird glanced hurriedly back to Brennen. Beyond the house, a dusky cloud arose billowing near the eastern outwall.

"Sight!" Phoena screamed. Ceremoniously, the Four House Guards brought up the D-rifles.

Brennen flung both arms forward. From where they had lain hidden, the handblazers flew into his palms. He deflected one toward Firebird. She dropped shooting to one knee and sighted on the nearest guard while Brennen extended an arm again, reaching into the gesture with his whole body. His crystace sailed from Phoena's cloak pocket. Phoena grabbed for it, lost her balance on the bucking ground, and fell facedown in the weeds. As the nearest guard sprawled on his back, Brennen caught and activated the crystace one-handed. To Firebird's amazement, he flung it away. It soared for the D-rifles and whirled through two, cleanly slicing them in half. By then Brennen was shooting.

Firebird crouched behind her blazer, holding it steady. One disarmed D-rifle carrier, recovering from his surprise, lunged for the weapon the dead guard had dropped. She felled him with a leg shot as Brennen got the other man. The horizon glowed. Her clumsy-numb hands began to feel warm. She swept the scattering crowd with her sights for the ample silhouette of His Grace, Muirnen Rattela. Had he drunk too much of Phoena's brandy to rise early?

So she saw Vultor Korda fall, fleeing for the Height, the satisfied look on Brennen's face, and the crystace returning to his hand.

A flashing bolt grazed Brennen's shoulder. Forgetting Rattela, Firebird returned fire. When the last secessionist in range was either down or fleeing, she relaxed her shooting hand.

Then she saw Tel Tellai across the tussocks of dry weeds, unarmed but bravely shielding Phoena with his body. Phoena waved wildly at several other men. Firebird's finger went back to the firing stud. Down the shaft of the energy pistol Tellai drew up, stretching tall. She hesitated. He *was* only a child. . . . Remembering his decency the night before, she lowered the blazer.

"Let's get out of here, Brenn!" The crystace's hum snapped off behind her.

From across the field, she could hear Phoena shouting again, and she caught the word "airstrip." Tellai and four others dashed down the field for the back gate.

"Brenn! If they can put a fighter into the air we're groundside targets!"

"Run, then!" he shouted. "We'll get one first!"

Finally she could release the flood of energy inside

her! She sprinted after Tellai, but before she had taken ten steps, Brennen shouted from far to her left. "Mari!"

She stumbled to a halt and looked for him. Running awkwardly, he was headed for the northern outwall instead of the gate. She angled back to join him. The sun crept at last over the horizon. At that moment he turned and shouted, "Drop!"

She plunged into the grass and prickly weeds. A brilliant bolt of green light, blowing a stone from the wall, pierced the spot where she had stood an instant before. Prone himself, Brennen fired once.

"This way!" He scrambled up and began to climb hand over hand. "Hurry—I missed. It's Friel, over in the trees."

"Squill! He must have ducked and played dead!" Fighting to hoist a foot onto the handrail inside the wall, she dropped her blazer. Another shot cracked a rock at her knee. She pushed up, caught the top of the wall, and peered down for the weapon in the weeds.

"Leave it!"

She linked her hand around Brennen's wrist, clambered over the top, and dropped with him onto the rim of the canyon. Far off to her right she saw the five men, halfway down the winding lane to the airstrip. Below on the apron lay four N'Taian tagwings, golden arrows glistening among the shadowy private craft.

Brennen snatched her hand and pulled her through the rocks and bushes to the steepest point of the rim, directly over the tagwings. "Up!" he directed. Firebird hesitated. Before she could protest that he was too weak to try it, he swung her into his arms and leaped.

She clung to his neck as the cliffs flew by and the permastone apron rushed up. He released her at the last second: she landed hard, tumbled over, and then sprang to her feet. With a backward glance to be sure he was coming, she dashed up the apron for the nearest fightercraft.

The stepstand had been taken away, but she had sprung onto these forewings a hundred times. Raising the bubble, she wriggled in. Close behind, Brennen jumped directly for the cockpit. He fell short. Firebird flung out a hand and pulled him aboard while he leaned heavily on her arm. Sliding the seat to its maximum forward position,

she watched him struggle behind it. "It's too small for you
back there, isn't it? Get on the seat—I'll sit in front of you."
They hurriedly repositioned as she ignited the laser-ion
generator.

Brennen tried to pull the flight harness around both of
them while she closed down the cockpit seals. "Too short,"
he gasped.

"We don't have any fighter pilots this big around.
Secure yourself." She leaned forward and hastily checked
her controls. When she pressed back, she felt his arms
tighten around her.

Motion down the apron caught her peripheral vision.
The runners had reached the breakaway. One man was
raising the canopy of the far tagwing and climbing aboard.
Others had nearly reached the next ships. Firebird pivoted
her fightercraft to starboard and fired its twin laser cannon
down the row, enveloping the golden ships with scarlet
lightning. Four men dove for cover as the nearest ship burst
into thousands of metal shards. Then the second.

The third hull merely twinkled. "His slip-shield's up,"
Firebird cried. "I can't take him broadside now. But I don't
think he'll oblige us by taking off first."

"We can't stay here." Brennen peered around her
head. The other tagwing's engines glowed. "Get up fast if
you want a good chance in a scrap. Do you know who that
is?"

"No. But I hope he's a Redjacket." Firebird cut the
braking system, raised shields, and careened off the apron
onto the strip, accelerating at max before she hit the canyon
straightaway. Then she pulled up and banked hard starboard to avoid being blasted from behind.

They skimmed Hunter Height, just clearing the
outwall, where a large area of the eastern slope had
collapsed inward. Brennen had done it: enough charges
had remained hidden and armed to bury the irradium lab
deep. But her stern sensors picked up her pursuer. The
display showed that he had dropped both shields, coaxing
extra speed from his engines. Apparently the pilot was no
amateur, and he intended to finish them quickly.

With double shields, she couldn't shake him. Spinning
full starboard, she singled the shield. The projectile protec-

tion dropped away, and a surge of acceleration pressed her body against Brennen's. *Let him leave those shields down,* she pleaded silently. *I wouldn't have to hit an engine port, I could take him with a side shot!* But his extra velocity kept him out of her sights, above and behind, and closing fast to make the kill.

All right, then. We die trying. Simultaneously, she cut out her last shield, angled straight up, and laid into a fast roll. For a terrifying moment she passed directly in front of him. An energy burst caught the very tip of her tailfin, and the sudden, horrible pitch threw her off the edge of the seat.

"*Hold* me, Brenn!"

His arms tightened again.

Suddenly inspired, she wrenched the emergency-blackout switch off her left-hand sideboard, cutting sensors and display to fly virtually blind and diverting the generator's last erg of output into the engines. Totally inverted now, her fighter looped back. The hillside spun crazily above the cockpit as she turned about, riding her instincts and pushing for the top of the tagwing's envelope.

Suddenly, incredibly, the other tagwing slid past the center of her cockpit bubble. She held down a firing stud and reactivated her particle shield. The flash momentarily blinded her, and the hull began to tinkle like singing, metallic rain.

"Kill!" she cried, blinking. "We did it!" Righting the tagwing, she cut her speed to ease the load on its generator. The horizon circled back down to where it belonged.

"Mari." Brennen exhaled the name like a sigh. "Firebird. Well flown." His head fell on her shoulder.

"Well. With his shields down it was like hitting a radio dish. Easy." Wishing her voice had a little less shake to it, she wagged the damaged rudder; it seemed stiff. "I don't suppose we'd better stay around."

"Probably not." She felt hair pulled back from her throat; a long kiss below her left ear.

It scarcely registered, her heart hammered so. "Sae Angelo, then?" She badly wanted to try that fast vertical roll again, with no one shooting.

"Yes, but just a drop-in with orders for Danton, and to

pick up a ship with a little . . ." He flexed his feet, sandwiched between hers and the hull. ". . . more room."

One-fingering a long, low, graceful arc to port, she laughed. "Orders? Who takes orders from whom, Brenn? You or Danton?"

"I'll let you guess—Princess."

"Lady!" she scolded. "Hang on!" And she sent the tagwing high into the morning sky, in the wildest victory roll ever negotiated over the mountains of Naetai.

Southward she soared, needing no instruments to set course down the Hunter Valley toward Sae Angelo's Tiggaree River. Abruptly she pulled her hands off the controls. "Cleary!" she gasped.

"Dead." Brennen shifted one hand on the sideboard. "When they took me I saw her in the chamber outside the irradium lab, wearing an oxygen mask and hunting explosives—carrying several."

"Oh!" She checked her altitude. "Then here's one"— she seized the stick—"for Cleary!" Again the horizon spun. "What *was* she building?"

"For security's sake, can you wait until I discuss it with my superiors?"

"Brenn?" She wriggled one foot. "This time, I would be glad to wait."

About half an hour farther south, a pair of elegant black Federate fighter-interceptors roared into escort position behind them and challenged them over the interlink. Brennen took the helmet communicator and answered; Firebird grinned at the chagrin in the pilots' voices as they acknowledged his security-code transmission and peeled away as neatly as skin from banam fruit.

She needed no warning to keep quiet herself, so she didn't object when Brennen reached for the transmitter on the approach to Sae Angelo and asked, "Would you mind waiting in the ship while I talk to Danton at the base? I'll hurry."

"That's all right with me," she answered absently, watching the familiar autumn browns of the outskirts of town sweep beneath her, flying on visual and savoring it. If her Academy flight trainer had spoken over the interlink, she wouldn't have been surprised.

Brennen obtained landing clearance from the Governor himself, then shut off the interlink and spoke quietly in her ear. "You can stay if you want, Mari. I'm certain you could make a niche for yourself here. Danton would help." He tangled his fingers into the hair over her shoulders. "But you're welcome to go back to Alta with me and face the consequences."

"Alta," she said. "Of course." Then an awkward thought crossed her mind. "Are you in trouble with Regional, do you think?"

"Danton will probably tell me."

She dropped the tagwing on the breakaway strip and halted near the largest of the strange new buildings. As Brennen squeezed out, she took a long look at his face: pale but no longer yellow, it glistened with sweat.

"I won't be long." Standing on the forewing, he bent and kissed her. Then he slid to the ground and strode off, slowly, but steadily.

Tel steadied himself with one arm against a wall of the master room. He couldn't believe what he was hearing. Carradee the jellyfish, standing up to Phoena!

After last night, he was almost glad.

"I told you," Phoena seethed into the tri-D pickup over her desk. "Caldwell was here—and with Firebird! Like a mated pair! And of course it was a laboratory. You would have known that already if you'd given half a brain to it. Catch them! Don't let them offplanet!"

"What *were* you building?" Carradee demanded. "You have played this secrecy game for long enough."

Phoena clenched her fists at her sides. "You'd better tell her," Tel whispered. "You may need her on your side."

"An ecological weapon." Phoena clipped each word. "Toxin-synthesizing algae, and a way to make it bloom through an entire ocean system."

"To—to foul an entire living world, as Cleary claimed."

"Within days. The irradium helps it along, somehow. But they've destroyed the entire tunnel, the spore stock, the irradium for—"

"Enough!" Carradee's nightrobed likeness stood as tall

and imperious as that of their mother. "I will send an escort
for you, and if you value your safety you'll cooperate fully.
We shall also send a team of engineers to see if the Height's
understructure is reparable."

"The Federates should pay to rebuild it." Phoena
glared back. "They gave no fair warning, made no requests
—they just obliterated the east end. It will take months to
rebuild."

"If you rebuild that laboratory you will face sedition
charges!" Carradee's passionate sincerity shocked Tel.
"You defiled the Height! You swore you were conducting a
cultural retreat, and I trusted you. I took your word. I
should have my head examined."

Tel glanced from sister to sister. For the first time, he
realized vengeance might be taken by the Federates on
Phoena, and—he swallowed—himself.

"Have you any more to say?" Carradee demanded.

"Don't let them get away, you incompetent! She's
betrayed us—taken Federate citizenship!"

Carradee gulped air like a skitter—Tel had never seen
her so angry. "If I find Firebird, I'll have her detained. But
if you break arrest, Phoena, so help me, I'll have the
Redjackets after you, too!"

Brennen slipped into the Governor's office without
waiting for the secretary to clear or announce him. Danton
looked up from his bluescreen and his face radiated alarm.
"Caldwell—what in Six-Alpha are you doing here? I've
been told to detain you on sight." He set down his stylus.
"So get out of my sight."

Brennen walked forward as quickly as his uncooperative legs would move. "You had a tetters' nest up north,
sir," he said. "Hunter Height, a private estate—"

"Yes, I had a message yesterday from Tierna Coll of the
Regional Council—but we couldn't find the locale on any
map. I put a query in to the Queen's office. . . ."

Brennen reached for the map projection on the wall
behind Danton's desk chair. "Here. They've kept it off
maps, so I'm not surprised you couldn't find it. Phoena
Angelo converted it into a nuclear laboratory—they were
modifying bombs. You'll want to send a mop-up crew: we

left about fifty very angry secessionists, probably armed. But they've no fightercraft now, and no ordnance lab."

Danton rubbed his chin. "Bombs? What are you talking about? They signed a treaty."

"Dig it out if you want, sir. I am leaving—quickly." He paused with one hand on a corner of Danton's desk. "What about Lady Firebird?"

"Caldwell, we have no idea where she is. None."

"Sir." Brennen nodded his thanks.

A small red light began to pulse beside the label on Danton's linkboard that read "Angelo."

Brennen took a step backward. "If I were looking for me, knowing I might be in trouble, I would try Procyel, the Sentinels' sanctuary world."

Brennen offered a hand, and Danton clasped it. *Stall her*, Brennen shot into an unguarded corner of the Governor's mind. Then he spun, caught his balance, and headed out. "Would you clear an unidentified 721 for takeoff?"

"Of course," Danton called after him. As the door closed, Brennen heard Danton say, "Madame?"

Working through the preflight sequence together, Firebird and Brennen checked the five-man shuttle for liftoff in short order. Instead of programming a course for Alta, however, Brennen gave the navcomputer liftoff instructions only. As the generator came up, Firebird felt the sweep of his awareness at the edge of her senses. She waited out the burst of recollection, a brief passing-over, more a caress than a questioning.

"Mari?"

She glanced curiously at him. The ready-lights flashed.

"We don't need to slip directly back to Alta. The intelligence I have from the laboratory will keep, for now. We could stop over at Hesed House."

Firebird pulled a lever to release the brakes. "Where?"

"Hesed is a sanctuary of my people." Thrust caught them, and they lifted. "A retreat—much like Hunter Height but more pastoral. Very restful. And it would be a beautiful place for a wedding. A simple one." He touched her hand on the console. "If you would want it, knowing what it would mean."

Yes, she knew. He offered the bonding like a gift; and others had survived it. There had been a time, she remembered, when she fought him for the right to die. What *had* kept her from accepting him, N'Taian tradition or cowardice?

"Brenn." She straightened. "If you're willing to take an outsider, I can face your pair bonding. You gave back my life."

His eyes shone under the blue striplights as he gave the computer final instructions.

Starpricks began to spring from the blackness of space, and Naetai's horizon curved far below. Unconsciously she began to hum, then almost laughed aloud. The melody was Iarla's Song, her ballad of the Wastling Queen who had triumphed over her fate: still unfinished, but swelling in her heart like an anthem. Somehow she suspected she would be able to write the other verses now.

Brennen was smiling; she guessed that he sensed her surge of exultation. "Ready to slip?"

"Go."

Like fire kissing water, the little ship winked out of space.

Coda

As Firebird stepped through golden double doors, she surveyed the underground hall to which Brennen had brought her. All was white and gold except ahead, where there shimmered a shallow man-made lake surrounded by a latticed rail, crossed and recrossed by paths of square stepping stones and broken by islands of greenery. Sunlight streamed down from countless skylights, dancing and refracting on the water, and from somewhere she could hear more water rushing and splashing.

The Master Sentinel Brennen had introduced as Jenner Dabarrah stepped around from behind them, very tall and thin, with blue-gray eyes as pale as his golden hair. Dressed all in white with an eight-rayed star, he wore his age well: forty, perhaps? or fifty?

"Have you eaten?" He touched a bell.

"Enough." Brennen squeezed Firebird's hand as she stood in motionless wonder. Three days in slip had virtually restored Brennen, and she was very glad, for at the moment she wanted all the support he could give.

A young girl in a pale blue gown approached along a walkway, through a high arch on the right. "Go with her, my lady," said Master Dabarrah. "Surely you would like to bathe and dress."

Firebird followed her leftward along the side of the sparkling pool, to another wide pavement. Her guide walked without hesitation to the fourth arching door, opened it, and stepped aside.

Firebird walked in. At first, the movement ahead startled her. It looked as though the inner wall were quaking. Then she sighed, delighted. As her eyes adjusted to the pale light she saw that the long wall hid behind a pale curtain of water that cascaded endlessly over smooth white stone.

The girl disappeared through an arch, but Firebird sat for a moment on the bed's white coverlet, watching and listening to the singing waters, wondering if she dared take the step ahead of her.

Then she rose and followed.

Dabarrah escorted Brennen across the stepping stones toward his own quarters. *We were alerted by Sentinel Kinsman that you had left Alta, of course,* the elder Master subvocalized as his long legs swung him from stone to stone, *and yesterday we received word from Naetai. You seem to have carried off a fine piece of work there, well within our codes. However . . .* He glanced sidelong. *You are wanted for questioning and censure by the Regional Command.*

Stepping silently to the next stone, Brennen sent a wordless general query for Dabarrah's reaction to that news.

Do not do this again, Brennen, Dabarrah sent back as they reached the paving at the far side of the reflecting pool. *Your brothers will shelter you and the woman you have chosen, if necessary, but we would prefer to see you elevated to the High Command one day.*

Brennen returned a pulse of gratitude.

*   *   *

The girl led Firebird to Master Dabarrah's rooms. Brennen stood inside, clothed in dress whites again, and on Dabarrah's desk lay a long document, rough-textured like ancient parchment. "I have completed all but one thing, Lady Firebird," he said. "What name will you take?"

"Firebird Mari Caldwell." She twisted an end of the long golden belt the girl had wound around her unfitted white gown. A broad smile spread across Brennen's face. "I like 'Mari,'" she whispered as Dabarrah filled the last blank space. "I would like to keep it."

Between the Sentinels she walked out upon the stepping stones. As the skylights dimmed, a band of light began to gleam around the edge of the waters, reflecting blue and green off Brennen's whites.

They halted on a paved island. Firebird faced Dabarrah; Brennen drew close beside her.

"You have no doubts?" Dabarrah asked softly. "You will hold this bond before all other loyalties, Firebird? And you, Brennen? Your path may not be easy."

She saw Brennen nod slightly, and did the same. Master Dabarrah placed his hands on their shoulders, speaking softly and musically in a tongue she did not know. A blessing, she guessed, or an invocation. Brennen answered briefly in what she thought was the same language.

Then Dabarrah dropped his right hand, leaving one on her left shoulder. "Firebird Mari," he said gently, "you have chosen a Sentinel. Your culture has done nothing to prepare you for this."

Firebird met the steady gaze of his pale eyes. "That is true, Master, but Brennen has explained bonding to me. I have accepted it—and him."

"Then, I ask to touch your spirits."

Brennen stepped behind her, circled her waist with one arm, and pressed into her mind, far deeper than he had ever gone before. For a sweet moment she held steady, but the feeling became a hurricane inside her, tearing her from her moorings even as it filled her with the presence she had come to love more than flight, more than freedom, more than life. As it became impossibly intense she let her body tumble against his.

He gathered her up into his arms. She sensed the

approach of Dabarrah's "otherness." "Yes," the elder Sentinel's voice echoed above the joyous roar of her senses. "It is right. I bless your bonding. It is yours to finish." A burst of light filled her mind's eye as Dabarrah spoke.

Resting against Brennen's chest, she half opened her eyes. Brennen took a step backward.

"I can walk," she murmured.

"Let me. Please?" He kissed her, then. Carrying her like a holy vessel, he walked back across the stones over the water, along the wide way, and through the arching door of their bedchamber.

ABOUT THE AUTHOR

Kathy Tyers, a California native, settled in Montana chiefly to see if she would find wilderness as inspiring in reality as in J.R.R. Tolkien's works (she did, and she stayed). She has earned degrees in microbiology and education, an amateur radio license and a SCUBA certificate, and has worked as an immunobiology tech and a primary teacher in a private school—but as the daughter of a flutist and a brassman, she has always considered music a necessity of life. A classical flutist turned semiprofessional folk artist, Kathy performs on flute and Irish harp with her guitarist–music teacher husband, Mark; their first album, *Leave Her, Johnny*, has been a regional sellout. They have one son, two cats, and about thirty assorted musical instruments.